The First Leonaur
Christmas Book of Great
Ghost Stories

The First Leonaur Christmas Book of Great Ghost Stories

Twenty-One Short Stories of the Strange and Unusual Including 'The Spectre of Tappington', 'To Let', 'The Story of the Inexperienced Ghost', and 'The Crooked Branch'

Eunice Hetherington

LEONAUR

The First Leonaur Christmas Book of Great Ghost Stories
Twenty Short Stories of the Strange and Unusual Including 'The Spectre of Tappington',
'To Let', 'The Story of the Inexperienced Ghost', and 'The Crooked Branch'

by Eunice Hetherington

FIRST EDITION

Leonaur is an imprint of Oakpast Ltd

Copyright in this form © 2017 Oakpast Ltd

ISBN: 978-1-78282-694-1 (hardcover)
ISBN: 978-1-78282-695-8 (softcover)

http://www.leonaur.com

Publisher's Notes

The views expressed in this book are not necessarily
those of the publisher.

Contents

Man-Size in Marble

Edith Nesbit

Although every word of this story is as true as despair, I do not expect people to believe it. Nowadays a "rational explanation" is required before belief is possible. Let me then, at once, offer the "rational explanation" which finds most favour among those who have heard the tale of my life's tragedy. It is held that we were "under a delusion," Laura and I, on that 31st of October; and that this supposition places the whole matter on a satisfactory and believable basis. The reader can judge, when he, too, has heard my story, how far this is an "explanation," and in what sense it is "rational." There were three who took part in this: Laura and I and another man. The other man still lives, and can speak to the truth of the least credible part of my story.

I never in my life knew what it was to have as much money as I required to supply the most ordinary needs—good colours, books, and cab-fares—and when we were married we knew quite well that we should only be able to live at all by "strict punctuality and attention to business." I used to paint in those days, and Laura used to write, and we felt sure we could keep the pot at least simmering. Living in town was out of the question, so we went to look for a cottage in the country, which should be at once sanitary and picturesque. So rarely do these two qualities meet in one cottage that our search was for some time quite fruitless. We tried advertisements, but most of the desirable rural residences which we did look at proved to be lacking in both essentials, and when a cottage chanced to have drains it always had stucco as well and was shaped like a tea-caddy. And if we found a vine or rose-covered porch, corruption invariably lurked within.

Our minds got so befogged by the eloquence of house-agents and the rival disadvantages of the fever-traps and outrages to beauty which we had seen and scorned, that I very much doubt whether either of us, on our wedding morning, knew the difference between a house and a haystack. But when we got away from friends and house-agents, on our honeymoon, our wits grew clear again, and we knew a pretty cottage when at last we saw one. It was at Brenzett—a little village set on a hill over against the southern marshes. We had gone there, from the seaside village where we were staying, to see the church, and two fields from the church we found this cottage. It stood quite by itself, about two miles from the village. It was a long, low building, with rooms sticking out in unexpected places. There was a bit of stone-work—ivy-covered and moss-grown, just two old rooms, all that was left of a big house that had once stood there—and round this stone-work the house had grown up. Stripped of its roses and jasmine it would have been hideous.

As it stood it was charming, and after a brief examination we took it. It was absurdly cheap. The rest of our honeymoon we spent in grubbing about in second-hand shops in the county town, picking up bits of old oak and Chippendale chairs for our furnishing. We wound up with a run up to town and a visit to Liberty's, and soon the low oak-beamed lattice-windowed rooms began to be home. There was a jolly old-fashioned garden, with grass paths, and no end of hollyhocks and sunflowers, and big lilies. From the window you could see the marsh-pastures, and beyond them the blue, thin line of the sea. We were as happy as the summer was glorious, and settled down into work sooner than we ourselves expected. I was never tired of sketching the view and the wonderful cloud effects from the open lattice, and Laura would sit at the table and write verses about them, in which I mostly played the part of foreground.

We got a tall old peasant woman to do for us. Her face and figure were good, though her cooking was of the homeliest; but she understood all about gardening, and told us all the old names of the coppices and cornfields, and the stories of the smugglers and highwaymen, and, better still, of the "things that walked," and of the "sights" which met one in lonely glens of a starlight night. She was a great comfort to us, because Laura hated housekeeping as much as I loved folklore, and we soon came to leave all the domestic business to Mrs. Dorman, and to use her legends in little magazine stories which brought in the jingling guinea.

We had three months of married happiness, and did not have a single quarrel. One October evening I had been down to smoke a pipe with the doctor—our only neighbour—a pleasant young Irishman.

Laura had stayed at home to finish a comic sketch of a village episode for the Monthly Marplot. I left her laughing over her own jokes, and came in to find her a crumpled heap of pale muslin weeping on the window seat.

"Good heavens, my darling, what's the matter?" I cried, taking her in my arms. She leaned her little dark head against my shoulder and went on crying. I had never seen her cry before—we had always been so happy, you see—and I felt sure some frightful misfortune had happened.

"What is the matter? Do speak."

"It's Mrs. Dorman," she sobbed.

"What has she done?" I inquired, immensely relieved.

"She says she must go before the end of the month, and she says her niece is ill; she's gone down to see her now, but I don't believe that's the reason, because her niece is always ill. I believe someone has been setting her against us. Her manner was so queer—"

"Never mind, Pussy," I said; "whatever you do, don't cry, or I shall have to cry too, to keep you in countenance, and then you'll never respect your man again!"

She dried her eyes obediently on my handkerchief, and even smiled faintly.

"But you see," she went on, "it is really serious, because these village people are so sheepy, and if one won't do a thing you may be quite sure none of the others will. And I shall have to cook the dinners, and wash up the hateful greasy plates; and you'll have to carry cans of water about, and clean the boots and knives—and we shall never have any time for work, or earn any money, or anything. We shall have to work all day, and only be able to rest when we are waiting for the kettle to boil!"

I represented to her that even if we had to perform these duties, the day would still present some margin for other toils and recreations. But she refused to see the matter in any but the greyest light. She was very unreasonable, my Laura, but I could not have loved her any more if she had been as reasonable as Whately.

"I'll speak to Mrs. Dorman when she comes back, and see if I can't come to terms with her," I said. "Perhaps she wants a rise in her screw. It will be all right. Let's walk up to the church."

The church was a large and lonely one, and we loved to go there, especially upon bright nights. The path skirted a wood, cut through it once, and ran along the crest of the hill through two meadows, and round the churchyard wall, over which the old yews loomed in black masses of shadow. This path, which was partly paved, was called "the bier-balk," for it had long been the way by which the corpses had been carried to burial. The churchyard was richly treed, and was shaded by great elms which stood just outside and stretched their majestic arms in benediction over the happy dead. A large, low porch let one into the building by a Norman doorway and a heavy oak door studded with iron. Inside, the arches rose into darkness, and between them the reticulated windows, which stood out white in the moonlight. In the chancel, the windows were of rich glass, which showed in faint light their noble colouring, and made the black oak of the choir pews hardly more solid than the shadows.

But on each side of the altar lay a grey marble figure of a knight in full plate armour lying upon a low slab, with hands held up in everlasting prayer, and these figures, oddly enough, were always to be seen if there was any glimmer of light in the church. Their names were lost, but the peasants told of them that they had been fierce and wicked men, marauders by land and sea, who had been the scourge of their time, and had been guilty of deeds so foul that the house they had lived in—the big house, by the way, that had stood on the site of our cottage—had been stricken by lightning and the vengeance of Heaven. But for all that, the gold of their heirs had bought them a place in the church. Looking at the bad hard faces reproduced in the marble, this story was easily believed.

The church looked at its best and weirdest on that night, for the shadows of the yew trees fell through the windows upon the floor of the nave and touched the pillars with tattered shade. We sat down together without speaking, and watched the solemn beauty of the old church, with some of that awe which inspired its early builders. We walked to the chancel and looked at the sleeping warriors. Then we rested some time on the stone seat in the porch, looking out over the stretch of quiet moonlit meadows, feeling in every fibre of our being the peace of the night and of our happy love; and came away at last with a sense that even scrubbing and blackleading were but small troubles at their worst.

Mrs. Dorman had come back from the village, and I at once invited her to a *tête-à-tête*.

"Now, Mrs. Dorman," I said, when I had got her into my painting room, "what's all this about your not staying with us?"

"I should be glad to get away, sir, before the end of the month," she answered, with her usual placid dignity.

"Have you any fault to find, Mrs. Dorman?"

"None at all, sir; you and your lady have always been most kind, I'm sure—"

"Well, what is it? Are your wages not high enough?"

"No, sir, I gets quite enough."

"Then why not stay?"

"I'd rather not"—with some hesitation—"my niece is ill."

"But your niece has been ill ever since we came."

No answer. There was a long and awkward silence. I broke it.

"Can't you stay for another month?" I asked.

"No, sir. I'm bound to go by Thursday."

And this was Monday!

"Well, I must say, I think you might have let us know before. There's no time now to get anyone else, and your mistress is not fit to do heavy housework. Can't you stay till next week?"

"I might be able to come back next week."

I was now convinced that all she wanted was a brief holiday, which we should have been willing enough to let her have, as soon as we could get a substitute.

"But why must you go this week?" I persisted. "Come, out with it."

Mrs. Dorman drew the little shawl, which she always wore, tightly across her bosom, as though she were cold. Then she said, with a sort of effort—

"They say, sir, as this was a big house in Catholic times, and there was a many deeds done here."

The nature of the "deeds" might be vaguely inferred from the inflection of Mrs. Dorman's voice—which was enough to make one's blood run cold. I was glad that Laura was not in the room. She was always nervous, as highly-strung natures are, and I felt that these tales about our house, told by this old peasant woman, with her impressive manner and contagious credulity, might have made our home less dear to my wife.

"Tell me all about it, Mrs. Dorman," I said; "you needn't mind about telling me. I'm not like the young people who make fun of such things."

Which was partly true.

"Well, sir"—she sank her voice—"you may have seen in the church, beside the altar, two shapes."

"You mean the effigies of the knights in armour," I said cheerfully.

"I mean them two bodies, drawed out man-size in marble," she returned, and I had to admit that her description was a thousand times more graphic than mine, to say nothing of a certain weird force and uncanniness about the phrase "drawed out man-size in marble."

"They do say, as on All Saints' Eve them two bodies sits up on their slabs, and gets off of them, and then walks down the aisle, in their marble"—(another good phrase, Mrs. Dorman)—"and as the church clock strikes eleven they walks out of the church door, and over the graves, and along the bier-balk, and if it's a wet night there's the marks of their feet in the morning."

"And where do they go?" I asked, rather fascinated.

"They comes back here to their home, sir, and if anyone meets them—"

"Well, what then?" I asked.

But no—not another word could I get from her, save that her niece was ill and she must go. After what I had heard I scorned to discuss the niece, and tried to get from Mrs. Dorman more details of the legend. I could get nothing but warnings.

"Whatever you do, sir, lock the door early on All Saints' Eve, and make the cross-sign over the doorstep and on the windows."

"But has anyone ever seen these things?" I persisted.

"That's not for me to say. I know what I know, sir."

"Well, who was here last year?"

"No one, sir; the lady as owned the house only stayed here in summer, and she always went to London a full month afore the night. And I'm sorry to inconvenience you and your lady, but my niece is ill and I must go on Thursday."

I could have shaken her for her absurd reiteration of that obvious fiction, after she had told me her real reasons.

She was determined to go, nor could our united entreaties move her in the least.

I did not tell Laura the legend of the shapes that "walked in their marble," partly because a legend concerning our house might perhaps trouble my wife, and partly, I think, from some more occult reason. This was not quite the same to me as any other story, and I did not want to talk about it till the day was over. I had very soon ceased to think of the legend, however. I was painting a portrait of Laura, against the lattice window, and I could not think of much else. I had got a splendid background of yellow and grey sunset, and was working away with enthusiasm at her lace. On Thursday Mrs. Dorman went. She

12

relented, at parting, so far as to say—

"Don't you put yourself about too much, ma'am, and if there's any little thing I can do next week, I'm sure I shan't mind."

From which I inferred that she wished to come back to us after Hallowe'en. Up to the last she adhered to the fiction of the niece with touching fidelity.

Thursday passed off pretty well. Laura showed marked ability in the matter of steak and potatoes, and I confess that my knives, and the plates, which I insisted upon washing, were better done than I had dared to expect.

Friday came. It is about what happened on that Friday that this is written. I wonder if I should have believed it, if anyone had told it to me. I will write the story of it as quickly and plainly as I can. Everything that happened on that day is burnt into my brain. I shall not forget anything, nor leave anything out.

I got up early, I remember, and lighted the kitchen fire, and had just achieved a smoky success, when my little wife came running down, as sunny and sweet as the clear October morning itself. We prepared breakfast together, and found it very good fun. The housework was soon done, and when brushes and brooms and pails were quiet again, the house was still indeed. It is wonderful what a difference one makes in a house. We really missed Mrs. Dorman, quite apart from considerations concerning pots and pans. We spent the day in dusting our books and putting them straight, and dined gaily on cold steak and coffee. Laura was, if possible, brighter and gayer and sweeter than usual, and I began to think that a little domestic toil was really good for her.

We had never been so merry since we were married, and the walk we had that afternoon was, I think, the happiest time of all my life. When we had watched the deep scarlet clouds slowly pale into leaden grey against a pale-green sky, and saw the white mists curl up along the hedgerows in the distant marsh, we came back to the house, silently, hand in hand.

"You are sad, my darling," I said, half-jestingly, as we sat down together in our little parlour. I expected a disclaimer, for my own silence had been the silence of complete happiness. To my surprise she said—

"Yes. I think I am sad, or rather I am uneasy. I don't think I'm very well. I have shivered three or four times since we came in, and it is not cold, is it?"

"No," I said, and hoped it was not a chill caught from the treacherous mists that roll up from the marshes in the dying light. No—she said, she did not think so. Then, after a silence, she spoke suddenly—

"Do you ever have presentiments of evil?"

"No," I said, smiling, "and I shouldn't believe in them if I had."

"I do," she went on; "the night my father died I knew it, though he was right away in the north of Scotland." I did not answer in words.

She sat looking at the fire for some time in silence, gently stroking my hand. At last she sprang up, came behind me, and, drawing my head back, kissed me.

"There, it's over now," she said. "What a baby I am! Come, light the candles, and we'll have some of these new Rubinstein duets."

And we spent a happy hour or two at the piano.

At about half-past ten I began to long for the good-night pipe, but Laura looked so white that I felt it would be brutal of me to fill our sitting-room with the fumes of strong cavendish.

"I'll take my pipe outside," I said.

"Let me come, too."

"No, sweetheart, not tonight; you're much too tired. I shan't be long. Get to bed, or I shall have an invalid to nurse tomorrow as well as the boots to clean."

I kissed her and was turning to go, when she flung her arms round my neck, and held me as if she would never let me go again. I stroked her hair.

"Come, Pussy, you're over-tired. The housework has been too much for you."

She loosened her clasp a little and drew a deep breath.

"No. We've been very happy today, Jack, haven't we? Don't stay out too long."

"I won't, my dearie."

I strolled out of the front door, leaving it unlatched. What a night it was! The jagged masses of heavy dark cloud were rolling at intervals from horizon to horizon, and thin white wreaths covered the stars. Through all the rush of the cloud river, the moon swam, breasting the waves and disappearing again in the darkness. When now and again her light reached the woodlands they seemed to be slowly and noiselessly waving in time to the swing of the clouds above them. There was a strange grey light over all the earth; the fields had that shadowy bloom over them which only comes from the marriage of dew and moonshine, or frost and starlight.

I walked up and down, drinking in the beauty of the quiet earth and the changing sky. The night was absolutely silent. Nothing seemed to be abroad. There was no scurrying of rabbits, or twitter of the half-asleep birds. And though the clouds went sailing across the sky, the wind that drove them never came low enough to rustle the dead leaves in the woodland paths. Across the meadows I could see the church tower standing out black and grey against the sky. I walked there thinking over our three months of happiness—and of my wife, her dear eyes, her loving ways. Oh, my little girl! my own little girl; what a vision came then of a long, glad life for you and me together!

I heard a bell-beat from the church. Eleven already! I turned to go in, but the night held me. I could not go back into our little warm rooms yet. I would go up to the church. I felt vaguely that it would be good to carry my love and thankfulness to the sanctuary whither so many loads of sorrow and gladness had been borne by the men and women of the dead years.

I looked in at the low window as I went by. Laura was half lying on her chair in front of the fire. I could not see her face, only her little head showed dark against the pale blue wall. She was quite still. Asleep, no doubt. My heart reached out to her, as I went on. There must be a God, I thought, and a God who was good. How otherwise could anything so sweet and dear as she have ever been imagined?

I walked slowly along the edge of the wood. A sound broke the stillness of the night, it was a rustling in the wood. I stopped and listened. The sound stopped too. I went on, and now distinctly heard another step than mine answer mine like an echo. It was a poacher or a wood-stealer, most likely, for these were not unknown in our Arcadian neighbourhood. But whoever it was, he was a fool not to step more lightly. I turned into the wood, and now the footstep seemed to come from the path I had just left. It must be an echo, I thought. The wood looked perfect in the moonlight. The large dying ferns and the brushwood showed where through thinning foliage the pale light came down.

The tree trunks stood up like Gothic columns all around me. They reminded me of the church, and I turned into the bier-balk, and passed through the corpse-gate between the graves to the low porch. I paused for a moment on the stone seat where Laura and I had watched the fading landscape. Then I noticed that the door of the church was open, and I blamed myself for having left it unlatched the other night. We were the only people who ever cared to come to the church except on Sundays, and I was vexed to think that through our carelessness the damp autumn airs had had a chance of getting in and injuring the old fabric. I went in. It will seem strange, perhaps, that I should have gone half-way up the aisle before I remembered—with a sudden chill, followed by as sudden a rush of self-contempt—that this was the very day and hour when, according to tradition, the "shapes drawed out man-size in marble" began to walk.

Having thus remembered the legend, and remembered it with a shiver, of which I was ashamed, I could not do otherwise than walk up towards the altar, just to look at the figures—as I said to myself; really what I wanted was to assure myself, first, that I did not believe the legend, and, secondly, that it was not true. I was rather glad that I had come. I thought now I could tell Mrs. Dorman how vain her fancies were, and how peacefully the marble figures slept on through the ghastly hour. With my hands in my pockets I passed up the aisle. In the grey dim light, the eastern end of the church looked larger than usual, and the arches above the two tombs looked larger too. The moon came out and showed me the reason. I stopped short, my heart gave a leap that nearly choked me, and then sank sickeningly.

The "bodies drawed out man-size" were gone, and their marble slabs lay wide and bare in the vague moonlight that slanted through the east window.

Were they really gone? or was I mad? Clenching my nerves, I stooped and passed my hand over the smooth slabs, and felt their flat unbroken surface. Had someone taken the things away? Was it some vile practical joke? I would make sure, anyway. In an instant I had made a torch of a newspaper, which happened to be in my pocket, and lighting it held it high above my head. Its yellow glare illumined the dark arches and those slabs. The figures were gone. And I was alone in the church; or was I alone?

And then a horror seized me, a horror indefinable and indescribable—an overwhelming certainty of supreme and accomplished calamity. I flung down the torch and tore along the aisle and out through the porch, biting my lips as I ran to keep myself from shrieking aloud. Oh, was I mad—or what was this that possessed me? I leaped the churchyard wall and took the straight cut across the fields, led by the light from our windows. Just as I got over the first stile, a dark figure seemed to spring out of the ground. Mad still with that certainty of misfortune, I made for the thing that stood in my path, shouting, "Get out of the way, can't you!"

But my push met with a more vigorous resistance than I had expected. My arms were caught just above the elbow and held as in a vice, and the raw-boned Irish doctor actually shook me.

"Would ye?" he cried, in his own unmistakable accents—"would ye, then?"

"Let me go, you fool," I gasped. "The marble figures have gone from the church; I tell you they've gone."

He broke into a ringing laugh. "I'll have to give ye a draught tomorrow, I see. Ye've bin smoking too much and listening to old wives' tales."

"I tell you, I've seen the bare slabs."

"Well, come back with me. I'm going up to old Palmer's—his daughter's ill; we'll look in at the church and let me see the bare slabs."

"You go, if you like," I said, a little less frantic for his laughter; "I'm going home to my wife."

"Rubbish, man," said he; "d'ye think I'll permit of that? Are ye to go saying all yer life that ye've seen solid marble endowed with vitality, and me to go all me life saying ye were a coward? No, sir—ye shan't do ut."

The night air—a human voice—and I think also the physical contact with this six feet of solid common sense, brought me back a little to my ordinary self, and the word "coward" was a mental shower-bath.

"Come on, then," I said sullenly; "perhaps you're right."

He still held my arm tightly. We got over the stile and back to the church. All was still as death. The place smelt very damp and earthy. We walked up the aisle. I am not ashamed to confess that I shut my eyes: I knew the figures would not be there. I heard Kelly strike a match.

"Here they are, ye see, right enough; ye've been dreaming or drinking, asking yer pardon for the imputation."

I opened my eyes. By Kelly's expiring vesta I saw two shapes lying "in their marble" on their slabs. I drew a deep breath, and caught his hand.

"I'm awfully indebted to you," I said. "It must have been some trick of light, or I have been working rather hard, perhaps that's it. Do you know, I was quite convinced they were gone."

"I'm aware of that," he answered rather grimly; "ye'll have to be careful of that brain of yours, my friend, I assure ye."

He was leaning over and looking at the right-hand figure, whose stony face was the most villainous and deadly in expression.

"By Jove," he said, "something has been afoot here—this hand is broken."

And so, it was. I was certain that it had been perfect the last time

Laura and I had been there.

"Perhaps someone has tried to remove them," said the young doctor.

"That won't account for my impression," I objected.

"Too much painting and tobacco will account for that, well enough."

"Come along," I said, "or my wife will be getting anxious. You'll come in and have a drop of whisky and drink confusion to ghosts and better sense to me."

"I ought to go up to Palmer's, but it's so late now I'd best leave it till the morning," he replied. "I was kept late at the Union, and I've had to see a lot of people since. All right, I'll come back with ye."

I think he fancied I needed him more than did Palmer's girl, so, discussing how such an illusion could have been possible, and deducing from this experience large generalities concerning ghostly apparitions, we walked up to our cottage. We saw, as we walked up the garden-path, that bright light streamed out of the front door, and presently saw that the parlour door was open too. Had she gone out?

"Come in," I said, and Dr. Kelly followed me into the parlour. It was all ablaze with candles, not only the wax ones, but at least a dozen guttering, glaring tallow dips, stuck in vases and ornaments in unlikely places. Light, I knew, was Laura's remedy for nervousness. Poor child! Why had I left her? Brute that I was.

We glanced round the room, and at first, we did not see her. The window was open, and the draught set all the candles flaring one way. Her chair was empty and her handkerchief and book lay on the floor. I turned to the window. There, in the recess of the window, I saw her. Oh, my child, my love, had she gone to that window to watch for me? And what had come into the room behind her? To what had she turned with that look of frantic fear and horror? Oh, my little one, had she thought that it was I whose step she heard, and turned to meet—what?

She had fallen back across a table in the window, and her body lay half on it and half on the window-seat, and her head hung down over the table, the brown hair loosened and fallen to the carpet. Her lips were drawn back, and her eyes wide, wide open. They saw nothing now. What had they seen last?

The doctor moved towards her, but I pushed him aside and sprang to her; caught her in my arms and cried—-

"It's all right, Laura! I've got you safe, wifie."

18

She fell into my arms in a heap. I clasped her and kissed her, and called her by all her pet names, but I think I knew all the time that she was dead. Her hands were tightly clenched. In one of them she held something fast. When I was quite sure that she was dead, and that nothing mattered at all any more, I let him open her hand to see what she held.

It was a grey marble finger.

The Spectre Bride

(A.k.a. The Baron's Bridal)

William Harrison Ainsworth

The castle of Hernswolf, at the close of the year 1655, was the resort of fashion and gaiety. The baron of that name was the most powerful nobleman in Germany, and equally celebrated for the patriotic achievements of his sons, and the beauty of his only daughter. The estate of Hernswolf, which was situated in the centre of the Black Forest, had been given to one of his ancestors by the gratitude of the nation, and descended with other hereditary possessions to the family of the present owner. It was a castellated, gothic mansion, built according to the fashion of the times, in the grandest style of architecture, and consisted principally of dark winding corridors, and vaulted tapestry rooms, magnificent indeed in their size, but ill-suited to private comfort, from the very circumstance of their dreary magnitude. A dark grove of pine and mountain ash encompassed the castle on every side, and threw an aspect of gloom around the scene, which was seldom enlivened by the cheering sunshine of heaven.

★★★★★★

The castle bells rung out a merry peal at the approach of a winter twilight, and the warder was stationed with his retinue on the battlements, to announce the arrival of the company who were invited to share the amusements that reigned within the walls. The Lady Clotilda, the baron's only daughter, had but just attained her seventeenth year, and a brilliant assembly was invited to celebrate the birthday. The large vaulted apartments were thrown open for the reception of the numerous guests, and the gaieties of the evening had scarcely commenced when the clock from the dungeon tower was heard to strike with unusual solemnity, and on the instant a tall stranger, arrayed in a deep suit of black, made his appearance in the ballroom. He bowed courteously on every side, but was received by all with the strictest reserve.

No one knew who he was or whence he came, but it was evident from his appearance, that he was a nobleman of the first rank, and though his introduction was accepted with distrust, he was treated by all with respect. He addressed himself particularly to the daughter of the baron, and was so intelligent in his remarks, so lively in his sallies, and so fascinating in his address, that he quickly interested the feelings of his young and sensitive auditor. In fine, after some hesitation on the part of the host, who, with the rest of the company, was unable to approach the stranger with indifference, he was requested to remain a few days at the castle, an invitation which was cheerfully accepted.

The dead of the night drew on, and when all had retired to rest, the dull heavy bell was heard swinging to and fro in the grey tower, though there was scarcely a breath to move the forest trees. Many of the guests, when they met the next morning at the breakfast table, averred that there had been sounds as of the most heavenly music, while all persisted in affirming that they had heard awful noises, proceeding, as it seemed, from the apartment which the stranger at that time occupied. He soon, however, made his appearance at the breakfast circle, and when the circumstances of the preceding night were alluded to, a dark smile of unutterable meaning played round his saturnine features, and then relapsed into an expression of the deepest melancholy.

He addressed his conversation principally to Clotilda, and when he talked of the different climes he had visited, of the sunny regions of Italy, where the very air breathes the fragrance of flowers, and the summer breeze sighs over a land of sweets; when he spoke to her of those delicious countries, where the smile of the day sinks into the softer beauty of the night, and the loveliness of heaven is never for an instant obscured, he drew tears of regret from the bosom of his fair auditor, and for the first time she regretted that she was yet at home

Days rolled on, and every moment increased the fervour of the inexpressible sentiments with which the stranger had inspired her. He never discoursed of love, but he looked it in his language, in his manner, in the insinuating tones of his voice, and in the slumbering softness of his smile, and when he found that he had succeeded in inspiring her with favourable sentiments, a sneer of the most diabolical meaning spoke for an instant, and died again on his dark featured countenance. When he met her in the company of her parents, he was at once respectful and submissive, and it was only when alone with her, in her ramble through the dark recesses of the forest, that he assumed the guise of the more impassioned admirer.

As he was sitting one evening with the baron in the wainscotted apartment of the library, the conversation happened to turn upon supernatural agency. The stranger remained reserved and mysterious during the discussion, but when the baron in a jocular manner denied the existence of spirits, and satirically mocked their appearance, his eyes glowed with unearthly lustre, and his form seemed to dilate to more than its natural dimensions. When the conversation had ceased, a fearful pause of a few seconds and a chorus of celestial harmony was heard pealing through the dark forest glade.

All were entranced with delight, but the stranger was disturbed and gloomy; he looked at his noble host with compassion, and something like a tear swam in his dark eye. After the lapse of a few seconds, the music died gently in the distance, and all was hushed as before. The baron soon after quitted the apartment, and was followed almost immediately by the stranger. He had not long been absent, when an awful noise, as of a person in the agonies of death, was heard, and the baron was discovered stretched dead along the corridors. His countenance was convulsed with pain, and the grip of a human hand was visible on his blackened throat. The alarm was instantly given, the castle searched in every direction, but the stranger was seen no more. The body of the baron, in the meantime, was quietly committed to the earth, and the remembrance of the dreadful transaction, recalled but as a thing that once was.

******

After the departure of the stranger, who had indeed fascinated her very senses, the spirits of the gentle Clotilda evidently declined. She loved to walk early and late in the walks that he had once frequented, to recall his last words; to dwell on his sweet smile; and wander to the spot where she had once discoursed with him of love. She avoided all society, and never seemed to be happy but when left alone in the solitude of her chamber. It was then that she gave vent to her affliction in tears; and the love that the pride of maiden modesty concealed in public, burst forth in the hours of privacy. So beauteous, yet so resigned was the fair mourner, that she seemed already an angel freed from the trammels of the world, and prepared to take her flight to heaven.

As she was one summer evening rambling to the sequestered spot that had been selected as her favourite residence, a slow step advanced towards her. She turned round, and to her infinite surprise discovered the stranger. He stepped gaily to her side, and commenced an animated conversation.

'You left me,' exclaimed the delighted girl; 'and I thought all happiness was fled from me for ever; but you return, and shall we not again be happy?'

'Happy,' replied the stranger, with a scornful burst of derision, 'Can I ever be happy again—can there;—but excuse the agitation, my love, and impute it to the pleasure I experience at our meeting. Oh! I have many things to tell you; aye! and many kind words to receive; is it not so, sweet one? Come, tell me truly, have you been happy in my absence? No! I see in that sunken eye, in that pallid cheek, that the poor wanderer has at least gained some slight interest in the heart of his beloved. I have roamed to other climes, I have seen other nations; I have met with other females, beautiful and accomplished, but I have met with but one angel, and she is here before me. Accept this simple offering of my affection, dearest,' continued the stranger, plucking a heath-rose from its stem; 'it is beautiful as the wild flowers that deck thy hair, and sweet as is the love I bear thee.'

'It is sweet, indeed,' replied Clotilda, 'but its sweetness must wither ere night closes around. It is beautiful, but its beauty is short-lived, as the love evinced by man. Let not this, then, be the type of thy attachment; bring me the delicate evergreen, the sweet flower that blossoms throughout the year, and I will say, as I wreathe it in my hair, "The violets have bloomed and died—the roses have flourished and decayed; but the evergreen is still young, and so is the love of heart!"—you will not—cannot desert me. I live but in you; you are my hopes, my thoughts, my existence itself: and if I lose you, I lose my all—I was but a solitary wild flower in the wilderness of nature, until you transplanted me to a more genial soil; and can you now break the fond heart you first taught to glow with passion?'

'Speak not thus,' returned the stranger, 'it rends my very soul to hear you; leave me—forget me—avoid me for ever—or your eternal ruin must ensue. I am a thing abandoned of God and man—and did you but see the scared heart that scarcely beats within this moving mass of deformity, you would flee me, as you would an adder in your path. Here is my heart, love, feel how cold it is; there is no pulse that betrays its emotion; for all is chilled and dead as the friends I once knew.'

'You are unhappy, love, and your poor Clotilda shall stay to succour you. Think not I can abandon you in your misfortunes. No! I will wander with thee through the wide world, and be thy servant, thy slave, if thou wilt have it so. I will shield thee from the night winds, that they blow not too roughly on thy unprotected head. I will defend thee from the tempest that howls around; and though the cold world may devote thy name to scorn—though friends may fall off, and associates wither in the grave, there shall be one fond heart who shall love thee better in thy misfortune, and cherish thee, bless thee still.' She ceased, and her blue eyes swam in tears, as she turned it glistening with affection towards the stranger.

He averted his head from her gaze, and a scornful sneer of the darkest, the deadliest malice passed over his fine countenance. In an instant, the expression subsided; his fixed glassy eye resumed its unearthly chillness, and he turned once again to his companion. 'It is the hour of sunset,' he exclaimed; 'the soft, the beauteous hour, when the hearts of lovers are happy, and nature smiles in unison with their feelings; but to me it will smile no longer—ere the morrow dawns I shall very far, from the house of my beloved; from the scenes where my heart is enshrined, as in a sepulchre. But must I leave thee, dearest flower of the wilderness, to be the sport of a whirlwind, the prey of the mountain blast?'

'No, we will not part,' replied the impassioned girl; 'where thou goest, will I go; thy home shall be my home; and thy God shall be my God.'

'Swear it, swear it,' resumed the stranger, wildly grasping her by the hand; 'swear to the fearful oath I shall dictate.' He then desired her to kneel, and holding his right hand in a menacing attitude towards heaven, and throwing back his dark raven locks, exclaimed in a strain of bitter imprecation with the ghastly smile of an incarnate fiend, 'May the curses of an offended God,' he cried, 'haunt thee, cling to thee for ever in the tempest and in the calm, in the day and in the night, in sickness and in sorrow, in life and in death, shouldst thou swerve from the promise thou hast here made to be mine. May the dark spirits of the damned howl in thine ears the accursed chorus of fiends—may the air rack thy bosom with the quenchless flames of hell! May thy soul be as the lazar-house of corruption, where the ghost of departed pleasure sits enshrined, as in a grave: where the hundred-headed worm never dies where the fire is never extinguished. May a spirit of evil lord it over thy brow, and proclaim, as thou passest by, "*this is the abandoned of God and man;"* may fearful spectres haunt thee in the night season; may thy dearest friends drop day by day into the grave, and curse thee with their dying breath: may all that is most horrible in human nature, more solemn than language can frame, or lips can utter, may this, and more than this, be thy eternal portion, shouldst thou violate the oath that thou has taken.'

He ceased—hardly knowing what she did, the terrified girl acceded to the awful adjuration, and promised eternal fidelity to him who was henceforth to be her lord.

'Spirits of the damned, I thank thee for thine assistance,' shouted the stranger; 'I have wooed my fair bride bravely. She is mine—mine forever.—Aye, body and soul both mine; mine in life, and mine in death. What in tears, my sweet one, ere yet the honeymoon is past? Why! indeed thou hast cause for weeping: but when next we meet we shall meet to sign the nuptial bond.' He then imprinted a cold salute on the cheek of his young bride, and softening down the unutterable horrors of his countenance, requested her to meet him at eight o'clock on the ensuing evening in the chapel adjoining to the castle of Hernswolf.

She turned round to him with a burning sigh, as if to implore protection from himself, but the stranger was gone.

On entering the castle, she was observed to be impressed with deepest melancholy. Her relations vainly endeavoured to ascertain the cause of her uneasiness; but the tremendous oath she had sworn completely paralysed her faculties, and she was fearful of betraying herself by even the slightest intonation of her voice, or the least variable expression of her countenance. When the evening was concluded, the family retired to rest; but Clotilda, who was unable to take repose, from the restlessness of her disposition, requested to remain alone in the library that adjoined her apartment.

All was now deep midnight; every domestic had long since retired to rest, and the only sound that could be distinguished was the sullen howl of the ban-dog as he bayed, the waning moon Clotilda remained in the library in an attitude of deep meditation. The lamp that burnt on the table, where she sat, was dying away, and the lower end of the apartment was already more than half obscured. The clock from the northern angle of the castle tolled out the hour of twelve, and the sound echoed dismally in the solemn stillness of the night. Sudden the oaken door at the farther end of the room was gently lifted on its latch, and a bloodless figure, apparelled in the habiliments of the grave, advanced slowly up the apartment.

No sound heralded its approach, as it moved with noiseless steps to the table where the lady was stationed. She did not at first perceive it, till she felt a death-cold hand fast grasped in her own, and heard a solemn voice whisper in her ear, 'Clotilda.' She looked up, a dark figure was standing beside her; she endeavoured to scream, but her voice was unequal to the exertion; her eye was fixed, as if by magic, on the form which, slowly removed the garb that concealed its countenance, and disclosed the livid eyes and skeleton shape of her father. It seemed to gaze on her with pity, an regret, and mournfully exclaimed—'Clotilda, the dresses and the servants are ready, the church bell has tolled, and the priest is at the altar, but where is the affianced bride? There is room for her in the grave, and tomorrow shall she be with me.'

'Tomorrow?' faltered out the distracted girl; 'the spirits of hell shall have registered it, and tomorrow must the bond be cancelled.'

The figure ceased—slowly retired, and was soon lost in the obscurity of distance.

The morning—evening—arrived; and already as the hall clock struck eight, Clotilda was on her road to the chapel. It was a dark, gloomy night, thick masses of dun clouds sailed across the firmament, and the roar of the winter wind echoed awfully through the forest trees. She reached the appointed place; a figure was in waiting for her—it advanced—and discovered the features of the stranger.

'Why! this is well, my bride,' he exclaimed, with a sneer; 'and well will I repay thy fondness. Follow me.'

They proceeded together in silence through the winding avenues of the chapel, until they reached the adjoining cemetery. Here they paused for an instant; and the stranger, in a softened tone, said, 'But one hour more, and the struggle will be over. And yet this heart of incarnate malice can feel, when it devotes so young, so pure a spirit to the grave. But it must—it must be,' he proceeded, as the memory of her past love rushed on her mind; 'for the fiend whom I obey has so willed it. Poor girl, I am leading thee indeed to our nuptials; but the priest will be death, thy parents the mouldering skeletons that rot in heaps around; and the witnesses to our union, the lazy worms that revel on the carious bones of the dead. Come, my young bride, the priest is impatient for his victim.'

As they proceeded, a dim blue light moved swiftly before them, and displayed at the extremity of the churchyard the portals of a vault. It was open, and they entered it in silence. The hollow wind came rushing through the gloomy abode of the dead; and on every side, were piled the mouldering remnants of coffins, which dropped piece by piece upon the damp mud. Every step they took was on a dead body; and the bleached bones rattled horribly beneath their feet. In the centre of the vault rose a heap of unburied skeletons, whereon was seated, a figure too awful even for the darkest imagination to conceive. As they approached it, the hollow vault rung with a hellish peal of laughter; and every mouldering corpse seemed endued with unholy life. The stranger paused, and as he grasped his victim in his hand, one sigh burst from his heart—one tear glistened in his eye. It was but for an instant; the figure frowned awfully at his vacillation, and waved his gaunt hand.

The stranger advanced; he made certain mystic circles in the air, uttered unearthly words, and paused in excess of terror. On a sudden he raised his voice and wildly exclaimed—'Spouse of the spirit of darkness, a few moments are yet thine; that thou may'st know to whom thou hast consigned thyself. I am the undying spirit of the wretch who curst his Saviour on the cross. He looked at me in the closing hour of his existence, and that look hath not yet passed away, for I am curst above all on earth. I am eternally condemned to hell and I must cater for my master's taste till the world is parched as is a scroll, and the heavens and the earth have passed away. I am he of whom thou may'st have read, and of whose feats thou may'st have heard. A million souls has my master condemned me to ensnare, and then my penance is accomplished, and I may know the repose of the grave. Thou art the thousandth soul that I have damned. I saw thee in thine hour of purity, and I marked thee at once for my home. Thy father did I murder for his temerity, and permitted to warn thee of thy fate; and myself have I beguiled for thy simplicity. Ha! the spell works bravely, and thou shall soon see, my sweet one, to whom thou hast linked thine undying fortunes, for as long as the seasons shall move on their course of nature—as long as the lightning shall flash, and the thunders roll, thy penance shall be eternal. Look below! and see to what thou art destined.'

She looked, the vault split in a thousand different directions; the earth yawned asunder; and the roar of mighty waters was heard. A living ocean of molten fire glowed in the abyss beneath her, and blending with the shrieks of the damned, and the triumphant shouts of the fiends, rendered horror more horrible than imagination. Ten millions of souls were writhing in the fiery flames, and as the boiling billows dashed them against the blackened rocks of adamant, they cursed with the blasphemies of despair; and each curse echoed in thunder cross the wave.

The stranger rushed towards his victim. For an instant he held her over the burning *vista*, looked fondly in her face and wept as he were a child. This was but the impulse of a moment; again, he grasped her in his arms, dashed her from him with fury; and as her last parting glance was cast in kindness on his face, shouted aloud, 'not mine is the crime, but the religion that thou professest; for is it not said that there is a fire of eternity prepared for the souls of the wicked; and hast not thou incurred its torments?'

She, poor girl, heard not, heeded not the shouts of the blasphemer. Her delicate form bounded from rock to rock, over billow, and over foam; as she fell, the ocean lashed itself as it were in triumph to receive her soul, and as she sunk deep in the burning pit, ten thousand voices reverberated from the bottomless abyss, 'Spirit of evil! here indeed is an eternity of torments prepared for thee; for here the worm never dies, and the fire is never quenched.'

The Story of the Rippling Train

A True Ghost Story

Mrs. Molesworth

"Let's tell ghost stories, then," said Gladys.

"Aren't you tired of them? One hears nothing else nowadays. And they're all 'authentic,' really vouched for, only you never see the person who saw or heard or felt the ghost. It is always somebody's sister or cousin, or friend's friend," objected young Mrs. Snowdon, another of the guests at the Quarries.

"I don't know that that is quite a reasonable ground for discrediting them *en masse*," said her husband. "It is natural enough, indeed inevitable, that the principal or principals in such cases should be much more rarely come across than the stories themselves. A hundred people can repeat the story, but the author, or rather hero, of it, can't be in a hundred places at once. You don't disbelieve in any other statement or narrative merely because you have never seen the prime mover in it?"

"But I didn't say I discredited them on that account," said Mrs. Snowdon. "You take one up so, Archie. I'm not logical and reasonable; I don't pretend to be. If I meant anything, it was that a ghost story would have a great pull over other ghost stories if one could see the person it happened to. One does get rather provoked at *never* coming across him or her," she added a little petulantly.

She was tired; they were all rather tired, for it was the first evening since the party had assembled at the large country house known as "the Quarries" on which there was not to be dancing, with the additional fatigue of "ten miles there and ten back again"; and three or four evenings of such doings without intermission tell even on the young and vigorous.

Tonight various less energetic ways of passing the evening had been proposed,—music, games, reading aloud, recitation,—none had

31

found favour in everybody's sight, and now Gladys Lloyd's proposal that they should "tell ghost stories" seemed likely to fall flat also.

For a moment or two no one answered Mrs. Snowdon's last remarks. Then, somewhat to everybody's surprise, the young daughter of the house turned to her mother.

"Mamma," she said, "don't be vexed with me—I know you warned me once to be careful how I spoke of it; but *wouldn't* it be nice if Uncle Paul would tell us his ghost story? And then, Mrs. Snowdon," she went on, "you could always say you had heard *one* ghost story at or from—which should I say?—headquarters."

Lady Denholme glanced round half nervously before she replied.

"Locally speaking, it would not be *at* headquarters, Nina," she said. "The Quarries was not the scene of your uncle's ghost story. But I almost think it is better not to speak about it—I am not sure that he would like it mentioned, and he will be coming in a moment. He had only a note to write."

"I do wish he would tell it to us," said Nina regretfully. "Don't you think, mamma, I might just run to the study and ask him, and if he did not like the idea he might say so to me, and no one would seem to know anything about it? Uncle Paul is so kind—I'm never afraid of asking him any favour."

"Thank you, Nina, for your good opinion of me; you see there is no rule without exceptions; listeners do sometimes hear pleasant things of themselves," said Mr. Marischal, as he at that moment came round the screen which half concealed the doorway. "What is the special favour you were thinking of asking me?"

Nina looked rather taken aback.

"How softly you opened the door, Uncle Paul," she said. "I would not have spoken of you if I had known you were there."

"But after all you were saying no harm," observed her brother Michael. "And for my part I don't believe Uncle Paul would mind our asking him what we were speaking of."

"What was it?" asked Mr. Marischal. "I think, as I have heard so much, you may as well tell me the whole."

"It was only——" began Nina, but her mother interrupted her.

"I have told Nina not to speak of it, Paul," she said anxiously; "but—it was only that all these young people are talking about ghost stories, and they want you to tell them your own strange experience. You must not be vexed with them."

"Vexed!" said Mr. Marischal, "not in the least." But for a moment or two he said no more, and even pretty, spoilt Mrs. Snowdon looked a little uneasy.

"You shouldn't have persisted, Nina," she whispered.

Mr. Marischal must have had unusually quick ears. He looked up and smiled.

"I really don't mind telling you all there is to hear," he said. "At one time I had a sort of dislike to mentioning the story, for the sake of others. The details would have led to its being recognised—and it might have been painful. But there is no one now living to whom it would matter—you know," he added, turning to his sister; "her husband is dead too."

Lady Denholme shook her head.

"No," she said, "I did not hear."

"Yes," said her brother, "I saw his death in the papers last year. He had married again, I believe. There is not now, therefore, any reason why I should not tell the story, if it will interest you," he went on, turning to the others. "And there is not very much to tell. Not worth making such a preamble about. It was—let me see—yes, it must be nearly fifteen years ago."

"Wait a moment, Uncle Paul," said Nina. "Yes, that's all right, Gladys. You and I will hold each other's hands, and pinch hard if we get very frightened."

"Thank you," Miss Lloyd replied. "On the whole I should prefer for you not to hold my hand."

"But I won't pinch you so as to hurt," said Nina reassuringly; "and it isn't as if we were in the dark."

"Shall I turn down the lamps?" asked Mr. Snowdon.

"No, no," exclaimed his wife.

"There really is nothing frightening—scarcely even 'creepy,' in my story at all," said Mr. Marischal, half apologetically. "You make me feel like an impostor."

"Oh no, Uncle Paul, don't say that. It is all my fault for interrupting," said Nina. "Now go on, please. I have Gladys's hand all the same," she added *sotto voce*, "it's just as well to be prepared."

"Well, then," began Mr. Marischal once more, "it must be nearly fifteen years ago; and I had not seen her for fully ten years before that again! I was not thinking of her in the least; in a sense I had really forgotten her: she had quite gone out of my life; that has always struck me as a very curious point in the story," he added parenthetically.

"Won't you tell us who 'she' was, Uncle Paul?" asked Nina half shyly.

"Oh yes, I was going to do so. I am not skilled in story-telling, you see. She was, at the time I first knew her—at the only time, indeed, that I knew her—a very sweet and attractive girl, named Maud Bertram. She was very pretty—more than pretty, for she had remarkably regular features—her profile was always admired, and a tall and graceful figure. And she was a bright and happy creature too; that, perhaps, was almost her greatest charm. You will wonder—I see the question hovering on your lips, Miss Lloyd, and on yours too, Mrs. Snowdon—why, if I admired her and liked her so much, I did not go further. And I will tell you frankly that I did not because I dared not. I had then no prospect of being able to marry for years to come, and I was not very young. I was already nearly thirty, and Maud was quite ten years younger. I was wise enough and old enough to realise the situation thoroughly, and to be on my guard."

"And Maud?" asked Mrs. Snowdon.

"She was surrounded by admirers; it seemed to me then that it would have been insufferable conceit to have even asked myself if it could matter to her. It was only in the light of after events that the possibility of my having been mistaken occurred to me. And I don't even now see that I could have acted otherwise——" Here Uncle Paul sighed a little. "We were the best of friends. She knew that I admired her, and she seemed to take a frank pleasure in its being so. I had always hoped that she really liked and trusted me as a friend, but no more. The last time I saw her was just before I started for Portugal, where I remained three years.

"When I returned to London Maud had been married for two years, and had gone straight out to India on her marriage, and except by some few friends who had known us both intimately, I seldom heard her mentioned. And time passed. I cannot say I had exactly forgotten her, but she was not much or often in my thoughts. I was a busy and much-absorbed man, and life had proved a serious matter to me. Now and then some passing resemblance would recall her to my mind—once especially when I had been asked to look in to see the young wife of one of my cousins in her court-dress; something in her figure and bearing brought back Maud to my memory, for it was thus, in full dress, that I had last seen her, and thus perhaps, unconsciously, her image had remained photographed on my brain.

"But as far as I can recollect at the time when the occurrence I am going to relate to you happened, I had not been thinking of

Maud Bertram for months. I was in London just then, staying with my brother, my eldest brother, who had been married for several years, and lived in our own old town-house in —— Square. It was in April, a clear spring day, with no fog or half-lights about, and it was not yet four o'clock in the afternoon—not very ghost-like circumstances, you will admit. I had come home early from my club—it was a sort of holiday-time with me just then for a few weeks—intending to get some letters written which had been on my mind for some days, and I had sauntered into the library, a pleasant, fair-sized room lined with books, on the first-floor.

"Before setting to work I sat down for a moment or two in an easy-chair by the fire, for it was still cool enough weather to make a fire desirable, and began thinking over my letters. No thought, no shadow of a thought of my old friend Miss Bertram was present with me; of that I am perfectly certain. The door was on the same side of the room as the fireplace; as I sat there, half facing the fire, I also half faced the door. I had not shut it properly on coming in—I had only closed it without turning the handle—and I did not feel surprised when it slowly and noiselessly swung open, till it stood right out into the room, concealing the actual doorway from my view.

"You will perhaps understand the position better if you think of the door as just then acting like a screen to the doorway. From where I sat I could not have seen anyone entering the room till he or she had got beyond the door itself. I glanced up, half expecting to see someone come in, but there was no one; the door had swung open of itself. For the moment I sat on, with only the vague thought passing through my mind, 'I must shut it before I begin to write.'

"But suddenly I found my eyes fixing themselves on the carpet; something had come within their range of vision, compelling their attention in a mechanical sort of way. What was it?

"'Smoke,' was my first idea. 'Can there be anything on fire?' But I dismissed the notion almost as soon as it suggested itself. The something, faint and shadowy, that came slowly rippling itself in as it were beyond the dark wood of the open door, was yet too material for 'smoke.' My next idea was a curious one. 'It looks like soapy water,' I said to myself; 'can one of the housemaids have been scrubbing, and upset a pail on the stairs?' For the stair to the next floor almost faced the library door. But—no; I rubbed my eyes and looked again; the soapy water theory gave way.

"The wavy something that kept gliding, rippling in, gradually assumed a more substantial appearance. It was—yes, I suddenly became convinced of it—it was ripples of soft silken stuff, creeping in as if in some mysterious way unfolded or unrolled, not jerkily or irregularly, but glidingly and smoothly, like little wavelets on the sea-shore.

"And I sat there and gazed. 'Why did you not jump up and look behind the door to see what it was?' you may reasonably ask. That question I cannot answer. Why I sat still, as if bewitched, or under some irresistible influence, I cannot tell, but so it was.

"And it—came always rippling in, till at last it began to rise as it still came on, and I saw that a figure—a tall, graceful woman's figure—was slowly advancing, backwards of course, into the room, and that the waves of pale silk—a very delicate shade of pearly gray I think it must have been—were in fact the lower portion of a long court-train, the upper part of which hung in deep folds from the lady's waist. She moved in—I cannot describe the motion, it was not like ordinary walking or stepping backwards—till the whole of her figure and the clear profile of her face and head were distinctly visible, and when at last she stopped and stood there full in my view just, but only just beyond the door, I saw—it came upon me like a flash—that she was no stranger to me, this mysterious visitant! I recognised, unchanged it seemed to me since the day, ten years ago, when I had last seen her, the beautiful features of Maud Bertram."

Mr. Marischal stopped a moment. Nobody spoke. Then he went on again.

"I should not have said 'unchanged.' There was one great change in the sweet face. You remember my telling you that one of my girl-friend's greatest charms was her bright sunny happiness—she never seemed gloomy or depressed or dissatisfied, seldom even pensive. But in this respect the face I sat there gazing at was utterly unlike Maud Bertram's. Its expression, as she—or 'it'—stood there looking, not to-wards me, but out beyond, as if at some one or something outside the doorway, was of the profoundest sadness. Anything *so* sad I had never seen in a human face, and I trust I never may. But I sat on, as motion-less almost as she, gazing at her fixedly, with no desire, no power per-haps, to move or approach more nearly to the phantom.

"I was not in the least frightened. I knew it *was* a phantom, but I felt paralysed, and as if I myself had somehow got outside of ordinary conditions. And there I sat—staring at Maud, and there she stood, gazing before her with that terrible, unspeakable sadness in her face, which, even though I felt no *fear*, seemed to freeze me with a kind of unutterable pity.

"I don't know how long I had sat thus, or how long I might have continued to sit there, almost as if in a trance, when suddenly I heard the front-door bell ring. It seemed to awaken me. I started up and glanced round, half-expecting that I should find the vision dispelled. But no; she was still there, and I sank back into my seat just as I heard my brother coming quickly upstairs. He came towards the library, and seeing the door wide open walked in, and I, still gazing, saw his figure *pass through that of the woman in the doorway* as you may walk through a wreath of mist or smoke—only, don't misunderstand me, the figure of Maud till that moment had had nothing unsubstantial about it. She had looked to me, as she stood there, literally and exactly like a living woman—the shade of her dress, the colour of her hair, the few ornaments she wore, all were as defined and clear as yours, Nina, at the present moment, and remained so, or perhaps became so again as soon as my brother was well within the room.

"He came forward addressing me by name, but I answered him in a whisper, begging him to be silent and to sit down on the seat opposite me for a moment or two. He did so, though he was taken aback by my strange manner, for I still kept my eyes fixed on the door. I had a queer consciousness that if I looked away *it* would fade, and I wanted to keep cool and see what would happen. I asked Herbert in a low voice if *he* saw nothing, but though he mechanically followed the direction of my eyes, he shook his head in bewilderment. And for a moment or two he remained thus.

"Then I began to notice that the figure was growing less clear, as if it were receding, yet without growing smaller to the sight; it grew fainter and vaguer, the colours grew hazy. I rubbed my eyes once or twice with a half idea that my long watching was making them misty, but it was not so. My eyes were not at fault—slowly but surely Maud Bertram, or her ghost, melted away, till all trace of her had gone. I saw again the familiar pattern of the carpet where she had stood and the objects of the room that had been hidden by her draperies—all again in the most commonplace way, but she was gone, quite gone.

"Then Herbert, seeing me relax my intense gaze, began to question me. I told him exactly what I have told you. He answered, as every "common-sensible" person of course would, that it was strange, but that such things did happen sometimes and were classed by the wise under the head of 'optical delusions.' I was not well, perhaps, he suggested. Been over-working? Had I not better see a doctor? But I shook my head. I was quite well, and I said so. And perhaps he was right, it might be an optical delusion only. I had never had any experience of such things.

"'All the same,' I said, 'I shall mark down the date.'

"Herbert laughed and said that was what people always did in such cases. If he knew where Mrs. —— then was he would write to her, just for the fun of the thing, and ask her to be so good as to look up her diary, if she kept one, and let us know what she had been doing on that particular day—'the 6th of April, isn't it?' he said—when I would have it her wraith had paid me a visit. I let him talk. It seemed to remove the strange painful impression—painful because of that terrible sadness in the sweet face. But we neither of us knew where she was, we scarcely remembered her married name! And so there was nothing to be done—except, what I did at once in spite of Herbert's rallying, to mark down the day and hour with scrupulous exactness in *my* diary.

"Time passed. I had not forgotten my strange experience, but of course the impression of it lessened by degrees till it seemed more like a curious dream than anything more real, when one day I *did* hear of poor Maud again. 'Poor' Maud I cannot help calling her. I heard of her indirectly, and probably, but for the sadness of her story, I should never have heard it at all. It was a friend of her husband's family who had mentioned the circumstances in the hearing of a friend of mine, and one day something brought round the conversation to old times, and he startled me by suddenly inquiring if I remembered Maud Bertram. I said, of course I did. Did he know anything of her? And then he told me.

"She was dead—she had died some months ago after a long and trying illness, the result of a terrible accident. She had caught fire one evening when dressed for some grand entertainment or other, and though her injuries did not seem likely to be fatal at the time, she had never recovered the shock.

"'She was so pretty,' my friend said, 'and one of the saddest parts of it was that I hear she was terrifically disfigured, and she took this most sadly to heart. The right side of her face was utterly ruined, and the sight of the right eye lost, though, strange to say, the left side entirely escaped, and seeing her in profile one would have had no notion of what had happened. Was it not sad? She was such a sweet, bright creature.'

"I did not tell him *my* story, for I did not want it chattered about, but a strange sort of shiver ran through me at his words. *It was the left side of her face only* that the wraith of my poor friend had allowed me to see."

"Oh, Uncle Paul!" exclaimed Nina.

"And—as to the dates?" inquired Mr. Snowdon.

"I never knew the exact date of the accident," said Mr. Marischal, "but that of her death was fully six months after I had seen her. And in my own mind, I have never made any doubt that it was at or about, probably a short time after, the accident, that she came to me. It seemed a kind of appeal for sympathy—and—a farewell also, poor child."

They all sat silent for some little time, and then Mr. Marischal got up and went off to his own quarters, saying something vaguely about seeing if his letters had gone.

"What a touching story!" said Gladys Lloyd. "I am afraid, after all, it has been more painful than he realised for Mr. Marischal to tell it. Did you know anything of Maud's husband, dear Lady Denholme? Was he kind to her? Was she happy?"

"We never heard much about her married life," her hostess replied. "But I have no reason to think she was unhappy. Her husband married again two or three years after her death, but that says nothing."

"N—no," said Nina. "All the same, mamma, I am sure she really did love Uncle Paul very much,—much more than he had any idea of. Poor Maud!"

"And he has never married," added Gladys.

"No," said Lady Denholme, "but there have been many practical difficulties in the way of his doing so. He has had a most absorbingly busy life, and now that he is more at leisure he feels himself too old to form new ties."

"But," persisted Nina, "if he had had any idea at the time that Maud cared for him so?"

"Ah well," Lady Denholme allowed, "in that case, in spite of the practical difficulties, things would probably have been different."

And again Nina repeated softly, "Poor Maud!"

The Story of Clifford House

Anonymous

This story I will tell to you now, as I have promised to do so, and yet I can hardly make you believe in the reluctance with which I even allow my thoughts to go back to the time which I spent in that house—my first town residence after I was married.

I had wished so much to go to town that spring—grown tired of my lovely country home, I suppose. Tired of wide lawns and quiet, glassy ponds and streams, bordered by luscious, blooming rhododendrons; of silent, mossy avenues, glorious with the flickering light that stole through pale green beech leaves; of rose gardens with grassy paths, jewel-sprinkled with shell-like petals of white, crimson, pink, and cream-like hues; of old-fashioned rooms with narrow, mullioned windows embowered in scarlet japonica and fragrant, starry jessamine.

I suppose I had grown tired of them all, and I begged George to see about getting a nice house in town for the season.

George 'saw about it'—*viz.*: he wrote one letter—from my dictation—to a house agent, and answered one advertisement, and yawned and grunted for a week afterwards about the 'bore of the thing'.

Of course, I had to make him accompany me to town, and to the house agent's, and to the houses too. Let him smoke and yawn as much as he liked, I was determined to take a house, and take a nice one as well.

We had looked at—George said fourteen—but, in fact, seven, or eight houses I think, before we saw Clifford House.

I had found out a new house-agent's office, and this was the very first house we were shown—pressed upon our notice, too, by the enthusiastic encomiums of the said house-agent. It was certainly a very fine house, both as to exterior and interior appearances. Large, massively built, agreeably darkened in woodwork and masonry by

Time's shading brush, in excellent repair, and the locality all that could be desired. Wide, lofty apartments, staircases, and landings; a handsome dining-room panelled in velvety dark-green 'flock' and gold; a handsome drawing-room panelled in pale cream-colour and gold; airy bed-chambers and dressing-rooms—one, in particular, attached to what seemed the principal bedroom, with a vast mirror occupying the whole side of the apartment which was opposite to the door leading into the bedchamber.

'What a nice dressing-room!' I exclaimed, having a weakness, I confess, for large, handsome mirrors in the rooms I inhabit—George says impertinent things about my 'wishing to see as much of myself as I can'. I know I am not tall, in fact, rather what he should call petite, if he wished to be polite—but that is not my reason for liking a large mirror.

As I spoke the words I looked about mechanically for the house-agent's clerk who had been sent with us—a nervous-looking little man, with a pasty complexion, and orange-coloured hair meekly plastered down at each side of his face. He had been untiringly trotting up and down stairs, unlocking doors, answering questions, and keeping up a harmless soliloquy of chatter about the beauties and excellencies of the 'mansion,' as he called it, ever since he entered its doors, but now he was nowhere to be seen.

'What door have you open?' I said, speaking aloud to him, for suddenly a cold blast of air swept up the wide staircase and into the dressing-room, making me shudder.

'No door, ma'am—not one, indeed!' said the little clerk, hurrying to the dressing-room door, but not entering. His face looked whiter than before, and in his accents, there was an almost terrified earnestness that puzzled me.

The shadows of the afternoon seemed to deepen. The aspect of the suites of rooms and long silent corridors, with their doors ajar, as if unseen inhabitants were stealthily crouching behind them, drearily impressed me with a sense of dull desolation; and it was with a sudden sensation of childish fear and loneliness that I rushed after my husband, and took his arm as he hastily descended the stairs.

'A spacious, handsome staircase, George?' I remarked.

'Yes; and a spacious; handsome rent, you may be sure,' George responded.

But, in this particular, he was exceedingly, and I agreeably, astonished.

The rent was but a hundred and fifty pounds a year; when, judging from the situation and appearance of the house, our lowest estimate had been double that sum.

'How cheap!' I whispered.

'A screw loose somewhere,' was George's oracular response.

He repeated his opinion to the clerk in a more business-like expression, to the effect that the rent seemed low, and that he trusted there was no—peculiar—eh?

'Drains, gas, water, all right, sir—right as—a—a trivet, sir,' said the clerk, looking over his shoulder oddly, as he spoke. 'Chimneys, ventilators, roof, tiles—everything in the perfectest repair and order, sir!'

'Hum!' said George, with a frown of thoroughly British dissatisfaction. 'Unpleasant neighbours, then?'

The little clerk coughed violently, and buried his nose and eyes in the depths of a red cotton handkerchief:

'Neighbours? Disagreeable, sir? Ah! dear me! Beg pardon, sir—a little cough. No, indeed, sir!

Mrs Carmichael—very high lady—very rich, widow of young Mr William Carmichael, just opposite, sir—old Lady Broadleigh within two doors—Sir Thomas—'

'Oh, very well!' said George impatiently. 'Come, Helen.'

Nevertheless, I was rather surprised to see how many faces were clustered at the windows of our aristocratic neighbours' houses, and with what intently curious looks they watched our exit and departure, as if visitors, or would-be tenants for Clifford House, were some very wonderful people indeed.

However, wonderful or not, the house seemed all that we could desire; the lowness of the rent made it a decided bargain, the season was advancing, our low-ceiled, country rooms seemed contracted, old-fashioned, and shabby, after those lofty, handsome suites of apartments; and, in three weeks, huge furniture vans, and a clever upholsterer, had carpeted, curtained, and furnished our town mansion from garret to basement, and George and I, our two babies, a nurse, two maids, a cook, and a butler, were installed in Clifford House.

Dear George had been very generous—nay, almost extravagant—in his provisions for the comfort and pleasure of his wife and children; and my dressing-room and their nursery were fitted up so luxuriously and tastefully, that my feeling at the first inspection of them was that of self-gratulation on being such a fortunate woman, in having such a home, such babies, and such a husband.

I arrayed myself for dinner that evening quite gleefully; standing before my splendid mirror amid the blue drapery, cushions, and couches of my charming dressing-room. I put on George's favourite dress—a bronze-brown lustrous silk, with sparkling gold ornaments: he invariably kissed me when he saw it on, stroked my brown curls and brunette face, and called me 'Maid Marian'—and was still standing before the glass smiling at myself, like the happy, foolish little woman I was, when I perceived to my discomfiture that George was standing in the doorway watching my doings, and grinning very visibly under his moustache.

'Don't mind me, my dear, I beg! don't mind me in the least. But when you have done admiring Mrs George Russell, perhaps you will be kind enough to let me know'—then, suddenly changing his tone, he exclaimed, 'Have you the window open, Helen, this chilly evening?'

'No, George,' I replied, glancing at it to make sure of the fact.

'Change in the weather, then,' my husband said. 'Come, Helen, there is no use in making yourself any prettier!' He had just uttered the last words when I saw him spring aside suddenly, and look around.

'What is the matter?' I said—'George, dear, what is the matter?' For his face had grown quite white, and with his back against the wall, he was staring about him wildly 'I don't know—Helen—something'—he ejaculated in a low tone; then recovering himself, with a laugh, he cried—'I struck myself against the door, I suppose! I declare one would think I was composed of old china, or wax, or sugar candy, it hurt and stunned me so! Come, dearest.'

He had not struck himself, for I had been watching him going out on the lobby, and I felt an uneasy conviction that he knew he had not done so, and only spoke as he did in order to deceive or satisfy me. Why? Why did I think so? As I live I cannot tell why I thought so then—I know now. We had the 'babies'—as George always called them—in with the dessert, after the time-honoured fashion of making olives as well as olive branches of them; and then, when the little ones had gone to bed, we sat side by side in the summer twilight, I lazily fanning myself, George bending over me like the lover-husband he was.

Then came the lamps, and I played for him, and we sang duets and spent as happy an evening in our new home as a married pair could wish to spend. I cannot tell why I felt so disinclined to go upstairs that night, tired as I was, too—for we had had a long journey up from the country. However, as eleven struck, I routed George out of the easy chair where he had been indulging in a preliminary doze, and, ringing for my maid, went up to my dressing-room.

I like gas in my dressing-room, though not in my bedroom, and the globes at either side the great mirror were a blaze of light. As I entered I caught the reflection of a woman's figure in the depth of the glass, not my maid's. The glimpse I had was of a tall woman, strongly built, and broad-shouldered, a quantity of light hair hanging in a disordered manner on her neck, and the profile of a white, hard, masculine face, with the keen glittering eye turned watchfully towards the door.

This may seem an elaborately detailed description for the momentary glance I obtained, but it is well known with what lightning rapidity the organs of vision will, in moments of terror and amazement, convey impressions to the startled brain, impressions accurate and indelible.

I had taken but one step on entering, the next step the figure had vanished, and the mirror reflected but my own terrified face, and the homely, cheerful one of my maid Harriet, as she stooped over the dressing-table opening a jewel case.

I dropped down on the nearest chair, and, in answer to the girl's alarmed questions, replied that I did not feel very well. I was sick and shuddering from head to foot.

Suddenly it flashed across me that it was from a similar cause I had seen my husband's face grow ghastly, and that strange, terrified look come into his eyes,—he, who had been a soldier and unflinchingly had fought amidst the dead and dying on bloody Indian battlefields, almost boy as he was then! What was it? What had he seen? Nonsense! was I going to believe I had seen a ghost? Nonsense, a thousand times over! I heard my husband's cheery voice as he ascended the stairs, and, quite angry with myself for giving way to such folly, I threw on my dressing gown, and, snatching up the brush from Harriet, I pulled my hair down and brushed it quite savagely, until my head ached well— for punishment.

If the bright morning light disperses sweet illusions formed overnight, as people say it does, it disperses gloomy ones as well. With the warmth and brightness of the unclouded summer's sun streaming in through softly coloured blinds, bringing out the velvety green of soft new carpets and lounges, the rainbow tints of glittering chandeliers, vases, and ornaments, the gilding on bright fresh wallpaper, and the spotless folds of snowy window drapery, it was impossible for an instant to connect anything dark or dismal with Clifford House. Why, my dressing-room even, where I had been so silly last evening, was like a woodland bower, with its deep purple-blue hangings and rose painted china flower-vases, filled with bouquets from our country home.

Clustering fragrant honeysuckle half-opened moss roses, drooping emerald-green fern, and masses of delicious jessamine dropping its over-blown blossoms on the white toilet-cover, lace-flounced and tied with blue ribbons, as Harriet delighted to have it.

'I think this such a charming room and such a charming house altogether, George!' I said; 'and you have been such a dear, thoughtful old darling!' For I had perceived that the dear fellow had had his own half-length portrait hung over my writing-table. Quite a pleasant surprise for me, for I thought he intended it to be hung in the dining-room, and I delighted in having the dear pleasant brown eyes looking down at me when I was busy writing or sewing.

'I am so glad you like everything, Nellie,' said he.

'Why, George, don't you?'

But George had walked off whistling, and presently I heard uproarious baby-laughter, and baby-chatter, and thumping, trotting of small fat feet, as George put the tidy nursery into dire confusion by his morning game of romps with his son and heir, and red-cheeked baby-daughter.

And it did seem as if I must have been dreaming or delirious, when this day and many a succeeding one passed away swiftly and pleasantly, without the slightest recurring event to remind me of my strange alarm on the night of our arrival.

We had been in Clifford House about a fortnight, when one morning I received a visit from our opposite neighbour—the young widow, Mrs Carmichael. A very pretty, lady-like person she was, and as we had some common acquaintances we chattered away very freely and pleasantly for half-an-hour or so. As she rose to go she asked suddenly if we liked the house. I replied in the affirmative rather warmly.

She was opposite the light, and I saw an involuntary elevation of her eye-brows and compression of her lips that puzzled me. I fancied it was because I had spoken so enthusiastically. Yet her own manner was anything but languidly fashionable, being very cordial and decided.

'Yes; it is a very nice house, roomy and well-built,' said she, after a moment's pause; 'I am so glad you like it—we may be permanent neighbours.'

We went out to dinner at a friend's house in Seymour Street that evening, and when we returned about half-past eleven, in spite of a yawning remonstrance from George, I tripped off softly to have a peep at my darlings, before I went to bed.

The nursery was a large, pleasant room at the end of the long corridor leading from our own apartments, and, gently turning the handle and gathering my rustling silk dress around me, I opened the door and went in. There was the night-lamp burning clearly, shining softly on the tiny cribs with the sweet flushed infant faces, the long golden-brown lashes lying on the dimpled apple-bloom cheeks, the waxen hands and little rounded arms thrown above the tossed golden curls, and the heavenly calm of the little sleeping forms and pure, peaceful breathing.

I wonder would any mother, no matter how cold and careless, have neglected doing what I did, as I bent over my treasures, and prayed God that His angels might keep watch over each cherub head on its little, soft, white pillow?

I had looked at and kissed them, and turned to go, when I glanced towards the nurse's bed.

'Are you not well, Mary? What is the matter?' I said in an anxious whisper.

She was a very respectable and trustworthy servant, as well as being a kind, gentle creature with the little ones, and consequently highly valued by me, but her health was never very good, and she was subject to severe attacks of nervous headache and sleeplessness. She was sitting up in bed, her hands grasping the bedclothes, her face and lips ashy white, and her eyes staring wildly, as if they would start from their sockets.

'Mary! Good Heavens! what is the matter?' I gasped.

'Ma'am! Oh, ma'am—oh, mistress, I am dying!' And with a stifled cry the poor girl fell back on the pillow, her eyes still retaining their frenzied stare. It was but the work of a few moments to ring bells and summon the household, to dispatch the man-servant for a doctor, and to have the sleeping children taken into my own bedchamber, while Harriet and I administered restoratives, and chafed the half-senseless girl's damp, cold hands.

I could imagine no cause for her sudden illness, and the other servants were very voluble in exclamations and laments. But when the physician—a pale, kindly, grave-looking man arrived—after a moment's examination, he demanded if she had been frightened? I replied in the negative, and was proceeding to describe to him the state in which I had found her, when I heard the housemaid and Harriet whispering energetically together.

'She has!'

'Hush!'

'I know she has!'

'What is it? Speak out at once my good girl!' said the doctor sternly to the housemaid; 'you know something of this.'

Both servants looked apprehensively at me and at George.

'Speak up at once, Margaret; the girl's life may depend on it! Tell the truth, my girl, and don't be afraid,' said her master kindly, but firmly.

'I don't know nothing, sir—indeed, no, ma'am,' said Margaret confusedly; 'but—I think, ma'am—she's seen the ghost, sir!'

'The what!' cried George angrily.

'She have, sir!' persisted Margaret eagerly, now that her confession was made. 'We're all afraid, sir; but she's been worser nor the rest of us. And she says to me only this morning, "Margaret", she says, "if I see it, I'll die!" '

'What ghost, you fool?' cried George more angrily. 'A pretty set you are!—great, grown men and women, afraid of some bogie story you have heard when you were gossipping with the servants on the terrace, I suppose!'

'No, indeed, sir,' said Margaret; 'I wasn't gossippin', sir; but the parlour-maid over the way, sir—Mrs Carmichael's parlour-maid, ma'am—she told me that there was somethin'—'

'I thought so!' interrupted George. 'You ought to be ashamed of yourselves not to have an ounce of brains among you.'

'But, sir!' Margaret burst out again, unheeding her master's rather uncomplimentary phrenological verdict, 'we didn't mind, sir, though we was a bit frightened, until we seen it, sir! The butler seen it, and he ran, and cook ran.'

'And you ran after them?' said George, with an indignant laugh.

'I did, sir, for I saw it too—a big woman with fair hair all over her shoulders,' said Margaret, in an awestruck whisper to Harriet, who nodded her head.

The doctor looked up, gravely and without a smile. The servants clustered together near the door, and muttered in undertones. George looked at me with a forced smile, which died away in an instant:

'You are not so foolish as to credit any of this nonsense, Helen?' he said.

The servants all turned eagerly to hear their mistress's opinion. I am afraid it was written in my pallid face. Was it true? Was it what I had seen? Could there be any reality in this, that here, in our pleasant, happy home, here, beneath the roof with our helpless little ones, was a dreadful, unblessed presence—a shadowy horror; that that thing with the watchful, cruel eyes had not been a mere vision of imagination, the mere offspring of an active brain, and the unstrung nerves of an overtired frame?

'Oh! they imagined something from the stories they heard, I dare say,' I faltered.

The butler shook his head solemnly:

'I could swear to it, ma'am.'

'And so, could I, ma'am!' chorused the cook and housemaid.

'Hush!' said the doctor, as the nurse, roused, at length, from her stupor, lay quietly, with closed eyes, from which the tears streamed down her face. 'Someone must sit up with her now,' said the doctor, looking around.

'I will, sir, if my mistress allows me,' said Harriet.

'Certainly, Harriet,' said I at once.

He communicated his instructions to her and took his leave, promising to call in the morning.

'Did you ever hear anything like this folly, doctor?' said George, as he shook hands with him at the head of the stairs.

'Oh! yes, sir, I often hear such stories,' said the doctor quietly, as he bade us both goodnight.

'George! what has frightened the girl? What has she seen?' I whispered, clasping my husband's arm.

'Nellie, go to bed, and don't be a goose,' was George's reply.

'George—I saw that thing—that woman, in my dressing-room,' I said, trembling, 'and oh! think if the children were to see it and be frightened like poor Mary!'

'Well, Helen,' said my husband sharply, 'if you are going to listen to ignorant servants' superstitions and run out of your house, just as we are comfortably settled in it, on account of a foolish sickly woman fainting from hearing a ghost story—I say—it is a pity you ever came into it.'

He spoke very decidedly and sternly, and yet I felt in my inmost heart that he uttered what he wished me to believe, not what he believed himself.

I said no more, but went to my bedroom—not into the dreaded

dressing-room—and lay awake listening and fevered with nervous anxiety until the morning dawned.

The nurse was better and able to speak next day, though extremely weak and unnerved yet. The doctor forbade much questioning, and all that could be got from her at intervals was that something had come up the staircase and ran through the corridor, that she heard struggling and scuffling outside, and then the nursery door opened and she saw a woman's face peering in, the eyes gleaming wickedly at her, and it had the yellow hair that 'belonged to the ghost'.

'The woman has had a bad fit of nightmare—that is all, Helen,' said George, rattling his paper unconcernedly, when I repeated to him the story I had just heard from poor Mary's trembling lips.

It might be so; but why were they all agreed as to what they had seen? Why did they all speak of the tangled fair hair, and the wicked gleaming eyes? Was our house haunted? Was this the mysterious cause of the exceedingly moderate rent and the house-agent's profuse civility? The nurse did not recover strength, and being worse than useless in her present weak, hysterical condition, I sent her down to her country home for change of air, and hired another temporarily in her place.

The newcomer was a stout, small, cheerful woman of about forty. I liked her face the moment I saw her; for, besides its smiling, honest expression, there was a good deal of decided character in the large firm features. 'You appear to be a sensible person,' I said, when giving her her first instructions in the nursery, 'and I think I can rely on you. You know my nurse is leaving because of illness, and that illness was caused by her being frightened by—a ghost-story.' I paused; but the woman remained unmoved, listening to me in respectful silence.

'The servants downstairs have got some nonsense of the kind into their heads,' I went on; 'they will try to frighten you, too, and tell you they have seen—' I could not go on. For my life, I could not calmly give her the description of that shadowy image of fear.

'They cannot frighten me, ma'am,' said my new nurse quietly. 'I am not afraid of spirits.'

I thought she spoke in jest, and smiled.

'I am not indeed, ma'-am,' she repeated. 'I have lived where there were such things seen, but they never harmed me.'

'You don't mean to say you believe such nonsense?' said I, hypocritically trying to speak carelessly.

'Oh yes, ma'am, I do! I could not disbelieve it,' said the nurse, opening her eyes with earnestness, 'I know the story of this house, ma'am.'

'What story?' I cried.

The woman coloured and looked confused.

'I beg your pardon, ma'am—I mean what people say is seen here.'

'What do they say? Do not frighten me,' I said, and my voice quivered in spite of me; 'I have heard nothing but what the servants said.'

The nurse looked deeply concerned.

'I am very stupid, ma'am; I beg your pardon for repeating such stories to you—I daresay it is only idle people's gossip.'

She went about her duties, and I went—not into my dressing-room—but down into the drawing-room, where I sat by the window looking out until my husband returned.

Two or three weeks more passed away without any more alarms. The summer had deepened into its longest days and hottest sunshine; the gay season had reached and passed its meridian of wealth, beauty, luxury, extravagance, success, misery, hopes, and disappointments. I had enjoyed it very much at first; but I soon wearied of it as my bodily strength weakened in the ordeal of constant excitement, late hours, hot rooms, heavy perfumed atmosphere, ices, and diaphanous ball-dresses.

'Poor Maid Marian,' George said, 'she is pining for her green wild woods.' However, by following the doctor's advice—the same whom he had summoned the night of the nurse's illness, and whom we both liked very much—and living more quietly, I was able to enjoy quiet entertainments and my favourite operas very fairly, although my red brunette cheeks had faded dismally.

'An invitation for us, Helen, I know, and that is Willesden's writing.'

It was a sultry morning at the close of June. I felt tired and languid, and it was with a bad grace I tore open the envelope lying beside the breakfast tray.

'Yes, "Colonel and Mrs Willesden request the pleasure"—why George, it is for this evening!'

'Written the day before yesterday, though—delayed somehow,' said George, reading over my shoulder. 'Well, Helen, what do you say? It is only for a quiet, friendly dinner, and I like Willesden very much.'

'No, dear,' I replied wearily. 'You can go and make apologies for me. I am tired of dinner-parties, and, besides, George is not well.'

'My dear, the young urchin is far better than yourself,' replied George, dissecting a sardine with amazing relish; 'but just as you like, Nellie. There's *Mudie's last* on the sofa-table, and perhaps it is as well you should stay quiet this evening, and amuse yourself reading it.'

But *Mudie's last* failed to possess either interest or the power of amusing me in the long, quiet evening hours, after I had fidgeted about George whilst he was dressing, until he spoiled two white ties, and played with my darlings, and heard them lisp their prayers, and sang them asleep; after the clock had struck eight, and through the open windows the echoes of footsteps in the hot, dusty street grew fewer and fewer. No, *Mudie's last'* was a failure, as far as I was concerned; and, after a faint attempt at practising an intricate Morceau de Salon, I lay down on my pet chintz-covered couch, near the window, to look at the sky and the stars—when they came.

The house was as still as the grave, save for the far-off sound of some of the servants' voices; for I had given leave to Harriet and the housemaid for an evening out, escorted and protected by Charles—gravest and most stupid of butlers, between whom and my maid there existed tender relations, which were to be consummated by 'the good-will of a public' from master, and a silk wedding-dress from mistress, some happy future day.

Accordingly, they had donned all their finery, and set off in high glee; at least, I had heard much giggling and rustling of ribbons, and Charles's dignified cockney accents, as he opened the area gate wide for the young ladies' crinolines, and then dead silence again. Cook and the nurse were ensconced in one of the garret windows comparing notes and chatting busily, and all the lower part of the house was left to darkness and to me.

Dead silence—and the *ting, ting'* of the little French clock on the mantelpiece marked the half-hour after eight. Dear me, how dark it was growing! this brooding storm I supposed, which had been making me feel so languid and restless. I wish it would come down and cool the air—not tonight, though. Dear me, how lonely it is! I wish George were home. Those women are talking very loudly—I wonder nurse would—here I got drowsy, and my eyes ached looking for the stars that had not come.

In a few minutes I roused again, my maternal anxiety changing into indignation as I heard the women's voices growing louder and shriller, and some doors opened and shut violently.

What can nurse be thinking of? They will wake the children most certainly, and Georgie was so long in falling asleep—quite feverish, my own boy! I shall really reprove her very plainly. I never needed to do so before. What could she be thinking of? Dead silence again.

Well, this was lonely; I was inclined to ring for lights, and turn on all the burners in the chandelier by way of company. Then I remembered there were some wax matches in one of the drawers of a writing-tray just at hand, and thought I would light the gas myself instead of bringing the servants down—yes—but—I wanted company. It was so dark and dreary, and—and—I was afraid.

Afraid to stir—afraid to get off the couch on which I was lying—afraid to look at the door! a numbing, chilling tide of icy fear ebbing through even vein—afraid to draw a breath—afraid to move hand or foot, in a nightmare of supernatural terror. At last, by a violent effort, I sprang at the bell-handle, and pulled it frantically, and as soon as I had done so, with a sudden revulsion of feeling, I felt thoroughly ashamed of my childish cowardice, although I could not have helped it, and it had overcome me as suddenly as unexpectedly. How George would have laughed at me!

There were those servants talking again, tramping about and banging the doors as before.

Really, this was unbearable; cook must be in one of her fits of temper, and certainly had forgotten herself strangely.

And, as the quarrelsome tones grew louder and louder—evidently in bitter recrimination, although I could not catch a word—my own anger rose proportionately, and, forgetting loneliness and darkness in my indignant anxiety lest my children should be waked by this most unseemly behaviour of the servants, I ran hastily out of the room and up the wide staircase.

The dim light from the clouded evening sky, still further subdued by the gold and purple-stained glass of the conservatory door, streamed faintly down the steps from the first landing, and by it, just as I had ascended halfway, I discovered the short, thick-set figure of the nurse rushing down—of course, in answer to my ring, I supposed.

Involuntarily I stepped aside to avoid coming in violent contact with her as she fled past. No, it was not the nurse; and the woman following her in headlong haste, sweeping by me so that the current of air from their floating dresses struck icily cold on my brow where the clammy dew of perspiration had started in great drops, was—was—Merciful Heavens! What was that tall figure, with the coarse, disordered, yellow hair, the white face, and glittering, steel-blue eyes, that glinted fiendishly on me for one dreadful instant, and then vanished? Vanished as the pursued and pursuing figures had vanished in the shadows of the wide, lofty hall, without sound of voice or footstep?

I would have cried out—would have shrieked, if every nerve had not been paralyzed. I could not doubt the evidence of my senses—if I could have done so the cold, unearthy horror which sickened my very soul would have borne its undeniable testimony that I had beheld the impersonation of the hidden curse that rested on this dwelling.

I stood there rigid and immovable, as if that blighting Medusa-glance had indeed changed me into stone.

It may have been but a very few minutes—it seemed to me a cycle of painful ages, when the light of a brightly burning lamp shone before me, and I heard the cheerful sound of the new nurse's voice in my ears:

'Come along, cook. Bless your heart my dear! you needn't be nervous; there's no occasion.

'Mrs Russell, ma'am, aren't you well, ma'am?'

'No,' I said faintly, staggering to the woman's outstretched hands. 'Not down there—upstairs to the children.'

She turned as I bade her, and supported me up the stairs and into the nursery, the cook following close at my shins, muttering fervent prayers and ejaculations.

The sight of the peacefully sleeping little ones did far more to restore me than all the essences and chafing and unlacing which the two women busily administered.

I had got suddenly ill when coming upstairs was the explanation I gave, which the cook, I plainly perceived, most thoroughly doubted, at least without the cause she suspected being assigned, which, even in the midst of my terror-stricken condition, I refrained from giving. I did not speak to the nurse either of what had happened, but I felt that she knew as well as if she had been by my side all the time. But when George returned I told him.

Distressed and alarmed on my account though he was, yet he did not, as before, refuse credence to my story. 'We must leave the house, George. I should die here very soon,' I said.

'Yes Helen; of course, we must leave if you have anything to distress or terrify you in this manner, though it does seem absurd to be driven out of one's house and home by a thing of this kind. Someone's practical joke, or a trick prompted by malice against the owner of the property in order to lessen its value. I have heard of such things often.'

'George, it is nothing of the kind,' I said earnestly; 'you know it is not.'

'No, I don't,' said George shortly and grimly, as he opened his case of revolvers, 'and I wish I did.'

The night passed away quietly, to our ears at least; but next morning when George had concluded the usual morning prayers, instead of the usual move of the servants, they remained clustered at the door, Charles with an exceedingly elongated visage standing slightly in advance of the group as spokesman.

'Please, sir and ma'am, we can't tell what to do.'

'Why, go and do your work,' retorted George, with a nervous tug at his moustache and an uneasy glance at me.

Charles shook his head slowly. 'It can't be done, sir—can't be done, ma am. Why, no living Christian, not to speak of humble, but respectable servants,' said Charles with a flourish, quite unconscious of the nice distinction he had made, 'could stand it any longer.'

'What is the matter, pray?' said my husband.

'Ghosts, sir—spirits, sir—unclean spirits,' said Charles, in an awestruck whisper which was re-echoed in the cook's 'Lor' 'a' mercy!' as she dodged back from the doorway with the housemaid holding fast to one of her ample sleeves, and the lady's maid holding fast to the other.

The new nurse, quietly dandling the baby in her arms, was alone unmoved.

'What stories have you been listening to now?' said their master, with a slight laugh and a frown.

'No stories, sir; but what we've seen with our eyes and understanded with our ears, and—and—comprehended with our hearts,' said Charles, with an unsuccessful attempt at quoting Scripture. 'What was it as walked the floors last night between one and two, sir? What was it as talked and shrieked and run and raced? What was it as frightened the mistress on the stairs last evening?' And the whole posse of them turned to me, triumphantly awaiting my testimony.

I was feeling very ill, and looking so, I daresay, having struggled downstairs in order to prevent the servants having any additional confirmation of their surmises.

'That is no affair of yours,' said George gravely; 'your mistress is in delicate health, and was feeling unwell all day.'

'Will you allow me to speak, please, sir?' said the nurse, and, as her master nodded assent, she turned to the frightened group with a pleasant smile.

'You have no cause to be afraid, cook, or Mr Charles, or any of you,' said she, addressing the most important functionary first—'not in the least. I am only a servant like the rest, and here a shorter time than any one; but I think you are very foolish to unsettle yourselves in a good situation and frighten yourselves. You needn't think they'll harm you. Fear God and do your duty, and you needn't mind wandering, poor, lonely souls—'

'Lor' 'a' mercy! 'ow you do talk, Mrs Hamley!' said the cook indignantly.

'I've seen them more times than one—many and many a time, Mrs Cook; and they never harmed a hair of my head,' said the nurse, 'nor they'll never harm yours.'

'Well, then,' said the cook, packing into the hall, followed by her satellites, 'not to be made Queen Victorier of, nor Hemperor of Rooshia neither, would I stay to be frightened out of my seven senses, and made into a lunatic creature like poor Mary was!'

'Please to make better omelettes for luncheon, cook, than you did yesterday,' said George calmly, though he looked pale and angry enough, 'and leave me to deal with the ghosts—I'll settle accounts with them!'

The nurse turned quickly and looked earnestly at him: 'I would not say that, sir—God forbid,' said she in an undertone, and the next moment was singing softly and blithely as she carried the children away to their morning bath.

George and I looked at each other in silence.

'I wish we had never come into this house, dear,' I said.

'I wish from my heart that we never had, Helen,' he responded; 'but we must manage to stay the season out, at all events. It would be too absurd to run away like frightened hares, not to speak of the expense and trouble we have gone to.'

'We can get it taken off our hands without loss, perhaps,' I suggested. 'See the house-agent, George.'

'I have seen him,' he replied.

'Oh! all politeness and amiability, of course. Deeply regretted that we should have any occasion to find fault. No other tenants ever did. Happy to do anything in the way of clearing up this little mystery, etcetera. Of course, he was laughing at me in his sleeve.'

Again, as after our previous alarms, days passed on and lengthened into weeks in undisturbed quietude. George had a good many business matters to arrange; the children looked as rosy and healthy as in their country home. From their constant walking and playing in the airy, pleasant parks. My own health was not very good; and Dr Winchester was kindest and wisest of grave, gentlemanly doctors; so, all things considered, we stayed in London until August—very willingly, too—and only spoke of an excursion of a few weeks to the Isle of Man as a probability in September. Only on my husband's account, I wished for any change. Something seemed to affect his health strangely, although he never complained of anything beyond the usual lassitude and want of tune which a gay London season might be expected to bequeath him. He was sleepless, frequently depressed, nervous, and irritable; and still he vehemently declared he was quite well, and seemed almost annoyed when I urged him to put his business aside for the present and leave town.

He had been induced to enter into a large mining speculation, and hid, besides, some heavy money matters to arrange, connected with his sister's marriage settlements, which he expected would be required about Christmas. So, all things considered, he had some cause for looking as haggard as he did.

'It will be as well for him to leave London, Mrs Russell, as soon as he can,' said Dr Winchester at the close of one of his pleasant 'run-in' visits. 'His nerves are shaky. We men get nervous nearly as often as the ladies, though we don't confess to the fact quite so openly. A link unstrung, you know—nothing more. A few weeks in sea or mountain air will quite brace him up again.'

And as I dressed for dinner that evening, I determined that if wifely entreaties, arguments, and authority, should not fail for the first time in our wedded life, George should have the sea or mountain air without another week's delay; and, of course, I determined, likewise, to back up entreaties, arguments, and authority with the prettiest dress I could put on. I cannot tell why wives, and young wives too, will neglect their personal appearance when 'only one's husband' is present. It is unpolitic, unbecoming, and unloving; and men and husbands don't like neglect—direct or implied, be sure of that, ladies—young, middle-aged, or old.

'Your brown silk, ma'am?—it is rather cold this evening for that cream-coloured grenadine,' said Harriet, rustling at my wardrobe.

'No, Harriet, I won't have that brown, I am tired of it,' I replied. If I had said I was afraid of it, I should have kept closer to the truth. It so happened that it was this dress which I had worn on the three occasions when I had been terrified by the strange occurrences in this house; and I had acquired a superstitious aversion for this particular robe. So, Harriet arrayed me in a particularly charming demi-toilette of pale yellow silk grenadine and white lace; and I felt myself to be a most amiable and affectionate little wife, as I went downstairs to await George's return for dinner.

I never sat in my pretty dressing-room alone. Truth to tell, I disliked the apartment secretly and intensely, and only for fear of troubling and displeasing George I would have shut it up from the first evening I spent in it.

He was late for dinner, and I was quite shocked to see how thin and ill he looked by the gas-light; and, as soon as it was concluded, and that by the aid of excellent coffee and a vast amount of petting, I had coaxed him into his usual smiles and good-humour, I began my petition—that he would leave town for his own sake.

He listened to me in silence, and then said, 'Very well, Helen, we will go as soon as we can get the house disposed of; I suppose you will not come back here again?'

'Oh! no, I think not,' I replied, 'we will spend the winter in Hertfordshire, in our dear old house, George.'

'Very well,' he said wearily, 'though you must know, Helen, I am not going on account of this thing. I would hardly quit my house, indeed, because of ghostly or bodily sights or sounds.'

He had started up from the couch on which he was lying, flushed and excited as he always was when the subject was mentioned, his eyes gleaming as brightly as the flashing scabbard which hung on the wall before him.

'Certainly not, dearest,' I said soothingly.

'I wish I could solve the mystery,' he pursued, more excitedly; 'I would make somebody suffer for it! One's peace destroyed, and people terrified, and servants driven away, as if one was living in the dark ages, with some cursed necromancer next door!'

'Oh! well, it is some time ago now, and the servants have got over their fright. Pray, don't distress yourself about it, dear George.'

'Ah well—you don't—never mind,' he muttered; 'but I mean to have tangible evidence before ever I leave this house—I have sworn it!'

He was not easily roused, and I felt both surprise and alarm to see him so now, and for so inadequate a cause. I had almost fancied he had forgotten the matter, as we, by tacit consent, never alluded to it.

'Don't you allow yourself to be alarmed, Helen, that is all I care about,' he went on, pacing the floor. 'I have been half mad with anxiety on your account, for fear those idiotic servants should manage to startle you to death some dark evening—cowards, every one of them; but I mean to have someone to stay here and sit up'—He paused suddenly, and listened, then stepped noiselessly to the door, and opening it, listened again intently.

'George,' I whispered.

He took no heed of me; but rapidly unlocking a cabinet drawer, he drew out a six-barrelled revolver, loaded and capped, and with his finger on the trigger stole softly to the door and into the hall, whither I followed him.

Everything was silent, and the hail and stairs lamps were burning clear and high. I could hear the throbbing of my own heart as I stood there watching. Suddenly we both heard heavy rapid footsteps, seemingly overhead; and then confused noises, as of struggling, and quarrelling, and sobbing, mingled in a swelling clamour which sounded now near, deafeningly near, and then far, far away; now overhead, now beside us, now beneath, undistinguishable, indescribable, and unearthly.

Then the rushing footsteps came nearer and nearer. And, clenching his teeth, while his face grew rigid and white in desperate resolve, George sprang up the staircase with a bound like a tiger.

It had all passed in less than half the time I have taken to relate it, and while I yet stood breathless and with straining eyes, George had nearly reached the last step when I saw him stagger backwards, the revolver raised in his hand.

There was a struggle, a rushing, swooping sound, two shots fired in rapid succession, a floating cloud of white smoke, through which I saw the streaming yellow hair and steel-blue eyes flash downwards, and then a shriek rang out—the dreadful cry of a man in mortal terror—a crashing fall, beneath which the house trembled to its foundations, and I saw my husband's body stretched before the conservatory door, whither he had toppled backwards—whether dead or dying I knew not.

I remember dimly hearing my own voice in agonized screams, and the terror-stricken servants hurrying from the kitchens below. I remember the kind face of my new nurse as she bravely rushed down and dispatched someone for the doctor, and made others help her to carry the senseless figure, with blood slowly dripping from the parted lips and staining the snowy linen shirt-front in great gouts and splashes, up to the chamber, where they laid him on his bed, and I, a wretched frenzied woman, knelt beside him with the sole, ceaseless prayer that brain or lips could form—'God help me!'

I remember the physician's arrival, and the grave face and low clear voice of Dr Winchester, as he made his enquiries; and then another physician summoned, and the low frightened voices, and peering frightened faces, and the lighted candles guttering away in currents of air from opening and shutting doors, and the long hours of night, and the cold grey dawning, and the heart-rending suspense, and speechless, tearless, wordless agony, and the sun rose, gloriously cloudless, smiling in radiance, as if there was not the shadow of death over the weary world beneath his rays, and I heard the verdict—'There was scarcely a hope.'

But God was merciful to me and to him, and my darling did not die.

With a fevered brain and a shattered limb he lay there for weeks— lay there with the dark portals half open to receive him; lay there, when I could no longer watch beside him, but lay prostrate and suffering in another apartment, tended by kind relatives and friends; but at length, when the mellow sunshine, and the crisp clear air of the soft shadowy October days stole into the sick room, George was able to be dressed and sit up for an hour or two amongst the pillows of his easy-chair by the window.

And there he was, longing to be gone away from London.

'Helen, darling, weak or strong I must go,' he said in his trembling uncertain voice, and with a restless longing in his faded eyes, 'I shall never get better in this house.'

And so, a few days afterwards, accompanied by the doctor and two nurses, we went down in a pleasant swift railroad journey to our dear, beautiful, peaceful home in Hertfordshire.

George never spoke of that night of horror but once, when Dr Winchester told us the story connected with Clifford House.

Thirty years before, the man who was both proprietor and tenant of Clifford House died, leaving his two daughters all he possessed.

He had been a bad man, led a bad wild life, and died in a fit brought on by drunkenness; and these two daughters, grown to womanhood, inherited with his ill-gotten gold his evil nature.

They were only half-sisters, and were believed to have been illegitimate also. The elder, a tall, masculine, strongly built woman, with masses of coarse fair hair, and bright, glittering blue eyes; and the younger, a plump, dark-haired rather pretty girl, but as treacherous, vain, and bold, as her elder sister was fierce, passionate, and cruel. They lived in this house, with only their servants, for several years after their father's death, a life of quarrelling and bickering, jealousy and heart-burnings, on various accounts. The elder strove to tyrannize over the younger, who repaid it by deceit and crafty selfishness. At length a lover came, whom the elder sister favoured; whom she loved as fiercely and rashly as such wild untamed natures do; and by falsehood and deep-laid treachery the younger sister won the man's fickle fancy from the great, harsh-featured, haughty, passionate elder one.

The elder woman soon perceived it, and there were dreadful scenes between the two sisters, when the younger taunted the elder, and the elder cursed the younger; and at length one night—when there had been a fiercer encounter of words than usual, and the dark-haired girl maddened her sister by insults, and the sudden information that she intended leaving the house in the morning, to stay with a relative until her marriage, which was to take place in one week from that time—the wronged woman, demon-possessed from that moment, waited in her dressing-room until her sister entered, and then she sprang on her, and, screaming and struggling, they both wrestled until they reached the staircase, where the younger sister, escaping for an instant, rushed wildly down, followed by her murderess, who overpowered her in spite of her frantic struggles, and with her strong, cruel, bony hands deliberately strangled her, until she lay a disfigured palpitating corpse at her feet.

The officers of justice arrested the murderess a few hours afterwards, but she died by poison self-administered on the second day of her imprisonment.

Clifford House had been shut up and silent for many a year afterwards, and when, at length, an enterprising landlord put it in habitable order, and found tenants for it again, he only found them to lose them.

Year after year passed away, its evil fame darkening with its massive masonry, for none could be found to sanctify with the sacred name and pleasures of home that dwelling blighted by an abiding curse.

'I never told you, Helen,' George said, 'although I told Dr Winchester, that from the first evening I led a haunted life in that dreadful house, and the more I struggled to disbelieve the evidence of my senses, and to keep the knowledge from you, the more unbearable it became, until I felt myself going mad. I knew I was haunted, but until that last night I had never witnessed what I dreaded day and night to see. And then, Helen, when I fired, and I saw the devilish murderess face, with its demon eyes blazing on me, and the tall unearthly figure hurrying down to meet me, dragging the other struggling, writhing figure, with her long sinewy fingers seemingly pressed around the convulsed face, then I knew it was all over with me. If there had been a flaming furnace beside me I think I should have leaped into it to escape that awful sight.'

That is years ago now. We have spent many a pleasant month in the great metropolis since, but love our country home best of all. But we never speak of that terrible time when we learned the story of Clifford House.

My New Year's Eve among the Mummies

Grant Allen (J. Arbuthnot Wilson pseudonym)

January 1880

I have been a wanderer and a vagabond on the face of the earth for a good many years now, and I have certainly had some odd adventures in my time; but I can assure you, I never spent twenty-four queerer hours than those which I passed some twelve months since in the great unopened Pyramid of Abu Yilla.

The way I got there was itself a very strange one. I had come to Egypt for a winter tour with the Fitz-Simkinses, to whose daughter Editha I was at that precise moment engaged. You will probably remember that old Fitz-Simkins belonged originally to the wealthy firm of Simkinson and Stokoe, worshipful vintners; but when the senior partner retired from the business and got his knighthood, the College of Heralds opportunely discovered that his ancestors had changed their fine old Norman name for its English equivalent some time about the reign of King Richard I; and they immediately authorised the old gentleman to resume the patronymic and the armorial bearings of his distinguished forefathers. It's really quite astonishing how often these curious coincidences crop up at the College of Heralds.

Of course it was a great catch for a landless and briefless barrister like myself—dependent on a small fortune in South American securities, and my precarious earnings as a writer of burlesque—to secure such a valuable prospective property as Editha Fitz-Simkins. To be sure, the girl was undeniably plain; but I have known plainer girls than she was, whom forty thousand pounds converted into My Ladies: and if Editha hadn't really fallen over head and ears in love with me, I suppose old Fitz-Simkins would never have consented to such a match.

As it was, however, we had flirted so openly and so desperately during the Scarborough season, that it would have been difficult for Sir Peter to break it off: and so I had come to Egypt on a tour of insurance to secure my prize, following in the wake of my future mother-in-law, whose lungs were supposed to require a genial climate though in my private opinion they were really as creditable a pair of pulmonary appendages as ever drew breath.

Nevertheless, the course of true love did not run so smoothly as might have been expected. Editha found me less ardent than a devoted squire should be; and on the very last night of the old year she got up a regulation lovers' quarrel, because I had sneaked away from the boat that afternoon under the guidance of our *dragoman*, to witness the seductive performances of some fair Ghawzi, the dancing girls of a neighbouring town. How she found it out heaven only knows, for I gave that rascal Dimitri five *piastres* to hold his tongue: but she did find it out somehow, and chose to regard it as an offence of the first magnitude: a mortal sin only to be expiated by three days of penance and humiliation.

I went to bed that night, in my hammock on deck, with feelings far from satisfactory. We were moored against the bank at Abu Yilla, the most pestiferous hole between the cataracts and the Delta. The mosquitoes were worse than the ordinary mosquitoes of Egypt, and that is saying a great deal. The heat was oppressive even at night, and the malaria from the lotus beds rose like a palpable mist before my eyes. Above all, I was getting doubtful whether Editha Fitz-Simkins might not after all slip between my fingers. I felt wretched and feverish: and yet I had delightful interlusive recollections, in between, of that lovely little Ghziyah, who danced that exquisite, marvellous, entrancing, delicious, and awfully oriental dance that I saw in the afternoon.

By Jove, she was a beautiful creature. Eyes like two full moons; hair like Milton's Penseroso; movements like a poem of Swinburne's set to action. If Editha was only a faint picture of that girl now! Upon my word, I was falling in love with a Ghziyah!

Then the mosquitoes came again. *Buzz—buzz—buzz.* I make a lunge at the loudest and biggest, a sort of *prima donna* in their infernal opera. I kill the *prima donna*, but ten more shrill performers come in its place. The frogs croak dismally in the reedy shallows. The night grows hotter and hotter still. At last, I can stand it no longer. I rise up, dress myself lightly, and jump ashore to find some way of passing the time.

Yonder, across the flat, lies the great unopened Pyramid of Abu

Yilla. We are going tomorrow to climb to the top; but I will take a turn to reconnoitre in that direction now. I walk across the moonlit fields, my soul still divided between Editha and the Ghziyah, and approach the solemn mass of huge, antiquated granite blocks standing out so grimly against the pale horizon. I feel half awake, half asleep, and altogether feverish: but I poke about the base in an aimless sort of way, with a vague idea that I may perhaps discover by chance the secret of its sealed entrance, which has ere now baffled so many pertinacious explorers and learned Egyptologists.

As I walk along the base, I remember old Herodotus's story, like a page from the *Arabian Nights*, of how King Rhampsinitus built himself a treasury, wherein one stone turned on a pivot like a door; and how the builder availed himself of this his cunning device to steal gold from the king's storehouse. Suppose the entrance to the unopened Pyramid should be by such a door. It would be curious if I should chance to light upon the very spot.

I stood in the broad moonlight, near the north-east angle of the great pile, at the twelfth stone from the corner. A random fancy struck me, that I might turn this stone by pushing it inward on the left side. I leant against it with all my weight, and tried to move it on the imaginary pivot. Did it give way a fraction of an inch? No, it must have been mere fancy. Let me try again. Surely it is yielding! Gracious Osiris, it has moved an inch or more! My heart beats fast, either with fever or excitement, and I try a third time. The rust of centuries on the pivot wears slowly off, and the stone turned ponderously round, giving access to a low dark passage.

It must have been madness which led me to enter the forgotten corridor, alone, without torch or match, at that hour of the evening; but at any rate I entered. The passage was tall enough for a man to walk erect, and I could feel, as I groped slowly along, that the wall was composed of smooth polished granite, while the floor sloped away downward with a slight but regular descent. I walked with trembling heart and faltering feet for some forty or fifty yards down the mysterious vestibule: and then I felt myself brought suddenly to a standstill by a block of stone placed right across the pathway. I had had nearly enough for one evening, and I was preparing to return to the boat, agog with my new discovery, when my attention was suddenly arrested by an incredible, a perfectly miraculous fact.

The block of stone which barred the passage was faintly visible as a square, by means of a struggling belt of light streaming through the seams. There must be a lamp or other flame burning within. What if this were a door like the outer one, leading into a chamber perhaps inhabited by some dangerous band of outcasts? The light was a sure evidence of human occupation: and yet the outer door swung rustily on its pivot as though it had never been opened for ages. I paused a moment in fear before I ventured to try the stone: and then, urged on once more by some insane impulse, I turned the massive block with all my might to the left. It gave way slowly like its neighbour, and finally opened into the central hall.

Never as long as I live shall I forget the ecstasy of terror, astonishment, and blank dismay which seized upon me when I stepped into that seemingly enchanted chamber. A blaze of light first burst upon my eyes, from jets of gas arranged in regular rows tier above tier, upon the columns and walls of the vast apartment. Huge pillars, richly painted with red, yellow, blue and green decorations, stretched in endless succession down the dazzling aisles. A floor of polished syenite reflected the splendour of the lamps, and afforded a base for red granite sphinxes and dark purple images in porphyry of the cat-faced goddess Pasht, whose form I knew so well at the Louvre and the British Museum. But I had no eyes for any of these lesser marvels, being wholly absorbed in the greatest marvel of all: for there, in royal state and with mitred head, a living Egyptian king, surrounded by his coiffured court, was banqueting in the flesh upon a real throne, before a table laden with Memphian delicacies!

I stood transfixed with awe and amazement, my tongue and my feet alike forgetting their office, and my brain whirling round and round, as I remember it used to whirl when my health broke down utterly at Cambridge after the Classical Tripos. I gazed fixedly at the strange picture before me, taking in all its details in a confused way, yet quite incapable of understanding or realizing any part of its true import. I saw the king in the centre of the hall, raised on a throne of granite inlaid with gold and ivory; his head crowned with the peaked cap of Rameses, and his curled hair flowing down his shoulders in a set and formal frizz. I saw priests and warriors on either side, dressed in the costumes which I had often carefully noted in our great collections; while bronze-skinned maids, with light garments round their waists, and limbs displayed in graceful picturesqueness, waited upon them, half nude, as in the wall paintings which we had lately examined at Karnak and Syene.

I saw the ladies, clothed from head to foot in dyed linen garments, sitting apart in the background, banqueting by themselves at a separate table; while dancing girls, like older representatives of my yesternoon friends, the Ghawzi, tumbled before them in strange attitudes, to the music of four-stringed harps and long straight pipes. In short, I beheld as in a dream the whole drama of everyday Egyptian royal life, playing itself out anew under my eyes, in its real original properties and personages.

Gradually, as I looked, I became aware that my hosts were no less surprised at the appearance of their anachronistic guest than was the guest himself at the strange living panorama which met his eyes. In a moment music and dancing ceased; the banquet paused in its course, and the king and his nobles stood up in undisguised astonishment to survey the strange intruder.

Some minutes passed before any one moved forward on either side. At last a young girl of royal appearance, yet strangely resembling the Ghziyah of Abu Yilla, and recalling in part the laughing maiden in the foreground of Mr Long's great canvas at the previous Academy, stepped out before the throng.

'May I ask you,' she said in Ancient Egyptian, 'who you are, and why you come hither to disturb us?'

I was never aware before that I spoke or understood the language of the hieroglyphics: yet I found I had not the slightest difficulty in comprehending or answering her question. To say the truth, Ancient Egyptian, though an extremely tough tongue to decipher in its written form, becomes as easy as love-making when spoken by a pair of lips like that Pharaonic princess's. It is really very much the same as English, pronounced in a rapid and somewhat indefinite whisper, and with all the vowels left out.

'I beg ten thousand pardons for my intrusion,' I answered apologetically: 'but I did not know that this Pyramid was inhabited, or I should not have entered your residence so rudely. As for the points you wish to know, I am an English tourist, and you will find my name upon this card;' saying which I handed her one from the case which I had fortunately put into my pocket, with conciliatory politeness. The princess examined it closely, but evidently did not understand its import.

'In return,' I continued, 'may I ask you in what august presence I now find myself by accident?'

A court official stood forth from the throng, and answered in a set heraldic tone: 'In the presence of the illustrious monarch, Brother of the Sun, Thothmes the Twenty-Seventh, king of the Eighteenth Dynasty.'

'Salute the Lord of the World,' put in another official in the same regulation drone.

I bowed low to his Majesty, and stepped out into the hall. Apparently my obeisance did not come up to Egyptian standards of courtesy, for a suppressed titter broke audibly from the ranks of bronze-skinned waiting-women. But the king graciously smiled at my attempt, and turning to the nearest nobleman, observed in a voice of great sweetness and self-contained majesty: 'This stranger, Ombos, is certainly a very curious person. His appearance does not at all resemble that of an Ethiopian or other savage, nor does he look like the pale-faced sailors who come to us from the Achaian land beyond the sea. His features, to be sure, are not very different from theirs; but his extraordinary and singularly inartistic dress shows him to belong to some other barbaric race.'

I glanced down at my waistcoat, and saw that I was wearing my tourist's check suit, of grey and mud colour, with which a Bond Street tailor had supplied me just before leaving town, as the latest thing out in fancy tweeds. Evidently these Egyptians must have a very curious standard of taste not to admire our pretty and graceful style of male attire.

'If the dust beneath your Majesty's feet may venture upon a suggestion,' put in the officer whom the king had addressed, 'I would hint that this young man is probably a stray visitor from the utterly uncivilized lands of the North. The headgear which he carries in his hand obviously betrays an Arctic habitat.'

I had instinctively taken off my round felt hat in the first moment of surprise, when I found myself in the midst of this strange throng, and I was standing now in a somewhat embarrassed posture, holding it awkwardly before me like a shield to protect my chest.

'Let the stranger cover himself,' said the king.

'Barbarian intruder, cover yourself,' cried the herald. I noticed throughout that the king never directly addressed anybody save the higher officials around him.

I put on my hat as desired. 'A most uncomfortable and silly form of tiara indeed,' said the great Thothmes.

'Very unlike your noble and awe-spiring mitre, Lion of Egypt,' answered Ombos.

'Ask the stranger his name,' the king continued.

It was useless to offer another card, so I mentioned it in a clear voice.

'An uncouth and almost unpronounceable designation truly,' commented His Majesty to the Grand Chamberlain beside him. 'These savages speak strange languages, widely different from the flowing tongue of Memnon and Sesostris.'

The chamberlain bowed his assent with three low genuflexions. I began to feel a little abashed at these personal remarks, and I almost think (though I shouldn't like it to be mentioned in the Temple) that a blush rose to my cheek.

The beautiful princess, who had been standing near me meanwhile in an attitude of statuesque repose, now appeared anxious to change the current of the conversation. 'Dear father,' she said with a respectful inclination, 'surely the stranger, barbarian though he be, cannot relish such pointed allusions to his person and costume. We must let him feel the grace and delicacy of Egyptian refinement. Then he may perhaps carry back with him some faint echo of its cultured beauty to his northern wilds.'

'Nonsense, Hatasou,' replied Thothmes XXVII testily. 'Savages have no feelings, and they are as incapable of appreciating Egyptian sensibility as the chattering crow is incapable of attaining the dignified reserve of the sacred crocodile.'

'Your Majesty is mistaken,' I said, recovering my self-possession gradually and realizing my position as a freeborn Englishman before the court of a foreign despot—though I must allow that I felt rather less confident than usual, owing to the fact that we were not represented in the Pyramid by a British Consul—'I am an English tourist, a visitor from a modern land whose civilization far surpasses the rude culture of early Egypt; and I am accustomed to respectful treatment from all other nationalities, as becomes a citizen of the First Naval Power in the World.'

My answer created a profound impression. 'He has spoken to the Brother of the Sun,' cried Ombos in evident perturbation. 'He must be of the Blood Royal in his own tribe, or he would never have dared to do so!'

'Otherwise,' added a person whose dress I recognised as that of a priest, 'he must be offered up in expiation to Amon-Ra immediately.'

As a rule I am a decent truthful person, but under these alarming circumstances I ventured to tell a slight fib with an air of nonchalant boldness. 'I am a younger brother of our reigning king,' I said without

69

a moment's hesitation; for there was nobody present to gainsay me, and I tried to salve my conscience by reflecting that at any rate I was only claiming consanguinity with an imaginary personage.

'In that case,' said King Thothmes, with more geniality in his tone, 'there can be no impropriety in my addressing you personally. Will you take a place at our table next to myself, and we can converse together without interrupting a banquet which must be brief enough in any circumstances? Hatasou, my dear, you may seat yourself next to the barbarian prince.'

I felt a visible swelling to the proper dimensions of a Royal Highness as I sat down by the king's right hand. The nobles resumed their places, the bronze-skinned waitresses left off standing like soldiers in a row and staring straight at my humble self, the goblets went round once more, and a comely maid soon brought me meat, bread, fruits and date wine.

All this time I was naturally burning with curiosity to inquire who my strange host might be, and how they had preserved their existence for so many centuries in this undiscovered hall; but I was obliged to wait until I had satisfied his Majesty of my own nationality, the means by which I had entered the Pyramid, the general state of affairs throughout the world at the present moment, and fifty thousand other matters of a similar sort. Thothmes utterly refused to believe my reiterated assertion that our existing civilization was far superior to the Egyptian; 'because,' he said, 'I see from your dress that your nation is utterly devoid of taste or invention;' but he listened with great interest to my account of modern society, the steam-engine, the Permissive Prohibitory Bill, the telegraph, the House of Commons, Home Rule, and other blessings of our advanced era, as well as to a brief resume of European history from the rise of the Greek culture to the Russo-Turkish war. At last his questions were nearly exhausted, and I got a chance of making a few counter inquiries on my own account.

'And now,' I said, turning to the charming Hatasou, whom I thought a more pleasing informant than her august papa, 'I should like to know who you are.'

'What, don't you know?' she cried with unaffected surprise. 'Why, we're mummies.'

She made this astonishing statement with just the same quiet unconsciousness as if she had said, 'we're French,' or 'we're Americans.' I glanced round the walls, and observed behind the columns, what I had not noticed till then—a large number of empty mummy-cases, with their lids placed carelessly by their sides.

'But what are you doing here?' I asked in a bewildered way.

'Is it possible,' said Hatasou, 'that you don't really know the object of embalming? Though your manners show you to be an agreeable and well-bred young man, you must excuse my saying that you are shockingly ignorant. We are made into mummies in order to preserve our immortality. Once in every thousand years we wake up for twenty-four hours, recover our flesh and blood, and banquet once more upon the mummied dishes and other good things laid by for us in the Pyramid. Today is the first day of a millennium, and so we have waked up for the sixth time since we were first embalmed.'

'The sixth time?' I inquired incredulously. 'Then you must have been dead six thousand years.'

'Exactly so.'

'But the world has not yet existed so long,' I cried, in a fervour of orthodox horror.

'Excuse me, barbarian prince. This is the first day of the three hundred and twenty-seven thousandth millennium.'

My orthodoxy received a severe shock. However, I had been accustomed to geological calculations, and was somewhat inclined to accept the antiquity of man; so I swallowed the statement without more ado. Besides, if such a charming girl as Hatasou had asked me at that moment to turn Mohammedan, or to worship Oysteries, I believe I should incontinently have done so.

'You wake up only for a single day and night, then?' I said.

'Only for a single day and night. After that, we go to sleep for another millennium.'

'Unless you are meanwhile burned as fuel on the Cairo Railway,' I added mentally. 'But how,' I continued aloud, 'do you get these lights?'

'The Pyramid is built above a spring of inflammable gas. We have a reservoir in one of the side chambers in which it collects during the thousand years. As soon as we awake, we turn it on at once from the tap, and light it with a lucifer match.'

'Upon my word,' I interposed, 'I had no notion you Ancient Egyptians were acquainted with the use of matches.'

'Very likely not. "There are more things in heaven and earth, Cephrenes, than are dreamt of in your philosophy," as the bard of Philae puts it.'

Further inquiries brought out all the secrets of that strange tomb-house, and kept me fully interested till the close of the banquet. Then the chief priest solemnly rose, offered a small fragment of meat to a deified crocodile, who sat in a meditative manner by the side of his deserted mummy-case, and declared the feast concluded for the night. All rose from their places, wandered away into the long corridors or side-aisles, and formed little groups of talkers under the brilliant gas-lamps.

For my part, I strolled off with Hatasou down the least illuminated of the colonnades, and took my seat beside a marble fountain, where several fish (gods of great sanctity, Hatasou assured me) were disport-ing themselves in a porphyry basin. How long we sat there I can-not tell, but I know that we talked a good deal about fish, and gods, and Egyptian habits, and Egyptian philosophy, and, above all, Egyptian love-making. The last-named subject we found very interesting, and when once we got fully started upon it, no diversion afterwards oc-curred to break the even tenour of the conversation. Hatasou was a lovely figure, tall, queenly, with smooth dark arms and neck of pol-ished bronze: her big black eyes full of tenderness, and her long hair bound up into a bright Egyptian headdress, that harmonized to a tone with her complexion and her robe. The more we talked, the more desperately did I fall in love, and the more utterly oblivious did I become of my duty to Editha Fitz-Simkins. The mere ugly daughter of a rich and vulgar brand-new knight, forsooth, to show off her airs before me, when here was a Princess of the Blood Royal of Egypt, obviously sensible to the attentions which I was paying her, and not unwilling to receive them with a coy and modest grace.

Well, I went on saying pretty things to Hatasou, and Hatasou went on deprecating them in a pretty little way, as who should say, 'I don't mean what I pretend to mean one bit;' until at last I may confess that we were both evidently as far gone in the disease of the heart called love as it is possible for two young people on first acquaintance to become. Therefore, when Hatasou pulled forth her watch—another piece of mechanism with which antiquaries used never to credit the Egyptian people—and declared that she had only three more hours to live, at least for the next thousand years, I fairly broke down, took out my handkerchief, and began to sob like a child of five years old.

Hatasou was deeply moved. Decorum forbade that she should console me with too much empressement; but she ventured to re-move the handkerchief gently from my face, and suggested that there was yet one course open by which we might enjoy a little more of one another's society. 'Suppose,' she said quietly, 'you were to become a mummy. You would then wake up, as we do, every thousand years; and after you have tried it once, you will find it just as natural to sleep for a millennium as for eight hours. Of course,' she added with a slight blush, 'during the next three or four solar cycles there would be plenty of time to conclude any other arrangements you might possibly contemplate, before the occurrence of another glacial epoch.'

This mode of regarding time was certainly novel and somewhat bewildering to people who ordinarily reckon its lapse by weeks and months; and I had a vague consciousness that my relations with Editha imposed upon me a moral necessity of returning to the outer world, instead of becoming a millennial mummy. Besides, there was the awkward chance of being converted into fuel and dissipated into space before the arrival of the next waking day. But I took one look at Hatasou, whose eyes were filling in turn with sympathetic tears, and that look decided me. I flung Editha, life, and duty to the dogs, and resolved at once to become a mummy.

There was no time to be lost. Only three hours remained to us, and the process of embalming, even in the most hasty manner, would take up fully two. We rushed off to the chief priest, who had charge of the particular department in question. He at once acceded to my wishes, and briefly explained the mode in which they usually treated the corpse.

That word suddenly aroused me. 'The corpse!' I cried; 'but I am alive. You can't embalm me living.'

'We can,' replied the priest, 'under chloroform.'

'Chloroform!' I echoed, growing more and more astonished: 'I had no idea you Egyptians knew anything about it.'

'Ignorant barbarian!' he answered with a curl of the lip; 'you imagine yourself much wiser than the teachers of the world. If you were versed in all the wisdom of the Egyptians, you would know that chloroform is one of our simplest and commonest anaesthetics.'

I put myself at once under the hands of the priest. He brought out the chloroform, and placed it beneath my nostrils, as I lay on a soft couch under the central court. Hatasou held my hand in hers, and watched my breathing with an anxious eye. I saw the priest leaning over me, with a clouded phial in his hand, and I experienced a vague sensation of smelling myrrh and spikenard. Next, I lost myself for a few moments, and when I again recovered my senses in a temporary break, the priest was holding a small greenstone knife, dabbled with blood, and I felt that a gash had been made across my breast. Then they applied the chloroform once more; I felt Hatasou give my hand a gentle squeeze; the whole panorama faded finally from my view; and I went to sleep for a seemingly endless time.

When I awoke again, my first impression led me to believe that the thousand years were over, and that I had come to life once more to feast with Hatasou and Thothmes in the Pyramid of Abu Yilla. But second thoughts, combined with closer observation of the surroundings, convinced me that I was really lying in a bedroom of Shepheard's Hotel at Cairo. An hospital nurse leant over me, instead of a chief priest; and I noticed no tokens of Editha Fitz-Simkins's presence. But when I endeavoured to make inquiries upon the subject of my whereabouts, I was peremptorily informed that I mustn't speak, as I was only just recovering from a severe fever, and might endanger my life by talking.

Some weeks later I learned the sequel of my night's adventure. The Fitz-Simkinses, missing me from the boat in the morning, at first imagined that I might have gone ashore for an early stroll. But after breakfast time, lunch time, and dinner time had gone past, they began to grow alarmed, and sent to look for me in all directions. One of their scouts, happening to pass the Pyramid, noticed that one of the stones near the north-east angle had been displaced, so as to give access to a dark passage, hitherto unknown. Calling several of his friends, for he was afraid to venture in alone, he passed down the corridor, and through a second gateway into the central hall. There the Fellahin found me, lying on the ground, bleeding profusely from a wound on the breast, and in an advanced stage of malarious fever. They brought me back to the boat, and the Fitz-Simkinses conveyed me at once to Cairo, for medical attendance and proper nursing.

Editha was at first convinced that I had attempted to commit suicide because I could not endure having caused her pain, and she accordingly resolved to tend me with the utmost care through my illness. But she found that my delirious remarks, besides bearing frequent reference to a princess, with whom I appeared to have been on unexpectedly intimate terms, also related very largely to our casus belli itself, the dancing girls of Abu Yilla.

Even this trial she might have borne, setting down the moral degeneracy which led me to patronize so degrading an exhibition as a first symptom of my approaching malady: but certain unfortunate observations, containing pointed and by no means flattering allusions to her personal appearance—which I contrasted, much to her disadvantage, with that of the unknown princess—these, I say, were things which she could not forgive; and she left Cairo abruptly with her parents for the Riviera, leaving behind a stinging note, in which she denounced my perfidy and empty-heartedness with all the flowers of feminine eloquence. From that day to this I have never seen her.

When I returned to London and proposed to lay this account before the Society of Antiquaries, all my friends dissuaded me on the grounds of its apparent incredibility. They declare that I must have gone to the Pyramid already in a state of delirium, discovered the entrance by accident, and sunk exhausted when I reached the inner chamber. In answer, I would point out three facts. In the first place, I undoubtedly found my way into the unknown passage—for which achievement I afterwards received the gold medal of the Societe Khediviale, and of which I retain a clear recollection, differing in no way from my recollection of the subsequent events.

In the second place, I had in my pocket, when found, a ring of Hatasou's, which I drew from her finger just before I took the chloroform, and put into my pocket as a keepsake. And in the third place, I had on my breast the wound which I saw the priest inflict with a knife of greenstone, and the scar may be seen on the spot to the present day. The absurd hypothesis of my medical friends, that I was wounded by falling against a sharp edge of rock, I must at once reject as unworthy of a moment's consideration.

My own theory is either that the priest had not time to complete the operation, or else that the arrival of the Fitz-Simkins' scouts frightened back the mummies to their cases an hour or so too soon. At any rate, there they all were, ranged around the walls undisturbed, the moment the Fellahin entered.

Unfortunately, the truth of my account cannot be tested for another thousand years. But as a copy of this book will be preserved for the benefit of posterity in the British Museum, I hereby solemnly call upon Collective Humanity to try the veracity of this history by sending a deputation of archaeologists to the Pyramid of Abu Yilla, on the last day of December, Two thousand eight hundred and seventy-seven. If they do not then find Thothmes and Hatasou feasting in the central hall exactly as I have described, I shall willingly admit that the story of my New Year's Eve among the Mummies is a vain hallucination, unworthy of credence at the hands of the scientific world.

An Eddy on the Floor

Bernard Capes

PART 1 OF POLYHISTOR'S NARRATIVE

Written for but never inserted in the —— *Family Magazine*

The eyes of Polyhistor—as he sat before the fire at night—took in the tawdry surroundings of his lodging-house room with nothing of that apathy of resignation to his personal *avaykn* which of all moods is to Fortune, the goddess of spontaneity, the most antipathetic. Indeed, he felt his wit, like Romeo's, to be of cheveril; and his conviction that it needed only the pull of circumstance to stretch it "from an inch narrow to an ell broad" expressed but the very wooing quality of a constitutional optimism.

Now this inherent optimism is at least a serviceable weapon when it takes the form of self-reliance. It is always at hand in an emergency—a guard of honour to the soul. The loneliness of individual life must learn self-respect from within, not without; and were all creeds to be mixed, that truism should be found their precipitate.

Therefore Polyhistor was content to draw grass-green rep curtains across window-panes sloughed with wintry sleet; to place his feet upon a rug flayed of colour to its dusty sinews; to admit to his close fellowship—and find a familiar comfort in them, too—three separate lithographs of affected babies inviting any canine confidences but the bite one desired for them, and a dismal daguerreotype of his landlady's deceased husband, slowly perishing in peg-tops and a yellow fog of despondency, out of which only his boots and a very tall hat frowned insistent, the tabernacles of enduring respectability:—he was content, because he knew these were only incidents in his career—the slums to be first traversed on a journey before the rounding breadths of open country were reached,—and the station in life he purposed stopping at eventually was the terminus of prosperity, intellectual and material.

With no present good fortune but the capacity for desiring it; with the right to affix a letter or so—like grace after skilly—to his name; with the consciousness that, having overcome theoretical pharmaceutics masterfully, he was now combatting practical dispensing slavishly; with full confidence in his social position (he stood under the shadow of "high connections," like the little winged "Victory" in a conqueror's hand, he chose to think) to help him to eventual distinction, he toasted his toes that sour winter evening and reviewed in comfort an army of prospects.

Also, his thoughts reverted indulgently to the incidents and experiences of the previous night.

He had had the pleasure of an invitation to one of those reunions or *séances* at the house, in a fashionable quarter, of his distant connection. Lady Barbara Grille, whereat it was his hostess's humour to gather together those many birds of alien feather and incongruous habit that will flock from the hedgerows to the least little flattering crumb of attention. And scarce one of them but thinks the simple feast is spread for him alone. And with so cheap a bait may a title lure.

Lady Barbara, to do her justice, trades upon her position only in so far as it shapes itself the straight road to her desires. She is a carpet adventurer—an explorer amongst the nerves of moral sensation, to whom the discovery of an untrodden mental tract is a pure delight, and the more delightful the more ephemeral. She flits from guest to guest, shooting out to each a little proboscis, as it were, and happy if its point touches a speck of honey. She gathers from all, and stores the sweet agglomerate, let us hope, to feed upon it in the winter of her life, when the hive of her busy brain shall be thatched with snow.

That reference to so charming a personality should be in this place a digression is Polyhistor's unhappiness. She affects his narrative only inasmuch as he happened to meet at her house a gentleman who for a time exerted a considerable influence over his fortunes.

★★★★★★

Here Polyhistor's narrative must give place to certain editorial marginalia by Miss Lucy ——, who "runs" the *Family Magazine*, she writes:—"Polyhistor, indeed! The conceit of some people! He seems to take himself for a sort of *Admirable Crichton*, and all because his chance meeting with the gentleman referred to (a very *interesting* person, who is, I understand, reforming our prisons) brought him the offer of an appointment quite beyond his deserts. I was very glad to hear of it, however, and I asked the creature to contribute a paper recording his first impressions of *this notable man*; instead of which he begins with an opinionated rigmarole about himself, and goes on from bad to worse by describing a long conversation he had about prison reform with that horrid, masculine Mrs. ——, whom all the officers call 'Charlie,' and who thinks that for men to grow humane is a sign of their decadence. Of course, I shall 'cut' the whole of their talk together (it is a blessed privilege to be an editor), and jump to the part where *Polyhistor* (!) describes the *notable person's* visit to him, which was due to his (the N.P.'s) having the night before overheard some of the conversation *between those two*.

Polyhistor's Narrative (continued).

Now as Polyhistor sat, he humoured his recollection (in the intervals of scribbling verses to the *beaux yeux* of a certain Miss L——) with some of "Charlie's" characteristic last-night utterances.

She had dated man's decadence from the moment when he began to "poor-fellow" irreclaimable savagery on the score of heredity.

She had repudiated the old humbug of sex superiority because she had seen it fall on its face to howl over a trodden worm, with the result that it discovered itself hollow behind, like the elf-maiden.

She had said: "Once you taught us divinely—*argumentum baculinum*," said she; "(for you are the sons of God, you know). But you have since so insisted upon the Rights of Humanity that we have learned ourselves in the phrase, and that the earthy have the best right to precedence on the earth."

And thereupon Charlie had launched into abuse of what she called the latest masculine fad—prison reform, to wit—and a heated discussion between her and Polyhistor had ensued, in the midst of which she had happened to glance behind her, to find that very notable person who is the subject of this narrative vouchsafing a silent attention to her diatribe. And then—

But at this period to his cogitations Polyhistor's landlady entered with a card, which she presented to his consideration:—

Major James Shrike,
H.M. Prison, D——.

All astonishment, Polyhistor bade his visitor up.

He entered briskly, fur-collared, hat in hand, and bowed as he stood on the threshold. He was a very short man—snub-nosed; rusty-whiskered; indubitably and unimpressively a cockney in appearance.

He might have walked out of a Cruikshank etching.

Polyhistor was beginning, "May I inquire——" when the other took him up with a vehement frankness that he found engaging at once.

"This is a great intrusion. Will you pardon me? I heard some remarks of yours last night that deeply interested me. I obtained your name and address of our hostess, and took the liberty of——"

"Oh! pray be seated. Say no more. My kinswoman's introduction is all-sufficient. I am happy in having caught your attention in so motley a crowd."

"She doesn't—forgive the impertinence—take herself seriously enough."

"Lady Barbara? Then you've found her out?"

"Ah!—you're not offended?"

"Not in the least."

"Good. It was a motley assemblage, as you say. Yet I'm inclined to think I found my pearl in the oyster. I'm afraid I interrupted—eh?"

"No, no, not at all. Only some idle scribbling. I'd finished."

"You are a poet?"

"Only a lunatic. I haven't taken my degree."

"Ah! it's a noble gift—the gift of song; precious through its rarity."

Polyhistor caught a note of emotion in his visitor's voice, and glanced at him curiously.

"Surely," he thought, "that vulgar, ruddy little face is transfigured."

"But," said the stranger, coming to earth, "I am lingering beside the mark. I must try to justify my solecism in manners by a straight reference to the object of my visit. That is, in the first instance, a matter of business."

"Business!"

"I am a man with a purpose, seeking the hopefullest means to an end. Plainly: if I could procure you the post of resident doctor at D—— gaol, would you be disposed to accept it?"

Polyhistor looked his utter astonishment.

"I can affect no surprise at yours," said the visitor, attentively regarding Polyhistor. "It is perfectly natural. Let me forestall some unnecessary expression of it. My offer seems unaccountable to you, seeing that we never met until last night. But I don't move entirely in the dark. I have ventured in the interval to inform myself as to the details of your career. I was entirely one with much of your expression of opinion as to the treatment of criminals, in which you controverted the crude and unpleasant scepticism of the lady you talked with."

(Poor New Charlie!) "Combining the two, I come to the immediate conclusion that you are the man for my purpose."

"You have dumbfounded me. I don't know what to answer. You have views, I know, as to prison treatment. Will you sketch them? Will you talk on, while I try to bring my scattered wits to a focus?"

"Certainly, I will. Let me, in the first instance, recall to you a few words of your own. They ran somewhat in this fashion: Is not the man of practical genius the man who is most apt at solving the little problems of resourcefulness in life? Do you remember them?"

"Perhaps I do, in a cruder form."

"They attracted me at once. It is upon such a postulate I base my practice. Their moral is this: To know the antidote the moment the snake bites. That is to have the intuition of divinity. We shall rise to it someday, no doubt, and climb the hither side of the new Olympus. Who knows? Over the crest the spirit of creation may be ours."

Polyhistor nodded, still at sea, and the other went on with a smile:—

"I once knew a world-famous engineer with whom I used to breakfast occasionally. He had a patent egg-boiler on the table, with a little double-sided ladle underneath to hold the spirit. He complained that his egg was always undercooked. I said, 'Why not reverse the ladle so as to bring the deeper cup uppermost?' He was charmed with my perspicacity. The solution had never occurred to him. You remember, too, no doubt, the story of Coleridge and the horse collar. We aim too much at great developments. If we cultivate resourcefulness, the rest will follow. Shall I state my system *in nuce?* It is to encourage this spirit of resourcefulness."

"Surely the habitual criminal has it in a marked degree?"

"Yes; but abnormally developed in a single direction. His one object is to outmanoeuvred in a game of desperate and immoral chances. The tactical spirit in him has none of the higher ambition. It has felt itself in the degree only that stops at defiance."

"That is perfectly true."

"It is half self-conscious of an individuality that instinctively assumes the hopelessness of a recognition by duller intellects. Leaning to resentment through misguided vanity, it falls 'all oblique.' What is the cure for this? I answer, the teaching of a divine egotism. The subject must be led to a pure devotion to self. What he wishes to respect he must be taught to make beautiful and interesting. The policy of sacrifice to others has so long stunted his moral nature because it is an hypocritical policy. We are responsible to ourselves in the first instance;

and to argue an eternal system of blind self-sacrifice is to undervalue the fine gift of individuality. In such he sees but an indefensible policy of force applied to the advantage of the community. He is told to be good—not that he may morally profit, but that others may not suffer inconvenience."

Polyhistor was beginning to grasp, through his confusion, a certain clue of meaning in his visitor's rapid utterance. The stranger spoke fluently, but in the dry, positive voice that characterizes men of will.

"Pray go on," Polyhistor said; "I am digesting in silence."

"We must endeavour to lead him to respect of self by showing him what his mind is capable of. I argue on no sectarian, no religious grounds even. Is it possible to make a man's self his most precious possession? Anyhow, I work to that end, A doctor purges before building up with a tonic. I eliminate cant and hypocrisy, and then introduce self-respect. It isn't enough to employ a man's hands only. Initiation in some labour that should prove wholesome and remunerative is a redeeming factor, but it isn't all. His mind must work also, and awaken to its capacities. If it rusts, the body reverts to inhuman instincts."

"May I ask how you—?"

"By intercourse—in my own person or through my officials. I wish to have only those about me who are willing to contribute to my designs, and with whom I can work in absolute harmony. All my officers are chosen to that end. No doubt a dash of constitutional sentimentalism gives colour to my theories. I get it from a human tract in me that circumstances have obliged me to put a hoarding round."

"I begin to gather daylight."

"Quite so. My patients are invited to exchange views with their guardians in a spirit of perfect friendliness; to solve little problems of practical moment; to acquire the pride of self-reliance. We have competitions, such as certain newspapers open to their readers, in a simple form. I draw up the questions myself. The answers give me insight into the mental conditions of the competitors. Upon insight I proceed. I am fortunate in private means, and I am in a position to offer modest prizes to the winners. Whenever such an one is discharged, he finds awaiting him the tools most handy to his vocation. I bid him go forth in no pharisaical spirit, and invite him to communicate with me. I wish the shadow of the gaol to extend no further than the road whereon it lies. Henceforth, we are acquaintances with a common interest at heart. Isn't it monstrous that a state-fixed degree of misconduct should earn a man social ostracism? Parents are generally inclined to rule extra tenderness towards a child whose peccadilloes have brought him a whipping. For myself, I have no faith in police supervision. Give a culprit his term and have done with it. I find the majority who come back to me are ticket-of-leave men.

"Have I said enough? I offer yon the reversion of the post. The present holder of it leaves in a month's time. Please to determine here and at once."

"Very good. I have decided."

"You will accept?"

"Yes."

★★★★★★

So far wrote Polyhistor in the bonny days of early manhood—an attempt made in a spasm of enthusiasm inspired in him and humoured by his most engaging Mentor, to record his first impressions of a notable personality not many days after its introduction to him. He has never taken up the tale again until now, when an insistent sense, as of a task left unfinished, compels him to the effort. Over his sweet Mentor the grass lies thick, and flowers of aged stalk bloom perennially, and "Oh, the difference to me!"

To me, for it is time to drop the poor conceit, the pseudonym that once served its little purpose to awaken tender derision.

I take up the old and stained manuscript, with its marginalia, that are like the dim call from a far-away voice, and I know that, so I am driven to record the sequel to that gay introduction, it must be in a spirit of sombreness most deadly by contrast. I look at the faded opening words. The fire of the first line of the narrative is long out; the grate is cold some forty years—forty years!—and I think I have been a little chill during all that time. But, though the room rustle with phantoms and menace stalk in the retrospect, I shall acquit my conscience of its burden, refusing to be bullied by the counsel of a destiny that subpoenaed me entirely against my will.

PART 2 OF POLYHISTOR'S NARRATIVE
Continued and Finished after a Lapse of Forty Years

With my unexpected appointment as doctor to D—— gaol, I seemed to have put on the seven-league boots of success. No doubt it was an extraordinary degree of good fortune, even to one who had looked forward with a broad view of confidence; yet, I think, perhaps on account of the very casual nature of my promotion, I never took the post entirely seriously.

At the same time, I was fully bent on justifying my little cockney patron's choice by a resolute subscription to his theories of prison management.

Major James Shrike inspired me with a curious conceit of impertinent respect. In person the very embodiment of that insignificant vulgarity, without extenuating circumstances, which is the type in caricature of the ultimate cockney, he possessed a force of mind and an earnestness of purpose that absolutely redeemed him on close acquaintanceship. I found him all he had stated himself to be, and something more.

He had a noble object always in view—the employment of sane and humanitarian methods in the treatment of redeemable criminals, and he strove towards it with completely untiring devotion. He was of those who never insist beyond the limits of their own understanding, clear-sighted in discipline, frank in relaxation, an altruist in the larger sense.

His undaunted persistence, as I learned, received ample illustration some few years prior to my acquaintance with him, when—his system being experimental rather than mature—a devastating endemic of typhoid in the prison had for the time stultified his efforts. He stuck to his post; but so virulent was the outbreak that the prison commissioners judged a complete evacuation of the building and overhauling of the drainage to be necessary. As a consequence, for some eighteen months—during thirteen of which the Governor and his household remained sole inmates of the solitary pile (so sluggishly do we redeem our condemned social bog-lands)—the "system" stood still for lack of material to mould. At the end of over a year of stagnation, a contract was accepted and workmen put in, and another five months saw the prison reordered for practical purposes.

The interval of forced inactivity must have sorely tried the patience of the Governor. Practical theorists condemned to rust too often eat out their own hearts. Major Shrike never referred to this period, and, indeed, laboriously snubbed any allusion to it.

He was, I have a shrewd notion, something of an officially petted reformer. Anyhow, to his abolition of the insensate barbarism of crank and treadmill in favour of civilizing methods no opposition was offered. Solitary confinement—a punishment outside all nature to a gregarious race—found no advocate in him. "A man's own suffering mind," he argued, "must be, of all moral food, the most poisonous for him to feed on. Surround a scorpion with fire and he stings himself to

84

death, they say. Throw a diseased soul entirely upon its own resources and moral suicide results."

To sum up: his nature embodied humanity without sentimentalism, firmness without obstinacy, individuality without selfishness; his activity was boundless, his devotion to his system so real as to admit no utilitarian sophistries into his scheme of personal benevolence. Before I had been with him a week, I respected him as I had never respected man before.

★★★★★★

One evening (it was during the second month of my appointment) we were sitting in his private study—a dark, comfortable room lined with books. It was an occasion on which a new characteristic of the man was offered to my inspection.

A prisoner of a somewhat unusual type had come in that day—a spiritualistic medium, convicted of imposture. To this person I casually referred.

"May I ask how you propose dealing with the newcomer?"

"On the familiar lines."

"But, surely—here we have a man of superior education, of imagination even?"

"No, no, no! A hawker's opportuneness; that describes it. These fellows would make death itself a vulgarity."

"You've no faith in their—"

"Not a tittle. Heaven forfend! A sheet and a turnip are poetry to their manifestations. It's as crude and sour soil for us to work on as any I know. "We'll cart it wholesale."

"I take you—excuse my saying so—for a supremely sceptical man."

"As to what?"

"The supernatural."

There was no answer during a considerable interval. Presently it came, with deliberate insistence:—

"It is a principle with me to oppose bullying. We are here for a definite purpose—his duty plain to any man who wills to read it. There may be disembodied spirits who seek to distress or annoy where they can no longer control. If there are, mine, which is not yet divorced from its means to material action, declines to be influenced by any irresponsible whimsey, emanating from a place whose denizens appear to be actuated by a mere frivolous antagonism to all human order and progress."

"But supposing you, a murderer, to be haunted by the presentment of your victim?"

"I will imagine that to be my case. Well, it makes no difference. My interest is with the great human system, in one of whose veins I am a circulating drop. It is my business to help to keep the system sound, to do my duty without fear or favour. If disease—say a fouled conscience—contaminates me, it is for me to throw off the incubus, not accept it, and transmit the poison. Whatever my lapses of nature, I owe it to the entire system to work for purity in my allotted sphere, and not to allow any microbe bugbear to ride me roughshod, to the detriment of my fellow drops."

I laughed.

"It should be for you," I said, "to learn to shiver, like the boy in the fairy tale."

"I cannot," he answered, with a peculiar quiet smile; "and yet prisons, above all places, should be haunted."

★★★★★★

Very shortly after his arrival I was called to the cell of the medium, F——. He suffered, by his own statement, from severe pains in the head.

I found the man to be nervous, anaemic; his manner characterized by a sort of hysterical effrontery.

"Send me to the infirmary," he begged. "This isn't punishment, but torture."

"What are your symptoms?"

"I see things; my case has no comparison with others. To a man of my super-sensitiveness close confinement is mere cruelty."

I made a short examination. He was restless under my hands.

"You'll stay where you are," I said.

He broke out into, violent abuse, and I left him.

Later in the day I visited him again. He was then white and sullen; but under his mood I could read real excitement of some sort.

"Now, confess to me, my man," I said, "what do you see?"

He eyed me narrowly, with his lips a little shaky.

"Will you have me moved if I tell you?"

"I can give no promise till I know."

He made up his mind after an interval of silence.

"There's something uncanny in my neighbourhood. Who's confined in the next cell—there, to the left?"

"To my knowledge it's empty."

He shook his head incredulously.

"Very well," I said, "I don't mean to bandy words with you"; and I turned to go.

At that he came after me with a frightened choke.

"Doctor, your mission's a merciful one. I'm not trying to sauce you. For God's sake have me moved! I can see further than most, I tell you!"

The fellow's manner gave me pause. He was patently and beyond the pride of concealment terrified.

"What do you see?" I repeated stubbornly.

"It isn't that I see, but I know. The cell's *not* empty!"

I stared at him in considerable wonderment.

"I will make inquiries," I said. "You may take that for a promise. If the cell proves empty, you stop where you are."

I noticed that he dropped his hands with a lost gesture as I left him. I was sufficiently moved to accost the warder who awaited me on the spot.

"Johnson," I said, "is that cell—"

"Empty, sir," answered the man sharply and at once.

Before I could respond, F—— came suddenly to the door, which I still held open.

"You lying cur!" he shouted. "You damned lying cur!"

The warder thrust the man back with violence.

"Now you, 49," he said, "dry up, and none of your sauce!" and he banged to the door with a sounding slap, and turned to me with a lowering face. The prisoner inside yelped and stormed at the studded panels.

"That cell's empty, sir," repeated Johnson.

"Will you, as a matter of conscience, let me convince myself? I promised the man."

"No, I can't."

"You can't?"

"No, sir."

"This is a piece of stupid discourtesy. You can have no reason, of course?"

"I can't open it—that's all."

"Oh, Johnson! Then I must go to the fountainhead."

"Very well, sir."

Quite baffled by the man's obstinacy, I said no more, but walked off. If my anger was roused, my curiosity was piqued in proportion.

★★★★★★

I had no opportunity of interviewing the Governor all day, but at night I visited him by invitation to play a game of piquet.

He was a man without "incumbrances"—as a severe conservatism designates the *lares* of the cottage—and, at home, lived at his ease and indulged his amusements without comment.

I found him "tasting" his books, with which the room was well lined, and drawing with relish at an excellent cigar in the intervals of the courses.

He nodded to me, and held out an open volume in his left hand.

"Listen to this fellow," he said, tapping the page with his fingers:—

"'The most tolerable sort of revenge, is for those wrongs which there is no law to remedy: but then, let a man take heed, the revenge be such, as there is no law to punish: else, a man's enemy, is still before-hand, and it is two for one. Some, when they take revenge, are desirous the party should know, whence it cometh. This is the more generous. For the delight seemeth to be, not so much in doing the hurt, as in making the party repent: but base and crafty cowards are like the ar-row that flyeth in the dark. Cosmus, Duke of Florence, had a desperate saying against perfidious or neglecting friends, as if these wrongs were unpardonable. You shall reade (saith he) that we are commanded to forgive our enemies: But you never ready that we are commanded, to forgive our friends.'

"Is he not a rare fellow?"

"Who?" said I.

"Francis Bacon, who screwed his wit to his philosophy, like a ham-mer-head to its handle, and knocked a nail in at every blow. How many of our friends round about here would be picking oakum now if they had made a gospel of that quotation?"

"You mean they take no heed that the Law may punish for that for which it gives no remedy?"

"Precisely; and specifically as to revenge. The criminal, from the murderer to the petty pilferer, is actuated solely by the spirit of venge-ance—vengeance blind and speechless—towards a system that forces him into a position quite outside his natural instincts."

"As to that, we have left Nature in the thicket. It is hopeless hunt-ing for her now."

"We hear her breathing sometimes, my friend. Otherwise Her Majesty's prison locks would rust. But, I grant yon, we have grown so unfamiliar with her that we call her simplest manifestations *super*natu-ral nowadays."

"That reminds me. I visited F—— this afternoon. The man was in a queer way—not foxing, in my opinion. Hysteria, probably."

"Oh! What was the matter with him?"

"The form it took was some absurd prejudice about the next cell—number 47. He swore it was not empty—was quite upset about it—said there was some infernal influence at work in his neighbourhood. Nerves, he finds, I suppose, may revenge themselves on one who has made a habit of playing tricks with them. To satisfy him, I asked Johnson to open the door of the next cell—"

"Well?"

"He refused."

"It is closed by my orders."

"That settles it, of course. The manner of Johnson's refusal was a bit uncivil, but—"

He had been looking at me intently all this time—so intently that I was conscious of a little embarrassment and confusion. His mouth was set like a dash between brackets, and his eyes glistened. Now his features relaxed, and he gave a short high neigh of a laugh.

"My dear fellow, you must make allowances for the rough old lurcher. He was a soldier. He is all cut and measured out to the regimental pattern. With him Major Shrike, like the king, can do no wrong. Did I ever tell you he served under me in India? He did; and, moreover, I saved his life there."

"In an engagement?"

"Worse—from the bite of a snake. It was a mere question of will. I told him to wake and walk, and he did. They had thought him already in *rigor mortis*; and, as for him—well, his devotion to me since has been single to the last degree."

"That's as it should be."

"To be sure. And he's quite in my confidence. You must pass over the old beggar's churlishness."

I laughed an assent. And then an odd thing happened. As I spoke, I had walked over to a bookcase on the opposite side of the room to that on which my host stood. Near this bookcase hung a mirror—an oblong affair, set in brass *repoussé* work—on the wall; and, happening to glance into it as I approached, I caught sight of the Major's reflection as he turned his face to follow my movement.

I say "turned his face"—a formal description only. What met my startled gaze was an image of some nameless horror—of features grooved, and battered, and shapeless, as if they had been torn by a wild beast.

I gave a little indrawn gasp and turned about. There stood the Major, plainly himself, with a pleasant smile on his face.

"What's up?" said he.

He spoke abstractedly, pulling at his cigar; and I answered rudely, "That's a damned bad looking-glass of yours!"

"I didn't know there was anything wrong with it," he said, still abstracted and apart. And, indeed, when by sheer mental effort I forced myself to look again, there stood my companion as he stood in the room.

I gave a tremulous laugh, muttered something or nothing, and fell to examining the books in the case. But my fingers shook a trifle as I aimlessly pulled out one volume after another.

"Am *I* getting fanciful?" I thought—"I whose business it is to give practical account of every bugbear of the nerves. Bah! My liver must be out of order. A speck of bile in one's eye may look a flying dragon."

I dismissed the folly from my mind, and set myself resolutely to inspecting the books marshalled before me. Roving amongst them, I pulled out, entirely at random, a thin, worn duodecimo, that was thrust well back at a shelf end, as if it shrank from comparison with its prosperous and portly neighbours. Nothing but chance impelled me to the choice; and I don't know to this day what the ragged volume was about. It opened naturally at a marker that lay in it—a folded slip of paper, yellow with age; and glancing at this, a printed name caught my eye.

With some stir of curiosity, I spread the slip out. It was a title-page to a volume, of poems, presumably; and the author was James Shrike.

I uttered an exclamation, and turned, book in hand.

"An author!" I said. "*You* an author. Major Shrike!"

To my surprise, he snapped round upon me with something like a glare of fury on his face. This the more startled me as I believed I had reason to regard him as a man whose principles of conduct had long disciplined a temper that was naturally hasty enough.

Before I could speak to explain, he had come hurriedly across the room and had rudely snatched the paper out of my hand.

"How did this get—" he began; then in a moment came to himself, and apologised for his ill manners.

"I thought every scrap of the stuff had been destroyed," he said, and tore the page into fragments. "It is an ancient effusion, doctor—perhaps the greatest folly of my life; but it's something of a sore subject with me, and I shall be obliged if you'll not refer to it again."

He courted my forgiveness so frankly that the matter passed without embarrassment; and we had our game and spent a genial evening together. But memory of the queer little scene stuck in my mind, and I could not forbear pondering it fitfully.

Surely here was a new side-light that played upon my friend and superior a little fantastically.

★★★★★★

Conscious of a certain vague wonder in my mind, I was traversing the prison, lost in thought, after my sociable evening with the Governor, when the fact that dim light was issuing from the open door of cell number 49 brought me to myself and to a pause in the corridor outside.

Then I saw that something was wrong with the cell's inmate, and that my services were required.

The medium was struggling on the floor, in what looked like an epileptic fit, and Johnson and another warder were holding him from doing an injury to himself.

The younger man welcomed my appearance with relief.

"Heerd him guggling," he said, "and thought as something were up. You come timely, sir."

More assistance was procured, and I ordered the prisoner's removal to the infirmary. For a minute, before following him, I was left alone with Johnson.

"It came to a climax, then?" I said, looking the man steadily in the face.

"He may be subject to 'em, sir," he replied, evasively.

I walked deliberately up to the closed door of the adjoining cell, which was the last on that side of the corridor. Huddled against the massive end wall, and half imbedded in it, as it seemed, it lay in a certain shadow, and bore every sign of dust and disuse. Looking closely, I saw that the trap in the door was not only firmly bolted, but *screwed into its socket.*

I turned and said to the warder quietly,—

"Is it long since this cell was in use?"

"You're very fond of asking questions," he answered doggedly.

It was evident he would baffle me by impertinence rather than yield a confidence. A queer insistence had seized me—a strange desire to know more about this mysterious chamber. But, for all my curiosity, I flushed at the man's tone.

91

"You have your orders," I said sternly, "and do well to hold by them. I doubt, nevertheless, if they include impertinence to your superiors."

"I look straight on my duty, sir," he said, a little abashed. "I don't wish to give offence."

He did not, I feel sore. He followed his instinct to throw me off the scent, that was all.

I strode off in a fume, and after attending F—— in the infirmary, went promptly to my own quarters.

I was in an odd frame of mind, and for long tramped my sitting-room to and fro, too restless to go to bed, or, as an alternative, to settle down to a book. There was a welling up in my heart of some emotion that I could neither trace nor define. It seemed neighbour to terror, neighbour to an intense fainting pity, yet was not distinctly either of these. Indeed, where was cause for one, or the subject of the other? F—— might have endured mental sufferings which it was only human to help to end, yet F—— was a swindling rogue, who, once relieved, merited no further consideration.

It was not on him my sentiments were wasted. Who, then, was responsible for them?

There is a very plain line of demarcation between the legitimate spirit of inquiry and mere apish curiosity. I could recognise it, I have no doubt, as a rule, yet in my then mood, under the influence of a kind of morbid seizure, inquisitiveness took me by the throat. I could not whistle my mind from the chase of a certain graveyard will-o'-the-wisp; and on it went stumbling and floundering through bog and mire, until it fell into a state of collapse, and was useful for nothing else.

I went to bed and to sleep without difficulty, but I was conscious of myself all the time, and of a shadowless horror that seemed to come stealthily out of comers and to bend over and look at me, and to be nothing but a curtain or a hanging coat when I started and stared.

Over and over again this happened, and my temperature rose by leaps, and suddenly I saw that if I failed to assert myself, and promptly, feyer would lap me in a consuming fire. Then in a moment I broke into a profuse perspiration, and sank exhausted into delicious unconsciousness.

Morning found me restored to vigour, but still with the maggot of curiosity boring in my brain. It worked there all day, and for many subsequent days, and at last it seemed as if my every faculty were honeycombed with its ramifications. Then "this will not do," I thought, but still the tunnelling process went on.

At first, I would not acknowledge to myself what all this mental to-do was about. I was ashamed of my new development, in fact, and nervous, too, in a degree of what it might reveal in the matter of moral degeneration; but gradually, as the curious devil mastered me, I grew into such harmony with it that I could shut my eyes no longer to the true purpose of its insistence. It was the closed cell about which my thoughts hovered like crows circling round carrion.

★★★★★★

"In the dead waste and middle" of a certain night I awoke with a strange, quick recovery of consciousness. There was the passing of a single expiration, and I had been asleep and was awake. I had gone to bed with no sense of premonition or of resolve in a particular direction; I sat up a monomaniac. It was as if, swelling in the silent hours, the tumour of curiosity had come to a head, and in a moment, it was necessary to operate upon it.

I make no excuse for my then condition. I am convinced I was the victim of some undistinguishable force, that I was an agent under the control of the supernatural, if you like. Some thought had been in my mind of late that in my position it was my duty to unriddle the mystery of the closed cell. This was a sop timidly held out to and rejected by my better reason. I sought—and I knew it in my heart—solution of the puzzle, because it was a puzzle with an atmosphere that vitiated my moral fibre. Now, suddenly, I knew I must act, or, by forcing self-control, imperil my mind's stability.

All strung to a sort of exaltation, I rose noiselessly and dressed myself with rapid, nervous hands. My every faculty was focussed upon a solitary point. Without and around there was nothing but shadow and uncertainty. I seemed conscious only of a shaft of light, as it were, traversing the darkness and globing itself in a steady disc of radiance on a lonely door.

Slipping out into the great echoing vault of the prison in stockinged feet, I sped with no hesitation of purpose in the direction of the corridor that was my goal. Surely some resolute Providence guided and encompassed me, for no meeting with the night patrol occurred at any point to embarrass or deter me. Like a ghost myself, I flitted along the stone flags of the passages, hardly waking a murmur from them in my progress.

Without, I knew, a wild and stormy wind thundered on the walls of the prison. Within, where the very atmosphere was self-contained, a cold and solemn peace held like an irrevocable judgment.

I found myself as if in a dream before the sealed door that had for days harassed my waking thoughts. Dim light from a distant gas jet made a patch of yellow upon one of its panels; the rest was buttressed with shadow.

A sense of fear and constriction was upon me as I drew softly from my pocket a screwdriver I had brought with me. It never occurred to me, I swear, that the quest was no business of mine, and that even now I could withdraw from it, and no one be the wiser. But I was afraid—I was afraid. And there was not even the negative comfort of knowing that the neighbouring cell was tenanted. It gaped like a ghostly garret next door to a deserted house.

What reason had I to be there at all, or, being there, to fear? I can no more explain than tell how it was that I, an impartial follower of my vocation, had allowed myself to be tricked by that in the nerves I had made it my interest to study and combat in others.

My hand that held the tool was cold and wet. The stiff little shriek of the first screw, as it turned at first uneasily in its socket, sent a jarring thrill through me. But I persevered, and it came out readily by-and-by, as did the four or five others that held the trap secure.

Then I paused a moment; and, I confess, the quick pant of fear seemed to come grey from my lips. There were sounds about me—the deep breathing of imprisoned men; and I envied the sleepers their hard-wrung repose.

At last, in one access of determination, I put out my hand, and sliding back the bolt, hurriedly flung open the trap. An acrid whiff of dust assailed my nostrils as I stepped back a pace and stood expectant of anything— or nothing. What did I wish, or dread, or foresee? The complete absurdity of my behaviour was revealed to me in a moment. I could shake off the incubus here and now, and be a sane man again.

I giggled, with an actual ring of self -contempt in my voice, as I made a forward movement to close the aperture. I advanced my face to it, and inhaled the sluggish air that stole forth, and—God in heaven!

I had staggered back with that cry in my throat, when I felt fingers like iron clamps close on my arm and hold it. The grip, more than the face I turned to look upon in my surging terror, was forcibly human.

It was the warder Johnson who had seized me, and my heart bounded as I met the cold fury of his eyes.

"Prying!" he said, in a hoarse, savage whisper. "So, you will, will you? And now let the devil help you!"

It was not this fellow I feared, though his white face was set like a demon's; and in the thick of my terror I made a feeble attempt to assert my authority.

"Let me go!" I muttered. "What! you dare?"

In his frenzy he shook my arm as a terrier shakes a rat, and, like a dog, he held on, daring me to release myself.

For the moment an instinct half -murderous leapt in me. It sank and was overwhelmed in a slough of some more secret emotion.

"Oh!" I whispered, collapsing, as it were, to the man's fury, even pitifully deprecating it. "What is it? What's there? It drew me—something unnameable."

He gave a snapping laugh Uke a cough. His rage waxed second by second. There was a maniacal suggestiveness in it; and not much longer, it was evident, could he have it under control. I saw it run and congest in his eyes; and, on the instant of its accumulation, he tore at me with a sudden wild strength, and drove me up against the very door of the secret cell.

The action, the necessity of self-defence, restored me to some measure of dignity and sanity.

"Let me go, you ruffian!" I cried, struggling to free myself from his grasp.

It was useless. He held me madly. There was no beating him off: and, so holding me, he managed to produce a single key from one of his pockets, and to slip it with a rusty clang into the lock of the door.

"You dirty, prying civilian!" he panted at me, as he swayed this way and that with the pull of my body. "You shall have your wish, by G—! You want to see inside, do you? Look, then!"

He dashed open the door as he spoke, and pulled me violently into the opening. A great waft of the cold, dank air came at us, and with it—what?

The warder had jerked his dark lantern from his belt, and now—an arm of his still clasped about one of mine—snapped the slide open.

"Where is it?" he muttered, directing the disc of light round and about the floor of the cell. I ceased struggling. Some counter influence was raising an odd curiosity in me.

"Ah!" he cried, in a stifled voice, "there you are, my friend!"

He was setting the light slowly travelling along the stone flags close by the wall over against us, and now, so guiding it, looked askance at me with a small, greedy smile.

"Follow the light, sir," he whispered jeeringly.

I looked, and saw twirling on the floor, in the patch of radiance cast by the lamp, *a little eddy of dust*, it seemed. This eddy was never still, but went circling in that stagnant place without apparent cause or influence; and, as it circled, it moved slowly on by wall and comer, so that presently in its progress it must reach us where we stood.

Now, draughts will play queer freaks in quiet places, and of this trifling phenomenon I should have taken little note ordinarily. But, I must say at once, that as I gazed upon the odd moving thing my heart seemed to fall in upon itself like a drained artery.

"Johnson!" I cried, " I must get out of this. I don't know what's the matter, or—— Why do you hold me? D—n it! man, let me go; let me go, I say!"

As I grappled with him he dropped the lantern with a crash and flung his arms violently about me.

"You don't!" he panted, the muscles of his bent and rigid neck seeming actually to cut into my shoulder-blade. "You don't, by G—! You came of your own accord, and now you shall take your bellyful!"

It was a struggle for life or death, or, worse, for life and reason. But I was young and wiry, and held my own, if I could do little more. Yet there was something to combat beyond the mere brute strength of the man I struggled with, for I fought in an atmosphere of horror unexplainable, and I knew that inch by inch the *thing* on the floor was circling round in our direction.

Suddenly in the breathing darkness I felt it close upon us, gave one mortal yell of fear, and, with a last despairing fury, tore myself from the encircling arms, and sprang into the corridor without. As I plunged and leapt, the warder clutched at me, missed, caught a foot on the edge of the door, and, as the latter whirled to with a clap, fell heavily at my feet in a fit. Then, as I stood staring down upon him, steps sounded along the corridor and the voices of scared men hurrying up.

★★★★★★

Ill and shaken, and, for the time, little in love with life, yet fearing death as I had never dreaded it before, I spent the rest of that horrible night huddled between my crumpled sheets, fearing to look forth, fearing to think, wild only to be far away, to be housed in some green and innocent hamlet, where I might forget the madness and the terror in learning to walk the unvext paths of placid souls. I had not fairly knocked under until alone with my new dread familiar. That unction I could lay to my heart, at least. I had done the manly part by the stricken warder, whom I had attended to his own home, in a row of little tenements that stood south of the prison walls. I

had replied to all inquiries with some dignity and spirit, attributing my ruffled condition to an assault on the part of Johnson, when he was already under the shadow of his seizure. I had directed his removal, and grudged him no professional attention that it was in my power to bestow. But afterwards, locked into my room, my whole nervous system broke up like a trodden ant-hill, leaving me conscious of nothing but an aimless scurrying terror and the black swarm of thoughts, so that I verily fancied my reason would give under the strain.

Yet I had more to endure and to triumph over.

Near morning I fell into a troubled sleep, throughout which the drawn twitch of muscle seemed an accent on every word of ill-omen I had ever spelt out of the alphabet of fear. If my body rested, my brain was an open chamber for any toad of ugliness that listed to "sit at squat" in.

Suddenly I woke to the fact that there was a knocking at my door—that there had been for some little time.

I cried, "Come in!" finding a weak restorative in the mere sound of my own human voice; then, remembering the key was turned, bade the visitor wait until I could come to him.

Scrambling, feeling dazed and white-livered, out of bed, I opened the door, and met one of the warders on the threshold. The man looked scared, and his lips, I noticed, were set in a somewhat boding fashion.

"Can you come at once, sir?" he said. "There's summat wrong with the Governor."

"Wrong? What's the matter with him?"

"Why,"—he looked down, rubbed an imaginary protuberance smooth with his foot, and glanced up at me again with a quick, furtive expression—"he's got his face set in the grating of 47, and danged if a man Jack of us can get him to move or speak."

I turned away, feeling sick. I hurriedly pulled on coat and trousers, and hurriedly went off with my summoner. Reason was all absorbed in a wildest phantasy of apprehension.

"Who found him?" I muttered, as we sped on.

"Vokins see him go down the corridor about half after eight, sir, and see him give a start like when he noticed the trap open. It's never been so before in my time. Johnson must ha' done it last night, before he were took."

"Yes, yes."

"The man said the Governor went to shut it, it seemed, and to draw his face to'ards the bars in so doin'. Then he see him a-lookin' through, as he thought; but nat'rally it weren't no business of his'n, and he went off about his work. But when hie come anigh agen, fifteen minutes later, there were the Governor in the same position; and he got scared over it, and called out to one or two of us."

"Why didn't one of you ask the Major if anything was wrong?"

"Bless you! we did; and no answer. And we pulled him, compatible with discipline, but—"

"But what?"

"He's stuck."

"Stuck!"

"See for yourself, sir. That's all I ask."

I did, a moment later. A little group was collected about the door of cell 47, and the members of it spoke together in whispers, as if they were frightened men. One young fellow, with a face white in patches, as if it had been floured, slid from them as I approached, and accosted me tremulously.

"Don't go anigh, sir. There's something wrong about the place."

I pulled myself together, forcibly beating down the excitement re-awakened by the associations of the spot. In the discomfiture of others' nerves, I found my own restoration.

"Don't be an ass!" I said, in a determined voice. "There's nothing here that can't be explained. Make way for me, please!"

They parted and let me through, and I saw him.

He stood, spruce, frock-coated, dapper, as he always was, with his face pressed against and into the grill, and either hand raised and clenched tightly round a bar of the trap. His posture was as of one caught and striving frantically to release himself; yet, the narrowness of the interval between the rails precluded so extravagant an idea. He stood quite motionless—taut and on the strain, as it were—and nothing of his face was visible but the back ridges of his jaw-bones, showing white through a bush of red whiskers.

"Major Shrike!" I rapped out, and, allowing myself no hesitation, reached forth my hand and grasped his shoulder. The body vibrated under my touch, but he neither answered nor made sign of hearing me. Then I pulled at him forcibly, and ever with increasing strength. His fingers held like steel braces. He seemed glued to the trap, like Theseus to the rock.

Hastily I peered round, to see if I could get glimpse of his face. I

98

noticed enough to send me back with a little stagger.

"Has none of you got a key to this door?" I asked, reviewing the scared faces about me, than which my own was no less troubled, I feel sure.

"Only the Governor, sir," said the warder who had fetched me. "There's not a man but him amongst us that ever seen this opened."

He was wrong there, I could have told him; but held my tongue, for obvious reasons.

"I want it opened. Will one of you feel in his pockets?"

Not a soul stirred. Even had not sense of discipline precluded, that of a certain inhuman atmosphere made fearful creatures of them all.

"Then," said I, "I must do it myself."

I turned once more to the stiff-strung figure, had actually put hand on it, when an exclamation from Vokins arrested me.

"There's a key—there, sir!" he said—"stickin' out yonder between its feet."

Sure enough there was—Johnson's, no doubt, that had been shot from its socket by the clapping to of the door, and afterwards kicked aside by the warder in his convulsive struggles.

I stooped, only too thankful for the respite, and drew it forth. I had seen it but once before, yet I recognised it at a glance.

Now, I confess, my heart felt ill as I slipped the key into the wards, and a sickness of resentment at the tyranny of Fate in making me its helpless minister surged up in my veins. Once, with my fingers on the iron loop, I paused, and ventured a fearful side glance at the figure whose crookt elbow almost touched my face; then, strung to the high pitch of inevitability, I shot the lock, pushed at the door, and in the act, made a back leap into the corridor.

Scarcely, in doing so, did I look for the totter and collapse outwards of the rigid form. I had expected to see it fall away, face down, into the cell, as its support swung from it. Yet it was, I swear, as if *something* from within had relaxed its grasp and given the fearful dead man a swingeing push outwards as the door opened.

It went on its back, with a dusty slap on the stone flags, and from all its spectators—me included—came a sudden drawn sound, like wind in a keyhole.

What can I say, or how describe it? A dead thing it was—but the face!

Barred with livid scars where the grating rails had crossed it, the rest seemed to have been worked and kneaded into a mere featureless plate of yellow and expressionless flesh.

And it was this I had seen in the glass!

★★★★★★

There was an interval following the experience above narrated, during which a certain personality that had once been mine was effaced or suspended, and I seemed a passive creature, innocent of the least desire of independence. It was not that I was actually ill or actually insane. A merciful Providence set my finer wits slumbering, that was all, leaving me a sufficiency of the grosser faculties that were necessary to the right ordering of my behaviour.

I kept to my room, it is true, and even lay a good deal in bed; but this was more to satisfy the busy scruples of a *locum tenens*—a practitioner of the neighbourhood, who came daily to the prison to officiate in my absence—than to cosset a complaint that in its inactivity was purely negative. I could review what had happened with a calmness as profound as if I had read of it in a book. I could have wished to continue my duties, indeed, had the power of insistence remained to me. But the saner *medicus* was acute where I had gone blunt, and bade me to the restful course. He was right. I was mentally stunned, and had I not slept off my lethargy, I should have gone mad in an hour—leapt at a bound, probably, from inertia to flaming lunacy.

I remembered everything, but through a fluffy atmosphere, so to speak. It was as if I looked on bygone pictures through ground glass that softened the ugly outlines.

Sometimes I referred to these to my substitute, who was wise to answer me according to my mood; for the truth left me unruffled, whereas an obvious evasion of it would have distressed me.

"Hammond," I said one day, "I have never yet asked you. How did I give my evidence at the inquest?"

"Like a doctor and a sane man."

"That's good. But it was a difficult course to steer. You conducted the *post-mortem*. Did any peculiarity in the dead man's face strike you?"

"Nothing but this: that the excessive contraction of the bicipital muscles had brought the features into such forcible contact with the bars as to cause bruising and actual abrasion. He must have been dead some little time when you found him."

"And nothing else? You noticed nothing else in his face—a sort of obliteration of what makes one human, I mean?"

"Oh, dear, no! nothing but the painful constriction that marks any ordinary fatal attack of *angina pectoris*.—There's a rum breach of promise case in the paper today. You should read it; it'll make you laugh?"

I had no more inclination to laugh than to sigh; but I accepted the change of subject with an equanimity now habitual to me.

★★★★★★

One morning I sat up in bed, and knew that consciousness was wide awake in me once more. It had slept, and now rose refreshed, but trembling. Looking back, all in a flutter of new responsibility, along the misty path by way of which I had recently loitered, I shook with an awful thankfulness at sight of the pitfalls I had skirted and escaped—of the demons my witlessness had baffled.

The joy of life was in my heart again, but chastened and made pitiful by experience.

Hammond noticed the change in me directly he entered, and congratulated me upon it.

"Go slow at first, old man," he said. "You've fairly sloughed the old skin; but give the sun time to toughen the new one. Walk in it at present, and be content."

I was, in great measure, and I followed his advice. I got leave of absence, and ran down for a month in the country to a certain house we wot of, where kindly ministration to my convalescence was only one of the many blisses to be put to an account of rosy days.

> *Then did my love awake.*
> *Most like a lily-flower,*
> *And as the lovely queene of heaven,*
> *So shone shee in her bower.*

Ah, me! ah, me! when was it? A year ago, or two-thirds of a lifetime? Alas! "Age with stealing steps hath clawde me with his crowch." And will the yews root in *my* heart, I wonder?

I was well, sane, recovered, when one morning, towards the end of my visit, I received a letter from Hammond, enclosing a packet addressed to me, and jealously sealed and fastened. My friend's communication ran as follows:—

There died here yesterday afternoon a warder, Johnson—he who had that apoplectic seizure, you will remember, the night before poor Shrike's exit. I attended him to the end, and, being alone with him an hour before the finish, he took the enclosed from under his pillow, and a solemn oath from me that I would forward it direct to you, sealed as you will find it, and permit no

101

other soul to examine or even touch it. I acquit myself of the charge, but, my dear fellow, with an uneasy sense of the responsibility I incur in thus possibly suggesting to you a retrospect of events which you had much best consign to the limbo of the—not unexplainable, but not worth trying to explain. It was patent from what I have gathered that you were in an overstrung and excitable condition at that time, and that your temporary collapse was purely nervous in its character. It seems there was some nonsense abroad in the prison about a certain cell, and that there were fools who thought fit to associate Johnson's attack and the other's death with the opening of that cell's door. I have given the new Governor a tip, and he has stopped all that. We have examined the cell in company, and found it, as one might suppose, a very ordinary chamber. The two men died perfectly natural deaths, and there is the last to be said on the subject. I mention it only from the fear that enclosed may contain some allusion to the rubbish, a perusal of which might check the wholesome convalescence of your thoughts. If you take my advice, you will throw the packet into the fire unread. At least, if you do examine it, postpone the duty till you feel yourself absolutely impervious to any mental trickery, and—bear in mind that you are a worthy member of a particularly matter-of-fact and unemotional profession.

I smiled at the last clause, for I was now in a condition to feel a rather warm shame over my erst weak-knee'd collapse before a sheet and an illuminated turnip. I took the packet to my bedroom, shut the door, and sat myself down by the open window. The garden lay below me, and the dewy meadows beyond. In the one, bees were busy ruffling the ruddy gillyflowers and April stocks; in the other, the hedge twigs were all frosted with Mary buds, as if Spring had brushed them with the fleece of her wings in passing.

I fetched a sigh of content as I broke the seal of the packet and brought out the enclosure. Somewhere in the garden a little sardonic laugh was clipt to silence. It came from groom or maid, no doubt; yet it thrilled me with an odd feeling of uncanniness, and I shivered slightly.

"Bah!" I said to myself determinedly. "There is a shrewd nip in the wind, for all the show of sunlight;" and I rose, pulled down the window, and resumed my seat.

Then in the closed room, that had become deathly quiet by contrast, I opened and read the dead man's letter.

Sir,—I hope you will read what I here put down. I lay it on you as a solemn injunction, for I am a dying man, and I know it. And to who is my death due, and the Governor's death, if not to you, for your pryin' and curiosity, as surely as if you had drove a nife through our harts? Therefore, I say, read this, and take my burden from me, for it has been a burden; and now it is right that you that interfered should have it on your own mortal shoulders. The Major is dead and I am dying, and in the first of my fit it went on in my head like cimbells that the trap was left open, and that if he passed he would look in and *it* would get him. For he knew not fear, neither would he submit to bullying by God or devil.

Now I will tell you the truth, and Heaven quit you of your responsibility in our destruction.

There wasn't another man to me like the Governor in all the countries of the world. Once he brought me to life after doctors had given me up for dead; but he willed it, and I lived; and ever afterwards I loved him as a dog loves its master. That was in the Punjab; and I came home to England with him, and was his servant when he got his appointment to the jail here. I tell you he was a proud and fierce man, but under control and tender to those he favoured; and I will tell you also a strange thing about him.

Though he was a soldier and an officer, and strict in discipline as made men fear and admire him, his hart at bottom was all for books, and literature, and such-like gentle crafts. I had his confidence, as a man gives his confidence to his dog, and before me sometimes he unbent as he never would before others. In this way I learnt the bitter sorrow of his life. He had once hoped to be a poet, acknowledged as such before the world. He was by natur' an idelist, as they call it, and God knows what it meant to him to come out of the woods, so to speak, and swet in the dust of cities; but he did it, for his will was of tempered steel. He buried his dreams in the clouds and came down to earth greatly resolved, but with one undying hate. It is not good to hate as he could, and worse to be hated by such as him; and I will tell you the story, and what it led to.

103

It was when he was a subaltern that he made up his mind to the plunge. For years he had placed all his hopes and confidents in a book of verses he had wrote, and added to, and improved during that time. A little encouragement, a little word of praise, was all he looked for, and then he was redy to buckle to again, profitin' by advice, and do better. He put all the love and beauty of his hart into that book, and at last, after doubt, and anguish, and much diffidents, he published it and give it to the world. Sir, it fell what they call still-born from the press. It was like a green leaf flutterin' down in a dead wood. To a proud and hopeful man, bubblin' with music, the pain of neglect, when he come to relize it, was terrible. But nothing was said, and there was nothing to say. In silence he had to endure and suffer.

But one day, during manoovers, there came to the camp a grey-faced man, a newspaper correspondent, and young Shrike nocked up a friendship with him. Now how it come about I cannot tell, but so it did that this skip-kennel wormed the lad's sorrow out of him, and his confidents, swore he'd been damnabilly used, and that when he got back he'd crack up the book himself in his own paper. He was a fool for his pains, and a serpent in his croolty. The notice come out as promised, and, my God! the author was laughed and mocked at from beginning to end. Even confidentses he had given to the creature was twisted to his ridicule, and his very appearance joked over. And the mess got wind of it, and made a rare story for the dog days. 'He bore it like a soldier, and that he became hart and liver from the moment. But he put something to the account of the grey-faced man and locked it up in his breast.

He come across him again years afterwards in India, and told him very politely that he hadn't forgotten him, and didn't intend to. But he was anigh losin' sight of him there for ever and a day, for the creature took cholera, or what looked like it, and rubbed shoulders with death and the devil before he pulled through. And he come across him again over here, and that was the last of him, as you shall see presently.

Once, after I knew the Major (he were Captain then), I was a-brushin' his coat, and he stood a long while before the glass. Then he twisted upon me, with a smile on his mouth, and says he,—

'The dog was right, Johnson: this isn't the face of a poet. I was a presumtious ass, and born to cast up figgers with a pen behind my ear.'

'Captain,' I says, 'if you was skinned, you'd look like any other man without his. The quality of a soul isn't expressed by a coat.'

'Well,' he answers, 'my soul's pretty clean-swept, I think, save for one Bluebeard chamber in it that's been kep' locked ever so many years. It's nice and dirty by this time, I expect,' he says. Then the grin comes on his mouth again. 'I'll open it someday,' he says, 'and look. There's something in it about comparing me to a dancing dervish, with the wind in my petticuts. Perhaps I'll get the chance to set somebody else dancing by-and-by.'

He did, and took it, and the Bluebeard chamber come to be opened in this very jail.

It was when the system was lying fallow, so to speak, and the prison was deserted. Nobody was there but him and me and the ecoes from the empty courts. The contract for restoration hadn't been signed, and for months, and more than a year, we lay idle, nothing bein' done.

Near the beginnin' of this period, one day comes, for the third time of the Major's seein' him, the grey-faced man. 'Let bygones be bygones,' he says. 'I was a good friend to you, though you didn't know it; and now, I expect, you're in the way to thank me.'

'I am,' says the Major.

'Of course,' he answers. 'Where would be your fame and reputation as one of the leadin' prison reformers of the day if you had kep' on in that riming nonsense?'

'Have you come for my thanks?' says the Governor.

'I've come,' says the grey-faced man, 'to examine and report upon your system.'

'For your paper?'

'Possibly; but to satisfy myself of its efficacy, in the first instance.'

'You aren't commissioned, then?'

'No; I come on my own responsibility.'

'Without consultation with anyone?'

'Absolutely without. I haven't even a wife to advise me,' he says, with a yellow grin. What once passed for cholera had set the bile on his skin like paint, and he had caught a manner of coughing behind his hand like a toastmaster.

'I know,' says the Major, looking him steady in the face, 'that what you say about me and my affairs is sure to be actuated by conscientious motives.'

'Ah,' he answers. 'You're sore about that review still, I see.'

'Not at all,' says the Major; 'and, in proof, I invite you to be my guest for the night, and tomorrow I'll show you over the prison and explain my system.'

The creature cried, 'Done!' and they set to and discussed jail matters in great earnestness. I couldn't guess the Governor's intentions, but, somehow, his manner troubled me. And yet I can remember only one point of his talk. He were always dead against making public show of his birds. 'They're there for reformation, not ignimony,' he'd say. Prisons in the old days were often, with the asylum and the work'us, made the holiday show-places of towns. I've heard of one Justice of the Peace, up North, who, to save himself trouble, used to sign a lot of blank orders for leave to view, so that applicants needn't bother him when they wanted to go over. They've changed all that, and the Governor were instrumental in the change.

'It's against my rule,' he said that night, 'to exhibit to a stranger without a Government permit; but, seein' the place is empty, and for old remembrance' sake, I'll make an exception in your favour, and you shall learn all I can show you of the inside of a prison.'

Now this was natural enough; but I was uneasy.

He treated his guest royly; so much that when we assembled the next momin' for the inspection, the grey-faced man were shaky as a wet dog. But the Major were all set prim and dry, like the soldier he was.

We went straight away down corridor B, and at cell 47 we stopped.

'We will begin our inspection here,' said the Governor. 'Johnson, open the door.'

I had the keys of the row; fitted in the right one, and pushed open the door.

'After you, sir,' said the Major; and the creature walked in, and he shut the door on him.

I think he smelt a rat at once, for he began beating on the wood and calling out to us. But the Major only turned round to me with his face like a stone.

'Take that key from the bunch,' he said, 'and give it to me.'

I obeyed, all in a tremble, and he took and put it in his pocket.
'My God, Major' I whispered, 'what are you going to do with
him?'

'Silence, sir!' he said. 'How dare you question your superior
officer!'

And the noise inside grew louder.

The Governor, he listened to it a moment like music; then he
unbolted and flung open the trap, and the creature's face came
at it like a wild beast's.

'Sir,' said the Major to it, 'you can't better understand my system
than by experiencing it. What an article for your paper you
could write already—almost as pungint a one as that in which
you ruined the hopes and prospects of a young cockney poet.'

The man mouthed at the bars. He was half-mad, I think, in that
one minute.

'Let me out!' he screamed. 'This is a hidius joke! Let me out!'

'When you are quite quiet—deathly quiet,' said the Major, 'you
shall come out. Not before;' and he shut the trap in its face very
softly.

'Come, Johnson, march!' he said, and took the lead, and we
walked out of the prison.

I was like to faint, but I dared not disobey, and the man's
screeching followed us all down the empty corridors and halls,
until we shut the first great door on it.

It may have gone on for hours, alone in that awful emptiness.
The creature was a reptile, but the thought sickened my heart.
And from that hour till his death, five months later, he rotted
and maddened in his dreadful tomb.

There was more, but I pushed the ghastly confession from me at
this point in uncontrollable loathing and terror. Was it possible—possible, that injured vanity could so falsify its victim's every tradition of
decency?

"Oh!" I muttered, "what a disease is ambition! Who takes one step
towards it puts his foot on Alsirat!"

It was minutes before my shocked nerves were equal to a resump-
tion of the task; but at last I took it up again, with a groan.

I don't think at first I relized the full mischief the Governor
intended to do. At least, I hoped he only meant to give the man
a good fright and then let him go. I might have known better.

107

How could he ever release him without ruining himself?

The next morning, he summoned me to attend him. There was a strange new look of triump in his face, and in his hand, he held a heavy hunting-crop. I pray to God he acted in madness, but my duty and obedience was to him.

'There is sport toward, Johnson,' he said. 'My dervish has got to dance.'

I followed him quiet. We listened when I opened the jail door, but the place was silent as the grave. But from the cell, when we reached it, came a low, whispering sound.

The Governor slipped the trap and looked through.

'All right,' he said, and put the key in the door and flung it open.

He were sittin' crouched on the ground, and he looked up at us vacant-like. His face were all fallen down, as it were, and his mouth never ceased to shake and whisper.

The Major shut the door and posted me in a comer. Then he moved to the creature with his whip.

'Up!' he cried. 'Up, you dervish, and dance to us!' and he brought the thong with a smack across his shoulders.

The creature leapt under the blow, and then to his feet with a cry, and the Major whipped him till he danced. All round the cell he drove him, lashing and cutting—and again, and many times again, until the poor thing rolled on the floor whimpering and sobbing. I shall have to give an account of this someday. I shall have to whip my master with a red-hot serpent round the blazing furnace of the pit, and I shall do it with agony, because here my love and my obedience was to him.

When it was finished, he bade me put down food and drink that I had brought with me, and come away with him; and we went, leaving him rolling on the floor of the cell, and shut him alone in the empty prison until we should come again at the same time tomorrow.

So, day by day this went on, and the dancing three or four times a week, until at last the whip could be left behind, for the man would scream and begin to dance at the mere turning of the key in the lock. And he danced for four months, but not the fifth.

Nobody official came near us all this time. The prison stood lonely as a deserted ruin where dark things have been done.

Once, with fear and trembling, I asked my master how he

would account for the inmate of 47 if he was suddenly called upon by authority to open the cell; and he answered, smiling,—'I should say it was my mad brother. By his own account, he showed me a brother's love, you know. It would be thought a liberty; but the authorities, I think, would stretch a point for me. But if I got sufficient notice, I should clear out the cell.'

I asked him how, with my eyes rather than my lips, and he answered me only with a look.

And all this time he was, outside the prison, living the life of a good man—helping the needy, ministering to the poor. He even entertained occasionally, and had more than one noisy party in his house.

But the fifth month the creature danced no more. He was a dumb, silent animal then, with matted hair and beard; and when one entered he would only look up at one pitifully, as if he said, 'My long punishment is nearly ended.' How it came that no inquiry was ever made about him I know not, but none ever was. Perhaps he was one of the wandering gentry that nobody ever knows where they are next. He was unmarried, and had apparently not told of his intended journey to a soul.

And at the last he died in the night. We found him lying stiff and stark in the morning, and scratched with a piece of black crust on a stone of the wall these strange words: '*An Eddy on the Floor.*' Just that—nothing else.

Then the Governor came and looked down, and was silent. Suddenly he caught me by the shoulder.

'Johnson,' he cried, 'if it was to do again, I would do it! I repent of nothing. But he has paid the penalty, and we call quits. May he rest in peace!'

'Amen!' I answered low. Yet I knew our turn must come for this. We buried him in quicklime under the wall where the murderers lie, and I made the cell trim and rubbed out the writing, and the Governor locked all up and took away the key. But he locked in more than he bargained for.

For months the place was left to itself, and neither of us went anigh 47. Then one day the workmen was to be put in, and the Major he took me round with him for a last examination of the place before they come.

He hesitated a bit outside a particular cell; but at last he drove in the key and kicked open the door.

'My God!' he says, 'he's dancing still!'

My heart was thumpin', I tell you, as I looked over his shoulder. What did we see? What you well understand, sir; but, for all it was no more than that, we knew as well as if it was shouted in our ears that it was him, dancin'. It went round by the walls and drew towards us, and as it stole near I screamed out, 'An Eddy on the Floor!' and seized and dragged the Major out and clapped to the door behind us.

'Oh!' I said, 'in another moment it would have had us.'

He looked at me gloomily.

'Johnson,' he said, ' I'm not to be frighted or coerced. He may dance, but he shall dance alone. Get a screwdriver and some screws and fasten up this trap. No one from this time looks into this cell'

I did as he bid me, swetin'; and I swear all the time I wrought I dreaded a hand would come through the trap and clutch mine. On one pretex' or another, from that day till the night you meddled with it, he kep' that cell as close shut as a tomb. And he went his ways, discardin' the past from that time forth. Now and again a over-sensitive prisoner in the next cell would complain of feelin' uncomfortable. If possible, he would be removed to another; if not, he was damd for his fancies. And so, it might be goin' on to now, if you hadn't pried and interfered. I don't blame you at this moment, sir. Likely you were an instrument in the hands of Providence; only, as the instrument, you must now take the burden of the truth on your own shoulders. I am a dying man, but I cannot die till I have confessed. Per'aps you may find it in your hart someday to give up a prayer for me—but it must be for the Major as well.

Your obedient servant,

J Johnson.

What comment of my own can I append to this wild narrative? Professionally, and apart from personal experiences, I should role it the composition of an epileptic. That a noted journalist, nameless as he was and is to me, however nomadic in habit, could disappear from human ken, and his fellows rest content to leave him unaccounted for, seems a tax upon credulity so stupendous that I cannot seriously endorse the statement.

Yet, also—there *is* that little matter of my personal experience.

Father Macclesfield's Tale

R H Benson

Monsignor Maxwell announced next day at dinner that he had already arranged for the evening's entertainment. A priest, whose acquaintance he had made on the Palatine, was leaving for England the next morning; and it was our only chance therefore of hearing his story. That he had a story had come to the Canon's knowledge in the course of a conversation on the previous afternoon.

'He told me the outline of it,' he said, 'I think it very remarkable. But I had a great deal of difficulty in persuading him to repeat it to the company this evening. But he promised at last. I trust, gentlemen, you do not think I have presumed in begging him to do so.'

Father Macclesfield arrived at supper.

He was a little unimposing dry man, with a hooked nose, and grey hair. He was rather silent at supper; but there was no trace of shyness in his manner as he took his seat upstairs, and without glancing round once, began in an even and dispassionate voice:

'I once knew a Catholic girl that married an old Protestant three times her own age. I entreated her not to do so; but it was useless. And when the disillusionment came she used to write to me piteous letters, telling me that her husband had in reality no religion at all. He was a convinced *infidel*; and scouted even the idea of the soul's immortality.

'After two years of married life the old man died. He was about sixty years old; but very hale and hearty till the end.

'Well, when he took to his bed, the wife sent for me; and I had half-a-dozen interviews with him; but it was useless. He told me plainly that he wanted to believe—in fact he said that the thought of annihilation was intolerable to him. If he had had a child he would not have hated death so much; if his flesh and blood in any manner

111

survived him, he could have fancied that he had a sort of vicarious life left; but as it was there was no kith or kin of his alive; and he could not bear that.'

Father Macclesfield sniffed cynically, and folded his hands.

'I may say that his death-bed was extremely unpleasant. He was a coarse old fellow, with plenty of strength in him; and he used to make remarks about the churchyard—and—and in fact the worms, that used to send his poor child of a wife half fainting out of the room. He had lived an immoral life too, I gathered.

Just at the last it was—well—disgusting. He had no consideration (God knows why she married him!). The agony was a very long one; he caught at the curtains round the bed; calling out; and all his words were about death, and the dark. It seemed to me that he caught hold of the curtains as if to hold himself into this world. And at the very end he raised himself clean up in bed, and stared horribly out of the window that was open just opposite.

'I must tell you that straight away beneath the window lay a long walk, between sheets of dead leaves with laurels on either side, and the branches meeting overhead, so that it was very dark there even in summer; and at the end of the walk away from the house was the churchyard gate.'

Father Macclesfield paused and blew his nose. Then he went on still without looking at us.

'Well the old man died; and he was carried along this laurel path, and buried.

'His wife was in such a state that I simply dared not go away. She was frightened to death; and, indeed, the whole affair of her husband's dying was horrible. But she would not leave the house. She had a fancy that it would be cruel to him. She used to go down twice a day to pray at the grave; but she never went along the laurel walk. She would go round by the garden and in at a lower gate, and come back the same way, or by the upper garden.

'This went on for three or four days. The man had died on a Saturday, and was buried on Monday; it was in July; and he had died about eight o'clock.

'I made up my mind to go on the Saturday after the funeral. My curate had managed along very well for a few days; but I did not like to leave him for a second Sunday.

'Then on the Friday at lunch—her sister had come down, by the way, and was still in the house—on the Friday the widow said something about never daring to sleep in the room where the old man had died. I told her it was nonsense, and so on; but you must remember she was in a dreadful state of nerves, and she persisted. So, I said I would sleep in the room myself. I had no patience with such ideas then.

'Of course, she said all sorts of things, but I had my way; and my things were moved in on Friday evening.

'I went to my new room about a quarter before eight to put on my cassock for dinner. The room was very much as it had been—rather dark because of the trees at the end of the walk outside. There was the four-poster there with the damask curtains; the table and chairs, the cupboard where his clothes were kept, and so on.

'When I had put my cassock on, I went to the window to look out.

To right and left were the gardens, with the sunlight just off them, but still very bright and gay, with the geraniums, and exactly opposite was the laurel walk, like a long green shady tunnel, dividing the upper and lower lawns.

'I could see straight down it to the churchyard gate, which was about a hundred yards away, I suppose. There were limes overhead, and laurels, as I said, on each side.

'Well—I saw someone coming up the walk; but it seemed to me at first that he was drunk. He staggered several times as I watched; I suppose he would be fifty yards away—and once I saw him catch hold of one of the trees and cling against it as if he were afraid of falling. Then he left it, and came on again slowly, going from side to side, with his hands out. He seemed desperately keen to get to the house.

'I could see his dress; and it astonished me that a man dressed so should be drunk; for he was quite plainly a gentleman. He wore a white top hat, and a grey cut-away coat, and grey trousers, and I could make out his white spats.

'Then it struck me he might be ill; and I looked harder than ever, wondering whether I ought to go down.

'When he was about twenty yards away he lifted his face; and, it struck me as very odd, but it seemed to me he was extraordinarily like the old man we had buried on Monday; but it was darkish where he was, and the next moment he dropped his face, threw up his hands and fell flat on his back.

'Well of course I was startled at that, and I leaned out of the window and called out something. He was moving his hands I could see, as if he were in convulsions; and I could hear the dry leaves rustling.

'Well, then I turned and ran out and downstairs.'

Father Macclesfield stopped a moment.

'Gentlemen,' he said abruptly, 'when I got there, there was not a sign of the old man. I could see that the leaves had been disturbed, but that was all.'

There was an odd silence in the room as he paused; but before any of us had time to speak he went on.

'Of course, I did not say a word of what I had seen. We dined as usual; I smoked for an hour or so by myself after prayers; and then I went up to bed. I cannot say I was perfectly comfortable, for I was not; but neither was I frightened.

'When I got to my room I lit all my candles, and then went to a big cupboard I had noticed, and pulled out some of the drawers. In the bottom of the third drawer I found a grey cut-away coat and grey trousers; I found several pairs of white spats in the top drawer; and a white hat on the shelf above. That is the first incident.'

Did you sleep there, Father?' said a voice softly.

'I did,' said the priest; 'there was no reason why I should not. I did not fall asleep for two or three hours; but I was not disturbed in any way; and came to breakfast as usual.

'Well, I thought about it all a bit; and finally, I sent a wire to my curate telling him I was detained. I did not like to leave the house just then.'

Father Macclesfield settled himself again in his chair and went on, in the same dry uninterested voice.

'On Sunday we drove over to the Catholic Church, six miles off, and I said Mass. Nothing more happened till the Monday evening.

'That evening I went to the window again about a quarter before eight, as I had done both on the Saturday and Sunday. Everything was perfectly quiet, till I heard the churchyard gate unlatch; and I saw a man come through.

'But I saw almost at once that it was not the same man I had seen before; it looked to me like a keeper, for he had a gun across his arm; then I saw him hold the gate open an instant, and a dog came through and began to trot up the path towards the house with his master following.

'When the dog was about fifty yards away he stopped dead, and pointed.

'I saw the keeper throw his gun forward and come up softly; and as he came the dog began to slink backwards. I watched very closely, clean forgetting why I was there; and the next instant something—it was too shadowy under the trees to see exactly what it was—but something about the size of a hare burst out of the laurels and made straight up the path, dodging from side to side, but coming like the wind.

'The beast could not have been more than twenty yards from me, when the keeper fired, and the creature went over and over in the dry leaves, and lay struggling and screaming. It was horrible! But what astonished me was that the dog did not come up. I heard the keeper snap out something, and then I saw the dog making off down the avenue in the direction of the churchyard as hard as he could go.

'The keeper was running now towards me; but the screaming of the hare, or of whatever it was, had stopped; and I was astonished to see the man come right up to where the beast was struggling and kicking, and then stop as if he was puzzled.

'I leaned out of the window and called to him. "Right in front of you, man," I said. "For God's sake kill the brute."

'He looked up at me, and then down again. "Where is it, sir," he said. "I can't see it any-where."

'And there lay the beast clear before him all the while, not a yard away, still kicking.

'Well, I went out of the room and downstairs and out to the avenue.

'The man was standing there still, looking terribly puzzled, but the hare was gone. There was not a sign of it. Only the leaves were disturbed, and the wet earth showed beneath.

'The keeper said that it had been a great hare; he could have sworn to it; and that he had orders to kill all hares and rabbits in the garden enclosure. Then he looked rather odd.

'"Did you see it plainly, sir," he asked.

'I told him, not very plainly; but I thought it a hare too.

'"Yes, sir," he said, "it was a hare, sure enough; but do you know, sir, I thought it to be a kind of silver grey with white feet. I never saw one like that before!"

'The odd thing was that not a dog would come near, his own dog was gone; but I fetched the yard dog—a retriever, out of his kennel in the kitchen yard; and if ever I saw a frightened dog it was this one. When we dragged him up at last, all whining and pulling back, he began to snap at us so fiercely that we let go, and he went back like the wind to his kennel. It was the same with the terrier.

'Well, the bell had gone, and I had to go in and explain Why I was late; but I didn't say anything about the colour of the hare. That was the second incident.'

Father Macclesfield stopped again, smiling reminiscently to himself. I was very much impressed by his quiet air and composure. I think it helped his story a good deal.

Again, before we had time to comment or question he went on.

'The third incident was so slight that I should not have mentioned it, or thought anything of it, if it had not been for the others; but it seemed to me there was a kind of diminishing gradation of energy, which explained. Well, now you shall hear.

'On the other nights of that week I was at my window again; but nothing happened till the Friday. I had arranged to go for certain next day; the widow was much better and more reasonable, and even talked of going abroad herself in the following week.

'On that Friday evening I dressed a little earlier, and went down to the avenue this time, instead of staying at my window, at about twenty minutes to eight.

'It was rather a heavy depressing evening, without a breath of wind; and it was darker than it had been for some days.

'I walked slowly down the avenue to the gate and back again; and, I suppose it was fancy, but I felt more uncomfortable than I had felt at all up to then. I was rather relieved to see the widow come out of the house and stand looking down the avenue. I came out myself then and went towards her. She started rather when she saw me and then smiled.

"I thought it was someone else," she said. "Father, I have made up my mind to go. I shall go to town tomorrow, and start on Monday. My sister will come with me."

'I congratulated her; and then we turned and began to walk back to the lime avenue. She stopped at the entrance, and seemed unwilling to come any further.

"Come down to the end," I said, "and back again. There will be time before dinner."

'She said nothing; but came with me; and we went straight down to the gate and then turned to come back.

'I don't think either of us spoke a word; I was very uncomfortable indeed by now; and yet I had to go on.

'We were half way back I suppose when I heard a sound like a gate rattling; and I whisked round in an instant, expecting to see someone at the gate. But there was no one.

'Then there came a rustling overhead in the leaves; it had been dead still before. Then I don't know why, but I took my friend suddenly by the arm and drew her to one side out of the path, so that we stood on the right hand, not a foot from the laurels.

'She said nothing, and I said nothing; but I think we were both looking this way and that, as if we expected to see something.

'The breeze died, and then sprang up again; but it was only a breath. I could hear the living leaves rustling overhead, and the dead leaves underfoot; and it was blowing gently from the churchyard.

'Then I saw a thing that one often sees; but I could not take my eyes off it, nor could she. It was a little column of leaves, twisting and turning and dropping and picking up again in the wind, coming slowly up the path. It was a capricious sort of draught, for the little scurry of leaves went this way and that, to and fro across the path. It came up to us, and I could feel the breeze on my hands and face. One leaf struck me softly on the cheek, and I can only say that I shuddered as if it had been a toad. Then it passed on.

'You understand, gentlemen, it was pretty dark; but it seemed to me that the breeze died and the column of leaves—it was no more than a little twist of them—sank down at the end of the avenue.

'We stood there perfectly still for a moment or two; and when I turned, she was staring straight at me, but neither of us said one word.

'We did not go up the avenue to the house. We pushed our way through the laurels, and came back by the upper garden.

'Nothing else happened; and the next morning we all went off by the eleven o'clock train.

'That is all, gentlemen.'

The Haunted Organist of Hurly Burly

Rosa Mulholland

There had been a thunderstorm in the village of Hurly Burly. Every door was shut, every dog in his kennel, every rut and gutter a flowing river after the deluge of rain that had fallen. Up at the great house, a mile from the town, the rooks were calling to one another about the fright they had been in, the fawns in the deer-park were venturing their timid heads from behind the trunks of trees, and the old woman at the gate-lodge had risen from her knees, and was putting back her prayer-book on the shelf.

In the garden, July roses, unwieldy with their full-blown richness, and saturated with rain, hung their heads heavily to the earth; others, already fallen, lay flat upon their blooming faces on the path, where Bess, Mistress Hurly's maid, would find them, when going on her morning quest of rose-leaves for her lady's potpourri. Ranks of white lilies, just brought to perfection by today's sun, lay dabbled in the mire of flooded mould. Tears ran down the amber cheeks of the plums on the south wall, and not a bee had ventured out of the hives, though the scent of the air was sweet enough to tempt the laziest drone. The sky was still lurid behind the boles of the upland oaks, but the birds had begun to dive in and out of the ivy that wrapped up the home of the Hurlys of Hurly Burly.

This thunderstorm took place more than half a century ago, and we must remember that Mistress Hurly was dressed in the fashion of that time as she crept out from behind the squire's chair, now that the lightning was over, and, with many nervous glances towards the window, sat down before her husband, the tea-urn, and the muffins. We can picture her fine lace cap, with its peachy ribbons, the frill on the hem of her cambric gown just touching her ankles, the embroidered clocks on her stockings, the rosettes on her shoes, but not so easily the lilac shade of her mild eyes, the satin skin, which still kept its delicate bloom, though wrinkled with advancing age, and the pale, sweet, puckered mouth, that time and sorrow had made angelic while trying vainly to deface its beauty.

The squire was as rugged as his wife was gentle, his skin as brown as hers was white, his grey hair as bristling as hers was glossed; the years had ploughed his face into ruts and channels; a bluff, choleric, noisy man he had been; but of late a dimness had come on his eyes, a hush on his loud voice, and a check on the spring of his hale step. He looked at his wife often, and very often she looked at him. She was not a tall woman, and he was only a head higher. They were a quaintly well-matched couple, despite their differences. She turned to you with nervous sharpness and revealed her tender voice and eye; he spoke and glanced roughly, but the turn of his head was courteous. Of late they fitted one another better than they had ever done in the heyday of their youthful love. A common sorrow had developed a singular likeness between them. In former years the cry from the wife had been, "Don't curb my son too much!" and from the husband, "You ruin the lad with softness." But now the idol that had stood between them was removed, and they saw each other better.

The room in which they sat was a pleasant old-fashioned drawing-room, with a general spider-legged character about the fittings; spinnet and guitar in their places, with a great deal of copied music beside them; carpet, tawny wreaths on pale blue; blue flutings on the walls, and faint gilding on the furniture. A huge urn, crammed with roses, in the open bay-window, through which came delicious airs from the garden, the twittering of birds settling to sleep in the ivy close by, and occasionally the pattering of a flight of raindrops, swept to the ground as a bough bent in the breeze. The urn on the table was ancient silver, and the china rare. There was nothing in the room for luxurious ease of the body, but everything of delicate refinement for the eye.

There was a great hush all over Hurly Burly, except in the neighbourhood of the rooks. Every living thing had suffered from heat for the past month, and now, in common with all Nature, was receiving the boon of refreshed air in silent peace. The mistress and master of Hurly Burly shared the general spirit that was abroad, and were not talkative over their tea.

"Do you know?" said Mistress Hurly, at last, "when I heard the first of the thunder beginning I thought it was—it was—"

The lady broke down, her lips trembling, and the peachy ribbons of her cap stirring with great agitation.

"Pshaw!" cried the old squire, making his cup suddenly ring upon the saucer, "we ought to have forgotten that. Nothing has been heard for three months."

At this moment a rolling sound struck upon the ears of both. The lady rose from her seat trembling, and folded her hands together, while the tea-urn flooded the tray.

"Nonsense, my love," said the squire; "that is the noise of wheels. Who can be arriving?"

"Who, indeed?" murmured the lady, reseating herself in agitation.

Presently pretty Bess of the rose-leaves appeared at the door in a flutter of blue ribbons.

"Please, madam, a lady has arrived, and says she is expected. She asked for her apartment, and I put her into the room that was got ready for Miss Calderwood. And she sends her respects to you, madam, and she'll be down with you presently."

The squire looked at his wife, and his wife looked at the squire.

"It is some mistake," murmured madam. "Some visitor for Calderwood or the Grange. It is very singular."

Hardly had she spoken when the door again opened, and the stranger appeared—a small creature, whether girl or woman it would be hard to say—dressed in a scanty black silk dress, her narrow shoulders covered with a white muslin pelerine. Her hair was swept up to the crown of her head, all but a little fringe hanging over her low forehead within an inch of her brows. Her face was brown and thin, eyes black and long, with blacker settings, mouth large, sweet, and melancholy. She was all head, mouth, and eyes; her nose and chin were nothing.

This visitor crossed the floor hastily, dropped a courtesy in the middle of the room, and approached the table, saying abruptly, with a soft Italian accent:

"Sir and madam, I am here. I am come to play your organ."

"The organ!" gasped Mistress Hurly.

"The organ!" stammered the squire.

"Yes, the organ," said the little stranger lady, playing on the back of a chair with her fingers, as if she felt notes under them. "It was but last week that the handsome *signor*, your son, came to my little house, where I have lived teaching music since my English father and my Italian mother and brothers and sisters died and left me so lonely."

Here the fingers left off drumming, and two great tears were brushed off, one from each eye with each hand, child's fashion. But the next moment the fingers were at work again, as if only whilst they were moving the tongue could speak.

"The noble *signor*, your son," said the little woman, looking trustfully from one to the other of the old couple, while a bright blush shone through her brown skin, "he often came to see me before that, always in the evening, when the sun was warm and yellow all through my little studio, and the music was swelling my heart, and I could play out grand with all my soul; then he used to come and say, 'Hurry, little Lisa, and play better, better still. I have work for you to do by-and-by.' Sometimes he said, '*Brava!*' and sometimes he said '*Eccellentissima!*' but one night last week he came to me and said, 'It is enough. Will you swear to do my bidding, whatever it may be?'

"Here the black eyes fell. And I said, 'Yes.'

"And he said, 'Now you are my betrothed.'

"And I said, 'Yes.'

"And he said, 'Pack up your music, little Lisa, and go off to England to my English father and mother, who have an organ in their house which must be played upon. If they refuse to let you play, tell them I sent you, and they will give you leave. You must play all day, and you must get up in the night and play. You must never tire. You are my betrothed, and you have sworn to do my work.' I said, 'Shall I see you there, *signor*?'

"And he said, 'Yes, you shall see me there.'

"I said, 'I will keep my vow, *signor*.' And so, sir and madam, I am come."

The soft foreign voice left off talking, the fingers left off thrumming on the chair, and the little stranger gazed in dismay at her auditors, both pale with agitation.

"You are deceived. You make a mistake," said they in one breath.

"Our son—" began Mistress Hurly, but her mouth twitched, her voice broke, and she looked piteously towards her husband.

"Our son," said the squire, making an effort to conquer the quavering in his voice, "our son is long dead."

"Nay, nay," said the little foreigner. "If you have thought him dead have good cheer, dear sir and madam. He is alive; he is well, and strong, and handsome. But one, two, three, four, five (on the fingers) days ago he stood by my side."

"It is some strange mistake, some wonderful coincidence!" said the mistress and master of Hurly Burly.

"Let us take her to the gallery," murmured the mother of this son who was thus dead and alive. "There is yet light to see the pictures. She will not know his portrait."

The bewildered wife and husband led their strange visitor away to a long gloomy room at the west side of the house, where the faint gleams from the darkening sky still lingered on the portraits of the Hurly family.

"Doubtless he is like this," said the squire, pointing to a fair-haired young man with a mild face, a brother of his own who had been lost at sea.

But Lisa shook her head, and went softly on tiptoe from one picture to another, peering into the canvas, and still turning away troubled. But at last a shriek of delight startled the shadowy chamber.

"Ah, here he is! See, here he is, the noble *signor*, the beautiful *signor*, not half so handsome as he looked five days ago, when talking to poor little Lisa! Dear sir and madam, you are now content. Now take me to the organ, that I may commence to do his bidding at once."

The mistress of Hurly Burly clung fast by her husband's arm.

"How old are you, girl?" she said faintly.

"Eighteen," said the visitor impatiently, moving towards the door.

"And my son has been dead for twenty years!" said his mother, and swooned on her husband's breast.

"Order the carriage at once," said Mistress Hurly; recovering from her swoon; "I will take her to Margaret Calderwood. Margaret will tell her the story. Margaret will bring her to reason. No, not tomorrow; I cannot bear tomorrow, it is so far away. We must go tonight."

The little *signora* thought the old lady mad, but she put on her cloak again obediently, and took her seat beside Mistress Hurly in the Hurly family coach. The moon that looked in at them through the pane as they lumbered along was not whiter than the aged face of the squire's wife, whose dim faded eyes were fixed upon it in doubt and awe too great for tears or words.

Lisa, too, from her corner gloated upon the moon, her black eyes shining with passionate dreams.

A carriage rolled away from the Calderwood door as the Hurly coach drew up at the steps. Margaret Calderwood had just returned from a dinner-party, and at the open door a splendid figure was standing, a tall woman dressed in brown velvet, the diamonds on her bosom glistening in the moonlight that revealed her, pouring, as it did, over the house from eaves to basement. Mistress Hurly fell into her out-stretched arms with a groan, and the strong woman carried her aged friend, like a baby, into the house. Little Lisa was overlooked, and sat down contentedly on the threshold to gloat awhile longer on the moon, and to thrum imaginary sonatas on the doorstep.

There were tears and sobs in the dusk, moonlit room into which Margaret Calderwood carried her friend. There was a long consulta-tion, and then Margaret, having hushed away the grieving woman into some quiet corner, came forth to look for the little dark-faced stranger, who had arrived, so unwelcome, from beyond the seas, with such wild communication from the dead.

Up the grand staircase of handsome Calderwood the little wom-an followed the tall one into a large chamber where a lamp burned, showing Lisa, if she cared to see it, that this mansion of Calderwood was fitted with much greater luxury and richness than was that of Hurly Burly. The appointments of this room announced it the sanc-tum of a woman who depended for the interest of her life upon resources of intellect and taste. Lisa noticed nothing but a morsel of biscuit that was lying on a plate.

"May I have it?" said she eagerly. "It is so long since I have eaten. I am hungry."

Margaret Calderwood gazed at her with a sorrowful, motherly look, and, parting the fringing hair on her forehead, kissed her. Lisa, staring at her in wonder, returned the caress with ardour. Margaret's large fair shoulders, Madonna face, and yellow braided hair, excited a rapture within her. But when food was brought her, she flew to it and ate.

"It is better than I have ever eaten at home!" she said gratefully.

And Margaret Calderwood murmured, "She is physically healthy, at least."

"And now, Lisa," said Margaret Calderwood, "come and tell me the whole history of the grand *signor* who sent you to England to play the organ."

Then Lisa crept in behind a chair, and her eyes began to burn and her fingers to thrum, and she repeated word for word her story as she had told it at Hurly Burly.

When she had finished, Margaret Calderwood began to pace up and down the floor with a very troubled face. Lisa watched her, fasci-nated, and, when she bade her listen to a story which she would relate to her, folded her restless hands together meekly, and listened.

"Twenty years ago, Lisa, Mr. and Mrs. Hurly had a son. He was handsome, like that portrait you saw in the gallery, and he had brilliant talents. He was idolised by his father and mother, and all who knew him felt obliged to love him. I was then a happy girl of twenty. I was an orphan, and Mrs. Hurly, who had been my mother's friend, was like a mother to me. I, too, was petted and caressed by all my friends, and I was very wealthy; but I only valued admiration, riches—every good gift that fell to my share—just in proportion as they seemed of worth in the eyes of Lewis Hurly. I was his affianced wife, and I loved him well.

"All the fondness and pride that were lavished on him could not keep him from falling into evil ways, nor from becoming rapidly more and more abandoned to wickedness, till even those who loved him best despaired of seeing his reformation. I prayed him with tears, for my sake, if not for that of his grieving mother, to save himself before it was too late. But to my horror I found that my power was gone, my words did not even move him; he loved me no more. I tried to think that this was some fit of madness that would pass, and still clung to hope. At last his own mother forbade me to see him."

Here Margaret Calderwood paused, seemingly in bitter thought, but resumed:

"He and a party of his boon companions, named by themselves the 'Devil's Club,' were in the habit of practising all kinds of unholy pranks in the country. They had midnight carousings on the tombstones in the village graveyard; they carried away helpless old men and children, whom they tortured by making believe to bury them alive; they raised the dead and placed them sitting round the tombstones at a mock feast. On one occasion there was a very sad funeral from the village. The corpse was carried into the church, and prayers were read over the coffin, the chief mourner, the aged father of the dead man, standing weeping by.

"In the midst of this solemn scene the organ suddenly pealed forth a profane tune, and a number of voices shouted a drinking chorus. A groan of execration burst from the crowd, the clergyman turned pale and closed his book, and the old man, the father of the dead, climbed the altar steps, and, raising his arms above his head, uttered a terrible curse. He cursed Lewis Hurly to all eternity, he cursed the organ he played, that it might be dumb henceforth, except under the fingers that had now profaned it, which, he prayed, might be forced to labour upon it till they stiffened in death. And the curse seemed to work, for the organ stood dumb in the church from that day, except when touched by Lewis Hurly.

"For a bravado he had the organ taken down and conveyed to his father's house, where he had it put up in the chamber where it now stands. It was also for a bravado that he played on it every day. But, by-and-by, the amount of time which he spent at it daily began to increase rapidly. We wondered long at this whim, as we called it, and his poor mother thanked God that he had set his heart upon an occupation which would keep him out of harm's way. I was the first to suspect that it was not his own will that kept him hammering at the organ so many laborious hours, while his boon companions tried vainly to draw him away. He used to lock himself up in the room with the organ, but one day I hid myself among the curtains, and saw him writhing on his seat, and heard him groaning as he strove to wrench his hands from the keys, to which they flew back like a needle to a magnet.

"It was soon plainly to be seen that he was an involuntary slave to the organ; but whether through a madness that had grown within himself, or by some supernatural doom, having its cause in the old man's curse, we did not dare to say. By-and-by there came a time when we were wakened out of our sleep at nights by the rolling of the organ. He wrought now night and day. Food and rest were denied him. His face got haggard, his beard grew long, his eyes started from their sockets. His body became wasted, and his cramped fingers like the claws of a bird. He groaned piteously as he stooped over his cruel toil. All save his mother and I were afraid to go near him. She, poor, tender woman, tried to put wine and food between his lips, while the tortured fingers crawled over the keys; but he only gnashed his teeth at her with curses, and she retreated from him in terror, to pray. At last, one dreadful hour, we found him a ghastly corpse on the ground before the organ.

"From that hour the organ was dumb to the touch of all human fingers. Many, unwilling to believe the story, made persevering endeavours to draw sound from it, in vain. But when the darkened empty room was locked up and left, we heard as loud as ever the well-known sounds humming and rolling through the walls. Night and day the tones of the organ boomed on as before. It seemed that the doom of the wretched man was not yet fulfilled, although his tortured body had been worn out in the terrible struggle to accomplish it. Even his own mother was afraid to go near the room then. So, the time went on, and the curse of this perpetual music was not removed from the house. Servants refused to stay about the place. Visitors shunned it.

"The squire and his wife left their home for years, and returned; left it, and returned again, to find their ears still tortured and their hearts wrung by the unceasing persecution of terrible sounds. At last, but a few months ago, a holy man was found, who locked himself up in the cursed chamber for many days, praying and wrestling with the demon. After he came forth and went away the sounds ceased, and the organ was heard no more. Since then there has been peace in the house. And now, Lisa, your strange appearance and your strange story convince us that you are a victim of a ruse of the Evil One. Be warned in time, and place yourself under the protection of God, that you may be saved from the fearful influences that are at work upon you. Come—"

Margaret Calderwood turned to the corner where the stranger sat, as she had supposed, listening intently. Little Lisa was fast asleep, her hands spread before her as if she played an organ in her dreams.

Margaret took the soft brown face to her motherly breast, and kissed the swelling temples, too big with wonder and fancy.

"We will save you from a horrible fate!" she murmured, and carried the girl to bed.

In the morning Lisa was gone. Margaret Calderwood, coming early from her own chamber, went into the girl's room and found the bed empty.

"She is just such a wild thing," thought Margaret, u as would rush out at sunrise to hear the larks!" and she went forth to look for her in the meadows, behind the beech hedges, and in the home park. Mistress Hurly, from the breakfast-room window, saw Margaret Calderwood, large and fair in her white morning gown, coming down the garden-path between the rose bushes, with her fresh draperies dabbled by the dew, and a look of trouble on her calm face. Her quest had been unsuccessful. The little foreigner had vanished.

A second search after breakfast proved also fruitless, and towards evening the two women drove back to Hurly Burly together. There all was panic and distress. The squire sat in his study with the doors shut, and his hands over his ears. The servants, with pale faces, were huddled together in whispering groups. The haunted organ was pealing through the house as of old.

Margaret Calderwood hastened to the fatal chamber, and there, sure enough, was Lisa, perched upon the high seat before the organ, beating the keys with her small hands, her slight figure swaying, and the evening sunshine playing about her weird head. Sweet unearthly music she wrung from the groaning heart of the organ—wild melodies, mounting to rapturous heights and falling to mournful depths. She wandered from Mendelssohn to Mozart, and from Mozart to Beethoven. Margaret stood fascinated awhile by the ravishing beauty of the sounds she heard, but, rousing herself quickly, put her arms round the musician and forced her away from the chamber. Lisa returned next day, however, and was not so easily coaxed from her post again. Day after day she laboured at the organ, growing paler and thinner and more weird-looking as time went on.

"I work so hard," she said to Mrs. Hurly. "The *signor*, your son, is he pleased? Ask him to come and tell me himself if he is pleased."

Mistress Hurly got ill and took to her bed. The squire swore at the young foreign baggage, and roamed abroad. Margaret Calderwood was the only one who stood by to watch the fate of the little organist. The curse of the organ was upon Lisa; it spoke under her hand, and her hand was its slave.

At last she announced rapturously that she had had a visit from the brave *signor*, who had commended her industry, and urged her to work yet harder. After that she ceased to hold any communication with the living. Time after time Margaret Calderwood wrapped her arms about the frail thing, and carried her away by force, locking the door of the fatal chamber. But locking the chamber and burying the key were of no avail. The door stood open again, and Lisa was labouring on her perch.

One night, wakened from her sleep by the well-known humming and moaning of the organ, Margaret dressed hurriedly and hastened to the unholy room. Moonlight was pouring down the staircase and passages of Hurly Burly. It shone on the marble bust of the dead Lewis Hurly, that stood in the niche above his mother's sitting-room door. The organ room was full of it when Margaret pushed open the door and entered—full of the pale green moonlight from the window, mingled with another light, a dull lurid glare which seemed to centre round a dark shadow, like the figure of a man standing by the organ, and throwing out in fantastic relief the slight form of Lisa writhing, rather than swaying, back and forward, as if in agony.

"The sounds that came from the organ were broken and meaningless, as if the hands of the player lagged and stumbled on the keys. Between the intermittent chords low moaning cries broke from Lisa, and the dark figure bent towards her with menacing gestures. Trembling with the sickness of supernatural fear, yet strong of will, Margaret Calderwood crept forward within the lurid light, and was drawn into its influence. It grew and intensified upon her, it dazzled and blinded her at first; but presently, by a daring effort of will, she raised her eyes, and beheld Lisa's face convulsed with torture in the burning glare, and bending over her the figure and the features of Lewis Hurly! Smitten with horror, Margaret did not even then lose her presence of mind. She wound her strong arms around the wretched girl and dragged her from her seat and out of the influence of the lurid light, which immediately paled away and vanished. She carried her to her own bed, where Lisa lay, a wasted wreck, raving about the cruelty of the pitiless *signor* who would not see that she was labouring her best. Her poor cramped hands kept beating the coverlet, as though she were still at her agonising task.

Margaret Calderwood bathed her burning temples, and placed fresh flowers upon her pillow. She opened the blinds and windows, and let in the sweet morning air and sunshine, and then, looking up at the newly awakened sky with its fair promise of hope for the day, and down at the dewy fields, and afar off at the dark green woods with the purple mists still hovering about them, she prayed that a way might be shown her by which to put an end to this curse. She prayed for Lisa, and then, thinking that the girl rested somewhat, stole from the room. She thought that she had locked the door behind her.

She went downstairs with a pale, resolved face, and, without consulting any one, sent to the village for a bricklayer. Afterwards she sat by Mistress Hurly's bedside, and explained to her what was to be done. Presently she went to the door of Lisa's room, and hearing no sound, thought the girl slept, and stole away. By-and-by she went downstairs, and found that the bricklayer had arrived and already begun his task of building up the organ-room door. He was a swift workman, and the chamber was soon sealed safely with stone and mortar.

Having seen this work finished, Margaret Calderwood went and listened again at Lisa's door; and still hearing no sound, she returned, and took her seat at Mrs. Hurly's bedside once more. It was towards evening that she at last entered her room to assure herself of the comfort of Lisa's sleep. But the bed and room were empty. Lisa had disappeared.

Then the search began, upstairs and downstairs, in the garden, in the grounds, in the fields and meadows. No Lisa. Margaret Calderwood ordered the carriage and drove to Calderwood to see if the strange little Will-o'-the-wisp might have made her way there; then to the village, and to many other places in the neighbourhood which it was not possible she could have reached. She made inquiries everywhere; she pondered and puzzled over the matter. In the weak, suffering state that the girl was in, how far could she have crawled?

After two days' search, Margaret returned to Hurly Burly. She was sad and tired, and the evening was chill. She sat over the fire wrapped in her shawl when little Bess came to her, weeping behind her muslin apron.

"If you'd speak to Mistress Hurly about it, please, ma'am," she said. "I love her dearly, and it breaks my heart to go away, but the organ haven't done yet, ma'am, and I'm frightened out of my life, so I can't stay."

"Who has heard the organ, and when?" asked Margaret Calderwood, rising to her feet.

"Please, ma'am, I heard it the night you went away—the night after the door was built up!"

"And not since?"

"No, ma'am," hesitatingly, "not since. Hist! hark, ma'am! Is not that like the sound of it now?"

"No," said Margaret Calderwood; "it is only the wind." But pale as death she flew down the stairs and laid her ear to the yet damp mortar of the newly-built wall. All was silent. There was no sound but the monotonous sough of the wind in the trees outside. Then Margaret began to dash her soft shoulder against the strong wall, and to pick the mortar away with her white fingers, and to cry out for the bricklayer who had built up the door.

It was midnight, but the bricklayer left his bed in the village, and obeyed the summons to Hurly Burly. The pale woman stood by and watched him undo all his work of three days ago, and the servants gathered about in trembling groups, wondering what was to happen next.

What happened next was this: When an opening was made the man entered the room with a light, Margaret Calderwood and others following. A heap of something dark was lying on the ground at the foot of the organ. Many groans arose in the fatal chamber. Here was little Lisa dead!

When Mistress Hurly was able to move, the squire and his wife went to live in France, where they remained till their death. Hurly

Burly was shut up and deserted for many years. Lately it has passed into new hands. The organ has been taken down and banished, and the room is a bedchamber, more luxuriously furnished than any in the house. But no one sleeps in it twice.

Margaret Calderwood was carried to her grave the other day a very aged woman.

The Man of Science
Jerome K. Jerome

I met a man in the Strand one day that I knew very well, as I thought, though I had not seen him for years. We walked together to Charing Cross, and there we shook hands and parted. Next morning, I spoke of this meeting to a mutual friend, and then I learnt, for the first time, that the man had died six months before.

The natural inference was that I had mistaken one man for another, an error that, not having a good memory for faces, I frequently fall into. What was remarkable about the matter, however, was that throughout our walk I had conversed with the man under the impression that he was that other dead man, and, whether by coincidence or not, his replies had never once suggested to me my mistake.

As soon as I finished, Jephson, who had been listening very thoughtfully, asked me if I believed in spiritualism "to its fullest extent."

"That is rather a large question," I answered. "What do you mean by 'spiritualism to its fullest extent'?"

"Well, do you believe that the spirits of the dead have not only the power of revisiting this earth at their will, but that, when here, they have the power of action, or rather, of exciting to action? Let me put a definite case. A spiritualist friend of mine, a sensible and by no means imaginative man, once told me that a table, through the medium of which the spirit of a friend had been in the habit of communicating with him, came slowly across the room towards him, of its own accord, one night as he sat alone, and pinioned him against the wall. Now can any of you believe that, or can't you?"

"I could," Brown took it upon himself to reply; "but, before doing so, I should wish for an introduction to the friend who told you the story. Speaking generally," he continued, "it seems to me that the difference between what we call the natural and the supernatural is merely the difference between frequency and rarity of occurrence. Having regard to the phenomena we are compelled to admit, I think it illogical to disbelieve anything we are unable to disprove."

"For my part," remarked MacShaughnassy, "I can believe in the ability of our spirit friends to give the quaint entertainments credited to them much easier than I can in their desire to do so."

"You mean," added Jephson, "that you cannot understand why a spirit, not compelled as we are by the exigencies of society, should care to spend its evenings carrying on a laboured and childish conversation with a room full of abnormally uninteresting people."

"That is precisely what I cannot understand," MacShaughnassy agreed.

"Nor I, either," said Jephson. "But I was thinking of something very different altogether. Suppose a man died with the dearest wish of his heart unfulfilled, do you believe that his spirit might have power to return to earth and complete the interrupted work?"

"Well," answered MacShaughnassy, "if one admits the possibility of spirits retaining any interest in the affairs of this world at all, it is certainly more reasonable to imagine them engaged upon a task such as you suggest, than to believe that they occupy themselves with the performance of mere drawing-room tricks. But what are you leading up to?"

"Why, to this," replied Jephson, seating himself straddle-legged across his chair, and leaning his arms upon the back. "I was told a story this morning at the hospital by an old French doctor. The actual facts are few and simple; all that is known can be read in the Paris police records of sixty-two years ago.

"The most important part of the case, however, is the part that is not known, and that never will be known.

"The story begins with a great wrong done by one man unto another man. What the wrong was I do not know. I am inclined to think, however, it was connected with a woman. I think that, because he who had been wronged hated him who had wronged him with a hate such as does not often burn in a man's brain, unless it be fanned by the memory of a woman's breath.

"Still that is only conjecture, and the point is immaterial. The man who had done the wrong fled, and the other man followed him. It became a point-to-point race, the first man having the advantage of a day's start. The course was the whole world, and the stakes were the first man's life.

"Travellers were few and far between in those days, and this made the trail easy to follow. The first man, never knowing how far or how near the other was behind him, and hoping now and again that he might have baffled him, would rest for a while. The second man, knowing always just how far the first one was before him, never paused, and thus each day the man who was spurred by Hate drew nearer to the man who was spurred by Fear.

"At this town the answer to the never-varied question would be:-

"'At seven o'clock last evening, *M'sieur.*'

"'Seven—ah; eighteen hours. Give me something to eat, quick, while the horses are being put to.'

"At the next the calculation would be sixteen hours.

"Passing a lonely chalet, *Monsieur* puts his head out of the window:—

"'How long since a carriage passed this way, with a tall, fair man inside?'

"'Such a one passed early this morning, M'sieur.'

"'Thanks, drive on, a hundred francs apiece if you are through the pass before daybreak.'

"'And what for dead horses, *M'sieur?*'

"'Twice their value when living.'

"One day the man who was ridden by Fear looked up, and saw before him the open door of a cathedral, and, passing in, knelt down and prayed. He prayed long and fervently, for men, when they are in sore straits, clutch eagerly at the straws of faith. He prayed that he might be forgiven his sin, and, more important still, that he might be pardoned the consequences of his sin, and be delivered from his adversary; and a few chairs from him, facing him, knelt his enemy, praying also.

"But the second man's prayer, being a thanksgiving merely, was short, so that when the first man raised his eyes, he saw the face of his enemy gazing at him across the chair-tops, with a mocking smile upon it.

"He made no attempt to rise, but remained kneeling, fascinated by the look of joy that shone out of the other man's eyes. And the other man moved the high-backed chairs one by one, and came towards him softly.

"Then, just as the man who had been wronged stood beside the man who had wronged him, full of gladness that his opportunity had come, there burst from the cathedral tower a sudden clash of bells, and the man, whose opportunity had come, broke his heart and fell back dead, with that mocking smile still playing round his mouth.

"And so he lay there.

"Then the man who had done the wrong rose up and passed out, praising God.

"What became of the body of the other man is not known. It was the body of a stranger who had died suddenly in the cathedral. There was none to identify it, none to claim it.

"Years passed away, and the survivor in the tragedy became a worthy and useful citizen, and a noted man of science.

"In his laboratory were many objects necessary to him in his researches, and, prominent among them, stood in a certain corner a human skeleton. It was a very old and much-mended skeleton, and one day the long-expected end arrived, and it tumbled to pieces.

"Thus it became necessary to purchase another.

"The man of science visited a dealer he well knew—a little parchment-faced old man who kept a dingy shop, where nothing was ever sold, within the shadow of the towers of Notre Dame.

"The little parchment-faced old man had just the very thing that *Monsieur* wanted—a singularly fine and well-proportioned 'study.' It should be sent round and set up in *Monsieur's* laboratory that very afternoon.

"The dealer was as good as his word. When *Monsieur* entered his laboratory that evening, the thing was in its place.

"*Monsieur* seated himself in his high-backed chair, and tried to collect his thoughts. But *Monsieur's* thoughts were unruly, and inclined to wander, and to wander always in one direction.

"*Monsieur* opened a large volume and commenced to read. He read of a man who had wronged another and fled from him, the other man following. Finding himself reading this, he closed the book angrily, and went and stood by the window and looked out. He saw before him the sun-pierced nave of a great cathedral, and on the stones lay a dead man with a mocking smile upon his face.

"Cursing himself for a fool, he turned away with a laugh. But his laugh was short-lived, for it seemed to him that something else in the room was laughing also. Struck suddenly still, with his feet glued to the ground, he stood listening for a while: then sought with starting eyes the corner from where the sound had seemed to come. But the white thing standing there was only grinning.

"*Monsieur* wiped the damp sweat from his head and hands, and stole out.

"For a couple of days he did not enter the room again. On the third, telling himself that his fears were those of a hysterical girl, he opened the door and went in. To shame himself, he took his lamp in his hand, and crossing over to the far corner where the skeleton stood, examined it. A set of bones bought for three hundred francs. Was he a child, to be scared by such a bogey!

"He held his lamp up in front of the thing's grinning head. The flame of the lamp flickered as though a faint breath had passed over it.

"The man explained this to himself by saying that the walls of the house were old and cracked, and that the wind might creep in anywhere. He repeated this explanation to himself as he recrossed the room, walking backwards, with his eyes fixed on the thing. When he reached his desk, he sat down and gripped the arms of his chair till his fingers turned white.

"He tried to work, but the empty sockets in that grinning head seemed to be drawing him towards them. He rose and battled with his inclination to fly screaming from the room. Glancing fearfully about him, his eye fell upon a high screen, standing before the door. He dragged it forward, and placed it between himself and the thing, so that he could not see it—nor it see him. Then he sat down again to his work. For a while he forced himself to look at the book in front of him, but at last, unable to control himself any longer, he suffered his eyes to follow their own bent.

"It may have been an hallucination. He may have accidentally placed the screen so as to favour such an illusion. But what he saw was a bony hand coming round the corner of the screen, and, with a cry, he fell to the floor in a swoon.

"The people of the house came running in, and lifting him up, carried him out, and laid him upon his bed. As soon as he recovered, his first question was, where had they found the thing—where was it when they entered the room? and when they told him they had seen it standing where it always stood, and had gone down into the room to look again, because of his frenzied entreaties, and returned trying to hide their smiles, he listened to their talk about overwork, and the necessity for change and rest, and said they might do with him as they would.

"So for many months the laboratory door remained locked. Then there came a chill autumn evening when the man of science opened it again, and closed it behind him.

"He lighted his lamp, and gathered his instruments and books around him, and sat down before them in his high-backed chair. And the old terror returned to him.

"But this time he meant to conquer himself. His nerves were stronger now, and his brain clearer; he would fight his unreasoning fear. He crossed to the door and locked himself in, and flung the key to the other end of the room, where it fell among jars and bottles with an echoing clatter.

"Later on, his old housekeeper, going her final round, tapped at his door and wished him goodnight, as was her custom. She received no response, at first, and, growing nervous, tapped louder and called again; and at length an answering 'good-night' came back to her.

"She thought little about it at the time, but afterwards she remembered that the voice that had replied to her had been strangely grating and mechanical. Trying to describe it, she likened it to such a voice as she would imagine coming from a statue.

"Next morning his door remained still locked. It was no unusual thing for him to work all night and far into the next day, so no one thought to be surprised. When, however, evening came, and yet he did not appear, his servants gathered outside the room and whispered, remembering what had happened once before.

"They listened, but could hear no sound. They shook the door and called to him, then beat with their fists upon the wooden panels. But still no sound came from the room.

"Becoming alarmed, they decided to burst open the door, and, after many blows, it gave way, and they crowded in.

He sat bolt upright in his high-backed chair. They thought at first he had died in his sleep. But when they drew nearer and the light fell upon him, they saw the livid marks of bony fingers round his throat; and in his eyes there was a terror such as is not often seen in human eyes."

Brown was the first to break the silence that followed. He asked me if I had any brandy on board. He said he felt he should like just a nip of brandy before going to bed. That is one of the chief charms of Jephson's stories: they always make you feel you want a little brandy.

The Spectre of Tappington

Richard Harris Barham

"It is very odd, though; what can have become of them?" said Charles Seaforth, as he peeped under the valance of an old-fashioned bedstead, in an old-fashioned apartment of a still more old-fashioned manor-house; "'tis confoundedly odd, and I can't make it out at all. Why, Barney, where are they?—and where the devil are you?"

No answer was returned to this appeal; and the lieutenant, who was, in the main, a reasonable person—at least as reasonable a person as any young gentleman of twenty-two in "the service" can fairly be expected to be—cooled when he reflected that his servant could scarcely reply extempore to a summons which it was impossible he should hear.

An application to the bell was the considerate result; and the footsteps of as tight a lad as ever put pipe-clay to belt sounded along the gallery.

"Come in!" said his master.—An ineffectual attempt upon the door reminded Mr Seaforth that he had locked himself in.—"By Heaven! this is the oddest thing of all," said he, as he turned the key and admitted Mr Maguire into his dormitory.

"Barney, where are my pantaloons?"

"Is it the breeches?" asked the valet, casting an inquiring eye round the apartment;—"is it the breeches, sir?"

"Yes; what have you done with them?"

"Sure then your honour had them on when you went to bed, and it's hereabout they'll be, I'll be bail;" and Barney lifted a fashionable tunic from a cane-backed armchair, proceeding in his examination. But the search was vain: there was the tunic aforesaid—there was a smart-looking kerseymere waistcoat; but the most important article of all in a gentleman's wardrobe was still wanting.

"Where *can* they be?" asked the master, with a strong accent on the auxiliary verb.

"Sorrow a know I knows," said the man.

"It *must* have been the devil, then, after all, who has been here and carried them off!" cried-Seaforth, staring full into Barney's face.

Mr Maguire was not devoid of the superstition of his countrymen, still he looked as if he did not quite subscribe to the *sequitur*.

His master read incredulity in his countenance. "Why, I tell you, Barney, I put them there, on that armchair, when I got into bed; and, by Heaven! I distinctly saw the ghost of the old fellow they told me of, come in at midnight, put on my pantaloons, and walk away with them.

"Maybe so," was the cautious reply.

"I thought, of course, it was a dream; but then—where the devil are the breeches?"

The question was more easily asked than answered. Barney renewed his search, while the lieutenant folded his arms, and, leaning against the toilet, sunk into a reverie.

"After all, it must be some trick of my laughter-loving cousins," said Seaforth.

"Ah! then, the ladies!" chimed in Mr Maguire, though the observation was not addressed to him; "and will it be Miss Caroline, or Miss Fanny, that's stole your honour's things?"

"I hardly know what to think of it," pursued the bereaved lieutenant, still speaking in soliloquy, with his eye resting dubiously on the chamber-door. "I locked myself in, that's certain; and—but there must be some other entrance to the room—pooh! I remember—the private staircase; how could I be such a fool?" and he crossed the chamber to where a low oaken doorcase was dimly visible in a distant corner. He paused before it. Nothing now interfered to screen it from observation; but it bore tokens of having been at some earlier period concealed by tapestry, remains of which yet clothed the walls on either side the portal.

"This way they must have come," said Seaforth; "I wish with all my heart I had caught them!"

"Och! the kittens!" sighed Mr Barney Maguire.

But the mystery was yet as far from being solved as before. True, there *was* the "other door;" but then that, too, on examination, was even more firmly-secured than the one which opened on the gallery—two heavy bolts on the inside effectually prevented any *coup de main* on the lieutenant's bivouac from that quarter. He was more puzzled than ever; nor did the minutest inspection of the walls and floor throw any light upon the subject! one thing only was clear—the breeches were gone!

"It is *very* singular," said the lieutenant.

★★★★★★

Tappington (generally called Tapton) Everard is an antiquated but commodious manor-house in the eastern division of the county of Kent. A former proprietor had been high-sheriff in the days of Elizabeth, and many a dark and dismal tradition was yet extant of the licentiousness of his life, and the enormity of his offences. The Glen, which the keeper's daughter was seen to enter, but never known to quit, still frowns darkly as of yore; while an ineradicable bloodstain on the oaken stair yet bids defiance to the united energies of soap and sand. But it is with one particular apartment that a deed of more especial atrocity is said to be connected.

A stranger guest—so runs the legend—arrived unexpectedly at the mansion of the "Bad Sir Giles." They met in apparent friendship; but the ill-concealed scowl on their master's brow told the domestics that the visit was not a welcome one; the banquet, however, was not spared; the wine-cup circulated freely—too freely, perhaps—for sounds of discord at length reached the ears of even the excluded serving-men as they were doing their best to imitate their betters in the lower hall. Alarmed, some of them ventured to approach the parlour; one, an old and favoured retainer of the house, went so far as to break in upon his master's privacy. Sir Giles, already high in oath, fiercely enjoined his absence, and he retired; not, however, before he had distinctly heard from the stranger's lips a menace that "There was that within his pocket which could disprove the knight's right to issue that or any other command within the walls of Tapton."

The intrusion, though momentary, seemed to have produced a beneficial effect; the voices of the disputants fell, and the conversation was carried on thenceforth in a more subdued tone, till, as evening closed in, the domestics, when summoned to attend with lights, found not only cordiality restored, but that a still deeper carouse was meditated. Fresh stoups, and from the choicest bins, were produced; nor was it till at a late, or rather early hour, that the revellers sought their chambers.

The one allotted to the stranger occupied the first floor of the eastern angle of the building, and had once been the favourite apartment of Sir Giles himself. Scandal-ascribed this preference to the facility

141

which a private staircase, communicating with the grounds, had afforded him, in the old knight's time, of following his wicked courses unchecked by parental observation; a consideration which ceased to be of weight when the death of his father left him uncontrolled master of his estate and actions. From that period Sir Giles had established himself in what were called the "state apartments;" and the "oaken chamber" was rarely tenanted, save on occasions of extraordinary festivity, or when the yule log drew an unusually large accession of guests around the Christmas hearth.

On this eventful night it was prepared for the unknown visitor, who sought his couch heated and inflamed from his midnight orgies, and in the morning, was found in his bed a swollen and blackened corpse. No marks of violence appeared upon the body; but the livid hue of the lips, and certain dark-coloured spots visible on the skin, aroused suspicions which those who entertained them were too timid to express. Apoplexy, induced by the excesses of the preceding night, Sir Giles's confidential leech pronounced to be the cause of his sudden dissolution; the body was buried in peace; and though some shook their heads as they witnessed the haste with which the funeral rites were hurried on, none ventured to murmur.

Other events arose to distract the attention of the retainers; men's minds became occupied by the stirring politics of the day, while the near approach of that formidable armada, so vainly arrogating to itself a title which the very elements joined with human valour to disprove, soon interfered to weaken, if not obliterate, all remembrance of the nameless stranger who had died within the walls of Tapton Everard.

Years rolled on: the "Bad Sir Giles" had—himself long since gone to his account, the last, as it was believed, of his immediate line; though a few of the older tenants were sometimes heard to speak of an elder brother, who had disappeared in early life, and never inherited the estate. Rumours, too, of his having left a son in foreign lands were at one time rife: but they died away, nothing occurring to support them: the property passed unchallenged to a collateral branch of the family, and the secret, if secret there were, was buried in Denton churchyard, in the lonely grave of the mysterious stranger.

One circumstance alone occurred, after a long-intervening period, to revive the memory of these transactions. Some workmen employed in grubbing an old plantation, for the purpose of raising on it site a modern shrubbery, dug up, in the execution of their task, the mill-dewed remnants of what seemed to have been once a garment.

On more minute inspection, enough remained of silken slashes and a coarse embroidery to identify the relics as having once formed part of a pair of trunk hose; while a few papers which fell from them, altogether illegible from damp and age, were by the unlearned rustics conveyed to the then owner of the estate.

Whether the squire was more successful in deciphering them was never known; he certainly never alluded to their contents; and little would have been thought of the matter but for the inconvenient memory of one old woman, who declared she heard her grandfather say that when the "stranger guest" was poisoned, though all the rest of his clothes were there, his breeches, the supposed repository of the supposed documents, could never be found.

The master of Tapton Everard smiled when he heard Dame Jones's hint of deeds which might impeach the validity of his own title in favour of some unknown descendant of some unknown heir; and the story was rarely alluded to, save by one or two miracle-mongers, who had heard that others had seen the ghost of old Sir Giles, in his nightcap, issue from the postern, enter the adjoining copse, and wring his shadowy hands in agony, as he seemed to search vainly for something hidden among the evergreens. The stranger's death-room had, of course, been occasionally haunted from the time of his decease; but the periods of visitation had latterly became very rare—even Mrs Botherby, the house-keeper, being forced to admit that, during her long sojourn at the manor, she had never "met with anything worse than herself;" though, as the old lady afterwards added upon more mature reflection, "I must say I think I saw the devil *once*."

Such was the legend attached to Tapton Everard, and such the story which the lively Caroline Ingoldsby detailed to her equally mercurial cousin Charles Seaforth, lieutenant in the Hon. East India Company's second regiment of Bombay Fencibles, as arm-in-arm they promenaded a gallery decked with some dozen grim-looking ancestral portraits, and, among others, with that of the redoubted Sir Giles himself. The gallant commander had that very morning paid his first visit to the house of his maternal uncle, after an absence of several years passed with his regiment on the arid plains of Hindostan, whence he was now returned on a three years' furlough. He had gone out a boy, he—returned a man, but the impression made upon his youthful fancy by his favourite cousin remained unimpaired, and to Tapton he directed his steps, even before he sought the home of his widowed mother—comforting himself in this breach of filial decorum by the reflection that, as the manor was so little out of his way, it would be unkind to pass, as it were, the door of his relatives without just looking in for a few hours.

But he found his uncle as hospitable and his cousin more charming than ever, and the looks of one, and the requests of the other, soon precluded the possibility of refusing to lengthen the "few hours" into a few days, though the house was at the moment full of visitors.

The Peterses were there from Ramsgate; and Mr, Mrs, and the two Miss Simpkinsons, from Bath, had come to pass a month with the family; and Tom Ingoldsby had brought down his college friend the Honourable Augustus Sucklethumbkin, with his groom and pointers, to take a fortnight's shooting. And then there was Mrs Ogleton, the rich young widow, with her large black eyes, who, people did say, was setting her cap at the young squire, though Mrs Botherby did not believe it; and, above all, here was Mademoiselle Pauline, her *femme de chambre*, who "*mon Dieu'd*" everything and everybody, and cried, "*Quel horreur!*" at Mrs Botherby's cap.

In short, to use the last-named and much-respected lady's own expression, the house was "choke-full" to the very attics—all, save the "oaken chamber," which, as the lieutenant expressed a most magnanimous disregard of ghosts, was forthwith appropriated to his particular accommodation. Mr Maguire meanwhile was fain to share the apartment of Oliver Dobbs, the squire's own man: a jocular proposal of joint occupancy having been first indignantly rejected by "*Mademoiselle*," though preferred with the "laste taste in life" of Mr Barney's most insinuating brogue.

★★★★★★

"Come, Charles, the urn is absolutely getting cold; your breakfast will be quite spoiled: what can have made you so idle?" Such was the morning salutation of Miss Ingoldsby to the *militaire* as he entered the breakfast-room half an hour after the latest of the party.

"A pretty gentleman, truly, to make an appointment with," chimed in Miss Frances. "What is become of our ramble to the rocks before breakfast?"

"Oh! the young men never think of keeping a promise now," said Mrs Peters, a little ferret-faced woman with underdone eyes.

"When I was a young man," said Mr Peters, "I remember I always made a point of—"

"Pray how long ago was that?" asked Mr Simpkinson from Bath.

"Why, sir, when I married Mrs Peters, I was—let me see—I was—"

"Do pray hold your tongue, P., and eat your breakfast!" interrupted his better half, who had a mortal horror of chronological references; it's very rude to tease people with your family-affairs."

The lieutenant had by this time taken his seat in silence—a good-humoured nod, and a glance, half-smiling, half-inquisitive, being the extent of his salutation. Smitten as he was, and in the immediate presence of her who had made so large a hole in his heart, his manner was evidently *distrait*, which the fair Caroline in her secret soul attributed to his being solely occupied by her *agrémens*—how would she have bridled had she known that they only shared his meditations with a pair of breeches!

Charles drank his coffee and spiked some half-dozen eggs, darting occasionally a penetrating glance at the ladies, in hope of detecting the supposed waggery by the evidence of some furtive smile or conscious look. But in vain; not dimple moved indicative of roguery, nor did the slightest elevation of eyebrow rise confirmative of his suspicions. Hints and insinuations passed unheeded—more particular inquiries were out of the question:—the subject was unapproachable.

In the meantime, "patent cords" were just the thing for a morning's ride; and, breakfast ended, away cantered the party over the downs, till, every faculty absorbed by the beauties, animate and inanimate, which surrounded him, Lieutenant Seaforth of the Bombay Fencibles bestowed no more thought upon his breeches than if he had been born the top of Ben Lomond.

******

Another night had passed away; the sun rose brilliantly, forming with his level beams a splendid rainbow in the far off west, whither the heavy cloud, which for the last two hours had been pouring its waters on the earth, was now flying before him.

"Ah! then, and it's little good it'll be the claning of ye," apostrophised Mr Barney Maguire, as he deposited, in front of his master's toilet, a pair of "bran-new" jockey boots, one of Hoby's primeest fits, which the lieutenant had purchased in his way through town. On that very morning had they come for the first time under the valet's depurating hand, so little soiled, indeed, from the turfy ride of the preceding day, that a less scrupulous domestic might, perhaps, have considered the application of "Warren's Matchless," or oxalic acid, altogether superfluous. Not so Barney: with the nicest care had he removed the slightest impurity from each polished surface and there they stood, rejoicing in their sable radiance. No wonder a pang shot across Mr Maguire s breast, as he thought on the work now cut out for them, so different from the light labours of the day before, no wonder he murmured with a sigh, as the scarce-dried window-panes disclosed a road now inch-deep in mud, "Ah! then, it's little good the claning of ye!"—for well had he learned in the hall below that eight miles of a stiff clay soil lay between the Manor and Bolsover Abbey, whose picturesque ruins,

"Like ancient Rome, majestic in decay,"

the party had determined to explore. The master-had already commenced dressing, and the man was fitting straps upon a light pair of crane-necked spurs, when his hand was arrested by the old question, "Barney, where are the breeches?"

They were nowhere to be found!

★★★★★★

Mr Seaforth descended that morning, whip in hand, and equipped in a handsome green riding-frock, but no "breeches and boots to match" were there: loose jean trowsers, surmounting a pair of diminutive Wellingtons, embraced, somewhat incongruously, his nether man, *vice* the "patent cords," returned, like yesterday's pantaloons, absent without leave. The "top-boots" had a holiday.

"A fine morning after the rain," said Mr Simpkinson from Bath.

"Just the thing for the 'ops," said Mr Peters. "I remember when I was a boy—"

"Do hold your tongue, P.," said Mrs Peters, advice which that exemplary matron was in the constant habit of administering to "her P.," as she called him, whenever he prepared to vent his reminiscences. Her precise reason for this it would be difficult to determine, unless, indeed, the story be true which a little bird had whispered into Mrs Botherby's ear—Mr Peters, though now a wealthy man, had received a liberal education at a charity-school and was apt to recur to the days of his muffin cap and leathers. As usual, he took his wife's hint in good part, and "paused in his reply."

"A glorious day for the ruins!" said young Ingoldsby. "But, Charles, what the deuce are you about?—you don't mean to ride through our lanes in such toggery as that?"

"Lassy me!" said Miss Julia Simpkinson, "won't you be very wet?"

"You had better take Tom's cab," quoth the squire.

But this proposition was at once overruled; Mrs Ogleton had already nailed the cab, a vehicle of all others the best adapted for a snug flirtation.

"Or drive Miss Julia in the phaeton?" No; that was the post of Mr Peters, who, indifferent as an equestrian, had acquired some fame as a whip while travelling through the midland counties for the firm of Bagshaw, Snivelby, and Ghrimes.

"Thank you, I shall ride with my cousins," said Charles, with as much nonchalance as he could assume—and he did so; Mr Ingoldsby, Mrs Peters, Mr Simpkinson from Bath, and his eldest daughter with her album, following in the family coach. The gentleman-commoner "voted the affair d——d slow," and declined the party altogether in favour of the gamekeeper and a cigar. "There was 'no fun' in looking at old houses!" Mrs Simpkinson preferred a short *sejour* in the still-room with Mrs Botherby, who had promised to initiate her in that grand *arcanum*, the transmutation of gooseberry jam into Guava jelly.

★★★★★★

"Did you ever see an old abbey before, Mr Peters?"

"Yes, miss, a French one; we have got one at Ramsgate; he teaches the Miss Joneses to *parley-voo*, and is turned of sixty."

Miss Simpkinson closed her album with an air of ineffable disdain.

Mr Simpkinson from Bath was a professed antiquary and one of the first water; he was master of Gwillim's *Heraldry*, and Milles's *History of the Crusades*; knew every plate the *Monasticon*; had written an essay on the origin and dignity of the office of overseer, and settled the date of a Queen Anne's farthing. An influential member of the Antiquarian Society, to whose *Beauties of Bagnigge Wells* he had been a liberal subscriber, procured him a seat at the board of that learned body, since which happy epoch Sylvanus Urban had not a more indefatigable correspondent. His inaugural essay on the President's cocked hat was considered a miracle of erudition: and his account of the earliest application of gilding to gingerbread, a masterpiece of antiquarian research.

His eldest daughter was of a kindred spirit: if her father's mantle had not fallen upon her, it was only because he had not thrown it off himself; she had caught hold of its tail, however, while it yet hung upon his honoured shoulders. To souls so congenial, what a sight was the magnificent ruin of Bolsover! its broken arches, its mouldering pinnacles, and the airy tracery of its half-demolished windows. The party were in raptures; Mr Simpkinson began to meditate an essay, and his daughter an ode: even Seaforth, as he gazed on these lonely relics of the olden time, was betrayed into a momentary forgetfulness of his love and losses; the widow's eye-glass turned from her cicisbeo's

147

whiskers to the mantling ivy: Mrs Peters wiped her spectacles; and "her P." supposed the central tower "had once been the county jail." The squire was a philosopher, and had been there often before, so he ordered out the cold tongue and chickens.

"Bolsover Priory," said Mr Simpkinson, with the air of a connoisseur—"Bolsover Priory was founded in the reign of Henry the Sixth, about the beginning of the eleventh century. Hugh de Bolsover had accompanied that monarch to the Holy Land, in the expedition undertaken by way of penance for the murder of his young nephews in the Tower. Upon the dissolution of the monasteries, the veteran was enfeoffed in the lands and manor, to which he gave his own name of Bowlsover, or Bee-owls-over (by corruption Bolsover)—a Bee in chief, over three Owls, all proper, being the armorial ensigns borne by this distinguished crusader at the siege of Acre."

"Ah! that was Sir Sidney Smith," said Mr Peters; "I've heard tell of him, and all about Mrs Partington, and—"

"P., be quiet, and don't expose yourself!" sharply interrupted his lady. P. was silenced, and betook himself to the bottled stout.

"These lands," continued the antiquary, "were held in grand sergeanty by the presentation of three white owls and a pot of honey—"

"Lassy me! how nice!" said Miss Julia. Mr Peters licked his lips.

"Pray give me leave, my dear—owls and honey, whenever the king should come a rat-catching into this part of the country."

"Rat-catching!" ejaculated the squire, pausing abruptly in the mastication of a drumstick.

"To be sure, my dear sir: don't you remember that rats once came under the forest law—a minor species of venison? 'Rats and mice, and such small deer,' eh?—Shakespeare, you know. Our ancestors ate rats ("The nasty fellows!" shuddered Miss Julia in a parenthesis); and owls, you now, are capital mousers—"

"I've seen a howl," said Mr Peters; "there's one in the Sohological Gardens—a little hook-nosed chap in a wig—only its feathers and—"

Poor P. was destined never to finish a speech.

"Do be quiet!" cried the authoritative voice, and the would-be naturalist shrank into his shell, like a snail in the "Sohological Gardens."

"You should read Blount's *Jocular Tenures*, Mr Ingoldsby," pursued Simpkinson. "A learned man was Blount! Why, sir, his Royal Highness the Duke of York once paid a silver horse-shoe to Lord Ferrers—"

"I've heard of him," broke in the incorrigible Peters; "he was hanged at the old Bailey in a silk rope for shooting Dr Johnson."

The antiquary vouchsafed no notice of the interruption; but, taking a pinch of snuff, continued his harangue.

"A silver horse-shoe, sir, which is due from every scion of royalty who rides across one of his manors; and if you look into the penny county histories, now publishing by an eminent friend of mine, you will find that Langhale in Co. Norf. was held by one Baldwin *per saltum sufflatum, et pettum*; that is, he was to come every Christmas into Westminster Hall, there to take a leap, cry hem! and—"

"Mr Simpkinson, a glass of sherry?" cried Tom Ingoldsby, hastily.

"Not any, thank you, sir. This Baldwin, surnamed *Le*—"

"Mrs Ogleton challenges you, sir; she insists upon it," said Tom, still more rapidly; at the same time filling a glass, and forcing it on the sçavant, who, thus arrested in the very crisis of his narrative, received and swallowed the potation as if it had been physic.

"What on earth has Miss Simpkinson discovered there?" continued Tom; "something of interest. See how fast she is writing."

The diversion was effectual: everyone looked towards Miss Simpkinson, who, far too ethereal for "creature comforts," was seated apart on the dilapidated remains of an altar-tomb, committing eagerly to paper something that had strongly impressed her: the air—the eye in a "fine frenzy rolling,"—all betokened that the divine *afflatus* was come. Her father rose, and stole silently towards her.

"What an old boar!" muttered young Ingoldsby; alluding, perhaps, to a slice of brawn which he had just begun to operate upon, but which, from the celerity with which it disappeared, did not seem so very difficult of mastication.

But what had become of Seaforth and his fair Caroline all this while? Why, it so happened that they had been simultaneously stricken with the picturesque appearance of one of those high and pointed arches, which that eminent antiquary, Mr Horseley Curties, has described in his *Ancient Records* as "a Gothic window of the *Saxon* order;"—and then the ivy clustered so thickly and so beautifully on the other side, that they went round to look at that;—and then their proximity deprived it of half its effect, and so they walked across to a little knoll, a hundred yards off, and in crossing a small ravine, they came to what in Ireland they call a "bad step," and Charles had to carry his cousin over it—and then, when they had to come back, she would not give him the trouble again for the world, so they followed a better but more circuitous route and there were hedges and ditches in the way, and stiles to get over, and gates to get through; so that an hour or more had elapsed before they were able to rejoin the party.

"Lassy me!" said Miss Julia Simpkinson, "how long you have been gone!"

And so, they had. The remark was a very just as well as a very natural one. They were gone a long while, and a nice cosy chat they had; and what do you think it was all about, my dear miss?

"O, lassy me! love, no doubt, and the moon, and eyes, and nightingales, and—"

Stay, stay, my sweet young lady; do not let the fervour of your feelings run away with you! I do not pretend to say, indeed, that one or more of these pretty subjects might not have been introduced; but the most important and leading topic of the conference was—Lieutenant Seaforth's breeches.

"Caroline," said Charles, "I have had some very odd dreams since I have been at Tappington."

"Dreams, have you?" smiled the young lady, arching her taper neck like a swan in pluming. "Dreams, have you?"

"Ay, dreams—or dream, perhaps, I should say; for, though repeated, it was still the same. And what do you imagine was its subject?"

"It is impossible for me to divine," said the tongue;—"I have not the least difficulty in guessing," said the eye, as plainly as ever eye spoke.

"I dreamt—of your great grandfather!"

There was a change in the glance—"My great grandfather?"

"Yes, the old Sir Giles, or Sir John, you told me about the other day: he walked into my bedroom in his short, cloak of murrey-coloured velvet, his long rapier, and his Raleigh-looking hat and feather, just as the picture represents him: but with one exception."

"And what was that?"

"Why, his lower extremities, which were visible, were—those of a skeleton."

"Well."

"Well, after taking a turn or two about the room, and looking round him with a wistful air, he came to the bed's foot, stared at me in a manner impossible to describe—and then he—he laid hold of my pantaloons; whipped his long bony legs into them in a twinkling; and strutting up to the glass, seemed to view himself in it with great complacency. I tried to speak, but in vain. The effort, however, seemed to excite his attention; for, wheeling about, he showed me the grimmest-looking death's head you can well imagine, and with an indescribable grin strutted out of the room."

"Absurd! Charles. How can you talk such nonsense?"

"But, Caroline—the breeches are really gone."

★★★★★★

On the following morning, contrary to his usual custom, Seaforth was the first person in the breakfast parlour. As no one else was present, he did precisely what nine young men out of ten so situated would have done; he walked up to the mantelpiece, established himself upon the rug, and subducting his coat-tails one under each arm, turned towards the fire that portion of the human frame which it is considered equally indecorous to present to a friend or enemy. A serious, not to say anxious, expression was visible upon his good-humoured countenance, and his mouth was fast buttoning itself up for an incipient whistle when little Flo, a tiny spaniel of the Blenheim breed—the pet object of Miss Julia Simpkinson's affections, bounced from beneath a sofa, and began to bark at—his pantaloons.

They were cleverly "built," of a light grey mixture, a broad stripe of the most vivid scarlet traversing each seam in a perpendicular direction from hip to ankle—in short, the regimental costume of the Royal Bombay Fencibles. The animal, educated in the country, had never seen such a pair of breeches in her life—*Omne ignotum pro magnifico!* The scarlet streak, inflamed as it was by the reflection of the fire, seemed to act on Flora's nerves as the same colour does on those of bulls and turkeys; she advanced at the *pas de charge*, and her vociferation, like her amazement, was unbounded. A sound kick from the disgusted officer changed its character, and induced a retreat at the very moment when the mistress of the pugnacious quadruped entered to the rescue.

"Lassy me! Flo! what is the matter?" cried the sympathising lady, with a scrutinising glance levelled at the gentleman.

It might as well have lighted on a feather bed.—His air of imperturbable unconsciousness defied examination; and as he would not, and Flora could not expound, that injured individual was compelled to pocket up her wrongs. Others of the household soon dropped in, and clustered round the board dedicated to the most sociable of meals; the urn was paraded "hissing hot," and the cups which "cheer, but not inebriate," steamed redolent of hyson and pekoe; muffins and marmalade, newspapers and Finnon haddies, left little room for observation on the character of Charles's warlike "turn-out." At length a

151

look from Caroline, followed by a smile that nearly ripened to a titter, caused him to turn abruptly and address his neighbour. It was Miss Simpkinson, who, deeply engaged in sipping her tea and turning over her album, seemed, like a female Chrononotonthologos, "immersed in cogibundity of cogitation." An interrogatory on the subject of her studies drew from her the confession that she was at that moment employed in putting the finishing touches to a poem inspired by the romantic shades of Bolsover. The entreaties of the company were of course urgent. Mr Peters, "who liked verses," was especially persevering, and Sappho at length compliant. After a preparatory hem! and a glance at the mirror to ascertain that her look was sufficiently sentimental, the poetess began:—

There is a calm, a holy feeling,
Vulgar minds can never know,
O'er the bosom softly stealing—
Chasten'd grief, delicious woe!
Oh! how sweet at eve regaining
Yon lone tower's sequester'd shade—
Sadly mute and uncomplaining—

Yow!—yeough!—yeough!—yow!—yow! yelled a hapless sufferer from beneath the table.—It was an unlucky hour for quadrupeds; and if "every dog will have his day," he could not have selected a more unpropitious one than this. Mrs Ogleton, too, had a pet—a favourite pug—whose squab figure, black muzzle, and tortuosity of tail, that curled like a head of celery in a salad-bowl, bespoke his Dutch extraction. *Yow! yow! yow!* continued the brute—a chorus in which Flo instantly joined. Sooth to say, pug had more reason to express his dissatisfaction than was given him by the muse of Simpkinson; the other only barked for company. Scarcely had the poetess got through her first stanza, when Tom Ingoldsby, in the enthusiasm of the moment, became so lost in the material world, that, in his abstraction, he unwarily laid his hand on the cock of the urn. Quivering with emotion, he gave it such an unlucky twist, that the full stream of its scalding contents descended on the gingerbread hide of the unlucky Cupid.— The confusion was complete—the whole economy of the table disarranged;—the company broke up most admired disorder—and "Vulgar minds will never know" anything more of Miss Simpkinson's ode till they peruse it in some forthcoming Annual.

Seaforth profited by the confusion to take the delinquent who had caused this "stramash" by the arm, and to lead him to the lawn, where he had a word or two for his private ear. The conference between the young gentlemen was neither brief in its duration nor unimportant in its result. The subject was what the lawyers call tripartite, embracing the information that Charles Seaforth was over head and ears in love with Tom Ingoldsby's sister; secondly, that the lady had referred him to "papa" for his sanction; thirdly and lastly, his nightly visitations, and consequent bereavement. At the two first items Tom smiled auspiciously; at the last he burst out into an absolute "guffaw."

"Steal your breeches!—Miss Bailey over again, by Jove," shouted Ingoldsby. "But a gentleman, you say—and Sir Giles too.—I am not sure, Charles, whether I ought not to call you out for aspersing the honour of the family."

"Laugh as you will, Tom—be as incredulous as you please. One fact is incontestable—the breeches are gone! Look here—I am reduced to my regimentals, and if these go, tomorrow I must borrow of you!"

Rochefoucault says, there is something in the misfortunes of our very best friends that does not displease us;—assuredly we can, most of us, laugh at their petty inconveniences, till called upon to supply them. Tom composed his features on the instant, and replied with more gravity, as well as with an expletive, which, if my Lord Mayor had been within hearing, might have cost him five shillings.

"There is something very queer in this, after all. The clothes, you say, have positively disappeared. Somebody is playing you a trick, and, ten to one, your servant has a hand in it. By the way, I heard something yesterday of his kicking up a bobbery in the kitchen, and seeing a ghost, or something of that kind, himself. Depend upon it, Barney is in the plot."

It now struck the lieutenant at once, that the usually buoyant spirits of his attendant had of late been materially sobered down, his loquacity obviously circumscribed, and that he, the said lieutenant, had actually rung his bell several times that very morning before he could procure his attendance. Mr Maguire was forthwith summoned, and underwent a close examination. The "bobbery" was easily explained. Mr Oliver Dobbs hinted his disapprobation of a flirtation carrying on between the gentleman from Minster and the lady from the Rue St Honoré. *Mademoiselle* had boxed Mr Maguire's ears, and Mr Maguire had pulled *Mademoiselle* upon his knee, and the lady had *not* cried *Mon Dieu!* And Mr Oliver Dobbs said it was very wrong; and Mrs Botherby said it was "scandalous," and what ought not to be done in any moral kitchen; and Mr Maguire had got hold of the Honourable Augustus Sucklethumbkin's powder-flask, and had put large pinches of the best double Dartford into Mr Dobbs's tobacco-box;—and Mr Dobbs's pipe had exploded, and set fire to Mrs Botherby's Sunday cap—and Mr Maguire had put it out with the slop-basin, "barring the wig";—and then they were all so "cantankerous," that Barney had gone to take a walk in the garden; and then—then Mr Barney had seen a ghost!

"A what? you blockhead!" asked Tom Ingoldsby.

"Sure then, and it's meself will tell your honour the rights of it," said the ghost-seer. "Meself and Miss Pauline, sir, or Miss Pauline and meself, for the ladies comes first anyhow, we got tired of the hobstroppylous skrimmaging among the ould servants, that didn't know a joke when they seen one: and we went out to look at the comet—that's the rorybory-alehouse, they calls him in this country—and we walked upon the lawn—and divil of any alehouse there was there at all; and Miss Pauline said it was because of the shrubbery maybe, and why wouldn't we see it better beyonst the trees?—and so we went to the trees, but sorrow a comet did meself see there, barring a big ghost instead of it."

"A ghost? And what sort of a ghost, Barney?"

"Och, then, devil a lie I'll tell your honour. A tall ould gentleman he was, all in white, with a shovel on the shoulder of him, and a big torch in his fist—though what he wanted with that it's meself can't tell, for his eyes were like gig-lamps, let alone the moon and the comet, which wasn't there at all—and 'Barney,' says he to me—'cause why he knew me—'Barney,' says he, 'what is it you're doing with the colleen there, Barney?'—Divil a word did I say. Miss Pauline screeched, and cried murther in French, and ran off with herself; and of course, meself was in a mighty hurry after the lady, and had no time to stop palavering with him anyway; so, I dispersed at once, and the ghost vanished in a flame of fire!"

Mr Maguire's account was received with avowed incredulity by both gentlemen; but Barney stuck to his text with unflinching pertinacity. A reference to *Mademoiselle* was suggested, but abandoned, as neither party had a taste for delicate investigations.

"I'll tell you what, Seaforth," said Ingoldsby, after Barney had received his dismissal, "that there is a trick here, is evident; and Barney's vision may possibly be a part of it. Whether he is most knave or fool, you best know. At all events, I will sit up with you to-night and see if I can convert my ancestor into a visiting acquaintance. Meanwhile your finger on your lip!"

> 'Twas now the very witching time of night,
> When churchyards yawn, and graves give up their dead.

Gladly would I grace my tale with decent horror, and therefore I do beseech the "gentle reader" to believe, that if all the succedanea to this mysterious narrative are not in strict keeping, he will ascribe it only to the disgraceful innovations of modern degeneracy upon the sober and dignified habits of our ancestors. I can introduce him, it is true, into an old and high-roofed chamber, its walls covered on three sides with black oak wainscotting, adorned with carvings of fruit and flowers long anterior to those of Grinling Gibbons; the fourth side is clothed with a curious remnant of dingy tapestry, once elucidatory of some Scriptural history, but of *which* not even Mrs Botherby could determine. Mr Simpkinson, who had examined it carefully, inclined to believe the principal figure to be either Bathsheba, or Daniel in the lions' den; while Tom Ingoldsby decided in favour of the King of Bashan. All, however, was conjecture, tradition being silent on the subject.

A lofty arched portal led into, and a little arched portal led out of, this apartment; they were opposite each other, and each possessed the security of massy bolts on its interior. The bedstead, too, was not one of yesterday, but manifestly coeval with days ere Seddons was, and, when a good four-post "article" was deemed worthy of being a royal bequest. The bed itself, with all the appurtenances of *palliasse*, mattresses, etc., was of far later date, and looked most incongruously comfortable; the casements, too, with their little diamond-shaped panes and iron binding, had given way to the modern heterodoxy of the sash-window. Nor was this all that conspired to ruin the costume, and render the room a meet haunt for such "mixed spirits" only as could condescend to don at the same time an Elizabethan doublet and Bond Street inexpressibles.

With their green morocco slippers on a modern fender in front of a disgracefully modern grate, sat two young gentlemen, clad in "shawl pattern" dressing gowns and black silk stocks, much at variance with the high cane-backed chairs which supported them. A bunch of abomination, called a cigar, reeked in the left-hand corner of the mouth of one, and in the right-hand corner of the mouth of the other;—an arrangement happily adapted for the escape of the noxious fumes up the chimney, without that unmerciful "funking" each other, which a less scientific disposition of the weed would have induced. A small Pembroke table filled up the intervening space between them, sustaining at each extremity, an elbow and a glass of toddy;—thus in "lonely pensive contemplation" were the two worthies occupied, when the "iron tongue of midnight had tolled twelve."

"Ghost-time's come!" said Ingoldsby, taking from his waistcoat pocket a watch like a gold half-crown, and consulting it as though he suspected the turret-clock over the stables of mendacity.

"Hush!" said Charles; "did I not hear a footstep?"

There was a pause:—there was a footstep—it sounded distinctly—it reached the door—it hesitated, stopped, and

Tom darted across the room, threw open the door, and became aware of Mrs Botherby toddling to her chamber, at the other end of the gallery, after dosing one of the housemaids with an approved, julep from the Countess of Kent's *Choice Manual*.

"Goodnight, sir!" said Mrs Botherby.

"Go to the devil!" said the disappointed ghost-hunter.

An hour—two—rolled on, and still no spectral visitation; nor did aught intervene to make night hideous; and when the turret-clock sounded at length the hour of three, Ingoldsby, whose patience and grog were alike exhausted, sprang from his chair, saying—

"This is all infernal nonsense, my good fellow. Deuce of any ghost shall we see to-night; it's long past the canonical hour. I'm off to bed; and as to your breeches, I'll insure them for the next twenty-four hours at least, at the price of the buckram."

"Certainly.—Oh! thankee—to be sure!" stammered Charles, rousing himself from a reverie, which had degenerated into an absolute snooze.

"Goodnight, my boy! Bolt the door behind me; and defy the Pope, the Devil and the Pretender!—"

Seaforth followed his friend's advice, and the next morning came down to breakfast dressed in the habiliments of the preceding day. The charm was broken, the demon defeated; the light greys with the red stripe down the seams were yet *in rerum natura*, and adorned the person of their lawful proprietor.

Tom felicitated himself and his partner of the watch on the result of their vigilance; but there is a rustic adage, which warns us against self-gratulation before we are quite "out of the wood."—Seaforth was yet within its verge.

A rap at Tom Ingoldsby's door the following morning startled him as he was shaving—he cut his chin.

"Come in, and be d—d to you!" said the martyr, pressing his thumb on the scarified epidermis.—The door opened, and exhibited Mr Barney Maguire.

"Well, Barney, what is it?" quoth the sufferer, adopting the vernacular of his visitant.

"The master, sir—"

"Well, what does he want?"

"The loanst of a breeches, plase your honour."

"Why, you don't mean to tell me—By Heaven, this is too good!" shouted Tom, bursting into a fit of uncontrollable laughter. "Why, Barney, you don't mean to say the ghost has got them again!"

Mr Maguire did not respond to the young squire's risibility; the cast of his countenance was decidedly serious.

"Faith, then, it's gone they are, sure enough! Hasn't meself been looking over the bed, and under the bed, and *in* the bed, for the matter of that, and divil a ha'p'orth of breeches is there to the fore at all:—I'm bothered entirely!"

"Hark'ee! Mr Barney," said Tom, incautiously removing his thumb, and letting a crimson stream "incarnadine the multitudinous" lather that plastered his throat—"this may be all very well with your master, but you don't humbug me, sir—tell me instantly what have you done with the clothes?"

This abrupt transition from "lively to severe" certainly took Maguire by surprise, and he seemed for an instant as much disconcerted as it is possible to disconcert an Irish gentleman's gentleman.

"Me? is it meself, then, that's the ghost to your honour's thinking?" said he, after a moment's pause, and with a slight shade of indignation in his tones: "is it I would stale the master's things?—and what would I do with them?"

"That you best know—what your purpose is I can't guess, for I don't think you mean to 'stale' them, as you call it; but that you are concerned in their disappearance, I am satisfied. Confound this blood!—give me a towel, Barney."

Maguire acquitted himself of the commission. "As I've a sowl, your honour," said he solemnly, "little it is meself knows of the matter: and after what I seen—"

"What you've seen! Why, what have you seen?—Barney, I don't want to enquire into your flirtations; but don't suppose you can palm

157

off your saucer eyes and gig-lamps upon me!"

"Then, as sure as your honour's standing there I saw him: and why wouldn't I, when Miss *Pauline* was to the fore as well as meself, and—"

"Get along with your nonsense, leave the room, sir!"

"But the master?" said Barney imploringly; "and without a breeches?—sure he'll be catching cowld!—"

"Take that, rascal!" replied Ingoldsby, throwing a pair of pantaloons at, rather than to, him: "but don't suppose, sir, you shall carry on your tricks here with impunity; recollect there is such a thing as a treadmill, and that my father is a county magistrate."

Barney's eye flashed fire—he stood erect, and was about to speak; but, mastering himself, not without an effort, he took up the garment, and left the room as perpendicular as a Quaker.

"Ingoldsby;" said Charles Seaforth, after breakfast, "this is now past a joke; today is the last of my stay; for, notwithstanding the ties which detain me, common decency obliges me to visit home after so long an absence. I shall come to an immediate explanation with your father on the subject nearest my heart, and depart while I have a change of dress left. On his answer will my return depend! In the meantime tell me candidly—I ask it in all seriousness and as a friend—am I not a dupe to your well-known propensity to hoaxing? have you not a hand in—"

"No, by heaven I Seaforth; I see what you mean: on my honour, I am as much mystified as yourself: and if your servant—"

"Not he:—if there be a trick, he at least is not privy to it."

"If there be a trick? Why, Charles, do you think—"

"I know not *what* to think, Tom. As surely as you are a living man, so surely did that spectral anatomy visit my room again last night, grin in my face, and walk away with my trousers, nor was I able to spring from my bed, or break the chain which seemed to bind me to my pillow."

"Seaforth!" said Ingoldsby, after a short pause, "I will—But hush! here are the girls and my father.—I will carry off the females, and leave you a clear field with the governor: carry your point with him, and we will talk about your breeches afterwards."

Tom's diversion was successful; he carried off the ladies *en masse* to look at a remarkable specimen of the class *Dodecandria Monogynia*—which they could not find:—while Seaforth marched boldly up to the encounter, and carried "the governor's" outworks by a *coup de main*. I shall not stop to describe the progress of the attack: suffice it that it

was as successful as could have been wished, and that Seaforth was referred back again to the lady. The happy lover was off at a tangent; the
botanical party was soon overtaken; and the arm of Caroline, whom a
vain endeavour to spell out the Linnaen name of a daffy-down-dilly
had detained a little in the rear of the others, was soon firmly locked
in his own.

What was the world to them,
Its noise, its nonsense, and its 'breeches' all?

Seaforth was in the seventh heaven; he retired to his room that
night as happy as if no such thing as a goblin had ever been heard
of, and personal chattels were as well fenced in by law as real property. Not so Tom Ingoldsby: the mystery—for mystery there evidently
was—had not only piqued his curiosity, but ruffled his temper. The
watch of the previous night had been unsuccessful, probably because
it was undisguised. Tonight he would "ensconce himself,"—not indeed "behind the arras,"—for the little that remained was, as we have
seen, nailed to the wall—but in a small closet which opened from one
corner of the room, and, by leaving the door ajar, would give to its
occupant a view of all that might pass in the apartment.

Here did the young ghost-hunter take up a position with a good
stout sapling under his arm, a full half-hour before Seaforth retired
for the night. Not even his friend did he let into his confidence, fully
determined that if his plan did not succeed, the failure should be attributed to himself alone.

At the usual hour of separation for the night, Tom saw, from his
concealment, the lieutenant enter his room, and after taking a few
turns in it, with an expression so joyous as to betoken that his thoughts
were mainly occupied by his approaching happiness, proceed slowly
to disrobe himself. The coat, the waistcoat, the black silk stock, were
gradually discarded; the green morocco slippers were kicked off, and
then—ay, and then—his countenance grew grave; it seemed to occur
to him all at once that this was his last stake—nay, that very breeches
he had on were not his own—that tomorrow morning was his last,
and that if he lost *them*—A glance showed that his mind was made up:
he replaced the single button he had just subducted, and threw himself
upon the bed in a state of transition—half chrysalis, half grub.

Wearily did Tom Ingoldsby watch the sleeper by the flickering
light of the night-lamp, till the clock, striking one, induced him to
increase the narrow opening which he had left for the purpose of

observation. The motion, slight as it was, seemed to attract Charles's attention; for he raised. himself suddenly to a sitting posture, listened for a moment, and then stood upright upon the floor. Ingoldsby was on the point of discovering himself, when, the light, flashing full upon his friend's countenance, he perceived that, though his eyes were open, "their sense was shut,"—that he was yet under the influence of sleep.

Seaforth advanced slowly to the toilet, lit his candle at the lamp that stood on it, then, going back to the bed's foot, appeared to search eagerly for something which he could not find.—For a few moments he seemed restless and uneasy, walking round the apartment and examining the chairs, till, coming fully in front of a large swing-glass that flanked the dressing-table, he paused, as if contemplating his figure in it. He now returned towards the bed; put on his slippers; and, with cautious and stealthy steps, proceeded towards the little arched doorway that opened on the private staircase.

As he drew the bolt, Tom Ingoldsby emerged from his hiding-place; but the sleep-walker heard him not; he proceeded softly down stairs, followed at a due distance by his friend; opened the door which led out upon the gardens; and stood at once among the thickest of the scrubs, which here clustered round the base of a corner turret, and screened the postern from common observation. At this moment Ingoldsby had nearly spoiled all by making a false step: the sound attracted Seaforth's attention—he paused and turned: and as the full moon shed her light directly upon his pale and troubled features, Tom marked, almost with dismay, the fixed and rayless appearance of his eyes:

There was no speculation in those orbs
That he did glare withal.

The perfect stillness preserved by his follower seemed to reassure him; he turned aside; and from the midst of a thicket laurustinus, drew forth a gardener's spade, shouldering which he proceeded with great rapidity into the midst of the shrubbery. Arrived at a certain point where the earth seemed to have been recently disturbed, he set himself heartily to the task of digging, till, having thrown up several shovelfuls of mould, he stopped, flung down his tool, and very composedly began to disencumber himself of his pantaloons.

Up to this moment Tom had watched him with a wary eye: he now advanced cautiously, and, as his friend was busily engaged in disentangling himself from his garment, made himself master of the spade. Seaforth, meanwhile, had accomplished his purpose: he stood for a moment with "His streamers waving in the wind," occupied in carefully rolling up the small-clothes into as compact a form as possible, and all heedless of the breath of heaven, which might certainly be supposed, at such a moment, and in such a plight, to "visit his frame too roughly."

He was in the act of stooping low to deposit the pantaloons in the grave which he had been digging for them, when Tom Ingoldsby came close behind him, and with the flat side of the spade—

******

The shock was effectual—never again was Lieutenant Seaforth known to act the part of a somnambulist. One by one, his breeches—his trousers—his pantaloons—his silk-net tights—his patent cords—his showy greys with the broad red stripe of the Bombay Fencibles were brought to light—rescued from the grave in which they had been buried, like the *strata* of a Christmas pie; and, after having been well aired by Mrs Botherby, became once again effective.

The family, the ladies especially, laughed—the Peterses laughed—the Simpkinsons laughed—Barney Maguire cried "Botheration!" and Ma'mselle Pauline "*Mon Dieu!*"

Charles Seaforth, unable to face the quizzing which awaited him on all sides, started off two hours earlier than he had proposed—he soon returned, however; and having, at his father-in-law's request, given up the occupation of *Rajah*-hunting and shooting *Nabobs*, led his blushing bride to the altar.

Mr Simpkinson from Bath did not attend the ceremony, being engaged at the Grand Junction meeting of *Sçavans*, then congregating from all parts of the known world in the city of Dublin. His essay, demonstrating that the globe is a great custard, whipped into coagulation by whirlwinds, and cooked by electricity—a little too much baked in the Isle of Portland, and a thought underdone about the Bog of Allen—was highly spoken of, and narrowly escaped obtaining a Bridgewater prize.

Miss Simpkinson and her sister acted as bridesmaids on the occasion; the former wrote an *epithalamium*, and the latter cried "Lassy me!" at the clergyman's wig.—Some years have since rolled on; the union has been crowned with two or three tidy little offshoots from the family tree of whom Master Neddy is "grandpapa's darling," and Mary-Anne mamma's particular "Sock." I shall only add that Mr and Mrs Seaforth are living together quite as happily as two good-hearted, good-tempered bodies, very fond, of each other, can possibly do: and, that since the day of his marriage Charles has shown no disposition to jump out of bed, or ramble out of doors o' nights—though, from his entire devotion to every wish and whim of his young wife, Tom insinuates that the fair Caroline does still occasionally take advantage of it so far as to "slip on the breeches."

The Open Door
Mrs Oliphant

I took the house of Brentwood on my return from India in 18—, for the temporary accommodation of my family, until I could find a permanent home for them. It had many advantages which made it peculiarly appropriate. It was within reach of Edinburgh; and my boy Roland, whose education had been considerably neglected, could go in and out to school; which was thought to be better for him than either leaving home altogether or staying there always with a tutor. The first of these expedients would have seemed preferable to me; the second commended itself to his mother. The doctor, like a judicious man, took the midway between. "Put him on his pony, and let him ride into the High School every morning; it will do him all the good in the world," Dr. Simson said; "and when it is bad weather, there is the train."

His mother accepted this solution of the difficulty more easily than I could have hoped; and our pale-faced boy, who had never known anything more invigorating than Simla, began to encounter the brisk breezes of the North in the subdued severity of the month of May. Before the time of the vacation in July we had the satisfaction of see-ing him begin to acquire something of the brown and ruddy com-plexion of his schoolfellows. The English system did not commend itself to Scotland in these days. There was no little Eton at Fettes; nor do I think, if there had been, that a genteel exotic of that class would have tempted either my wife or me. The lad was doubly precious to us, being the only one left us of many; and he was fragile in body, we believed, and deeply sensitive in mind. To keep him at home, and yet to send him to school,—to combine the advantages of the two sys-tems,—seemed to be everything that could be desired.

The two girls also found at Brentwood everything they wanted. They were near enough to Edinburgh to have masters and lessons as many as they required for completing that never-ending education which the young people seem to require nowadays. Their mother married me when she was younger than Agatha; and I should like to see them improve upon their mother! I myself was then no more than twenty-five,—an age at which I see the young fellows now groping about them, with no notion what they are going to do with their lives. However; I suppose every generation has a conceit of itself which elevates it, in its own opinion, above that which comes after it.

Brentwood stands on that fine and wealthy slope of country—one of the richest in Scotland—which lies between the Pentland Hills and the Firth. In clear weather you could see the blue gleam—like a bent bow, embracing the wealthy fields and scattered houses—of the great estuary on one side of you, and on the other the blue heights, not gigantic like those we had been used to, but just high enough for all the glories of the atmosphere, the play of clouds, and sweet reflections, which give to a hilly country an interest and a charm which nothing else can emulate. Edinburgh—with its two lesser heights, the Castle and the Calton Hill, its spires and towers piercing through the smoke, and Arthur's Seat lying crouched behind, like a guardian no longer very needful, taking his repose beside the well-beloved charge, which is now, so to speak, able to take care of itself without him—lay at our right hand. From the lawn and drawing-room windows we could see all these varieties of landscape. The colour was sometimes a little chilly, but sometimes, also, as animated and full of vicissitude as a drama. I was never tired of it. Its colour and freshness revived the eyes which had grown weary of arid plains and blazing skies. It was always cheery, and fresh, and full of repose.

The village of Brentwood lay almost under the house, on the other side of the deep little ravine, down which a stream—which ought to have been a lovely, wild, and frolicsome little river—flowed between its rocks and trees. The river, like so many in that district, had, however, in its earlier life been sacrificed to trade, and was grimy with paper-making. But this did not affect our pleasure in it so much as I have known it to affect other streams. Perhaps our water was more rapid; perhaps less clogged with dirt and refuse. Our side of the dell was charmingly *accidenté*, and clothed with fine trees, through which various paths wound down to the river-side and to the village bridge which crossed the stream. The village lay in the hollow, and climbed, with very prosaic houses, the other side.

Village architecture does not flourish in Scotland. The blue slates and the gray stone are sworn foes to the picturesque; and though I do not, for my own part, dislike the interior of an old-fashioned hewed and galleried church, with its little family settlements on all sides, the square box outside, with its bit of a spire like a handle to lift it by, is not an improvement to the landscape. Still a cluster of houses on differing elevations, with scraps of garden coming in between, a hedgerow with clothes laid out to dry, the opening of a street with its rural sociability, the women at their doors, the slow wagon lumbering along, gives a centre to the landscape. It was cheerful to look at, and convenient in a hundred ways. Within ourselves we had walks in plenty, the glen being always beautiful in all its phases, whether the woods were green in the spring or ruddy in the autumn.

In the park which surrounded the house were the ruins of the former mansion of Brentwood,—a much smaller and less important house than the solid Georgian edifice which we inhabited. The ruins were picturesque, however, and gave importance to the place. Even we, who were but temporary tenants, felt a vague pride in them, as if they somehow reflected a certain consequence upon ourselves. The old building had the remains of a tower,—an indistinguishable mass of mason-work, over-grown with ivy; and the shells of walls attached to this were half filled up with soil. I had never examined it closely, I am ashamed to say. There was a large room, or what had been a large room, with the lower part of the windows still existing, on the principal floor, and underneath other windows, which were perfect, though half filled up with fallen soil, and waving with a wild growth of brambles and chance growths of all kinds. This was the oldest part of all. At a little distance were some very commonplace and disjointed fragments of building, one of them suggesting a certain *pathos* by its very commonness and the complete wreck which it showed. This was the end of a low gable, a bit of gray wall, all incrusted with lichens, in which was a common doorway. Probably it had been a servants' entrance, a backdoor, or opening into what are called "the offices" in Scotland.

No offices remained to be entered,—pantry and kitchen had all been swept out of being; but there stood the doorway open and vacant, free to all the winds, to the rabbits, and every wild creature. It struck my eye, the first time I went to Brentwood, like a melancholy comment upon a life that was over. A door that led to nothing,—closed once, perhaps, with anxious care, bolted and guarded, now void of any meaning. It impressed me, I remember, from the first; so perhaps it may be said that my mind was prepared to attach to it an importance which nothing justified.

The summer was a very happy period of repose for us all. The warmth of Indian suns was still in our veins. It seemed to us that we could never have enough of the greenness, the dewiness, the freshness of the northern landscape. Even its mists were pleasant to us, taking all the fever out of us, and pouring in vigour and refreshment. In autumn we followed the fashion of the time, and went away for change which we did not in the least require. It was when the family had settled down for the winter, when the days were short and dark, and the rigorous reign of frost upon us, that the incidents occurred which alone could justify me in intruding upon the world my private affairs. These incidents were, however, of so curious a character, that I hope my inevitable references to my own family and pressing personal interests will meet with a general pardon.

I was absent in London when these events began. In London an old Indian plunges back into the interests with which all his previous life has been associated, and meets old friends at every step. I had been circulating among some half-dozen of these,—enjoying the return to my former life in shadow, though I had been so thankful in substance to throw it aside,—and had missed some of my home letters, what with going down from Friday to Monday to old Benbow's place in the country, and stopping on the way back to dine and sleep at Sellar's and to take a look into Cross's stables, which occupied another day.

It is never safe to miss one's letters. In this transitory life, as the Prayer-book says, how can one ever be certain what is going to happen? All was well at home. I knew exactly (I thought) what they would have to say to me: "The weather has been so fine, that Roland has not once gone by train, and he enjoys the ride beyond anything." "Dear papa, be sure that you don't forget anything, but bring us so-and-so, and so-and-so,"—a list as long as my arm. Dear girls and dearer mother! I would not for the world have forgotten their commissions, or lost their little letters, for all the Benbows and Crosses in the world.

But I was confident in my home-comfort and peacefulness. When I got back to my club, however, three or four letters were lying for one, upon some of which I noticed the "immediate," "urgent," which old-fashioned people and anxious people still believe will influence the post-office and quicken the speed of the mails. I was about to open one of these, when the club porter brought me two telegrams, one of which, he said, had arrived the night before. I opened, as was to be expected, the last first, and this was what I read:

Why don't you come or answer? For God's sake, come. He is much worse.

This was a thunderbolt to fall upon a man's head who had one only son, and he the light of his eyes! The other telegram, which I opened with hands trembling so much that I lost time by my haste, was to much the same purport:

No better; doctor afraid of brain-fever. Calls for you day and night. Let nothing detain you.

The first thing I did was to look up the timetables to see if there was any way of getting off sooner than by the night-train, though I knew well enough there was not; and then I read the letters, which furnished, alas! too clearly, all the details. They told me that the boy had been pale for some time, with a scared look. His mother had noticed it before I left home, but would not say anything to alarm me. This look had increased day by day: and soon it was observed that Roland came home at a wild gallop through the park, his pony panting and in foam, himself "as white as a sheet," but with the perspiration streaming from his forehead.

For a long time he had resisted all questioning, but at length had developed such strange changes of mood, showing a reluctance to go to school, a desire to be fetched in the carriage at night,—which was a ridiculous piece of luxury,—an unwillingness to go out into the grounds, and nervous start at every sound, that his mother had insisted upon an explanation. When the boy—our boy Roland, who had never known what fear was—began to talk to her of voices he had heard in the park, and shadows that had appeared to him among the ruins, my wife promptly put him to bed and sent for Dr. Simson, which, of course, was the only thing to do.

I hurried off that evening, as may be supposed, with an anxious heart. How I got through the hours before the starting of the train, I cannot tell. We must all be thankful for the quickness of the railway when in anxiety; but to have thrown myself into a postchaise as soon as horses could be put to, would have been a relief. I got to Edinburgh very early in the blackness of the winter morning, and scarcely dared look the man in the face, at whom I gasped, "What news?" My wife had sent the brougham for me, which I concluded, before the man spoke, was a bad sign. His answer was that stereotyped answer which leaves the imagination so wildly free,—"Just the same."

Just the same! What might that mean? The horses seemed to me to creep along the long dark country road. As we dashed through the park, I thought I heard someone moaning among the trees, and clenched my fist at him (whoever he might be) with fury. Why had the fool of a woman at the gate allowed any one to come in to disturb the quiet of the place? If I had not been in such hot haste to get home, I think I should have stopped the carriage and got out to see what tramp it was that had made an entrance, and chosen my grounds, of all places in the world,—when my boy was ill!—to grumble and groan in. But I had no reason to complain of our slow pace here. The horses flew like lightning along the intervening path, and drew up at the door all panting, as if they had run a race.

My wife stood waiting to receive me, with a pale face, and a candle in her hand, which made her look paler still as the wind blew the flame about. "He is sleeping," she said in a whisper, as if her voice might wake him. And I replied, when I could find my voice, also in a whisper, as though the jingling of the horses' furniture and the sound of their hoofs must not have been more dangerous. I stood on the steps with her a moment, almost afraid to go in, now that I was here; and it seemed to me that I saw without observing, if I may say so, that the horses were unwilling to turn round, though their stables lay that way, or that the men were unwilling. These things occurred to me afterwards, though at the moment I was not capable of anything but to ask questions and to hear of the condition of the boy.

I looked at him from the door of his room, for we were afraid to go near, lest we should disturb that blessed sleep. It looked like actual sleep, not the lethargy into which my wife told me he would sometimes fall. She told me everything in the next room, which communicated with his, rising now and then and going to the door of communication; and in this there was much that was very startling and confusing to the mind. It appeared that ever since the winter began—since it was early dark, and night had fallen before his return from school—he had been hearing voices among the ruins: at first only a groaning, he said, at which his pony was as much alarmed as he was, but by degrees a voice. The tears ran down my wife's cheeks as she described to me how he would start up in the night and cry out, "Oh, mother, let me in! oh, mother, let me in!" with a *pathos* which rent her heart. And she sitting there all the time, only longing to do everything his heart could desire!

But though she would try to soothe him, crying, "You are at home, my darling. I am here. Don't you know me? Your mother is here!" he would only stare at her, and after a while spring up again with the same cry. At other times he would be quite reasonable, she said, asking eagerly when I was coming, but declaring that he must go with me as soon as I did so, "to let them in."

"The doctor thinks his nervous system must have received a shock," my wife said. "Oh, Henry, can it be that we have pushed him on too much with his work—a delicate boy like Roland? And what is his work in comparison with his health? Even you would think little of honours or prizes if it hurt the boy's health."

Even I!—as if I were an inhuman father sacrificing my child to my ambition. But I would not increase her trouble by taking any notice. After awhile they persuaded me to lie down, to rest, and to eat, none of which things had been possible since I received their letters. The mere fact of being on the spot, of course, in itself was a great thing; and when I knew that I could be called in a moment, as soon as he was awake and wanted me, I felt capable, even in the dark, chill morning twilight, to snatch an hour or two's sleep. As it happened, I was so worn out with the strain of anxiety, and he so quieted and consoled by knowing I had come, that I was not disturbed till the afternoon, when the twilight had again settled down.

There was just daylight enough to see his face when I went to him; and what a change in a fortnight! He was paler and more worn, I thought, than even in those dreadful days in the plains before we left India. His hair seemed to me to have grown long and lank; his eyes were like blazing lights projecting out of his white face. He got hold of my hand in a cold and tremulous clutch, and waved to everybody to go away. "Go away—even mother," he said; "go away." This went to her heart; for she did not like that even I should have more of the boy's confidence than herself; but my wife has never been a woman to think of herself, and she left us alone.

"Are they all gone?" he said eagerly. "They would not let me speak. The doctor treated me as if I were a fool. You know I am not a fool, papa."

"Yes, yes, my boy, I know. But you are ill, and quiet is so necessary. You are not only not a fool, Roland, but you are reasonable and understand. When you are ill you must deny yourself; you must not do everything that you might do being well."

He waved his thin hand with a sort of indignation. "Then, father, I

169

am not ill," he cried. "Oh, I thought when you came you would not stop me,—you would see the sense of it! What do you think is the matter with me, all of you? Simson is well enough; but he is only a doctor. What do you think is the matter with me? I am no more ill than you are. A doctor, of course, he thinks you are ill the moment he looks at you—that's what he's there for—and claps you into bed."

"Which is the best place for you at present, my dear boy."

"I made up my mind," cried the little fellow, "that I would stand it till you came home. I said to myself, I won't frighten mother and the girls. But now, father," he cried, half jumping out of bed, "it's not illness: it's a secret."

His eyes shone so wildly, his face was so swept with strong feeling, that my heart sank within me. It could be nothing but fever that did it, and fever had been so fatal. I got him into my arms to put him back into bed. "Roland," I said, humouring the poor child, which I knew was the only way, "if you are going to tell me this secret to do any good, you know you must be quite quiet, and not excite yourself. If you excite yourself, I must not let you speak."

"Yes, father," said the boy. He was quiet directly, like a man, as if he quite understood. When I had laid him back on his pillow, he looked up at me with that grateful, sweet look with which children, when they are ill, break one's heart, the water coming into his eyes in his weakness. "I was sure as soon as you were here you would know what to do," he said.

"To be sure, my boy. Now keep quiet, and tell it all out like a man." To think I was telling lies to my own child! for I did it only to humour him, thinking, poor little fellow, his brain was wrong.

"Yes, father. Father, there is someone in the park—someone that has been badly used."

"Hush, my dear; you remember there is to be no excitement. Well, who is this somebody, and who has been ill-using him? We will soon put a stop to that."

"All," cried Roland, "but it is not so easy as you think. I don't know who it is. It is just a cry. Oh, if you could hear it! It gets into my head in my sleep. I heard it as clear—as clear; and they think that I am dreaming, or raving perhaps," the boy said, with a sort of disdainful smile.

This look of his perplexed me; it was less like fever than I thought. "Are you quite sure you have not dreamed it, Roland?" I said.

"Dreamed?—that!" He was springing up again when he suddenly

bethought himself, and lay down flat, with the same sort of smile on his face. "The pony heard it, too," he said. "She jumped as if she had been shot. If I had not grasped at the reins—for I was frightened, father—"

"No shame to you, my boy," said I, though I scarcely knew why.

"If I hadn't held to her like a leech, she'd have pitched me over her head, and never drew breath till we were at the door. Did the pony dream it?" he said, with a soft disdain, yet indulgence for my foolishness. Then he added slowly, "It was only a cry the first time, and all the time before you went away. I wouldn't tell you, for it was so wretched to be frightened. I thought it might be a hare or a rabbit snared, and I went in the morning and looked; but there was nothing. It was after you went I heard it really first; and this is what he says." He raised himself on his elbow close to me, and looked me in the face: "'Oh, mother, let me in! oh, mother, let me in!'" As he said the words a mist came over his face, the mouth quivered, the soft features all melted and changed, and when he had ended these pitiful words, dissolved in a shower of heavy tears.

Was it a hallucination? Was it the fever of the brain? Was it the disordered fancy caused by great bodily weakness? How could I tell? I thought it wisest to accept it as if it were all true.

"This is very touching, Roland," I said.

"Oh, if you had just heard it, father! I said to myself, if father heard it he would do something; but mamma, you know, she's given over to Simson, and that fellow's a doctor, and never thinks of anything but clapping you into bed."

"We must not blame Simson for being a doctor, Roland."

"No, no," said my boy, with delightful toleration and indulgence; "oh, no; that's the good of him; that's what he's for; I know that. But you—you are different; you are just father; and you'll do something—directly, papa, directly; this very night."

"Surely," I said. "No doubt it is some little lost child."

He gave me a sudden, swift look, investigating my face as though to see whether, after all, this was everything my eminence as "father" came to,—no more than that. Then he got hold of my shoulder, clutching it with his thin hand. "Look here," he said, with a quiver in his voice; "suppose it wasn't—living at all!"

"My dear boy, how then could you have heard it?" I said.

He turned away from me with a pettish exclamation,—"As if you didn't know better than that!"

171

"Do you want to tell me it is a ghost?" I said.

Roland withdrew his hand; his countenance assumed an aspect of great dignity and gravity; a slight quiver remained about his lips. "Whatever it was—you always said we were not to call names. It was something—in trouble. Oh, father, in terrible trouble!"

"But, my boy," I said (I was at my wits' end), "if it was a child that was lost, or any poor human creature—but, Roland, what do you want me to do?"

"I should know if I was you," said the child eagerly. "That is what I always said to myself,—Father will know. Oh, papa, papa, to have to face it night after night, in such terrible, terrible trouble, and never to be able to do it any good! I don't want to cry; it's like a baby, I know; but what can I do else? Out there all by itself in the ruin, and nobody to help it! I can't bear it! I can't bear it!" cried my generous boy. And in his weakness he burst out, after many attempts to restrain it, into a great childish fit of sobbing and tears.

I do not know that I ever was in a greater perplexity, in my life; and afterwards, when I thought of it, there was something comic in it too. It is bad enough to find your child's mind possessed with the conviction that he has seen, or heard, a ghost; but that he should require you to go instantly and help that ghost was the most bewildering experience that had ever come my way. I am a sober man myself, and not superstitious—at least any more than everybody is superstitious. Of course I do not believe in ghosts; but I don't deny, any more than other people, that there are stories which I cannot pretend to understand.

My blood got a sort of chill in my veins at the idea that Roland should be a ghost-seer; for that generally means a hysterical temperament and weak health, and all that men most hate and fear for their children. But that I should take up his ghost and right its wrongs, and save it from its trouble, was such a mission as was enough to confuse any man. I did my best to console my boy without giving any promise of this astonishing kind; but he was too sharp for me: he would have none of my caresses. With sobs breaking in at intervals upon his voice, and the raindrops hanging on his eyelids, he yet returned to the charge.

"It will be there now!—it will be there all the night! Oh, think, papa,—think if it was me! I can't rest for thinking of it. Don't!" he cried, putting away my hand,—"don't! You go and help it, and mother can take care of me."

"But, Roland, what can I do?"

172

My boy opened his eyes, which were large with weakness and fever, and gave me a smile such, I think, as sick children only know the secret of. "I was sure you would know as soon as you came. I always said, Father will know. And mother," he cried, with a softening of repose upon his face, his limbs relaxing, his form sinking with a luxurious ease in his bed,—"mother can come and take care of me."

I called her, and saw him turn to her with the complete dependence of a child; and then I went away and left them, as perplexed a man as any in Scotland. I must say, however, I had this consolation, that my mind was greatly eased about Roland. He might be under a hallucination; but his head was clear enough, and I did not think him so ill as everybody else did. The girls were astonished even at the ease with which I took it. "How do you think he is?" they said in a breath, coming round me, laying hold of me.

"Not half so ill as I expected," I said; "not very bad at all."

"Oh, papa, you are a darling!" cried Agatha, kissing me, and crying upon my shoulder; while little Jeanie, who was as pale as Roland, clasped both her arms round mine, and could not speak at all. I knew nothing about it, not half so much as Simson; but they believed in me: they had a feeling that all would go right now. God is very good to you when your children look to you like that. It makes one humble, not proud. I was not worthy of it; and then I recollected that I had to act the part of a father to Roland's ghost,—which made me almost laugh, though I might just as well have cried. It was the strangest mission that ever was intrusted to mortal man.

It was then I remembered suddenly the looks of the men when they turned to take the brougham to the stables in the dark that morning. They had not liked it, and the horses had not liked it. I remembered that even in my anxiety about Roland I had heard them tearing along the avenue back to the stables, and had made a memorandum mentally that I must speak of it. It seemed to me that the best thing I could do was to go to the stables now and make a few inquiries. It is impossible to fathom the minds of rustics; there might be some devilry of practical joking, for anything I knew; or they might have some interest in getting up a bad reputation for the Brentwood avenue. It was getting dark by the time I went out, and nobody who knows the country will need to be told how black is the darkness of a November night under high laurel-bushes and yew-trees.

I walked into the heart of the shrubberies two or three times, not seeing a step before me, till I came out upon the broader carriage-road, where the trees opened a little, and there was a faint gray glimmer of sky visible, under which the great limes and elms stood darkling like ghosts; but it grew black again as I approached the corner where the ruins lay. Both eyes and ears were on the alert, as may be supposed; but I could see nothing in the absolute gloom, and, so far as I can recollect, I heard nothing. Nevertheless there came a strong impression upon me that somebody was there. It is a sensation which most people have felt. I have seen when it has been strong enough to awake me out of sleep, the sense of someone looking at me. I suppose my imagination had been affected by Roland's story; and the mystery of the darkness is always full of suggestions.

I stamped my feet violently on the gravel to rouse myself, and called out sharply, "Who's there?" Nobody answered, nor did I expect anyone to answer, but the impression had been made. I was so foolish that I did not like to look back, but went sideways, keeping an eye on the gloom behind. It was with great relief that I spied the light in the stables, making a sort of oasis in the darkness. I walked very quickly into the midst of that lighted and cheerful place, and thought the clank of the groom's pail one of the pleasantest sounds I had ever heard. The coachman was the head of this little colony, and it was to his house I went to pursue my investigations. He was a native of the district, and had taken care of the place in the absence of the family for years; it was impossible but that he must know everything that was going on, and all the traditions of the place. The men, I could see, eyed me anxiously when I thus appeared at such an hour among them, and followed me with their eyes to Jarvis's house, where he lived alone with his old wife, their children being all married and out in the world. Mrs. Jarvis met me with anxious questions. How was the poor young gentleman? But the others knew, I could see by their faces, that not even this was the foremost thing in my mind.

★★★★★★

"Noises?—ou ay, there'll be noises,—the wind in the trees, and the water soughing down the glen. As for tramps, Cornel, no, there's little o' that kind o' cattle about here; and Merran at the gate's a careful body." Jarvis moved about with some embarrassment from one leg to another as he spoke. He kept in the shade, and did not look at me more than he could help. Evidently his mind was perturbed, and he had reasons for keeping his own counsel. His wife sat by, giving him a quick look now and then, but saying nothing. The kitchen was very snug and warm and bright,—as different as could be from the chill and mystery of the night outside.

"I think you are trifling with me, Jarvis," I said.

"Triflin', cornel? No me. What would I trifle for? If the deevil himsel was in the auld hoose, I have no interest in 't one way or another—"

"Sandy, hold your peace!" cried his wife imperatively.

"And what am I to hold my peace for, wi' the Cornel standing there asking a' thae questions? I'm saying, if the deevil himsel—"

"And I'm telling ye hold your peace!" cried the woman, in great excitement. "Dark November weather and lang nichts, and us that ken a' we ken. How daur ye name—a name that shouldna be spoken?" She threw down her stocking and got up, also in great agitation. "I tellt ye you never could keep it. It's no a thing that will hide, and the haill toun kens as weel as you or me. Tell the cornel straight out—or see, I'll do it. I dinna hold wi' your secrets, and a secret that the haill toun kens!" She snapped her fingers with an air of large disdain. As for Jarvis, ruddy and big as he was, he shrank to nothing before this decided woman.

He repeated to her two or three times her own adjuration, "Hold your peace!" then, suddenly changing his tone, cried out, "Tell him then, confound ye! I'll wash my hands o't. If a' the ghosts in Scotland were in the auld hoose, is that ony concern o' mine?"

After this I elicited without much difficulty the whole story. In the opinion of the Jarvises, and of everybody about, the certainty that the place was haunted was beyond all doubt. As Sandy and his wife warmed to the tale, one tripping up another in their eagerness to tell everything, it gradually developed as distinct a superstition as I ever heard, and not without poetry and pathos. How long it was since the voice had been heard first, nobody could tell with certainty. Jarvis's opinion was that his father, who had been coachman at Brentwood before him, had never heard anything about it, and that the whole thing had arisen within the last ten years, since the complete dismantling of the old house; which was a wonderfully modern date for a tale so well authenticated.

According to these witnesses, and to several whom I questioned afterwards, and who were all in perfect agreement, it was only in the months of November and December that "the visitation" occurred. During these months, the darkest of the year, scarcely a night passed without the recurrence of these inexplicable cries. Nothing, it was said, had ever been seen,—at least, nothing that could be identified. Some people, bolder or more imaginative than the others, had seen the darkness moving, Mrs. Jarvis said, with unconscious poetry. It began when night fell, and continued, at intervals, till day broke. Very often it was only all inarticulate cry and moaning, but sometimes the words which had taken possession of my poor boy's fancy had been distinctly audible,—"Oh, mother, let me in!"

The Jarvises were not aware that there had ever been any investigation into it. The estate of Brentwood had lapsed into the hands of a distant branch of the family, who had lived but little there; and of the many people who had taken it, as I had done, few had remained through two Decembers. And nobody had taken the trouble to make a very close examination into the facts.

"No, no," Jarvis said, shaking his head, "No, no, Cornel. Wha wad set themsels up for a laughin'-stock to a' the countryside, making a wark about a ghost? Naebody believes in ghosts. It bid to be the wind in the trees, the last gentleman said, or some effec' o' the water wrastlin' among the rocks. He said it was a' quite easy explained; but he gave up the hoose. And when you cam, cornel, we were awfu' anxious you should never hear. What for should I have spoiled the bargain and hairmed the property for no-thing?"

"Do you call my child's life nothing?" I said in the trouble of the moment, unable to restrain myself. "And instead of telling this all to me, you have told it to him,—to a delicate boy, a child unable to sift evidence or judge for himself, a tender-hearted young creature—"

I was walking about the room with an anger all the hotter that I felt it to be most likely quite unjust. My heart was full of bitterness against the stolid retainers of a family who were content to risk other people's children and comfort rather than let a house be empty. If I had been warned I might have taken precautions, or left the place, or sent Roland away, a hundred things which now I could not do; and here I was with my boy in a brain-fever, and his life, the most precious life on earth, hanging in the balance, dependent on whether or not I could get to the reason of a commonplace ghost-story! I paced about in high wrath, not seeing what I was to do; for to take Roland away, even if he were able to travel, would not settle his agitated mind; and I feared even that a scientific explanation of refracted sound or reverberation, or any other of the easy certainties with which we elder men are silenced, would have very little effect upon the boy.

"Cornel," said Jarvis solemnly, "and *she'll* bear me witness,—the young gentleman never heard a word from me—no, nor from either groom or gardener; I'll gie ye my word for that. In the first place, he's no a lad that invites ye to talk. There are some that are, and some that arena. Some will draw ye on, till ye've tellt them a' the clatter of the toun, and a' ye ken, and whiles mair. But Maister Roland, his mind's fu' of his books. He's aye civil and kind, and a fine lad; but no that sort. And ye see it's for a' our interest, cornel, that you should stay at Brentwood. I took it upon me mysel to pass the word,—'No a syllable to Maister Roland, nor to the young leddies—no a syllable.' The women-servants, that have little reason to be out at night, ken little or nothing about it. And some think it grand to have a ghost so long as they're no in the way of coming across it. If you had been tellt the story to begin with, maybe ye would have thought so yourself."

This was true enough, though it did not throw any light upon my perplexity. If we had heard of it to start with, it is possible that all the family would have considered the possession of a ghost a distinct advantage. It is the fashion of the times. We never think what a risk it is to play with young imaginations, but cry out, in the fashionable jargon, "A ghost!—nothing else was wanted to make it perfect." I should not have been above this myself. I should have smiled, of course, at the idea of the ghost at all, but then to feel that it was mine would have pleased my vanity. Oh, yes, I claim no exemption. The girls would have been delighted. I could fancy their eagerness, their interest, and excitement. No; if we had been told, it would have done no good,— we should have made the bargain all the more eagerly, the fools that we are. "And there has been no attempt to investigate it," I said, "to see what it really is?"

"Eh, cornel," said the coachman's wife, "wha would investigate, as ye call it, a thing that nobody believes in? Ye would be the laughin'- stock of a' the countryside, as my man says."

"But you believe in it," I said, turning upon her hastily. The woman was taken by surprise. She made a step backward out of my way.

"Lord, cornel, how ye frichten a body! Me!—there's awfu' strange things in this world. An unlearned person doesna ken what to think. But the minister and the gentry they just laugh in your face. Inquire into the thing that is not! Na, na, we just let it be."

"Come with me, Jarvis," I said hastily, "and we'll make an attempt at least. Say nothing to the men or to anybody. I'll come back after dinner, and we'll make a serious attempt to see what it is, if it is anything. If I hear it,—which I doubt,—you may be sure I shall never rest till I make it out. Be ready for me about ten o'clock."

"Me, cornel!" Jarvis said, in a faint voice. I had not been looking at him in my own preoccupation, but when I did so, I found that the greatest change had come over the fat and ruddy coachman. "Me, cornel!" he repeated, wiping the perspiration from his brow. His ruddy face hung in flabby folds, his knees knocked together, his voice seemed half extinguished in his throat. Then he began to rub his hands and smile upon me in a deprecating, imbecile way. "There's nothing I wouldna do to pleasure ye, cornel," taking a step further back. "I'm sure *she* kens I've aye said I never had to do with a mair fair, weel-spoken gentleman—" Here Jarvis came to a pause, again looking at me, rubbing his hands.

"Well?" I said.

"But eh, sir!" he went on, with the same imbecile yet insinuating smile, "if ye'll reflect that I am no used to my feet. With a horse atween my legs, or the reins in my hand, I'm maybe nae worse than other men; but on fit, cornel—It's no the—bogles—but I've been cavalry, ye see," with a little hoarse laugh, "a' my life. To face a thing ye dinna understan'—on your feet, cornel."

"Well, sir, if *I* do it," said I tartly, "why shouldn't you?"

"Eh, cornel, there's an awfu' difference. In the first place, ye tramp about the haill countryside, and think naething of it; but a walk tires me mair than a hunard miles' drive; and then ye're a gentleman, and do your ain pleasure; and you're no so auld as me; and it's for your ain bairn, ye see, cornel; and then—"

"He believes in it, cornel, and you dinna believe in it," the woman said.

"Will you come with me?" I said, turning to her.

She jumped back, upsetting her chair in her bewilderment. "Me!" with a scream, and then fell into a sort of hysterical laugh. "I wouldna say but what I would go; but what would the folk say to hear of Cornel Mortimer with an auld silly woman at his heels?"

The suggestion made me laugh too, though I had little inclination for it. "I'm sorry you have so little spirit, Jarvis," I said. "I must find someone else, I suppose."

Jarvis, touched by this, began to remonstrate, but I cut him short. My butler was a soldier who had been with me in India, and was not supposed to fear anything,—man or devil,—certainly not the former; and I felt that I was losing time. The Jarvises were too thankful to get rid of me. They attended me to the door with the most anxious courtesies. Outside, the two grooms stood close by, a little confused by my sudden exit. I don't know if perhaps they had been listening,—as least standing as near as possible, to catch any scrap of the conversation. I waved my hand to them as I went past, in answer to their salutations, and it was very apparent to me that they also were glad to see me go.

And it will be thought very strange, but it would be weak not to add, that I myself, though bent on the investigation I have spoken of, pledged to Roland to carry it out, and feeling that my boy's health, perhaps his life, depended on the result of my inquiry,—I felt the most unaccountable reluctance to pass these ruins on my way home. My curiosity was intense; and yet it was all my mind could do to pull my body along. I daresay the scientific people would describe it the other way, and attribute my cowardice to the state of my stomach. I went on; but if I had followed my impulse, I should have turned and bolted. Everything in me seemed to cry out against it: my heart thumped, my pulses all began, like sledge-hammers, beating against my ears and every sensitive part.

It was very dark, as I have said; the old house, with its shapeless tower, loomed a heavy mass through the darkness, which was only not entirely so solid as itself. On the other hand, the great dark cedars of which we were so proud seemed to fill up the night. My foot strayed out of the path in my confusion and the gloom together, and I brought myself up with a cry as I felt myself knock against something solid. What was it? The contact with hard stone and lime and prickly bramble-bushes restored me a little to myself. "Oh, it's only the old gable," I said aloud, with a little laugh to reassure myself. The rough feeling of the stones reconciled me. As I groped about thus, I shook off my visionary folly. What so easily explained as that I should have strayed from the path in the darkness?

This brought me back to common existence, as if I had been shaken by a wise hand out of all the silliness of superstition. How silly it was, after all! What did it matter which path I took? I laughed again, this time with better heart, when suddenly, in a moment, the blood was chilled in my veins, a shiver stole along my spine, my faculties seemed to forsake me. Close by me, at my side, at my feet, there was a sigh. No, not a groan, not a moaning, not anything so tangible,— a perfectly soft, faint, inarticulate sigh. I sprang back, and my heart stopped beating. Mistaken! no, mistake was impossible. I heard it as clearly as I hear myself speak; a long, soft, weary sigh, as if drawn to the utmost, and emptying out a load of sadness that filled the breast.

To hear this in the solitude, in the dark, in the night (though it was still early), had an effect which I cannot describe. I feel it now,—something cold creeping over me, up into my hair, and down to my feet, which refused to move. I cried out, with a trembling voice, "Who is there?" as I had done before; but there was no reply.

I got home I don't quite know how; but in my mind there was no longer any indifference as to the thing, whatever it was, that haunted these ruins. My scepticism disappeared like a mist. I was as firmly determined that there was something as Roland was. I did not for a moment pretend to myself that it was possible I could be deceived; there were movements and noises which I understood all about,— cracklings of small branches in the frost, and little rolls of gravel on the path, such as have a very eerie sound sometimes, and perplex you with wonder as to who has done it, *when there is no real mystery*; but I assure you all these little movements of nature don't affect you one bit *when there is something*. I understood *them*. I did not understand the sigh. That was not simple nature; there was meaning in it, feeling, the soul of a creature invisible. This is the thing that human nature trembles at,—a creature invisible, yet with sensations, feelings, a power somehow of expressing itself. I had not the same sense of unwillingness to turn my back upon the scene of the mystery which I had experienced in going to the stables; but I almost ran home, impelled by eagerness to get everything done that had to be done, in order to apply myself to finding it out.

Bagley was in the hall as usual when I went in. He was always there in the afternoon, always with the appearance of perfect occupation, yet, so far as I know, never doing anything. The door was open, so that I hurried in without any pause, breathless; but the sight of his calm regard, as he came to help me off with my overcoat, subdued me in a moment. Anything out of the way, anything incomprehensible, faded to nothing in the presence of Bagley. You saw and wondered how *he* was made: the parting of his hair, the tie of his white neckcloth, the fit of his trousers, all perfect as works of art; but you could see how they were done, which makes all the difference. I flung myself upon him, so to speak, without waiting to note the extreme unlikeness of the man to anything of the kind I meant. "Bagley," I said, "I want you to come out with me tonight to watch for—"

"Poachers, colonel?" he said, a gleam of pleasure running all over him.

"No, Bagley; a great deal worse," I cried.

"Yes, colonel; at what hour, sir?" the man said; but then I had not told him what it was.

It was ten o'clock when we set out. All was perfectly quiet indoors. My wife was with Roland, who had been quite calm, she said, and who (though, no doubt, the fever must run its course) had been better ever since I came. I told Bagley to put on a thick greatcoat over his evening coat, and did the same myself, with strong boots; for the soil was like a sponge, or worse. Talking to him, I almost forgot what we were going to do. It was darker even than it had been before, and Bagley kept very close to me as we went along. I had a small lantern in my hand, which gave us a partial guidance. We had come to the corner where the path turns. On one side was the bowling-green, which the girls had taken possession of for their croquet-ground,—a wonderful enclosure surrounded by high hedges of holly, three hundred years old and more; on the other, the ruins. Both were black as night; but before we got so far, there was a little opening in which we could just discern the trees and the lighter line of the road. I thought it best to pause there and take breath.

"Bagley," I said, "there is something about these ruins I don't understand. It is there I am going. Keep your eyes open and your wits about you. Be ready to pounce upon any stranger you see,—anything, man or woman. Don't hurt, but seize anything you see."

"Colonel," said Bagley, with a little tremor in his breath, "they do say there's things there—as is neither man nor woman."

There was no time for words.

"Are you game to follow me, my man? that's the question," I said. Bagley fell in without a word, and saluted. I knew then I had nothing to fear.

We went, so far as I could guess, exactly as I had come; when I heard that sigh. The darkness, however, was so complete that all marks, as of trees or paths, disappeared. One moment we felt our feet on the gravel, another sinking noiselessly into the slippery grass, that was all. I had shut up my lantern, not wishing to scare anyone, whoever it might be. Bagley followed, it seemed to me, exactly in my footsteps as I made my way, as I supposed, towards the mass of the ruined house. We seemed to take a long time groping along seeking this; the squash of the wet soil under our feet was the only thing that marked our progress.

After a while I stood still to see, or rather feel, where we were. The darkness was very still, but no stiller than is usual in a winter's night. The sounds I have mentioned—the crackling of twigs, the roll of a pebble, the sound of some rustle in the dead leaves, or creeping creature on the grass—were audible when you listened, all mysterious enough when your mind is disengaged, but to me cheering now as signs of the livingness of nature, even in the death of the frost. As we stood still there came up from the trees in the glen the prolonged hoot of an owl. Bagley started with alarm, being in a state of general nervousness, and not knowing what he was afraid of. But to me the sound was encouraging and pleasant, being so comprehensible.

"An owl," I said, under my breath.

"Y—es, colonel," said Bagley, his teeth chattering. We stood still about five minutes, while it broke into the still brooding of the air, the sound widening out in circles, dying upon the darkness. This sound, which is not a cheerful one, made me almost gay. It was natural, and relieved the tension of the mind. I moved on with new courage, my nervous excitement calming down.

When all at once, quite suddenly, close to us, at our feet, there broke out a cry. I made a spring backwards in the first moment of surprise and horror, and in doing so came sharply against the same rough masonry and brambles that had struck me before. This new sound came upwards from the ground,—a low, moaning, wailing voice, full of suffering and pain. The contrast between it and the hoot of the owl was indescribable,—the one with a wholesome wildness and naturalness that hurt nobody; the other, a sound that made one's blood curdle, full of human misery.

With a great deal of fumbling,—for in spite of everything I could do to keep up my courage my hands shook,—I managed to remove the slide of my lantern. The light leaped out like something living, and made the place visible in a moment. We were what would have been inside the ruined building had anything remained but the gable-wall which I have described. It was close to us, the vacant doorway in it going out straight into the blackness outside. The light showed the bit of wall, the ivy glistening upon it in clouds of dark green, the bramble-branches waving, and below, the open door,—a door that led to nothing. It was from this the voice came which died out just as the light flashed upon this strange scene. There was a moment's silence, and then it broke forth again. The sound was so near, so penetrating, so pitiful, that, in the nervous start I gave, the light fell out of my hand.

As I groped for it in the dark my hand was clutched by Bagley, who, I think, must have dropped upon his knees; but I was too much perturbed myself to think much of this. He clutched at me in the confusion of his terror, forgetting all his usual decorum. "For God's sake, what is it, sir?" he gasped. If I yielded, there was evidently an end of both of us.

"I can't tell," I said, "any more than you; that's what we've got to find out. Up, man, up!" I pulled him to his feet. "Will you go round and examine the other side, or will you stay here with the lantern?" Bagley gasped at me with a face of horror.

"Can't we stay together, colonel?" he said; his knees were trembling under him. I pushed him against the corner of the wall, and put the light into his hands.

"Stand fast till I come back; shake yourself together, man; let nothing pass you," I said. The voice was within two or three feet of us; of that there could be no doubt.

I went myself to the other side of the wall, keeping close to it. The light shook in Bagley's hand, but, tremulous though it was, shone out through the vacant door, one oblong block of light marking all the crumbling corners and hanging masses of foliage. Was that something dark huddled in a heap by the side of it? I pushed forward across the light in the doorway, and fell upon it with my hands; but it was only a juniper-bush growing close against the wall. Meanwhile, the sight of my figure crossing the doorway had brought Bagley's nervous excitement to a height: he flew at me, gripping my shoulder.

"I've got him, Colonel! I've got him!" he cried, with a voice of sudden exultation. He thought it was a man, and was at once relieved. But at that moment the voice burst forth again between us, at our feet,—more close to us than any separate being could be. He dropped off from me, and fell against the wall, his jaw dropping as if he were dying. I suppose, at the same moment, he saw that it was me whom he had clutched. I, for my part, had scarcely more command of myself. I snatched the light out of his hand, and flashed it all about me wildly. Nothing,—the juniper-bush which I thought I had never seen before, the heavy growth of the glistening ivy, the brambles waving. It was close to my ears now, crying, crying, pleading as if for life.

Either I heard the same words Roland had heard, or else, in my excitement, his imagination got possession of mine. The voice went on, growing into distinct articulation, but wavering about, now from one point, now from another, as if the owner of it were moving slowly back and forward. "Mother! mother!" and then an outburst of wailing. As my mind steadied, getting accustomed (as one's mind gets accustomed

183

to anything), it seemed to me as if some uneasy, miserable creature was pacing up and down before a closed door. Sometimes—but that must have been excitement—I thought I heard a sound like knocking, and then another burst, "Oh, mother! mother!" All this close, close to the space where I was standing with my lantern, now before me, now behind me: a creature restless, unhappy, moaning, crying, before the vacant doorway, which no one could either shut or open more.

"Do you hear it, Bagley? do you hear what it is saying?" I cried, stepping in through the doorway. He was lying against the wall, his eyes glazed, half dead with terror. He made a motion of his lips as if to answer me, but no sounds came; then lifted his hand with a curious imperative movement as if ordering me to be silent and listen. And how long I did so I cannot tell. It began to have an interest, an exciting hold upon me, which I could not describe. It seemed to call up visibly a scene any one could understand,—a something shut out, restlessly wandering to and fro; sometimes the voice dropped, as if throwing itself down, sometimes wandered off a few paces, growing sharp and clear. "Oh, mother, let me in! oh, mother, mother, let me in! oh, let me in!" Every word was clear to me. No wonder the boy had gone wild with pity. I tried to steady my mind upon Roland, upon his conviction that I could do something, but my head swam with the excitement, even when I partially overcame the terror. At last the words died away, and there was a sound of sobs and moaning.

I cried out, "In the name of God, who are you?" with a kind of feeling in my mind that to use the name of God was profane, seeing that I did not believe in ghosts or anything supernatural; but I did it all the same, and waited, my heart giving a leap of terror lest there should be a reply. Why this should have been I cannot tell, but I had a feeling that if there was an answer it would be more than I could bear. But there was no answer; the moaning went on, and then, as if it had been real, the voice rose a little higher again, the words recommenced, "Oh, mother, let me in! oh, mother, let me in!" with an expression that was heart-breaking to hear.

As if it had been real! What do I mean by that? I suppose I got less alarmed as the thing went on. I began to recover the use of my senses,—I seemed to explain it all to myself by saying that this had once happened, that it was a recollection of a real scene. Why there should have seemed something quite satisfactory and composing in this explanation I cannot tell, but so it was. I began to listen almost as if it had been a play, forgetting Bagley, who, I almost think, had fainted, leaning against the wall. I was startled out of this strange spectatorship that had fallen upon me by the sudden rush of something which made my heart jump once more, a large black figure in the doorway waving its arms.

"Come in! come in! come in!" it shouted out hoarsely at the top of a deep bass voice, and then poor Bagley fell down senseless across the threshold. He was less sophisticated than I,—he had not been able to bear it any longer. I took him for something supernatural, as he took me, and it was some time before I awoke to the necessities of the moment. I remembered only after, that from the time I began to give my attention to the man, I heard the other voice no more. It was some time before I brought him to. It must have been a strange scene: the lantern making a luminous spot in the darkness, the man's white face lying on the black earth, I over him, doing what I could for him, probably I should have been thought to be murdering him had any one seen us.

When at last I succeeded in pouring a little brandy down his throat, he sat up and looked about him wildly. "What's up?" he said; then recognizing me, tried to struggle to his feet with a faint "Beg your pardon, colonel." I got him home as best I could, making him lean upon my arm. The great fellow was as weak as a child. Fortunately he did not for some time remember what had happened. From the time Bagley fell the voice had stopped, and all was still.

★★★★★★

"You've got an epidemic in your house, colonel," Simson said to me next morning. "What's the meaning of it all? Here's your butler raving about a voice. This will never do, you know; and so far as I can make out, you are in it too."

"Yes, I am in it, doctor. I thought I had better speak to you. Of course you are treating Roland all right, but the boy is not raving, he is as sane as you or me. It's all true."

"As sane as—I—or you. I never thought the boy insane. He's got cerebral excitement, fever. I don't know what you've got. There's something very queer about the look of your eyes."

"Come," said I, "you can't put us all to bed, you know. You had better listen and hear the symptoms in full."

The doctor shrugged his shoulders, but he listened to me patiently. He did not believe a word of the story, that was clear; but he heard it all from beginning to end. "My dear fellow," he said, "the boy told me

185

just the same. It's an epidemic. When one person falls a victim to this sort of thing, it's as safe as can be,—there's always two or three."

"Then how do you account for it?" I said.

"Oh, account for it!—that's a different matter; there's no accounting for the freaks our brains are subject to. If it's delusion, if it's some trick of the echoes or the winds,—some phonetic disturbance or other—"

"Come with me tonight, and judge for yourself," I said.

Upon this he laughed aloud, then said, "That's not such a bad idea; but it would ruin me forever if it were known that John Simson was ghost-hunting."

"There it is," said I; "you dart down on us who are unlearned with your phonetic disturbances, but you daren't examine what the thing really is for fear of being laughed at. That's science!"

"It's not science,—it's common-sense," said the doctor. "The thing has delusion on the front of it. It is encouraging an unwholesome tendency even to examine. What good could come of it? Even if I am convinced, I shouldn't believe."

"I should have said so yesterday; and I don't want you to be convinced or to believe," said I. "If you prove it to be a delusion, I shall be very much obliged to you for one. Come; somebody must go with me."

"You are cool," said the doctor. "You've disabled this poor fellow of yours, and made him—on that point—a lunatic for life; and now you want to disable me. But, for once, I'll do it. To save appearance, if you'll give me a bed, I'll come over after my last rounds."

It was agreed that I should meet him at the gate, and that we should visit the scene of last night's occurrences before we came to the house, so that nobody might be the wiser. It was scarcely possible to hope that the cause of Bagley's sudden illness should not somehow steal into the knowledge of the servants at least, and it was better that all should be done as quietly as possible. The day seemed to me a very long one. I had to spend a certain part of it with Roland, which was a terrible ordeal for me, for what could I say to the boy? The improvement continued, but he was still in a very precarious state, and the trembling vehemence with which he turned to me when his mother left the room filled me with alarm. "Father?" he said quietly.

"Yes, my boy, I am giving my best attention to it; all is being done that I can do. I have not come to any conclusion—yet. I am neglecting nothing you said," I cried. What I could not do was to give his active mind any encouragement to dwell upon the mystery. It was a hard predicament, for some satisfaction had to be given him. He looked at me very wistfully, with the great blue eyes which shone so large and brilliant out of his white and worn face. "You must trust me," I said.

"Yes, father. Father understands," he said to himself, as if to soothe some inward doubt. I left him as soon as I could. He was about the most precious thing I had on earth, and his health my first thought; but yet somehow, in the excitement of this other subject, I put that aside, and preferred not to dwell upon Roland, which was the most curious part of it all.

That night at eleven I met Simson at the gate. He had come by train, and I let him in gently myself. I had been so much absorbed in the coming experiment that I passed the ruins in going to meet him, almost without thought, if you can understand that. I had my lantern; and he showed me a coil of taper which he had ready for use. "There is nothing like light," he said, in his scoffing tone. It was a very still night, scarcely a sound, but not so dark. We could keep the path without difficulty as we went along.

As we approached the spot we could hear a low moaning, broken occasionally by a bitter cry. "Perhaps that is your voice," said the doctor; "I thought it must be something of the kind. That's a poor brute caught in some of these infernal traps of yours; you'll find it among the bushes somewhere." I said nothing. I felt no particular fear, but a triumphant satisfaction in what was to follow. I led him to the spot where Bagley and I had stood on the previous night. All was silent as a winter night could be,—so silent that we heard far off the sound of the horses in the stables, the shutting of a window at the house. Simson lighted his taper and went peering about, poking into all the corners.

We looked like two conspirators lying in wait for some unfortunate traveller; but not a sound broke the quiet. The moaning had stopped before we came up; a star or two shone over us in the sky, looking down as if surprised at our strange proceedings. Dr. Simson did nothing but utter subdued laughs under his breath. "I thought as much," he said. "It is just the same with tables and all other kinds of ghostly apparatus; a sceptic's presence stops everything. When I am present nothing ever comes off. How long do you think it will be necessary to stay here? Oh, I don't complain; only when *you* are satisfied, *I* am—quite."

I will not deny that I was disappointed beyond measure by this result. It made me look like a credulous fool. It gave the Doctor such a pull over me as nothing else could. I should point all his morals for years to come; and his materialism, his scepticism, would be increased beyond endurance. "It seems, indeed," I said, "that there is to be no—"

"Manifestation," he said, laughing; "that is what all the mediums say. No manifestations, in consequence of the presence of an unbeliever."

His laugh sounded very uncomfortable to me in the silence; and it was now near midnight. But that laugh seemed the signal; before it died away the moaning we had heard before was resumed. It started from some distance off, and came towards us, nearer and nearer, like someone walking along and moaning to himself. There could be no idea now that it was a hare caught in a trap. The approach was slow, like that of a weak person, with little halts and pauses. We heard it coming along the grass straight towards the vacant doorway. Simson had been a little startled by the first sound. He said hastily, "That child has no business to be out so late."

But he felt, as well as I, that this was no child's voice. As it came nearer, he grew silent, and, going to the doorway with his taper, stood looking out towards the sound. The taper being unprotected blew about in the night air, though there was scarcely any wind. I threw the light of my lantern steady and white across the same space. It was in a blaze of light in the midst of the blackness. A little icy thrill had gone over me at the first sound, but as it came close, I confess that my only feeling was satisfaction. The scoffer could scoff no more. The light touched his own face, and showed a very perplexed countenance. If he was afraid, he concealed it with great success, but he was perplexed. And then all that had happened on the previous night was enacted once more.

It fell strangely upon me with a sense of repetition. Every cry, every sob seemed the same as before. I listened almost without any emotion at all in my own person, thinking of its effect upon Simson. He maintained a very bold front, on the whole. All that coming and going of the voice was, if our ears could be trusted, exactly in front of the vacant, blank doorway, blazing full of light, which caught and shone in the glistening leaves of the great hollies at a little distance. Not a rabbit could have crossed the turf without being seen; but there was nothing. After a time, Simson, with a certain caution and bodily reluctance, as it seemed to me, went out with his roll of taper into this space. His figure showed against the holly in full outline. Just at this moment the voice sank, as was its custom, and seemed to fling itself down at the door. Simson recoiled violently, as if someone had come up against him, then turned, and held his taper low, as if examining something.

"Do you see anybody?" I cried in a whisper, feeling the chill of nervous panic steal over me at this action.

"It's nothing but a—confounded juniper-bush," he said. This I knew very well to be nonsense, for the juniper-bush was on the other side. He went about after this round and round, poking his taper everywhere, then returned to me on the inner side of the wall. He scoffed no longer; his face was contracted and pale. "How long does this go on?" he whispered to me, like a man who does not wish to interrupt someone who is speaking. I had become too much perturbed myself to remark whether the successions and changes of the voice were the same as last night. It suddenly went out in the air almost as he was speaking, with a soft reiterated sob dying away. If there had been anything to be seen, I should have said that the person was at that moment crouching on the ground close to the door.

We walked home very silent afterwards. It was only when we were in sight of the house that I said, "What do you think of it?"

"I can't tell what to think of it," he said quickly. He took—though he was a very temperate man—not the claret I was going to offer him, but some brandy from the tray, and swallowed it almost undiluted. "Mind you, I don't believe a word of it," he said, when he had lighted his candle; "but I can't tell what to think," he turned round to add, when he was half-way upstairs.

All of this, however, did me no good with the solution of my problem. I was to help this weeping, sobbing thing, which was already to me as distinct a personality as anything I knew; or what should I say to Roland? It was on my heart that my boy would die if I could not find some way of helping this creature. You may be surprised that I should speak of it in this way. I did not know if it was man or woman; but I no more doubted that it was a soul in pain than I doubted my own being; and it was my business to soothe this pain,—to deliver it, if that was possible. Was ever such a task given to an anxious father trembling for his only boy? I felt in my heart, fantastic as it may appear, that I must fulfil this somehow, or part with my child; and you may conceive that rather than do that I was ready to die. But even my dying would not have advanced me, unless by bringing me into the same world with that seeker at the door.

189

Next morning Simson was out before breakfast, and came in with evident signs of the damp grass on his boots, and a look of worry and weariness, which did not say much for the night he had passed. He improved a little after breakfast, and visited his two patients,—for Bagley was still an invalid. I went out with him on his way to the train, to hear what he had to say about the boy. "He is going on very well," he said; "there are no complications as yet. But mind you, that's not a boy to be trifled with, Mortimer. Not a word to him about last night." I had to tell him then of my last interview with Roland, and of the impossible demand he had made upon me, by which, though he tried to laugh, he was much discomposed, as I could see.

"We must just perjure ourselves all round," he said, "and swear you exorcised it;" but the man was too kind-hearted to be satisfied with that. "It's frightfully serious for you, Mortimer. I can't laugh as I should like to. I wish I saw a way out of it, for your sake. By the way," he added shortly, "didn't you notice that juniper-bush on the left-hand side?"

"There was one on the right hand of the door. I noticed you made that mistake last night."

"Mistake!" he cried, with a curious low laugh, pulling up the collar of his coat as though he felt the cold,—"there's no juniper there this morning, left or right. Just go and see." As he stepped into the train a few minutes after, he looked back upon me and beckoned me for a parting word. "I'm coming back tonight," he said.

I don't think I had any feeling about this as I turned away from that common bustle of the railway which made my private preoccupations feel so strangely out of date. There had been a distinct satisfaction in my mind before, that his scepticism had been so entirely defeated. But the more serious part of the matter pressed upon me now. I went straight from the railway to the manse, which stood on a little *plateau* on the side of the river opposite to the woods of Brentwood. The minister was one of a class which is not so common in Scotland as it used to be. He was a man of good family, well educated in the Scotch way, strong in philosophy, not so strong in Greek, strongest of all in experience,—a man who had "come across," in the course of his life, most people of note that had ever been in Scotland, and who was said to be very sound in doctrine, without infringing the toleration with which old men, who are good men, are generally endowed. He was old-fashioned; perhaps he did not think so much about the troublous problems of theology as many of the young men, nor ask himself any hard questions about the Confession of Faith; but he understood human nature, which is perhaps better. He received me with a cordial welcome.

"Come away, Colonel Mortimer," he said; "I'm all the more glad to see you, that I feel it's a good sign for the boy. He's doing well?—God be praised,—and the Lord bless him and keep him. He has many a poor body's prayers, and that can do nobody harm."

"He will need them all, Dr. Moncrieff," I said, "and your counsel too." And I told him the story,—more than I had told Simson. The old clergyman listened to me with many suppressed exclamations, and at the end the water stood in his eyes.

"That's just beautiful," he said. "I do not mind to have heard anything like it; it's as fine as Burns when he wished deliverance to one— that is prayed for in no kirk. Ay, ay! so he would have you console the poor lost spirit? God bless the boy! There's something more than common in that, Colonel Mortimer. And also the faith of him in his father!—I would like to put that into a sermon." Then the old gentleman gave me an alarmed look, and said, "No, no; I was not meaning a sermon; but I must write it down for the 'Children's Record.'" I saw the thought that passed through his mind. Either he thought, or he feared I would think, of a funeral sermon. You may believe this did not make me more cheerful.

I can scarcely say that Dr. Moncrieff gave me any advice. How could anyone advise on such a subject? But he said, "I think I'll come too. I'm an old man; I'm less liable to be frightened than those that are further off the world unseen. It behooves me to think of my own journey there. I've no cut-and-dry beliefs on the subject. I'll come too; and maybe at the moment the Lord will put into our heads what to do."

This gave me a little comfort,—more than Simson had given me. To be clear about the cause of it was not my grand desire. It was another thing that was in my mind,—my boy. As for the poor soul at the open door, I had no more doubt, as I have said, of its existence than I had of my own. It was no ghost to me. I knew the creature, and it was in trouble. That was my feeling about it, as it was Roland's. To hear it first was a great shock to my nerves, but not now; a man will get accustomed to anything. But to do something for it was the great problem; how was I to be serviceable to a being that was invisible, that was mortal no longer? "Maybe at the moment the Lord will put it into our heads." This is very old-fashioned phraseology, and a week before, most likely, I should have smiled (though always with kindness) at Dr. Moncrieff's credulity; but there was a great comfort, whether rational or otherwise I cannot say, in the mere sound of the words.

The road to the station and the village lay through the glen, not by the ruins; but though the sunshine and the fresh air, and the beauty of the trees, and the sound of the water were all very soothing to the spirits, my mind was so full of my own subject that I could not refrain from turning to the right hand as I got to the top of the glen, and going straight to the place which I may call the scene of all my thoughts. It was lying full in the sunshine, like all the rest of the world. The ruined gable looked due east, and in the present aspect of the sun the light streamed down through the doorway as our lantern had done, throwing a flood of light upon the damp grass beyond. There was a strange suggestion in the open door,—so futile, a kind of emblem of vanity: all free around, so that you could go where you pleased, and yet that semblance of an enclosure,—that way of entrance, unnecessary, leading to nothing.

And why any creature should pray and weep to get in—to nothing, or be kept out—by nothing, you could not dwell upon it, or it made your brain go round. I remembered, however, what Simson said about the juniper, with a little smile on my own mind as to the inaccuracy of recollection which even a scientific man will be guilty of. I could see now the light of my lantern gleaming upon the wet glistening surface of the spiky leaves at the right hand,—and he ready to go to the stake for it that it was the left! I went round to make sure. And then I saw what he had said. Right or left there was no juniper at all! I was confounded by this, though it was entirely a matter of detail nothing at all,—a bush of brambles waving, the grass growing up to the very walls.

But after all, though it gave me a shock for a moment, what did that matter? There were marks as if a number of footsteps had been up and down in front of the door, but these might have been our steps; and all was bright and peaceful and still. I poked about the other ruin—the larger ruins of the old house—for some time, as I had done before. There were marks upon the grass here and there—I could not call them footsteps—all about; but that told for nothing one way or another. I had examined the ruined rooms closely the first day. They were half filled up with soil and *debris*, withered brackens and bramble,—no refuge for any one there. It vexed me that Jarvis should see me coming from that spot when he came up to me for his orders. I don't know whether my nocturnal expeditions had got wind among the servants, but there was a significant look in his face. Something in it I felt was like my own sensation when Simson in the midst of his scepticism was struck dumb. Jarvis felt satisfied that his veracity had been put beyond question. I never spoke to a servant of mine in such a peremptory tone before. I sent him away "with a flea in his lug," as the man described it afterwards. Interference of any kind was intolerable to me at such a moment.

But what was strangest of all was, that I could not face Roland. I did not go up to his room, as I would have naturally done, at once. This the girls could not understand. They saw there was some mystery in it. "Mother has gone to lie down," Agatha said; "he has had such a good night."

"But he wants you so, papa!" cried little Jeanie, always with her two arms embracing mine in a pretty way she had. I was obliged to go at last, but what could I say? I could only kiss him, and tell him to keep still,—that I was doing all I could. There is something mystical about the patience of a child.

"It will come all right, won't it, father?" he said.

"God grant it may! I hope so, Roland."

"Oh, yes, it will come all right." Perhaps he understood that in the midst of my anxiety I could not stay with him as I should have done otherwise. But the girls were more surprised than it is possible to describe. They looked at me with wondering eyes.

"If I were ill, papa, and you only stayed with me a moment, I should break my heart," said Agatha. But the boy had a sympathetic feeling. He knew that of my own will I would not have done it. I shut myself up in the library, where I could not rest, but kept pacing up and down like a caged beast. What could I do? and if I could do nothing, what would become of my boy? These were the questions that, without ceasing, pursued each other through my mind.

Simson came out to dinner, and when the house was all still, and most of the servants in bed, we went out and met Dr. Moncrieff, as we had appointed, at the head of the glen. Simson, for his part, was disposed to scoff at the Doctor. "If there are to be any spells, you know, I'll cut the whole concern," he said. I did not make him any reply. I had not invited him; he could go or come as he pleased. He was very talkative, far more so than suited my humour, as we went on. "One thing is certain, you know; there must be some human agency," he said. "It is all bosh about apparitions. I never have investigated the laws of sound to any great extent, and there's a great deal in ventriloquism that we don't know much about."

"If it's the same to you," I said, "I wish you'd keep all that to yourself, Simson. It doesn't suit my state of mind."

"Oh, I hope I know how to respect idiosyncrasy," he said. The very tone of his voice irritated me beyond measure. These scientific fellows, I wonder people put up with them as they do, when you have no mind for their cold-blooded confidence. Dr. Moncrieff met us about eleven o'clock, the same time as on the previous night. He was a large man, with a venerable countenance and white hair,—old, but in full vigour, and thinking less of a cold night walk than many a younger man. He had his lantern, as I had. We were fully provided with means of lighting the place, and we were all of us resolute men. We had a rapid consultation as we went up, and the result was that we divided to different posts.

Dr. Moncrieff remained inside the wall—if you can call that inside where there was no wall but one. Simson placed himself on the side next the ruins, so as to intercept any communication with the old house, which was what his mind was fixed upon. I was posted on the other side. To say that nothing could come near without being seen was self-evident. It had been so also on the previous night. Now, with our three lights in the midst of the darkness, the whole place seemed illuminated. Dr. Moncrieff's lantern, which was a large one, without any means of shutting up,—an old-fashioned lantern with a pierced and ornamental top,—shone steadily, the rays shooting out of it upward into the gloom. He placed it on the grass, where the middle of the room, if this had been a room, would have been. The usual effect of the light streaming out of the doorway was prevented by the illumination which Simson and I on either side supplied. With these differences, everything seemed as on the previous night.

And what occurred was exactly the same, with the same air of repetition, point for point, as I had formerly remarked. I declare that it seemed to me as if I were pushed against, put aside, by the owner of the voice as he paced up and down in his trouble,—though these are perfectly futile words, seeing that the stream of light from my lantern, and that from Simson's taper, lay broad and clear, without a shadow, without the smallest break, across the entire breadth of the grass. I had ceased even to be alarmed, for my part. My heart was rent with pity and trouble,—pity for the poor suffering human creature that moaned and pleaded so, and trouble for myself and my boy. God! if I could not find any help,—and what help could I find?—Roland would die.

We were all perfectly still till the first outburst was exhausted, as I knew, by experience, it would be. Dr. Moncrieff, to whom it was new, was quite motionless on the other side of the wall, as we were in our places. My heart had remained almost at its usual beating during the voice. I was used to it; it did not rouse all my pulses as it did at first. But just as it threw itself sobbing at the door (I cannot use other words), there suddenly came something which sent the blood coursing through my veins, and my heart into my mouth. It was a voice inside the wall,—the minister's well-known voice. I would have been prepared for it in any kind of adjuration, but I was not prepared for what I heard. It came out with a sort of stammering, as if too much moved for utterance. "Willie, Willie! Oh, God preserve us! is it you?"

These simple words had an effect upon me that the voice of the invisible creature had ceased to have. I thought the old man, whom I had brought into this danger, had gone mad with terror. I made a dash round to the other side of the wall, half crazed myself with the thought. He was standing where I had left him, his shadow thrown vague and large upon the grass by the lantern which stood at his feet. I lifted my own light to see his face as I rushed forward. He was very pale, his eyes wet and glistening, his mouth quivering with parted lips. He neither saw nor heard me. We that had gone through this experience before, had crouched towards each other to get a little strength to bear it. But he was not even aware that I was there. His whole being seemed absorbed in anxiety and tenderness. He held out his hands, which trembled, but it seemed to me with eagerness, not fear. He went on speaking all the time. "Willie, if it is you,—and it's you, if it is not a delusion of Satan,—Willie, lad! why come ye here frighting them that know you not? Why came ye not to me?"

He seemed to wait for an answer. When his voice ceased, his countenance, every line moving, continued to speak. Simson gave me another terrible shock, stealing into the open doorway with his light, as much awe-stricken, as wildly curious, as I. But the minister resumed, without seeing Simson, speaking to someone else. His voice took a tone of expostulation:—

"Is this right to come here? Your mother's gone with your name on her lips. Do you think she would ever close her door on her own lad? Do ye think the Lord will close the door, ye faint-hearted creature? No!—I forbid ye! I forbid ye!" cried the old man. The sobbing voice had begun to resume its cries. He made a step forward, calling out the last words in a voice of command.

"I forbid ye! Cry out no more to man. Go home, ye wandering spirit! go home! Do you hear me?—me that christened ye, that have struggled with ye, that have wrestled for ye with the Lord!" Here the loud tones of his voice sank into tenderness. "And her too, poor woman! poor woman! her you are calling upon. She's not here. You'll find her with the Lord. Go there and seek her, not here. Do you hear me, lad? go after her there. He'll let you in, though it's late. Man, take heart! if you will lie and sob and greet, let it be at heaven's gate, and not your poor mother's ruined door."

He stopped to get his breath; and the voice had stopped, not as it had done before, when its time was exhausted and all its repetitions said, but with a sobbing catch in the breath as if overruled. Then the minister spoke again, "Are you hearing me, Will? Oh, laddie, you've liked the beggarly elements all your days. Be done with them now. Go home to the Father—the Father! Are you hearing me?" Here the old man sank down upon his knees, his face raised upwards, his hands held up with a tremble in them, all white in the light in the midst of the darkness. I resisted as long as I could, though I cannot tell why; then I, too, dropped upon my knees. Simson all the time stood in the doorway, with an expression in his face such as words could not tell, his under lip dropped, his eyes wild, staring. It seemed to be to him, that image of blank ignorance and wonder, that we were praying. All the time the voice, with a low arrested sobbing, lay just where he was standing, as I thought.

"Lord," the minister said,—"Lord, take him into Thy everlasting habitations. The mother he cries to is with Thee. Who can open to him but Thee? Lord, when is it too late for Thee, or what is too hard for Thee? Lord, let that woman there draw him inower! Let her draw him inower!"

I sprang forward to catch something in my arms that flung itself wildly within the door. The illusion was so strong, that I never paused till I felt my forehead graze against the wall and my hands clutch the ground,—for there was nobody there to save from falling, as in my foolishness I thought. Simson held out his hand to me to help me up. He was trembling and cold, his lower lip hanging, his speech almost inarticulate. "It's gone," he said, stammering,—"it's gone!"

We leaned upon each other for a moment, trembling so much, both of us, that the whole scene trembled as if it were going to dissolve and disappear; and yet as long as I live I will never forget it,—the shining of the strange lights, the blackness all round, the kneeling figure with all the whiteness of the light concentrated on its white venerable head and uplifted hands. A strange solemn stillness seemed to close all round us. By intervals a single syllable, "Lord! Lord!" came from the old minister's lips. He saw none of us, nor thought of us. I never knew how long we stood, like sentinels guarding him at his prayers, holding our lights in a confused dazed way, not knowing what we did. But at last he rose from his knees, and standing up at his full height, raised his arms, as the Scotch manner is at the end of a religious service, and solemnly gave the apostolical benediction,—to what? to the silent earth, the dark woods, the wide breathing atmosphere; for we were but spectators gasping an Amen!

It seemed to me that it must be the middle of the night, as we all walked back. It was in reality very late. Dr. Moncrieff put his arm into mine. He walked slowly, with an air of exhaustion. It was as if we were coming from a death-bed. Something hushed and solemnized the very air. There was that sense of relief in it which there always is at the end of a death-struggle. And nature, persistent, never daunted, came back in all of us, as we returned into the ways of life. We said nothing to each other, indeed, for a time; but when we got clear of the trees and reached the opening near the house, where we could see the sky, Dr. Moncrieff himself was the first to speak. "I must be going," he said; "it's very late, I'm afraid. I will go down the glen, as I came."

"But not alone. I am going with you, doctor."

"Well, I will not oppose it. I am an old man, and agitation wearies more than work. Yes; I'll be thankful of your arm. Tonight, Colonel, you've done me more good turns than one."

I pressed his hand on my arm, not feeling able to speak. But Simson, who turned with us, and who had gone along all this time with his taper flaring, in entire unconsciousness, came to himself, apparently at the sound of our voices, and put out that wild little torch with a quick movement, as if of shame. "Let me carry your lantern," he said; "it is heavy." He recovered with a spring; and in a moment, from the awe-stricken spectator he had been, became himself, sceptical and cynical. "I should like to ask you a question," he said. "Do you believe in Purgatory, Doctor? It's not in the tenets of the Church, so far as I know."

"Sir," said Dr. Moncrieff, "an old man like me is sometimes not very sure what he believes. There is just one thing I am certain of— and that is the loving-kindness of God."

"But I thought that was in this life. I am no theologian—"

"Sir," said the old man again, with a tremor in him which I could feel going over all his frame, "if I saw a friend of mine within the gates of hell, I would not despair but his Father would take him by the hand still, if he cried like *you*."

"I allow it is very strange, very strange. I cannot see through it. That there must be human agency, I feel sure. Doctor, what made you decide upon the person and the name?"

The minister put out his hand with the impatience which a man might show if he were asked how he recognized his brother. "Tuts!" he said, in familiar speech; then more solemnly, "How should I not recognize a person that I know better—far better—than I know you?"

"Then you saw the man?"

Dr. Moncrieff made no reply. He moved his hand again with a little impatient movement, and walked on, leaning heavily on my arm. And we went on for a long time without another word, threading the dark paths, which were steep and slippery with the damp of the winter. The air was very still,—not more than enough to make a faint sighing in the branches, which mingled with the sound of the water to which we were descending. When we spoke again, it was about indifferent matters,—about the height of the river, and the recent rains. We parted with the minister at his own door, where his old housekeeper appeared in great perturbation, waiting for him. "Eh, me, minister! the young gentleman will be worse?" she cried.

"Far from that—better. God bless him!" Dr. Moncrieff said.

I think if Simson had begun again to me with his questions, I should have pitched him over the rocks as we returned up the glen; but he was silent, by a good inspiration. And the sky was clearer than it had been for many nights, shining high over the trees, with here and there a star faintly gleaming through the wilderness of dark and bare branches. The air, as I have said, was very soft in them, with a subdued and peaceful cadence. It was real, like every natural sound, and came to us like a hush of peace and relief. I thought there was a sound in it as of the breath of a sleeper, and it seemed clear to me that Roland must be sleeping, satisfied and calm. We went up to his room when we went in. There we found the complete hush of rest. My wife looked up out of a doze, and gave me a smile:

"I think he is a great deal better; but you are very late," she said in a whisper, shading the light with her hand that the Doctor might see his patient. The boy had got back something like his own colour.

He woke as we stood all round his bed. His eyes had the happy, half-awakened look of childhood, glad to shut again, yet pleased with the interruption and glimmer of the light. I stooped over him and kissed his forehead, which was moist and cool.

"All is well, Roland," I said. He looked up at me with a glance of pleasure, and took my hand and laid his cheek upon it, and so went to sleep.

★★★★★★

For some nights after, I watched among the ruins, spending all the dark hours up to midnight patrolling about the bit of wall which was associated with so many emotions; but I heard nothing, and saw nothing beyond the quiet course of nature; nor, so far as I am aware, has anything been heard again. Dr. Moncrieff gave me the history of the youth, whom he never hesitated to name. I did not ask, as Simson did, how he recognized him. He had been a prodigal,—weak, foolish, easily imposed upon, and "led away," as people say. All that we had heard had passed actually in life, the doctor said. The young man had come home thus a day or two after his mother died,—who was no more than the housekeeper in the old house,—and distracted with the news, had thrown himself down at the door and called upon her to let him in. The old man could scarcely speak of it for tears.

To me it seemed as if—Heaven help us, how little do we know about anything!—a scene like that might impress itself somehow upon the hidden heart of nature. I do not pretend to know how, but the repetition had struck me at the time as, in its terrible strangeness and incomprehensibility, almost mechanical,—as if the unseen actor could not exceed or vary, but was bound to re-enact the whole. One thing that struck me, however, greatly, was the likeness between the old minister and my boy in the manner of regarding these strange phenomena. Dr. Moncrieff was not terrified, as I had been myself, and all the rest of us. It was no "ghost," as I fear we all vulgarly considered it, to him,—but a poor creature whom he knew under these conditions, just as he had known him in the flesh, having no doubt of his identity.

And to Roland it was the same. This spirit in pain,—if it was a spirit,—this voice out of the unseen,—was a poor fellow-creature in misery, to be succoured and helped out of his trouble, to my boy. He spoke to me quite frankly about it when he got better. "I knew father would find out some way," he said. And this was when he was strong and well, and all idea that he would turn hysterical or become a seer

199

of visions had happily passed away.

★★★★★★

I must add one curious fact, which does not seem to me to have any relation to the above, but which Simson made great use of, as the human agency which he was determined to find somehow. We had examined the ruins very closely at the time of these occurrences; but afterwards, when all was over, as we went casually about them one Sunday afternoon in the idleness of that unemployed day, Simson with his stick penetrated an old window which had been entirely blocked up with fallen soil. He jumped down into it in great excitement, and called me to follow. There we found a little hole,—for it was more a hole than a room,—entirely hidden under the ivy and ruins, in which there was a quantity of straw laid in a corner, as if someone had made a bed there, and some remains of crusts about the floor. Someone had lodged there, and not very long before, he made out; and that this unknown being was the author of all the mysterious sounds we heard he is convinced.

"I told you it was human agency," he said triumphantly. He forgets, I suppose, how he and I stood with our lights, seeing nothing, while the space between us was audibly traversed by something that could speak, and sob, and suffer. There is no argument with men of this kind. He is ready to get up a laugh against me on this slender ground. "I was puzzled myself,—I could not make it out,—but I always felt convinced human agency was at the bottom of it. And here it is,—and a clever fellow he must have been," the doctor says.

Bagley left my service as soon as he got well. He assured me it was no want of respect, but he could not stand "them kind of things;" and the man was so shaken and ghastly that I was glad to give him a present and let him go. For my own part, I made a point of staying out the time—two years—for which I had taken Brentwood; but I did not renew my tenancy. By that time we had settled, and found for ourselves a pleasant home of our own.

I must add, that when the doctor defies me, I can always bring back gravity to his countenance, and a pause in his railing, when I remind him of the juniper-bush. To me that was a matter of little importance. I could believe I was mistaken. I did not care about it one way or other; but on his mind the effect was different. The miserable voice, the spirit in pain, he could think of as the result of ventriloquism, or reverberation, or—anything you please: an elaborate prolonged hoax, executed somehow by the tramp that had found a lodging in the old tower; but the juniper-bush staggered him. Things have effects so different on the minds of different men.

The Last House in C—— Street

Dinah Mulock

I am not a believer in ghosts in general; I see no good in them.
They come—that is, are reported to come—so irrelevantly, purpose-
lessly— so ridiculously, in short—that one's common sense as regards
this world, one's supernatural sense of the other, are alike revolted.
Then nine out of ten 'capital ghost stories' are so easily accounted
for; and in the tenth, when all natural explanation fails, one who has
discovered the extraordinary difficulty there is in all society in getting hold of that very slippery article called a fact, is strongly inclined
to shake a dubious head, ejaculating, 'Evidence! it is all a question of
evidence!'

But my unbelief springs from no dogged or contemptuous scepticism as to the possibility—however great the improbability—of that
strange impression upon, or communication to, spirit in matter, from
spirit wholly immaterialised, which is vulgarly called 'a ghost'. There is
no credulity more blind, no ignorance more childish, that that of the
sage who tries to measure 'heaven and earth and the things under the
earth', with the small two-foot rule of his own brains.

The presumption of mere folly alone would argue concerning any
mystery of the universe, 'It is inexplicable, and therefore impossible.'

Premising these opinions, though simply as opinions, I am about
to relate what I must confess seems to me a thorough ghost story;
its external and circumstantial evidence being indisputable, while its
psychological causes and results, though not easy of explanation, are
still more difficult to be explained away. The ghost, like Hamlet's, was
'an honest ghost'. From her daughter—an old lady, who, bless her
good and gentle memory! has since learned the secrets of all things—I
heard this veritable tale.

'My dear,' said Mrs MacArthur to me—it was in the early days of table-moving, when young folk ridiculed and elder folk were shocked at the notion of calling up one's departed ancestors into one's dinner-table, and learning the wonders of the angelic world by the bobbings of a hat or the twirlings of a plate;—'My dear,' continued the old lady, 'I do not like trifling with spirits.'

'Why not? Do you believe in them?'

'A little.'

'Did you ever see one?'

'Never. But once, I heard one.'

She looked serious, as if she hardly liked to speak about it, either from a sense of awe or from fear of ridicule. But it was impossible to laugh at any illusions of the gentle old lady, who never uttered a harsh or satirical word to a living soul. Likewise, the evident awe with which she mentioned the circumstance was rather remarkable in one who had a large stock of common sense, little wonder, and no ideality.

I was very curious to hear Mrs MacArthur's ghost story.

'My dear, it was a long time ago, so long that you may fancy I forget and confuse the circumstances. But I do not. Sometimes I think one recollects more clearly things that happened in one's teens—I was eighteen that year—than a great many nearer events. And besides, I had other reasons for remembering vividly everything belonging to this time,—for I was in love, you must know.'

She looked at me with a mild deprecating smile, as if hoping my youthfulness would not consider the thing so very impossible or ridiculous. No; I was all interest at once.

'In love with Mr MacArthur,' I said, scarcely as a question, being at that Arcadian time of life when one takes as a natural necessity, and believes in as an undoubted truth, that all people, that is, good people, marry their first love.

'No, my dear; not with Mr MacArthur.'

I was so astonished, so completely dumbfounded—for I had woven a sort of ideal round my good old friend—that I suffered Mrs MacArthur to knit in silence for full five minutes. My surprise was not lessened when she said, with a gratified little smile—'He was a young gentleman of good parts; and he was very fond of me. Proud, too, rather. For though you might not think it, my dear, I was actually a beauty in those days.'

I had very little doubt of it. The slight lithe figure, the tiny hands and feet,—if you had walked behind Mrs MacArthur down the street you might have taken her for a young woman still. Certainly, people lived slower and easier in the last generation than in ours.

'Yes, I was the beauty of Bath. Mr Everest fell in love with me there. I was much gratified; for I had just been reading Miss Burney's Cecilia, and I thought him exactly like Mortimer Delvil. A very pretty story, Cecilia; did you ever read it?'

'No.' And, to arrive quicker at her tale, I leaped to the only conclusion which could reconcile the two facts of my good old friend having had a lover named Everest, and being now Mrs MacArthur. 'Was it his ghost you saw?'

'No, my dear, no; thank goodness, he is alive still. He calls here sometimes; he has been a faithful friend to our family. Ah!' with a slow shake of the head, half pleased, half pensive, 'you would hardly believe, my dear, what a very pretty fellow he was.'

One could scarcely smile at the odd phrase, pertaining to last-century novels and to the loves of our great-grandmothers. I listened patiently to the wandering reminiscences which still further delayed the ghost story.

'But, Mrs MacArthur, was it in Bath that you saw or heard what I think you were going to tell me? The ghost, you know?'

'Don't call it that; it sounds as if you were laughing at it. And you must not, for it is really true; as true as that I sit here, an old lady of seventy-five, and that then I was a young gentlewoman of eighteen. Nay, my dear, I will tell you all about it.

'We had been staying in London, my father and mother, Mr Everest, and I. He had persuaded them to take me; he wanted to show me a little of the world, though even his world was but a narrow one, my dear,—for he was a law student, living poorly and working hard.

'He took lodgings for us near the Temple; in C—-street, the last house there, looking on to the river. He was very fond of the river; and often of evenings, when his work was too heavy to let him take us to Ranelagh or to the play, he used to walk with my father and mother and me up and down the Temple Gardens. Were you ever in the Temple Gardens? It is a pretty place now—a quiet, grey nook in the midst of noise and bustle; the stars look wonderful through those great trees; but still it is not like what it was then, when I was a girl.'

Ah! no; impossible.

'It was in the Temple Gardens, my dear, that I remember we took our last walk—my mother, Mr Everest, and I—before she went home to Bath. She was very anxious and restless to go, being too delicate for London gaieties. Besides, she had a large family at home, of which

I was the eldest; and we were anxiously expecting another baby in a month or two. Nevertheless, my dear mother had gone about with me, taken me to all the shows and sights that I, a hearty and happy girl, longed to see, and entered into them with almost as great enjoyment as my own.

'But tonight, she was pale, rather grave, and steadfastly bent on returning home.

'We did all we could to persuade her to the contrary, for on the next night but one was to have been the crowning treat of all our London pleasures: we were to see Hamlet at Drury-lane, with John Kemble and Sarah Siddons! Think of that, my dear. Ah! you have no such sights now. Even my grave father longed to go, and urged in his mild way that we should put off our departure.

'But my mother was determined.

'At last Mr Everest said—I could show you the very spot where he stood, with the river—it was high water—lapping against the wall, and the evening sun shining on the Southwark houses opposite. He said—it was very wrong, of course, my dear; but then he was in love, and might be excused—"Madam," said he, "it is the first time I ever knew you think of yourself alone."

'"Myself, Edmond?"

'"Pardon me, but would it not be possible for you to return home, leaving behind, for two days only, Dr Thwaite and Mistress Dorothy?"

'"Leave them behind—leave them behind!" She mused over the words. "What say you, Dorothy?"

'I was silent. In very truth, I had never been parted from her in all my life. It had never crossed my mind to wish to part from her, or to enjoy any pleasure without her, till—till within the last three months. "Mother, don't suppose I—"

'But here I caught sight of Mr Everest and stopped.

'"Pray continue, Mistress Dorothy."

'No, I could not. He looked so vexed, so hurt; and we had been so happy together. Also, we might not meet again for years, for the journey between London and Bath was then a serious one, even to lovers; and he worked very hard—had few pleasures in his life. It did indeed seem almost selfish of my mother.

'Though my lips said nothing, perhaps my sad eyes said only too much, and my mother felt it.

'She walked with us a few yards, slowly and thoughtfully. I could see her now, with her pale, tired face, under the cherry-coloured ribbons of her hood. She had been very handsome as a young woman, and was most sweet-looking still—my dear, good mother!

"'Dorothy, we will discuss this no more. I am very sorry, but I must go home. However, I will persuade your father to remain with you till the week's end. Are you satisfied!"

"'No," was the first filial impulse of my heart; but Edmund pressed my arm with such an entreating look, that almost against my will I answered "Yes."

'Mr Everest overwhelmed my mother with his delight and gratitude. She walked up and down for some time longer, leaning on his arm—she was very fond of him; then stood looking on the river, upwards and downwards.

"'I suppose this is my last walk in London. Thank you for all the care you have taken of me. And when I am gone home—mind, oh, mind, Edmond, that you take special care of Dorothy."

'These words, and the tone in which they were spoken, fixed themselves on my mind—first, from gratitude, not unmingled with regret, as if I had not been so considerate to her as she to me; afterwards— But we often err, my dear, in dwelling too much on that word. We finite creatures have only to deal with "now"—nothing whatever to do with "afterwards". In this case, I have ceased to blame myself or others. Whatever was, being past, was right to be, and could not have been otherwise.

'My mother went home next morning, alone. We were to follow in a few days, though she would not allow us to fix any time. Her departure was so hurried that I remember nothing about it, save her answer to my father's urgent desire—almost command—that if anything went amiss she would immediately let him know.

"'Under all circumstances, wife," he reiterated, "this you promise?"

"'I promise."

'Though when she was gone he declared she need not have said it so earnestly, since we should be at home almost as soon as the slow Bath coach could take her there and bring us back a letter.

'And besides, there was nothing likely to happen. But he fidgeted a good deal, being unused to her absence in their happy wedded life. He was, like most men, glad to blame anybody but himself, and the whole day, and the next, was cross at intervals with both Edmond and me; but we bore it—and patiently.

"'It will be all right when we get him to the theatre. He has no real cause for anxiety about her. What a dear woman she is, and a precious—your mother, Dorothy!"

'I rejoiced to hear my lover speak thus, and thought there hardly ever was young gentlewoman so blessed as I.

'We went to the play. Ah, you know nothing of what a play is, nowadays. You never saw *John Kemble and Mrs Siddons*. Though in dresses and shows it was far inferior to the *Hamlet* you took me to see last week, my dear—and though I perfectly well remember being on the point of laughing when in the most solemn scene, it became clearly evident that the Ghost had been drinking. Strangely enough, no after events connected therewith ever were able to drive from my mind the vivid impression of this my first play. Strange, also, that the play should have been Hamlet. Do you think that Shakespeare believed in—in what people call "ghosts?"

I could not say; but I thought Mrs MacArthur's ghost very long in coming.

'Don't, my dear—don't; do anything but laugh at it.'

She was visibly affected, and it was not without an effort that she proceeded in her story.

'I wish you to understand exactly my position that night—a young girl, her head full of the enchantment of the stage——-her heart of something not less engrossing. Mr Everest had supped with us, leaving us both in the best of spirits; indeed, my father had gone to bed, laughing heartily at the remembrance of the antics of Mr Grimaldi, which had almost obliterated the Queen and Hamlet from his memory, on which the ridiculous always took a far stronger hold than the awful or sublime.

'I was sitting—let me see—at the window, chatting with my maid Patty, who was brushing the powder out of my hair. The window was open half-way, and looking out on the Thames; and the summer night being very warm and starry, made it almost like sitting out of doors. There was none of the awe given by the solitude of a closed room, when every sound is magnified, and every shadow seems alive.

'As I said, we had been chatting and laughing; for Patty and I were both very young, and she had a sweetheart, too. She, like every one of our household, was a warm admirer of Mr Everest. I had just been half scolding, half smiling at her praises of him, when St Paul's great clock came booming over the silent river.

'"Eleven," counted Patty. "Terrible late we be, Mistress Dorothy: not like Bath hours, I reckon."

'"Mother will have been in bed an hour ago," said I, with a little self-reproach at not having thought of her till now.

'The next minute my maid and I both started up with a simultaneous exclamation.

'"Did you hear that?"

'"Yes, a bat flying against the window."

'"But the lattices are open, Mistress Dorothy."

'So, they were; and there was no bird or bat or living thing about—only the quiet summer night, the river, and the stars.

'"I be certain sure I heard it. And I think it was like—just a bit like—somebody tapping.

'"Nonsense, Patty!" But it had struck me thus—though I said it was a bat. It was exactly like the sound of fingers against a pane—very soft, gentle fingers, such as, in passing into her flower-garden, my mother used often to tap outside the schoolroom casement at home.

'"I wonder, did father hear anything. It—the bird, you know, Patty—might have flown at his window, too?"

'"Oh, Mistress Dorothy!" Patty would not be deceived. I gave her the brush to finish my hair, but her hand shook too much. I shut the window, and we both sat down facing it.

'At that minute, distinct, clear, and unmistakable, like a person giving a summons in passing by, we heard once more the tapping on the pane. But nothing was seen; not a single shadow came between us and the open air; the bright starlight.

'Startled I was, and awed, but I was not frightened. The sound gave me even an inexplicable delight. But I had hardly time to recognise my feelings, still less to analyse them, when a loud cry came from my father's room.

'"Dolly,—Dolly!"

'Now my mother and I had both one name, but he always gave her the old-fashioned pet name,—I was invariably Dorothy. Still I did not pause to think, but ran to his locked door and answered.

'It was a long time before he took any notice, though I heard him talking to himself, and moaning. He was subject to bad dreams, especially before his attacks of gout. So, my first alarm lightened. I stood listening, knocking at intervals, until at last he replied.

'"What do 'ee want, child?"

'"Is anything the matter, father?"

'"Nothing. Go to thy bed, Dorothy."

'"Did you not call? Do you want anyone?"

'"Not thee. O Dolly, my poor Dolly,"—and he seemed to be almost sobbing, "why did I let thee leave me?"

"'Father, you are not going to be ill? It is not the gout, is it? (for that was the time when he wanted my mother most, and, indeed, when he was wholly unmanageable by anyone but her.)"

"'Go away. Get to thy bed, girl; I don't want 'ee.'"

'I thought he was angry with me for having been in some sort the cause of our delay, and retired very miserable. Patty and I sat up a good while longer, discussing the dreary prospect of my father's having a fit of the gout here in London lodgings, with only us to nurse him, and my mother away. Our alarm was so great that we quite forgot the curious circumstance which had first attracted us, till Patty spoke up from her bed on the floor.

"'I hope master beant going to be very ill, and that noise—you know—came for a warning. Do 'ee think it was a bird, Mistress Dorothy?"

"'Very likely. Now, Patty, let us go to sleep.'"

'But I did not, for all night I heard my father groaning at intervals. I was certain it was the gout, and wished from the bottom of my heart that we had gone home with mother.

'What was my surprise when, quite early, I heard him rise and go down, just as if nothing was ailing him! I found him sitting at the breakfast-table in his travelling coat, looking very haggard and miserable, but evidently bent on a journey.

"'Father, you are not going to Bath?"

"'Yes, I be.'"

"'Not till the evening coach starts,' I cried, alarmed. "We can't, you know?"

"'I'll take a post-chaise, then. We must be off in an hour.'"

'An hour! The cruel pain of parting—(my dear, I believe I used to feel things keenly when I was young)—shot through me—through and through. A single hour, and I should have said goodbye to Edmond—one of those heart-breaking farewells when we seem to leave half of our poor young life behind us, forgetting that the only real parting is when there is no love left to part from. A few years, and I wondered how I could have crept away and wept in such intolerable agony at the mere bidding goodbye to Edmond—Edmond, who loved me!

'Every minute seemed a day till he came in, as usual, to breakfast. My red eyes and my father's corded trunk explained all.

"'Dr Thwaite, you are not going?"

'"Yes, I am," repeated my father. He sat moodily leaning on the table—would not taste his breakfast.

'"Not till the night coach, surely? I was to take you and Mistress Dorothy to see Mr Benjamin West, the king's painter."

'"Let king and painters alone, lad; I am going home to my Dolly."

'Mr Everest used many arguments, gay and grave, upon which I hung with earnest conviction and hope. He made things so clear always; he was a man of much brighter parts than my father, and had great influence over him.

'"Dorothy," he whispered, "help me to persuade the Doctor. It is so little time I beg for, only a few hours; and before so long a parting."—Ay, longer than he thought, or I.

'"Children," cried my father at last, "you are a couple of fools. Wait till you have been married twenty years. I must go to my Dolly. I know there is something amiss at home."

'I should have felt alarmed, but I saw Mr Everest smile; and besides, I was yet glowing under his fond look, as my father spoke of our being "married twenty years".

'"Father, you have surely no reason for thinking this? If you have, tell us."

'My father just lifted his head, and looked at me woefully in the face.

'"Dorothy, last night, as sure as I see you now, I saw your mother."

'"Is that all?" cried Mr Everest, laughing: "why, my good sir, very likely you did; you were dreaming about her."

'"I had not gone to sleep."

'"How did you see her?"

'"Coming into my room, just as she used to do in our bedroom at home, with the candle in her hand and the baby asleep on her arm."

'"Did she speak?" asked Mr Everest, with another and rather satirical smile; "remember, you saw *Hamlet* last night. Indeed, sir—indeed, Dorothy—it was a mere dream. I do not believe in ghosts; it would be an insult to common sense, to human wisdom—nay, even to Divinity itself."

'Edmond spoke so earnestly, justly, and withal so affectionately, that perforce I agreed; and even my father began to feel rather ashamed of his own weakness. He, a sensible man and the head of a family, to yield to a mere superstitious fancy, springing probably from a hot supper and an over-excited brain! To the same cause Mr Everest attributed the other incident, which somewhat hesitatingly I told him.

"'Dear, it was a bird; nothing but a bird. One flew in at my window last spring; it had hurt itself, and I kept it, and nursed it, and petted it. It was such a pretty gentle little thing, it put me in mind of Dorothy."

"'Did it?" said I.

"'And at last it got well and flew away."

"'Ah! that was not like Dorothy."

'Thus, my father being persuaded, it was not hard to persuade me. We settled to remain till evening. Edmond and I, with my maid Patty, went about together chiefly in Mr West's Gallery, and in the quiet shade of our favourite Temple Gardens. And if for those four stolen hours, and the sweetness in them, I afterwards suffered untold remorse and bitterness, I have entirely forgiven myself, as I know my dear mother would have forgiven me, long ago.

Mrs MacArthur stopped, wiped her eyes, and then continued— speaking more in the matter-of-fact way that old people speak in, than she had been lately doing.

'Well, my dear, where was I?'

'In the Temple Gardens.'

'Yes, yes. Then we came home to dinner. My father always enjoyed his dinner, and his nap afterwards; he had nearly recovered himself now: only looked tired from loss of rest. Edmond and I sat in the window, watching the barges and wherries down the Thames; there were no steamboats then, you know.

'Someone knocked at the door with a message for my father, but he slept so heavily he did not hear. Mr Everest went to see what it was; I stood at the window. I remember mechanically watching the red sail of a Margate hoy that was going down the river, and thinking with a sharp pang how dark the room seemed to grow, in a moment, with Edmond not there.

'Re-entering, after a somewhat long absence, he never looked at me, but went straight to my father.

"'Sir, it is almost time for you to start;" (oh! Edmond). "There is a coach at the door; and, pardon me, but I think you should travel quickly."

'My father sprang to his feet.

"Dear sir, wait one moment; I have received news from Bath. You have another little daughter, sir, and—"

"'Dolly, my Dolly!" Without another word my father rushed away, leaped into the post-chaise that was waiting and drove off.

"'Edmond!" I gasped.

'"My poor little girl—my own Dorothy!"

'By the tenderness of his embrace, less lover-like than brother-like—by his tears, for I could feel them on my neck—I knew, as well as if he had told me, that I should never see my dear mother anymore.—'She had died in childbirth' continued the old lady after a long pause—'died at night, at the same hour and minute that I had heard the tapping on the window-pane, and my father had thought he saw her coming into his room with a baby on her arm.'

'Was the baby dead, too?'

'They thought so then, but it afterwards revived.'

'What a strange story!'

'I do not ask you to believe in it. How and why and what it was I cannot tell; I only know that it assuredly was as I have told it.'

'And Mr Everest?' I inquired, after some hesitation.

The old lady shook her head. 'Ah, my dear, you may perhaps learn—though I hope you will not—how very, very seldom things turn out as one expects when one is young. After that day, I did not see Mr Everest for twenty years.

'How wrong of him—how—'

'Don't blame him; it was not his fault. You see, after that time my father took a prejudice against him—not unnatural, perhaps; and she was not there to make things straight. Besides, my own conscience was very sore, and there were the six children at home, and the little baby had no mother: so, at last I made up my mind. I should have loved him just the same if we had waited twenty years. I told him so: but he could not see things in that light. Don't blame him, my dear, don't blame him. It was as well, perhaps, as it happened.'

'Did he marry?'

'Yes, after a few years; and loved his wife dearly. When I was about one-and-thirty, I married Mr MacArthur. So, neither of us was unhappy, you see—at least, not more so than most people; and we became sincere friends afterwards. Mr and Mrs Everest come to see me still, almost every Sunday. Why, you foolish child, you are not crying?'

Ay, I was—but scarcely at the ghost story.

The Shadows on the Wall

Mary E. Wilkins Freeman

"Henry had words with Edward in the study the night before Edward died," said Caroline Glynn.

She was elderly, tall, and harshly thin, with a hard colourlessness of face. She spoke not with acrimony, but with grave severity. Rebecca Ann Glynn, younger, stouter and rosy of face between her crinkling puffs of gray hair, gasped, by way of assent. She sat in a wide flounce of black silk in the corner of the sofa, and rolled terrified eyes from her sister Caroline to her sister Mrs. Stephen Brigham, who had been Emma Glynn, the one beauty of the family. She was beautiful still, with a large, splendid, full-blown beauty; she filled a great rocking-chair with her superb bulk of femininity, and swayed gently back and forth, her black silks whispering and her black frills fluttering. Even the shock of death (for her brother Edward lay dead in the house,) could not disturb her outward serenity of demeanour. She was grieved over the loss of her brother: he had been the youngest, and she had been fond of him, but never had Emma Brigham lost sight of her own importance amidst the waters of tribulation. She was always awake to the consciousness of her own stability in the midst of vicissitudes and the splendour of her permanent bearing.

But even her expression of masterly placidity changed before her sister Caroline's announcement and her sister Rebecca Ann's gasp of terror and distress in response.

"I think Henry might have controlled his temper, when poor Edward was so near his end," said she with an asperity which disturbed slightly the roseate curves of her beautiful mouth.

"Of course he did not *know*," murmured Rebecca Ann in a faint tone strangely out of keeping with her appearance.

One involuntarily looked again to be sure that such a feeble pipe came from that full-swelling chest.

"Of course he did not know it," said Caroline quickly. She turned on her sister with a strange sharp look of suspicion. "How could he have known it?" said she. Then she shrank as if from the other's possible answer. "Of course you and I both know he could not," said she conclusively, but her pale face was paler than it had been before.

Rebecca gasped again. The married sister, Mrs. Emma Brigham, was now sitting up straight in her chair; she had ceased rocking, and was eyeing them both intently with a sudden accentuation of family likeness in her face. Given one common intensity of emotion and similar lines showed forth, and the three sisters of one race were evident.

"What do you mean?" said she impartially to them both. Then she, too, seemed to shrink before a possible answer. She even laughed an evasive sort of laugh. "I guess you don't mean anything," said she, but her face wore still the expression of shrinking horror.

"Nobody means anything," said Caroline firmly. She rose and crossed the room toward the door with grim decisiveness.

"Where are you going?" asked Mrs. Brigham.

"I have something to see to," replied Caroline, and the others at once knew by her tone that she had some solemn and sad duty to perform in the chamber of death.

"Oh," said Mrs. Brigham.

After the door had closed behind Caroline, she turned to Rebecca. "Did Henry have many words with him?" she asked.

"They were talking very loud," replied Rebecca evasively, yet with an answering gleam of ready response to the other's curiosity in the quick lift of her soft blue eyes.

Mrs. Brigham looked at her. She had not resumed rocking. She still sat up straight with a slight knitting of intensity on her fair forehead, between the pretty rippling curves of her auburn hair.

"Did you—hear anything?" she asked in a low voice with a glance toward the door.

"I was just across the hall in the south parlour, and that door was open and this door ajar," replied Rebecca with a slight flush.

"Then you must have—"

"I couldn't help it."

"Everything?"

"Most of it."

"What was it?"

"The old story."

"I suppose Henry was mad, as he always was, because Edward was living on here for nothing, when he had wasted all the money father left him."

Rebecca nodded with a fearful glance at the door.

When Emma spoke again her voice was still more hushed. "I know how he felt," said she. "He had always been so prudent himself, and worked hard at his profession, and there Edward had never done anything but spend, and it must have looked to him as if Edward was living at his expense, but he wasn't."

"No, he wasn't."

"It was the way father left the property—that all the children should have a home here—and he left money enough to buy the food and all if we had all come home."

"Yes."

"And Edward had a right here according to the terms of father's will, and Henry ought to have remembered it."

"Yes, he ought."

"Did he say hard things?"

"Pretty hard from what I heard."

"What?"

"I heard him tell Edward that he had no business here at all, and he thought he had better go away."

"What did Edward say?"

"That he would stay here as long as he lived and afterward, too, if he was a mind to, and he would like to see Henry get him out; and then—"

"What?"

"Then he laughed."

"What did Henry say."

"I didn't hear him say anything, but—"

"But what?"

"I saw him when he came out of this room."

"He looked mad?"

"You've seen him when he looked so."

Emma nodded; the expression of horror on her face had deepened.

"Do you remember that time he killed the cat because she had scratched him?"

"Yes. Don't!"

Then Caroline re-entered the room. She went up to the stove in which a wood fire was burning—it was a cold, gloomy day of fall—and she warmed her hands, which were reddened from recent washing in cold water.

Mrs. Brigham looked at her and hesitated. She glanced at the door, which was still ajar, as it did not easily shut, being still swollen with the damp weather of the summer. She rose and pushed it together with a sharp thud which jarred the house. Rebecca started painfully with a half exclamation. Caroline looked at her disapprovingly.

"It is time you controlled your nerves, Rebecca," said she.

"I can't help it," replied Rebecca with almost a wail. "I am nervous. There's enough to make me so, the Lord knows."

"What do you mean by that?" asked Caroline with her old air of sharp suspicion, and something between challenge and dread of its being met.

Rebecca shrank.

"Nothing," said she.

"Then I wouldn't keep speaking in such a fashion."

Emma, returning from the closed door, said imperiously that it ought to be fixed, it shut so hard.

"It will shrink enough after we have had the fire a few days," replied Caroline. "If anything is done to it it will be too small; there will be a crack at the sill."

"I think Henry ought to be ashamed of himself for talking as he did to Edward," said Mrs. Brigham abruptly, but in an almost inaudible voice.

"Hush!" said Caroline, with a glance of actual fear at the closed door.

"Nobody can hear with the door shut."

"He must have heard it shut, and—"

"Well, I can say what I want to before he comes down, and I am not afraid of him."

"I don't know who is afraid of him! What reason is there for anybody to be afraid of Henry?" demanded Caroline.

Mrs. Brigham trembled before her sister's look. Rebecca gasped again. "There isn't any reason, of course. Why should there be?"

"I wouldn't speak so, then. Somebody might overhear you and think it was queer. Miranda Joy is in the south parlour sewing, you know."

"I thought she went upstairs to stitch on the machine."

"She did, but she has come down again."

"Well, she can't hear."

"I say again I think Henry ought to be ashamed of himself. I shouldn't think he'd ever get over it, having words with poor Edward the very night before he died. Edward was enough sight better disposition than Henry, with all his faults. I always thought a great deal of poor Edward, myself."

Mrs. Brigham passed a large fluff of handkerchief across her eyes; Rebecca sobbed outright.

"Rebecca," said Caroline admonishingly, keeping her mouth stiff and swallowing determinately.

"I never heard him speak a cross word, unless he spoke cross to Henry that last night. I don't know, but he did from what Rebecca overheard," said Emma.

"Not so much cross as sort of soft, and sweet, and aggravating," sniffled Rebecca.

"He never raised his voice," said Caroline; "but he had his way."

"He had a right to in this case."

"Yes, he did."

"He had as much of a right here as Henry," sobbed Rebecca, "and now he's gone, and he will never be in this home that poor father left him and the rest of us again."

"What do you really think ailed Edward?" asked Emma in hardly more than a whisper. She did not look at her sister.

Caroline sat down in a nearby armchair, and clutched the arms convulsively until her thin knuckles whitened.

"I told you," said she.

Rebecca held her handkerchief over her mouth, and looked at them above it with terrified, streaming eyes.

"I know you said that he had terrible pains in his stomach, and had spasms, but what do you think made him have them?"

"Henry called it gastric trouble. You know Edward has always had dyspepsia."

Mrs. Brigham hesitated a moment. "Was there any talk of an—examination?" said she.

Then Caroline turned on her fiercely.

"No," said she in a terrible voice. "No."

The three sisters' souls seemed to meet on one common ground of terrified understanding though their eyes. The old-fashioned latch of the door was heard to rattle, and a push from without made the door shake ineffectually. "It's Henry," Rebecca sighed rather than whispered.

Mrs. Brigham settled herself after a noiseless rush across the floor into her rocking-chair again, and was swaying back and forth with her head comfortably leaning back, when the door at last yielded and Henry Glynn entered. He cast a covertly sharp, comprehensive glance at Mrs. Brigham with her elaborate calm; at Rebecca quietly huddled in the corner of the sofa with her handkerchief to her face and only one small reddened ear as attentive as a dog's uncovered and revealing her alertness for his presence; at Caroline sitting with a strained composure in her armchair by the stove. She met his eyes quite firmly with a look of inscrutable fear, and defiance of the fear and of him.

Henry Glynn looked more like this sister than the others. Both had the same hard delicacy of form and feature, both were tall and almost emaciated, both had a sparse growth of gray blond hair far back from high intellectual foreheads, both had an almost noble aquilinity of feature. They confronted each other with the pitiless immovability of two statues in whose marble lineaments emotions were fixed for all eternity.

Then Henry Glynn smiled and the smile transformed his face. He looked suddenly years younger, and an almost boyish recklessness and irresolution appeared in his face. He flung himself into a chair with a gesture which was bewildering from its incongruity with his general appearance. He leaned his head back, flung one leg over the other, and looked laughingly at Mrs. Brigham.

"I declare, Emma, you grow younger every year," he said.

She flushed a little, and her placid mouth widened at the corners. She was susceptible to praise.

"Our thoughts today ought to belong to the one of us who will *never* grow older," said Caroline in a hard voice.

Henry looked at her, still smiling. "Of course, we none of us forget that," said he, in a deep, gentle voice, "but we have to speak to the living, Caroline, and I have not seen Emma for a long time, and the living are as dear as the dead."

"Not to me," said Caroline.

She rose, and went abruptly out of the room again. Rebecca also rose and hurried after her, sobbing loudly.

Henry looked slowly after them.

"Caroline is completely unstrung," said he. Mrs. Brigham rocked. A confidence in him inspired by his manner was stealing over her. Out of that confidence she spoke quite easily and naturally.

"His death was very sudden," said she.

Henry's eyelids quivered slightly but his gaze was unswerving.

"Yes," said he; "it was very sudden. He was sick only a few hours."

"What did you call it?"

"Gastric."

"You did not think of an examination?"

"There was no need. I am perfectly certain as to the cause of his death."

Suddenly Mrs. Brigham felt a creep as of some live horror over her very soul. Her flesh prickled with cold, before an inflection of his voice. She rose, tottering on weak knees.

"Where are you going?" asked Henry in a strange, breathless voice.

Mrs. Brigham said something incoherent about some sewing which she had to do, some black for the funeral, and was out of the room. She went up to the front chamber which she occupied. Caroline was there. She went close to her and took her hands, and the two sisters looked at each other.

"Don't speak, don't, I won't have it!" said Caroline finally in an awful whisper.

"I won't," replied Emma.

That afternoon the three sisters were in the study, the large front room on the ground floor across the hall from the south parlour, when the dusk deepened.

Mrs. Brigham was hemming some black material. She sat close to the west window for the waning light. At last she laid her work on her lap.

"It's no use, I cannot see to sew another stitch until we have a light," said she.

Caroline, who was writing some letters at the table, turned to Rebecca, in her usual place on the sofa.

"Rebecca, you had better get a lamp," she said.

Rebecca started up; even in the dusk her face showed her agitation.

"It doesn't seem to me that we need a lamp quite yet," she said in a piteous, pleading voice like a child's.

"Yes, we do," returned Mrs. Brigham peremptorily. "We must have a light. I must finish this tonight or I can't go to the funeral, and I can't see to sew another stitch."

"Caroline can see to write letters, and she is farther from the window than you are," said Rebecca.

"Are you trying to save kerosene or are you lazy, Rebecca Glynn?"

cried Mrs. Brigham. "I can go and get the light myself, but I have this work all in my lap."

Caroline's pen stopped scratching.

"Rebecca, we must have the light," said she.

"Had we better have it in here?" asked Rebecca weakly.

"Of course! Why not?" cried Caroline sternly.

"I am sure I don't want to take my sewing into the other room, when it is all cleaned up for tomorrow," said Mrs. Brigham.

"Why, I never heard such a to-do about lighting a lamp."

Rebecca rose and left the room. Presently she entered with a lamp—a large one with a white porcelain shade. She set it on a table, an old-fashioned card-table which was placed against the opposite wall from the window. That wall was clear of bookcases and books, which were only on three sides of the room. That opposite wall was taken up with three doors, the one small space being occupied by the table. Above the table on the old-fashioned paper, of a white satin gloss, traversed by an indeterminate green scroll, hung quite high a small gilt and black-framed ivory miniature taken in her girlhood of the mother of the family. When the lamp was set on the table beneath it, the tiny pretty face painted on the ivory seemed to gleam out with a look of intelligence.

"What have you put that lamp over there for?" asked Mrs. Brigham, with more of impatience than her voice usually revealed. "Why didn't you set it in the hall and have done with it. Neither Caroline nor I can see if it is on that table."

"I thought perhaps you would move," replied Rebecca hoarsely.

"If I do move, we can't both sit at that table. Caroline has her paper all spread around. Why don't you set the lamp on the study table in the middle of the room, then we can both see?"

Rebecca hesitated. Her face was very pale. She looked with an appeal that was fairly agonizing at her sister Caroline.

"Why don't you put the lamp on this table, as she says?" asked Caroline, almost fiercely. "Why do you act so, Rebecca?"

"I should think you *would* ask her that," said Mrs. Brigham. "She doesn't act like herself at all."

Rebecca took the lamp and set it on the table in the middle of the room without another word. Then she turned her back upon it quickly and seated herself on the sofa, and placed a hand over her eyes as if to shade them, and remained so.

"Does the light hurt your eyes, and is that the reason why you didn't want the lamp?" asked Mrs. Brigham kindly.

"I always like to sit in the dark," replied Rebecca chokingly. Then she snatched her handkerchief hastily from her pocket and began to weep. Caroline continued to write, Mrs. Brigham to sew.

Suddenly Mrs. Brigham as she sewed glanced at the opposite wall. The glance became a steady stare. She looked intently, her work suspended in her hands. Then she looked away again and took a few more stitches, then she looked again, and again turned to her task. At last she laid her work in her lap and stared concentratedly. She looked from the wall around the room, taking note of the various objects; she looked at the wall long and intently. Then she turned to her sisters.

"What *is* that?" said she.

"What?" asked Caroline harshly; her pen scratched loudly across the paper.

Rebecca gave one of her convulsive gasps.

"That strange shadow on the wall," replied Mrs. Brigham.

Rebecca sat with her face hidden: Caroline dipped her pen in the inkstand.

"Why don't you turn around and look?" asked Mrs. Brigham in a wondering and somewhat aggrieved way.

"I am in a hurry to finish this letter, if Mrs. Wilson Ebbit is going to get word in time to come to the funeral," replied Caroline shortly.

Mrs. Brigham rose, her work slipping to the floor, and she began walking around the room, moving various articles of furniture, with her eyes on the shadow.

Then suddenly she shrieked out:

"Look at this awful shadow! What is it? Caroline, look, look! Rebecca, look! *What is it?*"

All Mrs. Brigham's triumphant placidity was gone. Her handsome face was livid with horror. She stood stiffly pointing at the shadow.

"Look!" said she, pointing her finger at it. "Look! What is it?"

Then Rebecca burst out in a wild wail after a shuddering glance at the wall:

"Oh, Caroline, there it is again! There it is again!"

"Caroline Glynn, you look!" said Mrs. Brigham. "Look! What is that dreadful shadow?"

Caroline rose, turned, and stood confronting the wall.

"How should I know?" she said.

"It has been there every night since he died," cried Rebecca.

"Every night?"

"Yes. He died Thursday and this is Saturday; that makes three nights," said Caroline rigidly. She stood as if holding herself calm with a vise of concentrated will.

"It—it looks like—like—" stammered Mrs. Brigham in a tone of intense horror.

"I know what it looks like well enough," said Caroline. "I've got eyes in my head."

"It looks like Edward," burst out Rebecca in a sort of frenzy of fear. "Only—"

"Yes, it does," assented Mrs. Brigham, whose horror-stricken tone matched her sister's, "only— Oh, it is awful! What is it, Caroline?"

"I ask you again, how should I know?" replied Caroline. "I see it there like you. How should I know any more than you?"

"It *must* be something in the room," said Mrs. Brigham, staring wildly around.

"We moved everything in the room the first night it came," said Rebecca; "it is not anything in the room."

Caroline turned upon her with a sort of fury. "Of course it is something in the room," said she. "How you act! What do you mean by talking so? Of course it is something in the room."

"Of course, it is," agreed Mrs. Brigham, looking at Caroline suspiciously. "Of course it must be. It is only a coincidence. It just happens so. Perhaps it is that fold of the window curtain that makes it. It must be something in the room."

"It is not anything in the room," repeated Rebecca with obstinate horror.

The door opened suddenly and Henry Glynn entered. He began to speak, then his eyes followed the direction of the others'. He stood stock still staring at the shadow on the wall. It was life size and stretched across the white parallelogram of a door, half across the wall space on which the picture hung.

"What is that?" he demanded in a strange voice.

"It must be due to something in the room," Mrs. Brigham said faintly.

"It is not due to anything in the room," said Rebecca again with the shrill insistency of terror.

"How you act, Rebecca Glynn," said Caroline.

Henry Glynn stood and stared a moment longer. His face showed a gamut of emotions—horror, conviction, then furious incredulity. Suddenly he began hastening hither and thither about the room. He moved the furniture with fierce jerks, turning ever to see the effect upon the shadow on the wall. Not a line of its terrible outlines wavered.

"It must be something in the room!" he declared in a voice which seemed to snap like a lash.

His face changed. The inmost secrecy of his nature seemed evident until one almost lost sight of his lineaments. Rebecca stood close to her sofa, regarding him with woeful, fascinated eyes. Mrs. Brigham clutched Caroline's hand. They both stood in a corner out of his way. For a few moments he raged about the room like a caged wild animal. He moved every piece of furniture; when the moving of a piece did not affect the shadow, he flung it to the floor, the sisters watching.

Then suddenly he desisted. He laughed and began straightening the furniture which he had flung down.

"What an absurdity," he said easily. "Such a to-do about a shadow."

"That's so," assented Mrs. Brigham, in a scared voice which she tried to make natural. As she spoke she lifted a chair near her.

"I think you have broken the chair that Edward was so fond of," said Caroline.

Terror and wrath were struggling for expression on her face. Her mouth was set, her eyes shrinking. Henry lifted the chair with a show of anxiety.

"Just as good as ever," he said pleasantly. He laughed again, looking at his sisters. "Did I scare you?" he said. "I should think you might be used to me by this time. You know my way of wanting to leap to the bottom of a mystery, and that shadow does look—queer, like—and I thought if there was any way of accounting for it I would like to without any delay."

"You don't seem to have succeeded," remarked Caroline dryly, with a slight glance at the wall.

Henry's eyes followed hers and he quivered perceptibly.

"Oh, there is no accounting for shadows," he said, and he laughed again. "A man is a fool to try to account for shadows."

Then the supper bell rang, and they all left the room, but Henry kept his back to the wall, as did, indeed, the others.

Mrs. Brigham pressed close to Caroline as she crossed the hall. "He looked like a demon!" she breathed in her ear.

Henry led the way with an alert motion like a boy; Rebecca brought up the rear; she could scarcely walk, her knees trembled so.

"I can't sit in that room again this evening," she whispered to Caroline after supper.

"Very well, we will sit in the south room," replied Caroline. "I think we will sit in the south parlour," she said aloud; "it isn't as damp as the study, and I have a cold."

So they all sat in the south room with their sewing. Henry read the newspaper, his chair drawn close to the lamp on the table. About nine o'clock he rose abruptly and crossed the hall to the study. The three sisters looked at one another. Mrs. Brigham rose, folded her rustling skirts compactly around her, and began tiptoeing toward the door.

"What are you going to do?" inquired Rebecca agitatedly.

"I am going to see what he is about," replied Mrs. Brigham cautiously.

She pointed as she spoke to the study door across the hall; it was ajar. Henry had striven to pull it together behind him, but it had somehow swollen beyond the limit with curious speed. It was still ajar and a streak of light showed from top to bottom. The hall lamp was not lit.

"You had better stay where you are," said Caroline with guarded sharpness.

"I am going to see," repeated Mrs. Brigham firmly.

Then she folded her skirts so tightly that her bulk with its swelling curves was revealed in a black silk sheath, and she went with a slow toddle across the hall to the study door. She stood there, her eye at the crack.

In the south room Rebecca stopped sewing and sat watching with dilated eyes. Caroline sewed steadily. What Mrs. Brigham, standing at the crack in the study door, saw was this:

Henry Glynn, evidently reasoning that the source of the strange shadow must be between the table on which the lamp stood and the wall, was making systematic passes and thrusts all over and through the intervening space with an old sword which had belonged to his father. Not an inch was left unpierced. He seemed to have divided the space into mathematical sections. He brandished the sword with a sort of cold fury and calculation; the blade gave out flashes of light, the shadow remained unmoved. Mrs. Brigham, watching, felt herself cold with horror.

Finally Henry ceased and stood with the sword in hand and raised as if to strike, surveying the shadow on the wall threateningly. Mrs. Brigham toddled back across the hall and shut the south room door behind her before she related what she had seen.

"He looked like a demon!" she said again. "Have you got any of that old wine in the house, Caroline? I don't feel as if I could stand much more."

Indeed, she looked overcome. Her handsome placid face was worn and strained and pale.

"Yes, there's plenty," said Caroline; "you can have some when you go to bed."

"I think we had all better take some," said Mrs. Brigham. "Oh, my God, Caroline, what—"

"Don't ask and don't speak," said Caroline.

"No, I am not going to," replied Mrs. Brigham; "but—"

Rebecca moaned aloud.

"What are you doing that for?" asked Caroline harshly.

"Poor Edward," returned Rebecca.

"That is all you have to groan for," said Caroline. "There is nothing else."

"I am going to bed," said Mrs. Brigham. "I sha'n't be able to be at the funeral if I don't."

Soon the three sisters went to their chambers and the south parlour was deserted. Caroline called to Henry in the study to put out the light before he came upstairs. They had been gone about an hour when he came into the room bringing the lamp which had stood in the study. He set it on the table and waited a few minutes, pacing up and down. His face was terrible, his fair complexion showed livid; his blue eyes seemed dark blanks of awful reflections.

Then he took the lamp up and returned to the library. He set the lamp on the centre table, and the shadow sprang out on the wall. Again he studied the furniture and moved it about, but deliberately, with none of his former frenzy. Nothing affected the shadow. Then he returned to the south room with the lamp and again waited. Again he returned to the study and placed the lamp on the table, and the shadow sprang out upon the wall. It was midnight before he went upstairs. Mrs. Brigham and the other sisters, who could not sleep, heard him.

The next day was the funeral. That evening the family sat in the south room. Some relatives were with them. Nobody entered the study until Henry carried a lamp in there after the others had retired for the night. He saw again the shadow on the wall leap to an awful life before the light.

The next morning at breakfast Henry Glynn announced that he had to go to the city for three days. The sisters looked at him with surprise. He very seldom left home, and just now his practice had been neglected on account of Edward's death. He was a physician.

"How can you leave your patients now?" asked Mrs. Brigham wonderingly.

"I don't know how to, but there is no other way," replied Henry easily. "I have had a telegram from Doctor Mitford."

"Consultation?" inquired Mrs. Brigham.

"I have business," replied Henry.

Doctor Mitford was an old classmate of his who lived in a neighbouring city and who occasionally called upon him in the case of a consultation.

After he had gone Mrs. Brigham said to Caroline that after all Henry had not said that he was going to consult with Doctor Mitford, and she thought it very strange.

"Everything is very strange," said Rebecca with a shudder.

"What do you mean?" inquired Caroline sharply.

"Nothing," replied Rebecca.

Nobody entered the library that day, nor the next, nor the next. The third day Henry was expected home, but he did not arrive and the last train from the city had come.

"I call it pretty queer work," said Mrs. Brigham. "The idea of a doctor leaving his patients for three days anyhow, at such a time as this, and I know he has some very sick ones; he said so. And the idea of a consultation lasting three days! There is no sense in it, and *now* he has not come. I don't understand it, for my part."

"I don't either," said Rebecca.

They were all in the south parlour. There was no light in the study opposite, and the door was ajar.

Presently Mrs. Brigham rose—she could not have told why; something seemed to impel her, some will outside her own. She went out of the room, again wrapping her rustling skirts around that she might pass noiselessly, and began pushing at the swollen door of the study.

"She has not got any lamp," said Rebecca in a shaking voice.

Caroline, who was writing letters, rose again, took a lamp (there were two in the room) and followed her sister. Rebecca had risen, but she stood trembling, not venturing to follow.

The doorbell rang, but the others did not hear it; it was on the south door on the other side of the house from the study. Rebecca, after hesitating until the bell rang the second time, went to the door; she remembered that the servant was out.

Caroline and her sister Emma entered the study. Caroline set the lamp on the table. They looked at the wall. "Oh, my God," gasped Mrs. Brigham, "there are—there are *two*—shadows." The sisters stood clutching each other, staring at the awful things on the wall. Then Rebecca came in, staggering, with a telegram in her hand. "Here is—a telegram," she gasped. "Henry is—dead."

The Last Stage Coachman
Wilkie Collins

The last stage coachman! It falls upon the ear of everyone but a shareholder in railways, with a boding, melancholy sound. In spite of our natural reverence for the wonders of science, our hearts grow heavy at the thought of never again beholding the sweet-smelling nosegay, the unimpeachable top boots, and fair white breeches; once so prominent as the uniform of the fraternity. With all respect for expeditious and business-like travelling, we experience a feeling nearly akin to disgust, at being marshalled to our places by a bell and a fellow with a badge on his shoulder; instead of hearing the cheery summons 'Now then, gentlemen,' and being regaled by a short and instructive conversation with a ruddy-faced personage in a dustless olive green coat and prismatic belcher handkerchief.

What did we want with smoke? Had we not the coachman's cigar, if we were desirous of observing its shapes and appearances? Who would be so unreasonable as to languish for steam, when he could inhale it on a cool, autumnal morning, naturally concocted from the backs of four blood horses? Who!—Alas! We may propose questions and find out answers to the end of the chapter, and yet fail in reforming the perverted taste of the present generation; we know that the attempt is useless, and we give up in sorrowful and philosophic resignation, and proceed undaunted by the probable sneers of railway directors, to the recital of—

A Vision
Methought I walked forth one autumn evening to observe the arrival of a stage coach. I wandered on, yet nothing of the kind met my eye. I tried many an old public road—they were now grass-grown and miry, or desecrated by the abominable presence of a 'station.' I wended my way towards a famous roadside

inn: it was desolate and silent, or in other words, 'To Let.' I looked for 'the commercial room:' not a pot of beer adorned the mouldering tables, and not a pipe lay scattered over the wild and beautiful seclusions of its once numerous 'boxes.' It was deserted and useless; the voice of the traveller rung no longer round its walls, and the merry horn of the guard startled no more the sleepy few, who once congregated round its hospitable door. The chill fireplace and broad, antiquated mantelpiece presented but one bill—the starting time of an adjacent railroad; surmounted by a representation of those engines of destruction, in dull, frowsy lithograph.

I turned to the yard. Where was the ostler with his unbraced breeches and his upturned shirt sleeves? Where was the stable boy with his wisp of straw and his sieve of oats? Where were the coquettish mares and the tall blood horses? Where was the manger and the stable door?—All gone—all disappeared: the buildings dilapidated and tottering—of what use is a stable to a stoker? The ostler and stable boy had passed away—what fellowship have either with a boiler?

The inn yard was no more! The very dunghill in its farthest corner was choked by dust and old bricks, and the cock, the pride of the country round, clamoured no longer on the ruined and unsightly wall. I thought it was possible that he had satisfied long since the cravings of a railway committee; and I sat down on a ruined water-tub to give way to the melancholy reflections called up by the sight before me.

I know not how long I meditated. There was no officious waiter to ask me, 'What I would please to order?' No chambermaid to simper out 'This way, Sir,'—not even a stray cat to claim acquaintance with the calves of my legs, or a horse's hoof to tread upon my toe. There was nothing to disturb my miserable reverie, and I anathematised railways without distinction or exception.

The distant sound of slow and stealthy footsteps at last attracted my attention. I looked to the far end of the yard. Heavens above! A stage coachman was pacing its worn and weedy pavement.

There was no mistaking him—he wore the low-crowned, broadbrimmed, whitey-brown, well-brushed hat; the voluminous checked neckcloth; the ample-skirted coat; the striped waistcoat; the white cords; and last, not least, the immortal boots. But alas! The calf that had once filled them out, had disappeared; they clanked heavily on the pavement, instead of creaking tightly and noisily wherever he went.

His waistcoat, evidently once filled almost to bursting, hung in loose, uncomfortable folds about his emaciated waist: large wrinkles marred the former beauty of the fit of his coat: and his face was all lines and furrows, instead of smiles and jollity. The spirit of the fraternity had passed away from him—he was the stage coachman only in dress.

He walked backwards and forwards for some time without turning his head one way or the other, except now and then to peer into the deserted stable, or to glance mournfully at the whip held in his hand: at last the sound of the arrival of a train struck upon his ear!

He drew himself up to his full height, slowly and solemnly shook his clenched fist in the direction of the sound, and looked—Oh that look! it spoke annihilation to the mightiest engine upon the rail, it scoffed at steam, and flashed furious derision at the largest terminus that ever was erected; it was an awfully comprehensive look—the concentrated essence of the fierce and deadly enmity of all the stage coachmen in England to steam conveyance.

To my utter astonishment, not, it must be owned, unmixed with fear, he suddenly turned his eyes towards my place of shelter, and walked up to me.

'That's the rail,' said he, between his set teeth.

'It is,' said I, considerably embarrassed.

'Damn it!' returned the excited Stage Coachman.

There was something inexpressibly awful about this execration; and I confess I felt a strong internal conviction that the next day's paper would teem with horrible railway accidents in every column.

'I did my utmost to hoppose 'em,' said the Stage Coachman, in softened accents. 'I wos the last that guv' in, I kep' a losing day after day, and yet I worked on; I wos determined to do my dooty, and I drove a coach the last day with an old hooman and a carpet bag inside, and three little boys and seven whopping empty portmanteaus outside. I wos determined my last kick to have some passengers to show to the rail, so I took my wife and children 'cos nobody else wouldn't go, and then we guv' in. Hows'ever, the last time as I wos on the road I didn't go and show 'em an empty coach—we wasn't full, but we wasn't empty; we wos game to the last!'

A grim smile of triumph lit up the features of the deposed Coachman as he gave vent to this assertion. He took hold of me by the button-hole, and led the way into the house.

'This landlord wos an austerious sort of a man,' said he; 'he used to hobserve, that he only wished a Railway Committee would dine at his house, he'd pison 'em all, and emigrate; and he'd ha' done it, too!'

I did not venture to doubt this, so the Stage Coachman continued.

'I've smoked my pipe by the hour together in that fireplace; I've read *The Times* advertisements and Perlice Reports in that box till I fell asleep; I've walked up and down this here room a saying all sorts of things about the rail, and a busting for happiness. Outside this wery door I've bin a drownded in thankys from ladies for never lettin' nobody step through their band-boxes. The chambermaids used to smile, and the dogs used to bark, wherever I came.—But it's all hover now—the poor feller as kep' this place takes tickets at a Station, and the chambermaids makes scalding hot tea behind a mahuggany counter for people as has no time to drink it in!'

As the Stage Coachman uttered these words, a contemptuous sneer puckered in his sallow cheek. He led me back into the yard; the ruined appearance of which, looked doubly mournful, under the faint rays of moonlight that every here and there stole through the dilapidated walls of the stable. An owl had taken up his abode, where the chief ostler's bedroom had once rejoiced in the grotesque majesty of huge portraits of every winner of every 'Derby,' since the first days of Epsom. The bird of night flew heavily off at our approach, and my companion pointed gloomily up to the fragments of mouldy, worm-eaten wood, the last relics of the stable loft.

'He wos a great friend of mine, was that h'ostler,' said the Coachman, 'but he's left this railway-bothered world—he wos finished by the train.'

At my earnest entreaty to hear further, he continued,

'When this h'old place wos guv' up and ruinated; the h'ostler as 'ud never look at the rail before, went down to have a sight of it, and as he wos a leaning his elbows on the wall, and a wishing as how he had the stabling of all the steam h'ingines (he'd ha' done 'em justice!) wot should he see, but one of his osses as wos thrown out of employ by the rail, a walking along jist where the train wos coming.

'Bill jumped down, and as he wos a leading of him h'off, up comes the train, and went over his leg and cut the 'os in two—"Tom," says he to me when we picked him up; "I'm a going eleven mile an hour, to the last stage as is left for me to do. I've always done my dooty with the osses; I've bin and done it now—bury that ere poor os and me out of the noise of the rail." We got the surgeons to him, but he never spoke no more, Poor Bill! Poor Bill!'

This last recollection seemed too much for the Stage Coachman, he wrung my hand, and walked abruptly to the farthest corner of the yard.

I took care not to interrupt him, and watched him carefully from a distance.

At first, the one expression of his countenance was melancholy; but by degrees, other thoughts came crowding from his mind, and mantled on his woe-be-gone visage. Poor fellow, I could see that he was again in imagination the beloved of the ladies and the adored of the chambermaids: a faint reflection of the affable, yet majestic demeanour, required by his calling, flitted occasionally over his pinched, attenuated features: and brightened the cold, melancholy expression of his countenance.

As I still looked, it grew darker and darker, yet the face of the Stage Coachman was never for an instant hidden from me. The same artificial expression of pleasure characterised its lineaments as before. Suddenly I heard a strange, unnatural noise in the air—now it seemed like the distant trampling of horses; and now again, like the rumbling of a heavily laden coach along a public road.

A faint, sickly light, spread itself over that part of the Heavens whence the sounds proceeded; and after an interval, a fully equipped Stage Coach appeared in the clouds, with a railway director strapped fast to each wheel, and a stoker between the teeth of each of the four horses.

In place of luggage, fragments of broken steam carriages, and red carpet bags filled with other mementos of railway accidents, occupied the roof. Chance passengers appeared to be the only tenants of the outside places. In front sat Julius Cæsar and Mrs Hannah Moore; and behind, Sir Joseph Banks and Mrs Brownrigge. Of all the 'insides,' I could, I grieve to say, see nothing.

On the box was a little man with fuzzy hair and large iron grey whiskers; clothed in a coat of engineers' skin, with gloves of the hide of railway police. He pulled up opposite my friend, and bowing profoundly motioned to him to the box seat.

A gleam of unutterable joy irradiated the Stage Coachman's countenance, as he stepped lightly into his place, seized the reins, and with one hearty 'good night,' addressed to an imaginary inn-full of people, started the horses.

Off they drove! My friend in the plenitude of his satisfaction cracking the whip every instant as he drove the phantom coach into the air. And amidst the shrieks of the railway directors at the wheel, the groans of James Watt, the bugle of the guard, and the tremendous cursing of the invisible 'insides,' fast and furiously disappeared from my eyes.

The Story of the Inexperienced Ghost

H. G. Wells

The scene amidst which Clayton told his last story comes back very vividly to my mind. There he sat, for the greater part of the time, in the corner of the authentic settle by the spacious open fire, and Sanderson sat beside him smoking the Broseley clay that bore his name. There was Evans, and that marvel among actors, Wish, who is also a modest man. We had all come down to the Mermaid Club that Saturday morning, except Clayton, who had slept there overnight—which indeed gave him the opening of his story. We had golfed until golfing was invisible; we had dined, and we were in that mood of tranquil kindliness when men will suffer a story. When Clayton began to tell one, we naturally supposed he was lying. It may be that indeed he was lying—of that the reader will speedily be able to judge as well as I. He began, it is true, with an air of matter-of-fact anecdote, but that we thought was only the incurable artifice of the man.

"I say!" he remarked, after a long consideration of the upward rain of sparks from the log that Sanderson had thumped, "you know I was alone here last night?"

"Except for the domestics," said Wish.

"Who sleep in the other wing," said Clayton. "Yes. Well—" He pulled at his cigar for some little time as though he still hesitated about his confidence. Then he said, quite quietly, "I caught a ghost!"

"Caught a ghost, did you?" said Sanderson. "Where is it?"

And Evans, who admires Clayton immensely and has been four weeks in America, shouted, "Caught a ghost, did you, Clayton? I'm glad of it! Tell us all about it right now."

Clayton said he would in a minute, and asked him to shut the door.

He looked apologetically at me. "There's no eavesdropping of course, but we don't want to upset our very excellent service with any rumours of ghosts in the place. There's too much shadow and oak panelling to trifle with that. And this, you know, wasn't a regular ghost. I don't think it will come again—ever."

"You mean to say you didn't keep it?" said Sanderson.

"I hadn't the heart to," said Clayton.

And Sanderson said he was surprised.

We laughed, and Clayton looked aggrieved. "I know," he said, with the flicker of a smile, "but the fact is it really was a ghost, and I'm as sure of it as I am that I am talking to you now. I'm not joking. I mean what I say."

Sanderson drew deeply at his pipe, with one reddish eye on Clayton, and then emitted a thin jet of smoke more eloquent than many words.

Clayton ignored the comment. "It is the strangest thing that has ever happened in my life. You know, I never believed in ghosts or anything of the sort, before, ever; and then, you know, I bag one in a corner; and the whole business is in my hands."

He meditated still more profoundly, and produced and began to pierce a second cigar with a curious little stabber he affected.

"You talked to it?" asked Wish.

"For the space, probably, of an hour."

"Chatty?" I said, joining the party of the sceptics.

"The poor devil was in trouble," said Clayton, bowed over his cigar-end and with the very faintest note of reproof.

"Sobbing?" some one asked.

Clayton heaved a realistic sigh at the memory. "Good Lord!" he said; "yes." And then, "Poor fellow! yes."

"Where did you strike it?" asked Evans, in his best American accent.

"I never realised," said Clayton, ignoring him, "the poor sort of thing a ghost might be," and he hung us up again for a time, while he sought for matches in his pocket and lit and warmed to his cigar.

"I took an advantage," he reflected at last.

We were none of us in a hurry. "A character," he said, "remains just the same character for all that it's been disembodied. That's a thing we too often forget. People with a certain strength or fixity of purpose may have ghosts of a certain strength and fixity of purpose—most haunting ghosts, you know, must be as one-idea'd as monomaniacs and as obstinate as mules to come back again and again. This poor creature wasn't." He suddenly looked up rather queerly, and his eye went round the room. "I say it," he said, "in all kindliness, but that is the plain truth of the case. Even at the first glance he struck me as weak."

He punctuated with the help of his cigar.

"I came upon him, you know, in the long passage. His back was towards me and I saw him first. Right off I knew him for a ghost. He was transparent and whitish; clean through his chest I could see the glimmer of the little window at the end. And not only his physique but his attitude struck me as being weak. He looked, you know, as though he didn't know in the slightest whatever he meant to do. One hand was on the panelling and the other fluttered to his mouth. Like—*So!*"

"What sort of physique?" said Sanderson.

"Lean. You know that sort of young man's neck that has two great flutings down the back, here and here—so! And a little, meanish head with scrubby hair—And rather bad ears. Shoulders bad, narrower than the hips; turn-down collar, ready-made short jacket, trousers baggy and a little frayed at the heels. That's how he took me. I came very quietly up the staircase. I did not carry a light, you know—the candles are on the landing table and there is that lamp—and I was in my list slippers, and I saw him as I came up. I stopped dead at that—taking him in. I wasn't a bit afraid. I think that in most of these affairs one is never nearly so afraid or excited as one imagines one would be. I was surprised and interested. I thought, 'Good Lord! Here's a ghost at last! And I haven't believed for a moment in ghosts during the last five-and-twenty years.'"

"Um," said Wish.

"I suppose I wasn't on the landing a moment before he found out I was there. He turned on me sharply, and I saw the face of an immature young man, a weak nose, a scrubby little moustache, a feeble chin. So for an instant we stood—he looking over his shoulder at me and regarded one another. Then he seemed to remember his high calling. He turned round, drew himself up, projected his face, raised his arms, spread his hands in approved ghost fashion—came towards me. As he did so his little jaw dropped, and he emitted a faint, drawn-out 'Boo.' No, it wasn't—not a bit dreadful. I'd dined. I'd had a bottle of champagne, and being all alone, perhaps two or three—perhaps even four or five—whiskies, so I was as solid as rocks and no more frightened than if I'd been assailed by a frog. 'Boo!' I said. 'Nonsense. You don't belong to this place. What are you doing here?'

"I could see him wince. 'Boo-oo,' he said.

"'Boo—be hanged! Are you a member?' I said; and just to show I didn't care a pin for him I stepped through a corner of him and made to light my candle. 'Are you a member?' I repeated, looking at him sideways.

"He moved a little so as to stand clear of me, and his bearing became crestfallen. 'No,' he said, in answer to the persistent interrogation of my eye; 'I'm not a member—I'm a ghost.'

"'Well, that doesn't give you the run of the Mermaid Club. Is there any one you want to see, or anything of that sort?' and doing it as steadily as possible for fear that he should mistake the carelessness of whisky for the distraction of fear, I got my candle alight. I turned on him, holding it. 'What are you doing here?' I said.

"He had dropped his hands and stopped his booing, and there he stood, abashed and awkward, the ghost of a weak, silly, aimless young man. 'I'm haunting,' he said.

"'You haven't any business to,' I said in a quiet voice.

"'I'm a ghost,' he said, as if in defence.

"'That may be, but you haven't any business to haunt here. This is a respectable private club; people often stop here with nursemaids and children, and, going about in the careless way you do, some poor little mite could easily come upon you and be scared out of her wits. I suppose you didn't think of that?'

"'No, sir,' he said, 'I didn't.'

"'You should have done. You haven't any claim on the place, have you? Weren't murdered here, or anything of that sort?'

"'None, sir; but I thought as it was old and oak-panelled—'

"'That's no excuse.' I regarded him firmly. 'Your coming here is a mistake,' I said, in a tone of friendly superiority. I feigned to see if I had my matches, and then looked up at him frankly. 'If I were you I wouldn't wait for cock-crow—I'd vanish right away.'

"He looked embarrassed. 'The fact is, sir—' he began.

"'I'd vanish,' I said, driving it home.

"'The fact is, sir, that—somehow—I can't.'

"'You can't?'

"'No, sir. There's something I've forgotten. I've been hanging about here since midnight last night, hiding in the cupboards of the empty bedrooms and things like that. I'm flurried. I've never come haunting before, and it seems to put me out.'

"'Put you out?'

"'Yes, sir. I've tried to do it several times, and it doesn't come off. There's some little thing has slipped me, and I can't get back.'

"That, you know, rather bowled me over. He looked at me in such an abject way that for the life of me I couldn't keep up quite the high, hectoring vein I had adopted. 'That's queer,' I said, and as I spoke I fancied I heard some one moving about down below. 'Come into my room and tell me more about it,' I said. 'I didn't, of course, understand this,' and I tried to take him by the arm. But, of course, you might as well have tried to take hold of a puff of smoke! I had forgotten my number, I think; anyhow, I remember going into several bedrooms—it was lucky I was the only soul in that wing—until I saw my traps. 'Here we are,' I said, and sat down in the arm-chair; 'sit down and tell me all about it. It seems to me you have got yourself into a jolly awkward position, old chap.'

"Well, he said he wouldn't sit down! he'd prefer to flit up and down the room if it was all the same to me. And so he did, and in a little while we were deep in a long and serious talk. And presently, you know, something of those whiskies and sodas evaporated out of me, and I began to realise just a little what a thundering rum and weird business it was that I was in. There he was, semi-transparent— the proper conventional phantom, and noiseless except for his ghost of a voice—flitting to and fro in that nice, clean, chintz-hung old bedroom. You could see the gleam of the copper candlesticks through him, and the lights on the brass fender, and the corners of the framed engravings on the wall,—and there he was telling me all about this wretched little life of his that had recently ended on earth. He hadn't a particularly honest face, you know, but being transparent, of course, he couldn't avoid telling the truth."

"Eh?" said Wish, suddenly sitting up in his chair.

"What?" said Clayton.

"Being transparent—couldn't avoid telling the truth—I don't see it," said Wish.

"I don't see it," said Clayton, with inimitable assurance. "But it is so, I can assure you nevertheless. I don't believe he got once a nail's breadth off the Bible truth. He told me how he had been killed— he went down into a London basement with a candle to look for a leakage of gas—and described himself as a senior English master in a London private school when that release occurred."

"Poor wretch!" said I.

"That's what I thought, and the more he talked the more I thought it. There he was, purposeless in life and purposeless out of it. He talked of his father and mother and his schoolmaster, and all who had ever been anything to him in the world, meanly. He had been too sensitive, too nervous; none of them had ever valued him properly or understood him, he said. He had never had a real friend in the world, I think; he had never had a success. He had shirked games and failed examinations. 'It's like that with some people,' he said; 'whenever I got into the examination-room or anywhere everything seemed to go.' Engaged to be married of course—to another over-sensitive person, I suppose—when the indiscretion with the gas escape ended his affairs. 'And where are you now?' I asked. 'Not in——?'

"He wasn't clear on that point at all. The impression he gave me was of a sort of vague, intermediate state, a special reserve for souls too non-existent for anything so positive as either sin or virtue. I don't know. He was much too egotistical and unobservant to give me any clear idea of the kind of place, kind of country, there is on the Other Side of Things. Wherever he was, he seems to have fallen in with a set of kindred spirits: ghosts of weak Cockney young men, who were on a footing of Christian names, and among these there was certainly a lot of talk about 'going haunting' and things like that. Yes—going haunting! They seemed to think 'haunting' a tremendous adventure, and most of them funked it all the time. And so primed, you know, he had come."

"But really!" said Wish to the fire.

"These are the impressions he gave me, anyhow," said Clayton, modestly. "I may, of course, have been in a rather uncritical state, but that was the sort of background he gave to himself. He kept flitting up and down, with his thin voice going talking, talking about his wretched self, and never a word of clear, firm statement from first to last. He was thinner and sillier and more pointless than if he had been real and alive. Only then, you know, he would not have been in my bedroom here—if he had been alive. I should have kicked him out."

"Of course," said Evans, "there are poor mortals like that."

"And there's just as much chance of their having ghosts as the rest of us," I admitted.

"What gave a sort of point to him, you know, was the fact that he did seem within limits to have found himself out. The mess he had made of haunting had depressed him terribly. He had been told it would be a 'lark'; he had come expecting it to be a 'lark,' and here it was, nothing but another failure added to his record! He proclaimed himself an utter out-and-out failure. He said, and I can quite believe it, that he had never tried to do anything all his life that he hadn't made a perfect mess of—and through all the wastes of eternity he never would. If he had had sympathy, perhaps—. He paused at that, and stood regarding me. He remarked that, strange as it might seem to me, nobody, not any one, ever, had given him the amount of sympathy I was doing now. I could see what he wanted straight away, and I determined to head him off at once. I may be a brute, you know, but being the Only Real Friend, the recipient of the confidences of one of these egotistical weaklings, ghost or body, is beyond my physical endurance. I got up briskly. 'Don't you brood on these things too much,' I said. 'The thing you've got to do is to get out of this get out of this—sharp. You pull yourself together and try.' 'I can't,' he said. 'You try,' I said, and try he did."

"Try!" said Sanderson. "How?"

"Passes," said Clayton.

"Passes?"

"Complicated series of gestures and passes with the hands. That's how he had come in and that's how he had to get out again. Lord! what a business I had!"

"But how could any series of passes—?" I began.

"My dear man," said Clayton, turning on me and putting a great emphasis on certain words, "you want everything clear. I don't know how. All I know is that you do—that he did, anyhow, at least. After a fearful time, you know, he got his passes right and suddenly disappeared."

"Did you," said Sanderson, slowly, "observe the passes?"

"Yes," said Clayton, and seemed to think. "It was tremendously queer," he said. "There we were, I and this thin vague ghost, in that silent room, in this silent, empty inn, in this silent little Friday-night town. Not a sound except our voices and a faint panting he made when he swung. There was the bedroom candle, and one candle on the dressing-table alight, that was all—sometimes one or other would flare up into a tall, lean, astonished flame for a space. And queer things happened. 'I can't,' he said; 'I shall never—!' And suddenly he sat down on a little chair at the foot of the bed and began to sob and sob. Lord! what a harrowing, whimpering thing he seemed!

"'You pull yourself together,' I said, and tried to pat him on the back, and . . . my confounded hand went through him! By that time, you know, I wasn't nearly so—massive as I had been on the landing. I got the queerness of it full. I remember snatching back my hand out of him, as it were, with a little thrill, and walking over to the dressing-table. 'You pull yourself together,' I said to him, 'and try.' And in order to encourage and help him I began to try as well."

"What!" said Sanderson, "the passes?"

"Yes, the passes."

"But—" I said, moved by an idea that eluded me for a space.

"This is interesting," said Sanderson, with his finger in his pipe-bowl. "You mean to say this ghost of yours gave away—"

"Did his level best to give away the whole confounded barrier? Yes."

"He didn't," said Wish; "he couldn't. Or you'd have gone there too."

"That's precisely it," I said, finding my elusive idea put into words for me.

"That is precisely it," said Clayton, with thoughtful eyes upon the fire.

For just a little while there was silence.

"And at last he did it?" said Sanderson.

"At last he did it. I had to keep him up to it hard, but he did it at last—rather suddenly. He despaired, we had a scene, and then he got up abruptly and asked me to go through the whole performance, slowly, so that he might see. 'I believe,' he said, 'if I could see I should spot what was wrong at once.' And he did. 'I know,' he said. 'What do you know?' said I. 'I know,' he repeated. Then he said, peevishly, 'I can't do it if you look at me—I really can't; it's been that, partly, all along. I'm such a nervous fellow that you put me out.' Well, we had a bit of an argument. Naturally I wanted to see; but he was as obstinate as a mule, and suddenly I had come over as tired as a dog—he tired me out. 'All right,' I said, 'I won't look at you,' and turned towards the mirror, on the wardrobe, by the bed.

He started off very fast. I tried to follow him by looking in the looking-glass, to see just what it was had hung. Round went his arms and his hands, so, and so, and so, and then with a rush came to the last gesture of all—you stand erect and open out your arms—and so, don't you know, he stood. And then he didn't! He didn't! He wasn't! I wheeled round from the looking-glass to him. There was nothing! I was alone, with the flaring candles and a staggering mind. What had happened? Had anything happened? Had I been dreaming? . . . And then, with an absurd note of finality about it, the clock upon the landing discovered the moment was ripe for striking one. So!—Ping! And I was as grave and sober as a judge, with all my champagne and whisky gone into the vast serene. Feeling queer, you know—confoundedly queer! Queer! Good Lord!"

He regarded his cigar-ash for a moment. "That's all that happened," he said.

"And then you went to bed?" asked Evans.

"What else was there to do?"

I looked Wish in the eye. We wanted to scoff, and there was something, something perhaps in Clayton's voice and manner, that hampered our desire.

"And about these passes?" said Sanderson.

"I believe I could do them now."

"Oh!" said Sanderson, and produced a penknife and set himself to grub the dottel out of the bowl of his clay.

"Why don't you do them now?" said Sanderson, shutting his penknife with a click.

"That's what I'm going to do," said Clayton.

"They won't work," said Evans.

"If they do—" I suggested.

"You know, I'd rather you didn't," said Wish, stretching out his legs.

"Why?" asked Evans.

"I'd rather he didn't," said Wish.

"But he hasn't got 'em right," said Sanderson, plugging too much tobacco in his pipe.

"All the same, I'd rather he didn't," said Wish.

We argued with Wish. He said that for Clayton to go through those gestures was like mocking a serious matter. "But you don't believe—?" I said. Wish glanced at Clayton, who was staring into the fire, weighing something in his mind. "I do—more than half, anyhow, I do," said Wish.

"Clayton," said I, "you're too good a liar for us. Most of it was all right. But that disappearance . . . happened to be convincing. Tell us, it's a tale of cock and bull."

He stood up without heeding me, took the middle of the hearthrug, and faced me. For a moment he regarded his feet thoughtfully, and then for all the rest of the time his eyes were on the opposite wall, with an intent expression. He raised his two hands slowly to the level of his eyes and so began. . . .

Now, Sanderson is a Freemason, a member of the lodge of the Four

Kings, which devotes itself so ably to the study and elucidation of all the mysteries of Masonry past and present, and among the students of this lodge Sanderson is by no means the least. He followed Clayton's motions with a singular interest in his reddish eye. "That's not bad," he said, when it was done. "You really do, you know, put things together, Clayton, in a most amazing fashion. But there's one little detail out."

"I know," said Clayton. "I believe I could tell you which."

"Well?"

"This," said Clayton, and did a queer little twist and writhing and thrust of the hands.

"Yes."

"That, you know, was what he couldn't get right," said Clayton. "But how do you—?"

"Most of this business, and particularly how you invented it, I don't understand at all," said Sanderson, "but just that phase—I do." He reflected. "These happen to be a series of gestures—connected with a certain branch of esoteric Masonry. Probably you know. Or else—how?" He reflected still further. "I do not see I can do any harm in telling you just the proper twist. After all, if you know, you know; if you don't, you don't."

"I know nothing," said Clayton, "except what the poor devil let out last night."

"Well, anyhow," said Sanderson, and placed his churchwarden very carefully upon the shelf over the fireplace. Then very rapidly he gesticulated with his hands.

"So?" said Clayton, repeating.

"So," said Sanderson, and took his pipe in hand again.

"Ah, now," said Clayton, "I can do the whole thing—right."

He stood up before the waning fire and smiled at us all. But I think there was just a little hesitation in his smile. "If I begin—" he said.

"I wouldn't begin," said Wish.

"It's all right!" said Evans. "Matter is indestructible. You don't think any jiggery-pokery of this sort is going to snatch Clayton into the world of shades. Not it! You may try, Clayton, so far as I'm concerned, until your arms drop off at the wrists."

"I don't believe that," said Wish, and stood up and put his arm on Clayton's shoulder. "You've made me half believe in that story somehow, and I don't want to see the thing done!"

"Goodness!" said I, "here's Wish frightened!"

"I am," said Wish, with real or admirably feigned intensity. "I be-

246

lieve that if he goes through these motions right he'll go."

"He'll not do anything of the sort," I cried. "There's only one way out of this world for men, and Clayton is thirty years from that. Besides . . . And such a ghost! Do you think—?"

Wish interrupted me by moving. He walked out from among our chairs and stopped beside the tole and stood there. "Clayton," he said, "you're a fool."

Clayton, with a humorous light in his eyes, smiled back at him. "Wish," he said, "is right and all you others are wrong. I shall go. I shall get to the end of these passes, and as the last swish whistles through the air, Presto!—this hearthrug will be vacant, the room will be blank amazement, and a respectably dressed gentleman of fifteen stone will plump into the world of shades. I'm certain. So will you be. I decline to argue further. Let the thing be tried."

"No," said Wish, and made a step and ceased, and Clayton raised his hands once more to repeat the spirit's passing.

By that time, you know, we were all in a state of tension—largely because of the behaviour of Wish. We sat all of us with our eyes on Clayton—I, at least, with a sort of tight, stiff feeling about me as though from the back of my skull to the middle of my thighs my body had been changed to steel. And there, with a gravity that was imperturbably serene, Clayton bowed and swayed and waved his hands and arms before us. As he drew towards the end one piled up, one tingled in one's teeth. The last gesture, I have said, was to swing the arms out wide open, with the face held up. And when at last he swung out to this closing gesture I ceased even to breathe. It was ridiculous, of course, but you know that ghost-story feeling. It was after dinner, in a queer, old shadowy house. Would he, after all—?

There he stood for one stupendous moment, with his arms open and his upturned face, assured and bright, in the glare of the hanging lamp. We hung through that moment as if it were an age, and then came from all of us something that was half a sigh of infinite relief and half a reassuring "No!" For visibly—he wasn't going. It was all nonsense. He had told an idle story, and carried it almost to conviction, that was all! . . . And then in that moment the face of Clayton, changed.

It changed. It changed as a lit house changes when its lights are suddenly extinguished. His eyes were suddenly eyes that were fixed, his smile was frozen on his lips, and he stood there still. He stood there, very gently swaying.

That moment, too, was an age. And then, you know, chairs were

247

scraping, things were falling, and we were all moving. His knees seemed to give, and he fell forward, and Evans rose and caught him in his arms. . . .

It stunned us all. For a minute I suppose no one said a coherent thing. We believed it, yet could not believe it. . . . I came out of a muddled stupefaction to find myself kneeling beside him, and his vest and shirt were torn open, and Sanderson's hand lay on his heart. . . .

Well—the simple fact before us could very well wait our convenience; there was no hurry for us to comprehend. It lay there for an hour; it lies athwart my memory, black and amazing still, to this day. Clayton had, indeed, passed into the world that lies so near to and so far from our own, and he had gone thither by the only road that mortal man may take. But whether he did indeed pass there by that poor ghost's incantation, or whether he was stricken suddenly by apoplexy in the midst of an idle tale—as the coroner's jury would have us believe—is no matter for my judging; it is just one of those inexplicable riddles that must remain unsolved until the final solution of all things shall come. All I certainly know is that, in the very moment, in the very instant, of concluding those passes, he changed, and staggered, and fell down before us—dead!

The Festival
H. P. Lovecraft

*Efficiunt Daemones, ut quae non sunt, sic tamen
quasi sint, conspicienda hominibus exhibeant.*
—Lactantius.

I was far from home, and the spell of the eastern sea was upon me.
In the twilight I heard it pounding on the rocks, and I knew it lay just
over the hill where the twisting willows writhed against the clearing
sky and the first stars of evening. And because my fathers had called
me to the old town beyond, I pushed on through the shallow, new-
fallen snow along the road that soared lonely up to where Aldebaran
twinkled among the trees; on toward the very ancient town I had
never seen but often dreamed of.

It was the Yuletide, that men call Christmas though they know
in their hearts it is older than Bethlehem and Babylon, older than
Memphis and mankind. It was the Yuletide, and I had come at last to
the ancient sea town where my people had dwelt and kept festival
in the elder time when festival was forbidden; where also they had
commanded their sons to keep festival once every century, that the
memory of primal secrets might not be forgotten. Mine were an old
people, and were old even when this land was settled three hundred
years before. And they were strange, because they had come as dark
furtive folk from opiate southern gardens of orchids, and spoken another tongue before they learnt the tongue of the blue-eyed fishers.
And now they were scattered, and shared only the rituals of mysteries
that none living could understand. I was the only one who came back
that night to the old fishing town as legend bade, for only the poor
and the lonely remember.

Then beyond the hill's crest I saw Kingsport outspread frostily in
the gloaming; snowy Kingsport with its ancient vanes and steeples,

ridgepoles and chimney-pots, wharves and small bridges, willow-trees and graveyards; endless labyrinths of steep, narrow, crooked streets, and dizzy church-crowned central peak that time durst not touch; ceaseless mazes of colonial houses piled and scattered at all angles and levels like a child's disordered blocks; antiquity hovering on grey wings over winter-whitened gables and gambrel roofs; fanlights and small-paned windows one by one gleaming out in the cold dusk to join Orion and the archaic stars. And against the rotting wharves the sea pounded; the secretive, immemorial sea out of which the people had come in the elder time.

Beside the road at its crest a still higher summit rose, bleak and windswept, and I saw that it was a burying-ground where black gravestones stuck ghoulishly through the snow like the decayed fingernails of a gigantic corpse. The printless road was very lonely, and sometimes I thought I heard a distant horrible creaking as of a gibbet in the wind. They had hanged four kinsmen of mine for witchcraft in 1692, but I did not know just where.

As the road wound down the seaward slope I listened for the merry sounds of a village at evening, but did not hear them. Then I thought of the season, and felt that these old Puritan folk might well have Christmas customs strange to me, and full of silent hearthside prayer. So, after that I did not listen for merriment or look for wayfarers, but kept on down past the hushed lighted farmhouses and shadowy stone walls to where the signs of ancient shops and sea-taverns creaked in the salt breeze, and the grotesque knockers of pillared doorways glistened along deserted, unpaved lanes in the light of little, curtained windows.

I had seen maps of the town, and knew where to find the home of my people. It was told that I should be known and welcomed, for village legend lives long; so, I hastened through Back Street to Circle Court, and across the fresh snow on the one full flagstone pavement in the town, to where Green Lane leads off behind the Market house. The old maps still held good, and I had no trouble; though at Arkham they must have lied when they said the trolleys ran to this place, since I saw not a wire overhead. Snow would have hid the rails in any case. I was glad I had chosen to walk, for the white village had seemed very beautiful from the hill; and now I was eager to knock at the door of my people, the seventh house on the left in Green Lane, with an ancient peaked roof and jutting second story, all built before 1650.

There were lights inside the house when I came upon it, and I saw from the diamond window-panes that it must have been kept very close to its antique state. The upper part overhung the narrow grass-grown street and nearly met the overhanging part of the house opposite, so that I was almost in a tunnel, with the low stone doorstep wholly free from snow. There was no sidewalk, but many houses had high doors reached by double flights of steps with iron railings. It was an odd scene, and because I was strange to New England I had never known its like before. Though it pleased me, I would have relished it better if there had been footprints in the snow, and people in the streets, and a few windows without drawn curtains.

When I sounded the archaic iron knocker I was half afraid. Some fear had been gathering in me, perhaps because of the strangeness of my heritage, and the bleakness of the evening, and the queerness of the silence in that aged town of curious customs. And when my knock was answered I was fully afraid, because I had not heard any footsteps before the door creaked open. But I was not afraid long, for the gowned, slippered old man in the doorway had a bland face that reassured me; and though he made signs that he was dumb, he wrote a quaint and ancient welcome with the stylus and wax tablet he carried.

He beckoned me into a low, candle-lit room with massive exposed rafters and dark, stiff, sparse furniture of the seventeenth century. The past was vivid there, for not an attribute was missing. There was a cavernous fireplace and a spinning-wheel at which a bent old woman in loose wrapper and deep poke-bonnet sat back toward me, silently spinning despite the festive season. An indefinite dampness seemed upon the place, and I marvelled that no fire should be blazing.

The high-backed settle faced the row of curtained windows at the left, and seemed to be occupied, though I was not sure. I did not like everything about what I saw, and felt again the fear I had had. This fear grew stronger from what had before lessened it, for the more I looked at the old man's bland face the more its very blandness terrified me. The eyes never moved, and the skin was too like wax. Finally, I was sure it was not a face at all, but a fiendishly cunning mask. But the flabby hands, curiously gloved, wrote genially on the tablet and told me I must wait a while before I could be led to the place of festival.

Pointing to a chair, table, and pile of books, the old man now left the room; and when I sat down to read I saw that the books were hoary and mouldy, and that they included old Morryster's wild *Marvells of Science,* the terrible *Saducismus Triumphatus* of Joseph Glanvill, published in 1681, the shocking *Daemonolatreia* of Remigius, printed in 1595 at Lyons, and worst of all, the unmentionable *Necronomicon* of the mad Arab Abdul Alhazred, in Olaus Wormius' forbidden Latin translation; a book which I had never seen, but of which I had heard monstrous things whispered. No one spoke to me, but I could hear the creaking of signs in the wind outside, and the whir of the wheel as the bonneted old woman continued her silent spinning, spinning. I thought the room and the books and the people very morbid and disquieting, but because an old tradition of my fathers had summoned me to strange feastings, I resolved to expect queer things. So, I tried to read, and soon became tremblingly absorbed by something I found in that accursed *Necronomicon;* a thought and a legend too hideous for sanity or consciousness.

But I disliked it when I fancied I heard the closing of one of the windows that the settle faced, as if it had been stealthily opened. It had seemed to follow a whirring that was not of the old woman's spinning-wheel. This was not much, though, for the old woman was spinning very hard, and the aged clock had been striking. After that I lost the feeling that there were persons on the settle, and was reading intently and shudderingly when the old man came back booted and dressed in a loose antique costume, and sat down on that very bench, so that I could not see him. It was certainly nervous waiting, and the blasphemous book in my hands made it doubly so.

When eleven struck, however, the old man stood up, glided to a massive carved chest in a corner, and got two hooded cloaks; one of which he donned, and the other of which he draped round the old woman, who was ceasing her monotonous spinning. Then they both started for the outer door; the woman lamely creeping, and the old man, after picking up the very book I had been reading, beckoning me as he drew his hood over that unmoving face or mask.

We went out into the moonless and tortuous network of that in-credibly ancient town; went out as the lights in the curtained win-dows disappeared one by one, and the Dog Star leered at the throng of cowled, cloaked figures that poured silently from every doorway and formed monstrous processions up this street and that, past the creaking signs and antediluvian gables, the thatched roofs and dia-mond-paned windows; threading precipitous lanes where decaying houses overlapped and crumbled together, gliding across open courts and churchyards where the bobbing lanthorns made eldritch drunken constellations.

Amid these hushed throngs I followed my voiceless guides; jostled by elbows that seemed preternaturally soft, and pressed by chests and stomachs that seemed abnormally pulpy; but seeing never a face and hearing never a word. Up, up, up the eerie columns slithered, and I saw that all the travellers were converging as they flowed near a sort of focus of crazy alleys at the top of a high hill in the centre of the town, where perched a great white church. I had seen it from the road's crest when I looked at Kingsport in the new dusk, and it had made me shiver because Aldebaran had seemed to balance itself a moment on the ghostly spire.

There was an open space around the church; partly a churchyard with spectral shafts, and partly a half-paved square swept nearly bare of snow by the wind, and lined with unwholesomely archaic houses having peaked roofs and overhanging gables. Death-fires danced over the tombs, revealing gruesome *vistas*, though queerly failing to cast any shadows. Past the churchyard, where there were no houses, I could see over the hill's summit and watch the glimmer of stars on the harbour, though the town was invisible in the dark. Only once in a while a lanthorn bobbed horribly through serpentine alleys on its way to overtake the throng that was now slipping speechlessly into the church. I waited till the crowd had oozed into the black doorway, and till all the stragglers had followed.

The old man was pulling at my sleeve, but I was determined to be the last. Then I finally went, the sinister man and the old spinning woman before me. Crossing the threshold into that swarming temple of unknown darkness, I turned once to look at the outside world as the churchyard phosphorescence cast a sickly glow on the hill-top pavement. And as I did so I shuddered. For though the wind had not left much snow, a few patches did remain on the path near the door; and in that fleeting backward look it seemed to my troubled eyes that they bore no mark of passing feet, not even mine.

The church was scarce lighted by all the lanthorns that had entered it, for most of the throng had already vanished. They had streamed up the aisle between the high white pews to the trap-door of the vaults which yawned loathsomely open just before the pulpit, and were now squirming noiselessly in. I followed dumbly down the footworn steps and into the dank, suffocating crypt. The tail of that sinuous line of night-marchers seemed very horrible, and as I saw them wriggling into a venerable tomb they seemed more horrible still. Then I noticed that the tomb's floor had an aperture down which the throng was sliding, and in a moment, we were all descending an ominous staircase of rough-hewn stone; a narrow spiral staircase damp and peculiarly odorous, that wound endlessly down into the bowels of the hill past monotonous walls of dripping stone blocks and crumbling mortar.

It was a silent, shocking descent, and I observed after a horrible interval that the walls and steps were changing in nature, as if chiselled out of the solid rock. What mainly troubled me was that the myriad footfalls made no sound and set up no echoes. After more aeons of descent, I saw some side passages or burrows leading from unknown recesses of blackness to this shaft of nighted mystery. Soon they became excessively numerous, like impious catacombs of nameless menace; and their pungent odour of decay grew quite unbearable. I knew we must have passed down through the mountain and beneath the earth of Kingsport itself, and I shivered that a town should be so aged and maggoty with subterraneous evil.

Then I saw the lurid shimmering of pale light, and heard the insidious lapping of sunless waters. Again, I shivered, for I did not like the things that the night had brought, and wished bitterly that no forefather had summoned me to this primal rite. As the steps and the passage grew broader, I heard another sound, the thin, whining mockery of a feeble flute; and suddenly there spread out before me the boundless *vista* of an inner world—a vast fungous shore litten by a belching column of sick greenish flame and washed by a wide oily river that flowed from abysses frightful and unsuspected to join the blackest gulfs of immemorial ocean.

Fainting and gasping, I looked at that unhallowed Erebus of titan toadstools, leprous fire, and slimy water, and saw the cloaked throngs forming a semicircle around the blazing pillar. It was the Yule-rite, older than man and fated to survive him; the primal rite of the solstice and of spring's promise beyond the snows; the rite of fire and evergreen, light and music. And in the Stygian grotto I saw them do the rite, and adore the sick pillar of flame, and throw into the water handfuls gouged out of the viscous vegetation which glittered green in the chlorotic glare. I saw this, and I saw something amorphously squatted far away from the light, piping noisomely on a flute; and as the thing piped I thought I heard noxious muffled flutterings in the foetid darkness where I could not see.

But what frightened me most was that flaming column; spouting volcanically from depths profound and inconceivable, casting no shadows as healthy flame should, and coating the nitrous stone above with a nasty, venomous *verdigris*. For in all that seething combustion no warmth lay, but only the clamminess of death and corruption.

The man who had brought me now squirmed to a point directly beside the hideous flame, and made stiff ceremonial motions to the semicircle he faced. At certain stages of the ritual they did grovelling obeisance, especially when he held above his head that abhorrent *Necronomicon* he had taken with him; and I shared all the obeisances because I had been summoned to this festival by the writings of my forefathers. Then the old man made a signal to the half-seen flute-player in the darkness, which player thereupon changed its feeble drone to a scarce louder drone in another key; precipitating as it did so a horror unthinkable and unexpected. At this horror I sank nearly to the lichened earth, transfixed with a dread not of this nor any world, but only of the mad spaces between the stars.

Out of the unimaginable blackness beyond the gangrenous glare of that cold flame, out of the Tartarean leagues through which that oily river rolled uncanny, unheard, and unsuspected, there flopped rhythmically a horde of tame, trained, hybrid winged things that no sound eye could ever wholly grasp, or sound brain ever wholly remember. They were not altogether crows, nor moles, nor buzzards, nor ants, nor vampire bats, nor decomposed human beings; but something I cannot and must not recall. They flopped limply along, half with their webbed feet and half with their membraneous wings; and as they reached the throng of celebrants the cowled figures seized and mounted them, and rode off one by one along the reaches of that unlighted river, into pits and galleries of panic where poison springs feed frightful and undiscoverable cataracts.

The old spinning woman had gone with the throng, and the old man remained only because I had refused when he motioned me to seize an animal and ride like the rest. I saw when I staggered to my feet that the amorphous flute-player had rolled out of sight, but that two of the beasts were patiently standing by. As I hung back, the old man produced his stylus and tablet and wrote that he was the true deputy of my fathers who had founded the Yule worship in this ancient place; that it had been decreed I should come back, and that the most secret mysteries were yet to be performed. He wrote this in a very ancient hand, and when I still hesitated he pulled from his loose robe a seal ring and a watch, both with my family arms, to prove that he was what he said. But it was a hideous proof, because I knew from old papers that that watch had been buried with my great-great-great-great-grandfather in 1698.

Presently the old man drew back his hood and pointed to the family resemblance in his face, but I only shuddered, because I was sure that the face was merely a devilish waxen mask. The flopping animals were now scratching restlessly at the lichens, and I saw that the old man was nearly as restless himself. When one of the things began to waddle and edge away, he turned quickly to stop it; so that the suddenness of his motion dislodged the waxen mask from what should have been his head. And then, because that nightmare's position barred me from the stone staircase down which we had come, I flung myself into the oily underground river that bubbled somewhere to the caves of the sea; flung myself into that putrescent juice of earth's inner horrors before the madness of my screams could bring down upon me all the charnel legions these pest-gulfs might conceal.

At the hospital they told me I had been found half frozen in Kingsport Harbour at dawn, clinging to the drifting spar that accident sent to save me. They told me I had taken the wrong fork of the hill road the night before, and fallen over the cliffs at Orange Point; a thing they deduced from prints found in the snow. There was nothing I could say, because everything was wrong. Everything was wrong, with the broad window shewing a sea of roofs in which only about one in five was ancient, and the sound of trolleys and motors in the streets below. They insisted that this was Kingsport, and I could not deny it.

When I went delirious at hearing that the hospital stood near the old churchyard on Central Hill, they sent me to St. Mary's Hospital in Arkham, where I could have better care. I liked it there, for the doctors were broad-minded, and even lent me their influence in obtaining the carefully sheltered copy of Alhazred's objectionable *Necronomicon* from the library of Miskatonic University. They said something about a "psychosis", and agreed I had better get any harassing obsessions off my mind.

So, I read again that hideous chapter, and shuddered doubly because it was indeed not new to me. I had seen it before, let footprints tell what they might; and where it was I had seen it were best forgotten. There was no one—in waking hours—who could remind me of it; but my dreams are filled with terror, because of phrases I dare not quote. I dare quote only one paragraph, put into such English as I can make from the awkward Low Latin.

The mad Arab wrote:

The nethermost caverns, are not for the fathoming of eyes that see; for their marvels are strange and terrific. Cursed the ground where dead thoughts live new and oddly bodied, and evil the mind that is held by no head. Wisely did Ibn Schacabao say, that happy is the tomb where no wizard hath lain, and happy the town at night whose wizards are all ashes. For it is of old rumour that the soul of the devil-bought hastes not from his charnel clay, but fats and instructs *the very worm that gnaws;* till out of corruption horrid life springs, and the dull scavengers of earth wax crafty to vex it and swell monstrous to plague it. Great holes secretly are digged where earth's pores ought to suffice, and things have learnt to walk that ought to crawl.

The Upper Berth
F. Marion Crawford

1

Somebody asked for the cigars. We had talked long, and the conversation was beginning to languish; the tobacco smoke had got into the heavy curtains, the wine had got into those brains which were liable to become heavy, and it was already perfectly evident that, unless somebody did something to rouse our oppressed spirits, the meeting would soon come to its natural conclusion, and we, the guests, would speedily go home to bed, and most certainly to sleep. No one had said anything very remarkable; it may be that no one had anything very remarkable to say. Jones had given us every particular of his last hunting adventure in Yorkshire. Mr. Tompkins, of Boston, had explained at elaborate length those working principles, by the due and careful maintenance of which the Atchison, Topeka, and Santa Fé Railroad not only extended its territory, increased its departmental influence, and transported live stock without starving them to death before the day of actual delivery, but, also, had for years succeeded in deceiving those passengers who bought its tickets into the fallacious belief that the corporation aforesaid was really able to transport human life without destroying it.

Signor Tombola had endeavoured to persuade us, by arguments which we took no trouble to oppose, that the unity of his country in no way resembled the average modern torpedo, carefully planned, constructed with all the skill of the greatest European arsenals, but, when constructed, destined to be directed by feeble hands into a region where it must undoubtedly explode, unseen, unfeared, and unheard, into the illimitable wastes of political chaos.

It is unnecessary to go into further details. The conversation had assumed proportions which would have bored Prometheus on his rock, which would have driven Tantalus to distraction, and which would have impelled Ixion to seek relaxation in the simple but instructive dialogues of Herr Ollendorff, rather than submit to the greater evil of listening to our talk. We had sat at table for hours; we were bored, we were tired, and nobody showed signs of moving.

Somebody called for cigars. We all instinctively looked towards the speaker. Brisbane was a man of five-and-thirty years of age, and remarkable for those gifts which chiefly attract the attention of men. He was a strong man. The external proportions of his figure presented nothing extraordinary to the common eye, though his size was above the average. He was a little over six feet in height, and moderately broad in the shoulder; he did not appear to be stout, but, on the other hand, he was certainly not thin; his small head was supported by a strong and sinewy neck; his broad, muscular hands appeared to possess a peculiar skill in breaking walnuts without the assistance of the ordinary cracker, and, seeing him in profile, one could not help remarking the extraordinary breadth of his sleeves, and the unusual thickness of his chest. He was one of those men who are commonly spoken of among men as deceptive; that is to say, that though he looked exceedingly strong he was in reality very much stronger than he looked. Of his features I need say little. His head was small, his hair is thin, his eyes are blue, his nose is large, he has a small moustache, and a square jaw. Everybody knows Brisbane, and when he asked for a cigar everybody looked at him.

"It is a very singular thing," said Brisbane.

Everybody stopped talking. Brisbane's voice was not loud, but possessed a peculiar quality of penetrating general conversation, and cutting it like a knife. Everybody listened. Brisbane, perceiving that he had attracted their general attention, lit his cigar with great equanimity.

"It is very singular," he continued, "that thing about ghosts. People are always asking whether anybody has seen a ghost. I have."

"Bosh! What, you? You don't mean to say so, Brisbane? Well, for a man of his intelligence!"

A chorus of exclamations greeted Brisbane's remarkable statement. Everybody called for cigars, and Stubbs, the butler, suddenly appeared from the depths of nowhere with a fresh bottle of dry champagne. The situation was saved; Brisbane was going to tell a story.

I am an old sailor, said Brisbane, and as I have to cross the Atlantic pretty often, I have my favourites. Most men have their favourites. I have seen a man wait in a Broadway bar for three-quarters of an hour for a particular car which he liked. I believe the bar-keeper made at least one-third of his living by that man's preference. I have a habit of waiting for certain ships when I am obliged to cross that duck-pond. It may be a prejudice, but I was never cheated out of a good passage but once in my life. I remember it very well; it was a warm morning in June, and the Custom House officials, who were hanging about waiting for a steamer already on her way up from the Quarantine, presented a peculiarly hazy and thoughtful appearance.

I had not much luggage—I never have. I mingled with the crowd of passengers, porters, and officious individuals in blue coats and brass buttons, who seemed to spring up like mushrooms from the deck of a moored steamer to obtrude their unnecessary services upon the independent passenger. I have often noticed with a certain interest the spontaneous evolution of these fellows. They are not there when you arrive; five minutes after the pilot has called 'Go ahead!' they, or at least their blue coats and brass buttons, have disappeared from deck and gangway as completely as though they had been consigned to that locker which tradition ascribes to Davy Jones. But, at the moment of starting, they are there, clean shaved, blue coated, and ravenous for fees. I hastened on board.

The *Kamtschatka* was one of my favourite ships. I saw was, because she emphatically no longer is. I cannot conceive of any inducement which could entice me to make another voyage in her. Yes, I know what you are going to say. She is uncommonly clean in the run aft, she has enough bluffing off in the bows to keep her dry, and the lower berths are most of them double. She has a lot of advantages, but I won't cross in her again. Excuse the digression. I got on board. I hailed a steward, whose red nose and redder whiskers were equally familiar to me.

"One hundred and five, lower berth," said I, in the businesslike tone peculiar to men who think no more of crossing the Atlantic than taking a whisky cocktail at down-town Delmonico's.

The steward took my portmanteau, greatcoat, and rug. I shall never forget the expression on his face. Not that he turned pale. It is maintained by the most eminent divines that even miracles cannot change the course of nature. I have no hesitation in saying that he did not turn pale; but, from his expression, I judged that he was either about to shed tears, to sneeze, or to drop my portmanteau. As the latter contained two bottles of particularly fine old sherry presented to me for my voyage by my old friend Snigginson van Pickyns, I felt extremely nervous. But the steward did none of these things.

"Well, I'm d——d!" said he in a low voice, and led the way.

I supposed my Hermes, as he led me to the lower regions, had had a little grog, but I said nothing, and followed him. One hundred and five was on the port side, well aft. There was nothing remarkable about the state-room. The lower berth, like most of those upon the *Kamtschatka*, was double. There was plenty of room; there was the usual washing apparatus, calculated to convey an idea of luxury to the mind of a North American Indian; there were the usual inefficient racks of brown wood, in which it is more easy to hand a large-sized umbrella than the common tooth-brush of commerce. Upon the uninviting mattresses were carefully bolded together those blankets which a great modern humorist has aptly compared to cold buckwheat cakes.

The question of towels was left entirely to the imagination. The glass decanters were filled with a transparent liquid faintly tinged with brown, but from which an odour less faint, but not more pleasing, ascended to the nostrils, like a far-off sea-sick reminiscence of oily machinery. Sad-coloured curtains half-closed the upper berth. The hazy June daylight shed a faint illumination upon the desolate little scene. Ugh! how I hate that state-room!

The steward deposited my traps and looked at me, as though he wanted to get away—probably in search of more passengers and more fees. It is always a good plan to start in favour with those functionaries, and I accordingly gave him certain coins there and then.

"I'll try and make yer comfortable all I can," he remarked, as he put the coins in his pocket. Nevertheless, there was a doubtful intonation in his voice which surprised me. Possibly his scale of fees had gone up, and he was not satisfied; but on the whole I was inclined to think that, as he himself would have expressed it, he was "the better for a glass". I was wrong, however, and did the man injustice.

2

Nothing especially worthy of mention occurred during that day. We left the pier punctually, and it was very pleasant to be fairly under way, for the weather was warm and sultry, and the motion of the steamer produced a refreshing breeze. Everybody knows what the first day at sea is like. People pace the decks and stare at each other, and occasionally meet acquaintances whom they did not know to be on board. There is the usual uncertainty as to whether the food will be good, bad, or indifferent, until the first two meals have put the matter beyond a doubt; there is the usual uncertainty about the weather, until the ship is fairly off Fire Island. The tables are crowded at first, and then suddenly thinned. Pale-faced people spring from their seats and precipitate themselves towards the door, and each old sailor breathes more freely as his sea-sick neighbour rushes from his side, leaving him plenty of elbow-room and an unlimited command over the mustard.

One passage across the Atlantic is very much like another, and we who cross very often do not make the voyage for the sake of novelty. Whales and icebergs are indeed always objects of interest, but, after all, one whale is very much like another whale, and one rarely sees an iceberg at close quarters. To the majority of us the most delightful moment of the day on board an ocean steamer is when we have taken our last turn on deck, have smoked our last cigar, and having succeeded in tiring ourselves, feel at liberty to turn in with a clear conscience. On that first night of the voyage I felt particularly lazy, and went to bed in one hundred and five rather earlier than I usually do. As I turned in, I was amazed to see that I was to have a companion. A portmanteau, very like my own, lay in the opposite corner, and in the upper berth had been deposited a neatly-folded rug, with a stick and umbrella. I had hoped to be alone, and I was disappointed; but I wondered who my room-mate was to be, and I determined to have a look at him.

Before I had been long in bed he entered. He was, as far as I could see, a very tall man, very thin, very pale, with sandy hair and whiskers and colourless grey eyes. He had about him, I thought, an air of rather dubious fashion; the short of man you might see in Wall Street, without being able precisely to say what he was doing there—the sort of man who frequents the Café Anglais, who always seems to be alone and who drinks champagne; you might meet him on a racecourse, but he would never appear to be doing anything there either. A little over-dressed—a little odd. There are three or four of his kind on every ocean steamer. I made up my mind that I did not care to make his acquaintance, and I went to sleep saying to myself that I would study his habits in order to avoid him. If he rose early, I would rise late; if he went to bed late, I would go to bed early. I did not care to know him. If you once know people of that kind they are always turning up. Poor fellow! I need not have taken the trouble to come to so many decisions about him, for I never saw him again after that first night in one hundred and five.

I was sleeping soundly when I was suddenly waked by a loud noise. To judge from the sound, my room-mate must have sprung with a single leap from the upper berth to the floor. I heard him fumbling with the latch and bolt of the door, which opened almost immediately, and then I heard his footsteps as he ran at full speed down the passage, leaving the door open behind him. The ship was rolling a little, and I expected to hear him stumble or fall, but he ran as though he were running for his life. The door swung on its hinges with the motion of the vessel, and the sound annoyed me. I got up and shut it, and groped my way back to my berth in the darkness. I went to sleep again; but I have no idea how long I slept.

When I awoke it was still quite dark, but I felt a disagreeable sensation of cold, and it seemed to me that the air was damp. You know the peculiar smell of a cabin which has been wet with sea-water. I covered myself up as well as I could and dozed off again, framing complaints to be made the next day, and selecting the most powerful epithets in the language. I could hear my room-mate turn over in the upper berth. He had probably returned while I was asleep. Once I thought I heard him groan, and I argued that he was sea-sick. That is particularly unpleasant when one is below. Nevertheless I dozed off and slept till early daylight.

The ship was rolling heavily, much more than on the previous evening, and the grey light which came in through the porthole changed in tint with every movement according as the angle of the vessel's side turned the glass seawards or skywards. It was very cold—unaccountably so for the month of June. I turned my head and looked at the porthole, and saw to my surprise that it was wide open and hooked back. I believe I swore audibly. Then I got up and shut it. As I turned back I glanced at the upper berth. The curtains were drawn close together; my companion had probably felt cold as well as I. It struck me that I had slept enough. The state-room was uncomfortable, though, strange to say, I could not smell the dampness which had annoyed me in the night. My room-mate was still asleep—excellent opportunity for avoiding him, so I dressed at once and went on deck. The day was warm and cloudy, with an oily smell on the water. It was seven o'clock as I came out—much later than I had imagined. I came across the doctor, who was taking his first sniff of the morning air. He was a young man from the West of Ireland—a tremendous fellow, with black hair and blue eyes, already inclined to be stout; he had a happy-go-lucky, healthy look about him which was rather attractive.

"Fine morning," I remarked, by way of introduction.

"Well," said he, eyeing me with an air of ready interest, "it's a fine morning and it's not a fine morning. I don't think it's much of a morning."

"Well, no—it is not so very fine," said I.

"It's just what I call fuggly weather," replied the doctor.

"It was very cold last night, I thought," I remarked. "However, when I looked about, I found that the porthole was wide open. I had not noticed it when I went to bed. And the state-room was damp, too."

"Damp!" said he. "Whereabouts are you?"

"One hundred and five------"

To my surprise the doctor started visibly, and stared at me.

"What is the matter?" I asked.

"Oh—nothing," he answered; "only everybody has complained of that state-room for the last three trips."

"I shall complain too," I said. "It has certainly not been properly aired. It is a shame!"

"I don't believe it can be helped," answered the doctor. "I believe there is something—well, it is not my business to frighten passengers."

"You need not be afraid of frightening me," I replied. "I can stand any amount of damp. If I should get a bad cold I will come to you."

I offered the doctor a cigar, which he took and examined very critically.

"It is not so much the damp," he remarked. "However, I dare say you will get on very well. Have you a room-mate?"

"Yes; a deuce of a fellow, who bolts out in the middle of the night, and leaves the door open."

Again the doctor glanced curiously at me. Then he lit the cigar and looked grave.

"Did he come back?" he asked presently.

"Yes. I was asleep, but I waked up, and heard him moving. Then I felt cold and went to sleep again. This morning I found the porthole open."

"Look here," said the doctor quietly, "I don't care much for this ship. I don't care a rap for her reputation. I tell you what I will do. I have a good-sized place up here. I will share it with you, though I don't know you from Adam."

I was very much surprised at the proposition. I could not imagine why he should take such a sudden interest in my welfare. However, his manner as he spoke of the ship was peculiar.

"You are very good, doctor," I said. "But, really, I believe even now the cabin could be aired, or cleaned out, or something. Why do you not care for the ship?"

"We are not superstitious in our profession, sir," replied the doctor, "but the sea makes people so. I don't want to prejudice you, and I don't want to frighten you, but if you will take my advice you will move in here. I would as soon see you overboard," he added earnestly, "as know that you or any other man was to sleep in one hundred and five."

"Good gracious! Why?" I asked.

"Just because on the last three trips the people who have slept there actually have gone overboard," he answered gravely.

The intelligence was startling and exceedingly unpleasant, I confess. I looked hard at the doctor to see whether he was making game of me, but he looked perfectly serious. I thanked him warmly for his offer, but told him I intended to be the exception to the rule by which everyone who slept in that particular state-room went overboard. He did not say much, but looked as grave as ever, and hinted that, before we got across, I should probably reconsider his proposal. In the course of time we went to breakfast, at which only an inconsiderable number of passengers assembled. I noticed that one or two of the officers who breakfasted with us looked grave. After breakfast I went into my state-room in order to get a book. The curtains of the upper berth were still closely drawn. Not a word was to be heard. My room-mate was probably still asleep.

As I came out I met the steward whose business it was to look after me. He whispered that the captain wanted to see me, and then scuttled away down the passage as if very anxious to avoid any questions. I went toward the captain's cabin, and found him waiting for me.

"Sir," said he, "I want to ask a favour of you."

I answered that I would do anything to oblige him.

"Your room-mate had disappeared," he said. "He is known to have turned in early last night. Did you notice anything extraordinary in his manner?"

The question coming, as it did, in exact confirmation of the fears the doctor had expressed half an hour earlier, staggered me.

"You don't mean to say he has gone overboard?" I asked.

"I fear he has," answered the captain.

"This is the most extraordinary thing——" I began.

"Why?" he asked.

"He is the fourth, then?" I exclaimed. In answer to another question from the captain, I explained, without mentioning the doctor, that I had heard the story concerning one hundred and five. He seemed very much annoyed at hearing that I knew of it. I told him what had occurred in the night.

"What you say," he replied, "coincides almost exactly with what was told me by the room-mates of two of the other three. They bolt out of bed and run down the passage. Two of them were seen to go overboard by the watch; we stopped and lowered boats, but they were not found. Nobody, however, saw or heard the man who was lost last night—if he is really lost. The steward, who is a superstitious fellow, perhaps, and expected something to go wrong, went to look for him, this morning, and found his berth empty, but his clothes lying about, just as he had left them. The steward was the only man on board who knew him by sight, and he has been searching everywhere for him. He has disappeared! Now, sir, I want to beg you not to mention the circumstance to any of the passengers; I don't want the ship to get a bad name, and nothing hangs about an ocean-goer like stories of suicides. You shall have your choice of any one of the officers' cabins you like, including my own, for the rest of the passage. Is that a fair bargain?"

"Very," said I; "and I am much obliged to you. But since I am alone, and have the state-room to myself, I would rather not move. If the steward will take out that unfortunate man's things, I would as leave stay where I am. I will not say anything about the matter, and I think I can promise you that I will not follow my room-mate."

The captain tried to dissuade me from my intention, but I preferred having a state-room alone to being the chum of any officer on board. I do not know whether I aced foolishly, but if I had taken his advice I should have had nothing more to tell. There would have remained the disagreeable coincidence of several suicides occurring among men who had slept in the same cabin, but that would have been all.

That was not the end of the matter, however, by any means. I obstinately made up my mind that I would not be disturbed by such tales, and I even went so far as to argue the question with the captain. There was something wrong about the state-room, I said. It was rather damp. The porthole had been left open last night. My room-mate might have been ill when he came on board, and he might have become delirious after he went to bed. He might even now be hiding somewhere on board, and might be found later. The place ought to be aired and the fastening on the port looked to. If the captain would give me leave, I would see that what I thought necessary were done immediately.

"Of course you have a right to stay where you are if you please," he replied, rather petulantly; "but I wish you would turn out and let me lock the place up, and be done with it."

I did not see it in the same light, and left the captain, after promising to be silent concerning the disappearance of my companion. The latter had had no acquaintances on board, and was not missed in the course of the day. Towards evening I met the doctor again, and he asked me whether I had changed my mind. I told him I had not.

"Then you will before long," he said, very gravely.

3

We played whist in the evening, and I went to bed late. I will confess now that I felt a disagreeable sensation when I entered my state-room. I could not help thinking of the tall man I had seen on the previous night, who was now dead, drowned, tossing about in the long swell, two or three hundred miles astern. His face rose very distinctly before me as I undressed, and I even went so far as to draw back the curtains of the upper berth, as though to persuade myself that he was actually gone. I also bolted the door of the state-room. Suddenly I became aware that the porthole was open, and fastened back. This was more than I could stand. I hastily threw on my dressing-gown and went in search of Robert, the steward of my passage. I was very angry, I remember, and when I found him I dragged him roughly to the door of one hundred and five, and pushed him towards the open porthole.

"What the deuce do you mean, you scoundrel, by leaving that port open every night? Don't you know it is against the regulations? Don't you know that if the ship heeled and the water began to come in, ten men could not shut it? I will report you to the captain, you blackguard, for endangering the ship!"

I was exceedingly wroth. The man trembled and turned pale, and then began to shut the round glass plate with the heavy brass fittings.

"Why don't you answer me?" I said roughly.

"If you please, sir," faltered Robert, "there's nobody on board as can keep this 'ere port shut at night. You can try it yourself, sir. I ain't a-going to stop hany longer on board o' this vessel, sir; I ain't, indeed. But if I was you, sir, I'd just clear out and go and sleep with the surgeon, or something, I would. Look 'ere, sir, is that fastened what you may call securely, or not, sir? Try it, sir, see if it will move a hinch."

I tried the port, and found it perfectly tight.

"Well, sir," continued Robert triumphantly, "I wager my reputation as a A1 steward that in 'arf an hour it will be open again; fasteneed back, too, sir, that's the horful thing—fastened back!"

I examined the great screw and the looped nut that ran on it.

"If I find it open in the night, Robert, I will give you a sovereign. It is not possible. You may go."

"Soverin' did you say, sir? Very good, sir. Thank ye, sir. Goodnight, sir. Pleasant reepose, sir, and all manner of hinchantin' dreams, sir."

Robert scuttled away, delighted at being released. Of course, I thought he was trying to account for his negligence by a silly story, intended to frighten me, and I disbelieved him. The consequence was that he got his sovereign, and I spent a very peculiarly unpleasant night.

I went to bed, and five minutes after I had rolled myself up in my blankets the inexorable Robert extinguished the light that burned steadily behind the ground-glass pane near the door. I lay quite still in the dark trying to go to sleep, but I soon found that impossible. It had been some satisfaction to be angry with the steward, and the diversion had banished that unpleasant sensation I had at first experienced when I thought of the drowned man who had been my chum; but I was no longer sleepy, and I lay awake for some time, occasionally glancing at the porthole, which I could just see from where I lay, and which, in the darkness, looked like a faintly-luminous soup-plate suspended in blackness. I believe I must have lain there for an hour, and, as I remember, I was just dozing into sleep when I was roused by a draught of cold air, and by distinctly feeling the spray of the sea blown upon my face. I started to my feet, and not having allowed in the dark for the motion of the ship, I was instantly thrown violently across the state-room upon the couch which was placed beneath the port-hole. I recovered myself immediately, however, and climbed upon my knees. The port-hole was again wide open and fastened back!

Now these things are facts. I was wide awake when I got up, and I should certainly have been waked by the fall had I still been dozing. Moreover, I bruised my elbows and knees badly, and the bruises were there on the following morning to testify to the fact, if I myself had doubted it. The porthole was wide open and fastened back—a thing so unaccountable that I remember very well feeling astonishment rather that fear when I discovered it. I at once closed the plate again, and screwed down the loop nut with all my strength. It was very dark in the state-room. I reflected that the port had certainly been opened within an hour after Robert had at first shut it in my presence, and I determined to watch it, and see whether it would open again. Those brass fittings are very heavy and by no means easy to move; I could not believe that the clamp had been turned by the shaking of the screw. I stood peering out through the thick glass at the alternate white and grey streaks of the sea that foamed beneath the ship's side. I must have remained there a quarter of an hour.

Suddenly, as I stood, I distinctly heard something moving behind me in one of the berths, and a moment afterwards, just as I turned instinctively to look—though I could, of course, see nothing in the darkness—I heard a very faint groan. I sprang across the state-room, and tore the curtains of the upper berth aside, thrusting in my hands to discover if there were any one there. There was some one.

I remember that the sensation as I put my hands forward was as though I were plunging them into the air of a damp cellar, and from behind the curtains came a gust of wind that smelled horribly of stagnant sea-water. I laid hold of something that had the shape of a man's arm, but was smooth, and wet, and icy cold. But suddenly, as I pulled, the creature sprang violently forward against me, a clammy oozy mass, as it seemed to me, heavy and wet, yet endowed with a sort of supernatural strength. I reeled across the state-room, and in an instant the door opened and the thing rushed out. I had not had time to be frightened, and quickly recovering myself, I sprang through the door and gave chase at the top of my speed, but I was too late. Ten yards before me I could see—I am sure I saw it—a dark shadow moving in the dimly lighted passage, quickly as the shadow of a fast horse thrown before a dog-cart by the lamp on a dark night. But in a moment it had disappeared, and I found myself holding on to the polished rail that ran along the bulkhead where the passage turned towards the companion. My hair stood on end, and the cold perspiration rolled down my face. I am not ashamed of it in the least: I was very badly frightened.

Still I doubted my senses, and pulled myself together. It was absurd, I thought. The Welsh rare-bit I had eaten had disagreed with me. I had been in a nightmare. I made my way back to my state-room, and entered it with an effort. The whole place smelled of stagnant sea-water, as it had when I had waked on the previous evening. It required my utmost strength to go in, and grope among my things for a box of wax lights. As I lighted a railway reading lantern which I always carry in case I want to read after the lamps are out, I perceived that the porthole was again open, and a sort of creeping horror began to take possession of me which I never felt before, nor wish to feel again. But I got a light and proceeded to examine the upper berth, expecting to find it drenched with sea-water.

But I was disappointed. The bed had been slept in, and the smell of the sea was strong; but the bedding was as dry as a bone. I fancied that Robert had not had the courage to make the bed after the accident of the previous night—it had all been a hideous dream. I drew the curtains back as far as I could and examined the place very carefully. It was perfectly dry. But the porthole was open again. With a sort of dull bewilderment of horror I closed it and screwed it down, and thrusting my heavy stick through the brass loop, wrenched it with all my might, till the thick metal began to bend under the pressure. Then I hooked my reading lantern into the red velvet at the head of the couch, and sat down to recover my senses if I could. I sat there all night, unable to think of rest—hardly able to think at all. But the porthole remained closed, and I did not believe it would now open again without the application of a considerable force.

The morning dawned at last, and I dressed myself slowly, think-ing over all that had happened in the night. It was a beautiful day and I went on deck, glad to get out into the early, pure sunshine, and to smell the breeze from the blue water, so different from the noisome, stagnant odour of my state-room. Instinctively I turned aft, towards the surgeon's cabin. There he stood, with a pipe in his mouth, taking his morning airing precisely as on the preceding day.

"Good-morning," said he quietly, but looking at me with evident curiosity.

"Doctor, you were quite right," said I. "There is something wrong about that place."

"I thought you would change your mind," he answered, rather triumphantly. "You have had a bad night, eh? Shall I make you a pick-me-up? I have a capital recipe."

"No, thanks," I cried. "But I would like to tell you what happened."

I then tried to explain as clearly as possible precisely what had oc-curred, not omitting to state that I had been scared as I had never been scared in my whole life before. I dwelt particularly on the phenom-enon of the porthole, which was a fact to which I could testify, even if the rest had been an illusion. I had closed it twice in the night, and the second time I had actually bent the brass in wrenching it with my stick. I believe I insisted a good deal on this point.

"You seem to think I am likely to doubt the story," said the doctor, smiling at my detailed account of the state of the porthole. "I do not doubt in the least. I renew my invitation to you. Bring your traps here, and take half my cabin."

"Come and take half of mine for one night," I said. "Help me to get at the bottom of this thing."

"You will get to the bottom of something else if you try," answered the doctor.

"What?" I asked.

"The bottom of the sea. I am going to leave this ship. It is not canny."

"Then you will not help me to find out----"

"Not I," said the doctor quickly. "It is my business to keep my wits about me—not to go fiddling about with ghosts and things."

"Do you really believe it is a ghost?" I enquired, rather contemptuously. But as I spoke I remembered very well the horrible sensation of the supernatural which had got possession of me during the night. The doctor turned sharply on me—

"Have you any reasonable explanation of these things to offer?" he asked. "No; you have not. Well, you say you will find an explanation. I say that you won't, sir, simply because there is not any."

"But, my dear sir," I retorted, "do you, a man of science, mean to tell me that such things cannot be explained?"

"I do," he answered stoutly. "And, if they could, I would not be concerned in the explanation."

I did not care to spend another night alone in the state-room, and yet I was obstinately determined to get at the root of the disturbances. I do not believe there are many men who would have slept there alone, after passing two such nights. But I made up my mind to try it, if I could not get anyone to share a watch with me. The doctor was evidently not inclined for such an experiment. He said he was a surgeon, and that in case any accident occurred on board he must be always in readiness. He could not afford to have his nerves unsettled. Perhaps he was quite right, but I am inclined to think that his precaution was prompted by his inclination. On enquiry, he informed me that there was no one on board who would be likely to join me in my investigations, and after a little more conversation I left him. A little later I met the captain, and told him my story. I said that, if no one

272

would spend the night with me, I would ask leave to have the light burning all night, and would try it alone.

"Look here," said he, "I will tell you what I will do. I will share your watch myself, and we will see what happens. It is my belief that we can find out between us. There may be some fellow skulking on board, who steals a passage by frightening the passengers. It is just possible that there may be something queer in the carpentering of that berth."

I suggested taking the ship's carpenter below and examining the place; but I was overjoyed at the captain's offer to spend the night with me. He accordingly sent for the workman and ordered him to do anything I required. We went below at once. I had all the bedding cleared out of the upper berth, and we examined the place thoroughly to see if there was a board loose anywhere, or a panel which could be opened or pushed aside. We tried the planks everywhere, tapped the flooring, unscrewed the fittings of the lower berth and took it to pieces—in short, there was not a square inch of the state-room which was not searched and tested. Everything was in perfect order, and we put everything back in its place. As we were finishing our work, Robert came to the door and looked in.

"Well, sir—find anything, sir?" he asked, with a ghastly grin.

"You were right about the porthole, Robert," I said, and I gave him the promised sovereign. The carpenter did his work silently and skilfully, following my directions. When he had done he spoke.

"I'm a plain man, sir," he said. "But it's my belief you had better just turn out your things, and let me run half a dozen four-inch screws through the door of this cabin. There's no good never came o' this cabin yet, sir, and that's all about it. There's been four lives lost out o' here to my own remembrance, and that is four trips. Better give it up, sir—better give it up!"

"I will try it for one night more," I said.

"Better give it up, sir—better give it up! It's a precious bad job," repeated the workman, putting his tools in his bag and leaving the cabin.

But my spirits had risen considerably at the prospect of having the captain's company, and I made up my mind not to be prevented from going to the end of this strange business. I abstained from Welsh rarebits and grog that evening, and did not even join in the customary game of whist. I wanted to be quite sure of my nerves, and my vanity made me anxious to make a good figure in the captain's eyes.

The captain was one of those splendidly tough and cheerful speci-
mens of seafaring humanity whose combined courage, hardihood, and
calmness in difficulty leads them naturally into high positions of trust.
He was not the man to be led away by an idle tale, and the mere fact
that he was willing to join me in the investigation was proof that he
thought there was something seriously wrong, which could not be
accounted for on ordinary theories, nor laughed down as a common
superstition. To some extent, too, his reputation was at stake, as well as
the reputation of the ship. It is no light thing to lose passengers overboard, and he knew it.

About ten o'clock that evening, as I was smoking a last cigar, he
came up to me, and drew me aside from the beat of the other passengers who were patrolling the deck in the warm darkness.

"This is a serious matter, Mr. Brisbane," he said. "We must make up
our minds either way—to be disappointed or to have a pretty rough
time of it. You see I cannot afford to laugh at the affair, and I will ask
you to sign your name to a statement of whatever occurs. If nothing
happens tonight we will try it again tomorrow and next day. Are you
ready?"

So we went below, and entered the state-room. As we went in I
could see Robert the steward, who stood a little further down the
passage, watching us, with his usual grin, as though certain that something dreadful was about to happen. The captain closed the door behind us and bolted it.

"Supposing we put your portmanteau before the door," he suggested. "One of us can sit on it. Nothing can get out then. Is the port
screwed down?"

I found it as I had left it in the morning. Indeed, without using
a lever, as I had done, no one could have opened it. I drew back the
curtains of the upper berth so that I could see well into it. By the
captain's advice I lighted my reading lantern, and placed it so that it
shone upon the white sheets above. He insisted upon sitting on the
portmanteau, declaring that he wished to be able to swear that he had
sat before the door.

Then he requested me to search the state-room thoroughly, an
operation very soon accomplished, as it consisted merely in looking
beneath the lower berth and under the couch below the porthole. The
spaces were quite empty.

"It is impossible for any human being to get in," I said, "or for any human being to open the port."

"Very good," said the captain calmly. "If we see anything now, it must be either imagination or something supernatural."

I sat down on the edge of the lower berth.

"The first time it happened," said the captain, crossing his legs and leaning back against the door, "was in March. The passenger who slept here, in the upper berth, turned out have been a lunatic—at all events, he was known to have been a little touched, and he had taken his passage without the knowledge of his friends. He rushed out in the middle of the night, and threw himself overboard, before the officer who had the watch could stop him. We stopped and lowered a boat; it was a quiet night, just before that heavy weather came on; but we could not find him. Of course his suicide was afterwards accounted for on the ground of his insanity."

"I suppose that often happens?" I remarked, rather absently.

"Not often—no," said the captain; "never before in my experience, though I have heard of it happening on board of other ships. Well, as I was saying, that occurred in March. On the very next trip——What are you looking at?" he asked, stopping suddenly in his narration.

I believe I gave no answer. My eyes were riveted upon the porthole. It seemed to me that the brass loop-nut was beginning to turn very slowly upon the screw—so slowly, however, that I was not sure it moved at all. I watched it intently, fixing its position in my mind, and trying to ascertain whether it changed. Seeing where I was looking, the captain looked too.

"It moves!" he exclaimed, in a tone of conviction. "No, it does not," he added, after a minute.

"If it were the jarring of the screw," said I, "it would have opened during the day; but I found it this evening jammed tight as I left it this morning."

I rose and tried the nut. It was certainly loosened, for by an effort I could move it with my hands.

"The queer thing," said the captain, "is that the second man who was lost is supposed to have got through that very port. We had a terrible time over it. It was in the middle of the night, and the weather was very heavy; there was an alarm that one of the ports was open and the sea running in. I came below and found everything flooded, the water pouring in every time she rolled, and the whole port swinging from the top bolts—not the porthole in the middle. Well, we managed to shut it, but the water did some damage. Ever since that the place

275

smells of sea-water from time to time. We supposed the passenger had thrown himself out, though the Lord only knows how he did it. The steward kept telling me that he cannot keep anything shut here. Upon my word—I can smell it now, cannot you?" he enquired, sniffing the air suspiciously.

"Yes—distinctly," I said, and I shuddered as that same odour of stagnant sea-water grew stronger in the cabin. "Now, to smell like this, the place must be damp," I continued, "and yet when I examined it with the carpenter this morning everything was perfectly dry. It is most extraordinary—hallo!"

My reading lantern, which had been placed in the upper berth, was suddenly extinguished. There was still a good deal of light from the pane of ground glass near the door, behind which loomed the regulation lamp. The ship rolled heavily, and the curtain of the upper berth swung far out into the state-room and back again. I rose quickly from my seat on the edge of the bed, and the captain at the same moment started to his feet with a loud cry of surprise. I had turned with the intention of taking down the lantern to examine it, when I heard his exclamation, and immediately afterwards his call for help.

I sprang towards him. He was wrestling with all his might with the brass loop of the port. It seemed to turn against his hands in spite of all his efforts. I caught up my cane, a heavy oak stick I always used to carry, and thrust it through the ring and bore on it with all my strength. But the strong wood snapped suddenly and I fell upon the couch. When I rose again the port was wide open, and the captain was standing with his back against the door, pale to the lips.

"There is something in that berth!" he cried, in a strange voice, his eyes almost starting from his head. "Hold the door, while I look—it shall not escape us, whatever it is!"

But instead of taking his place, I sprang upon the lower bed, and seized something which lay in the upper berth.

It was something ghostly, horrible beyond words, and it moved in my grip. It was like the body of a man long drowned, and yet it moved, and had the strength of ten men living; but I gripped it with all my might—the slippery, oozy, horrible thing—the dead white eyes seemed to stare at me out of the dusk; the putrid odour of rank sea-water was about it, and its shiny hair hung in foul wet curls over its dead face. I wrestled with the dead thing; it thrust itself upon me and forced me back and nearly broke my arms; it wound its corpse's arms about my neck, the living death, and overpowered me, so that I, at last, cried aloud and fell, and left my hold.

As I fell the thing sprang across me, and seemed to throw itself upon the captain. When I last saw him on his feet his face was white and his lips set. It seemed to me that he struck a violent blow at the dead being, and then he, too, fell forward upon his face, with an inarticulate cry of horror.

The thing paused an instant, seeming to hover over his prostrate body, and I could have screamed again for very fright, but I had no voice left. The thing vanished suddenly, and it seemed to my disturbed senses that it made its exit through the open port, though how that was possible, considering the smallness of the aperture, is more than anyone can tell. I lay a long time on the floor, and the captain lay beside me. At last I partially recovered my senses and moved, and instantly I knew that my arm was broken—the small bone of my left forearm near the wrist.

I got upon my feet somehow, and with my remaining hand I tried to raise the captain. He groaned and moved, and at last came to himself. He was not hurt, but he seemed badly stunned.

Well, do you want to hear any more? There is nothing more. That is the end of my story. The carpenter carried out his scheme of running half a dozen four-inch screws through the door of one hundred and five; and if ever you take a passage in the *Kamtschatka*, you may ask for a berth in that state-room. You will be told that it is engaged—yes—it is engaged by that dead thing.

I finished the trip in the surgeon's cabin. He doctored my broken arm, and advised me not to "fiddle about with ghosts and things" any more. The captain was very silent, and never sailed again in that ship, though it is still running. And I will not sail in her either. It was a very disagreeable experience, and I was very badly frightened, which is a thing I do not like. That is all. That is how I saw a ghost—if it was a ghost. It was dead, anyhow.

To Let

B M Croker

Some years ago, when I was a slim young spin, I came out to India
to live with my brother Tom: he and I were members of a large and
somewhat impecunious family, and I do not think my mother was
sorry to have one of her four grown-up daughters thus taken off her
hands. Tom's wife, Aggie, had been at school with my eldest sister; we
had known and liked her all our lives, and regarded her as one of ourselves; and as she and the children were at home when Tom's letter was
received, and his offer accepted, she helped me to choose my slender
outfit, with judgment, zeal, and taste; endowed me with several pretty
additions to my wardrobe; superintended the fitting of my gowns and
the trying on of my hats, with most sympathetic interest, and finally
escorted me out to Lucknow, under her own wing, and installed me
in the only spare room in her comfortable bungalow in Dilkousha.

My sister-in-law is a pretty little brunette, rather pale, with dark
hair, brilliant black eyes, a resolute mouth, and a bright, intelligent
expression. She is orderly, trim, feverishly energetic, and seems to live
every moment of her life. Her children, her wardrobe, her house, her
servants, and last, not least, her husband, are all models in their way;
and yet she has plenty of time for tennis, and dancing, and talking and
walking. She is, undoubtedly, a remarkably talented little creature, and
especially prides herself on her nerve, and her power of will, or will
power. I suppose they are the same thing? and I am sure they are all
the same to Tom, who worships the sole of her small slipper.

Strictly between ourselves, she is the ruling member of the family,
and turns her lord and master round her little finger. Tom is big and
fair (of course), the opposite to his wife, quiet, rather easy-going and
inclined to be indolent; but Aggie rouses him up, and pushes him to
the front, and keeps him there. She knows all about his department,

his prospects of promotion, his prospects of furlough, of getting acting appointments, and so on, even better than he does himself. The
chief of Tom's department—have I said that Tom is in the Irritation
Office?—has placed it solemnly on record that he considers little Mrs.
Shandon a surprisingly clever woman. The two children, Bob and Tor,
are merry, oppressively active monkeys, aged three and five years re-
spectively. As for myself, I am tall, fair—and I wish I could add pretty!
but this is a true story. My eyes are blue, my teeth are white, my hair is
red—alas, a blazing red; and I was, at this period, nineteen years of age;
and now I think I have given a sufficient outline of the whole family.

We arrived at Lucknow in November, when the cold weather is
delightful, and everything was delightful to me. The bustle and life of
a great Indian station, the novelty of my surroundings, the early morning rides, picnics down the river, and dances at the "Chutter Munzil,"
made me look upon Lucknow as a paradise on earth; and in this light
I still regarded it, until a great change came over the temperature, and
the month of April introduced me to red-hot winds, sleepless nights,
and the intolerable "brain fever" bird. Aggie had made up her mind
definitely on one subject: we were not to go away to the hills until the
rains. Tom could only get two months' leave (July and August), and she
did not intend to leave him to grill on the plains alone.

As for herself and the children—not to speak of me—we had all
come out from home so recently that we did not require a change.
The trip to Europe had made a vast hole in the family stocking, and
she wished to economise; and who can economize with two estab-
lishments in full swing? Tell me this, ye Anglo Indian matrons? With
a large, cool bungalow, plenty of *punkhas*, *khuskhus* tatties, ice, and a
thermantidote, surely, we could manage to brave May and June—at
any rate the attempt was made. Gradually the hills drained Lucknow
week by week; family after family packed up, warned us of our folly in
remaining on the plains, offered to look for houses for us, and left by
the night mail. By the middle of May, the place was figuratively empty.

Nothing can be more dreary than a large station in the hot weather—unless it is an equally forsaken hill station in the depths of winter, when the mountains are covered with snow, the mall no longer
resounds with gay voices and the tramp of *Jampanies*, but is visited by
bears and panthers, and the houses are closed, and, as it were, put to
bed in straw! As for Lucknow in the summer, it was a melancholy spot;
the public gardens were deserted, the chairs at the Chutter Munzil
stood empty, the very bands had gone to the hills! the shops were shut,

the baked white roads, no longer thronged with carriages and bamboo carts, gave ample room to the humble *ekka*, or a *dhobie's* meagre donkey, shuffling along in the dust.

Of course, we were not the *only* people remaining in the place, grumbling at the heat and dust and life in general; but there can be no sociability with the thermometer above 100° in the shade. Through the long, long Indian day we sat and gasped, in darkened rooms, and consumed quantities of "Nimbo pegs," *i.e.* limes and soda water, and listened to the fierce hot wind roaring along the road and driving the roasted leaves before it; and in the evening, when the sun had set, we went for a melancholy drive through the Wingfield Park, or round by Martiniere College, and met our friends at the library, and compared sensations and thermometers.

The season was exceptionally bad (but people say that every year), and presently Bobby and Tor began to fade: their little white faces and listless eyes appealed to Aggie as Tom's anxious expostulations had never done. "Yes, they must go to the hills with *me*." But this idea I repudiated at once; I refused to undertake the responsibility—I, who could scarcely speak a word to the servants—who had no experience! Then Bobbie had a bad go of fever—intermittent fever; the beginning of the end to his alarmed mother; the end being represented by a large gravestone! She now became as firmly determined to go, as she had previously been resolved to stay; but it was so late in the season to take a house.

Alas, alas, for the beautiful tempting advertisements in the *Pioneer*, which we had seen and scorned! Aggie wrote to a friend in a certain hill station, called (for this occasion only) "Kantia," and Tom wired to a house agent, who triumphantly replied by letter, that there was not *one* unlet bungalow on his books. This missive threw us into the depths of despair; there seemed no alternative but a hill hotel, and the usual quarters that await the last comers, and the proverbial welcome for children and dogs (we had only four); but the next day brought us good news from Aggie's friend Mrs. Chalmers, she said:

Dear Mrs. Shandon,
I received your letter, and went at once to Cursitjee, the agent. Every hole and corner up here seems full, and he had not a single house to let. Today I had a note from him, saying that Briarwood is vacant; the people who took it are not coming up, they have gone to Naini Tal. You *are* in luck. I have just been

out to see the house, and have secured it for you. It is a mile and a half from the club, but I know that you and your sister are capital walkers. I envy you. Such a charming place—two sitting-rooms, four bedrooms, four bathrooms, a hall, servants' go-downs, stabling, and a splendid view from a very pretty garden, and only *Rs*. 800 for the season! Why, I am paying *Rs*. 1000 for a *very* inferior house, with scarcely a stick of furniture and no view. I feel so proud of myself, and I am longing to show you my treasure-trove. Telegraph when you start, and I shall have a milkman in waiting and fires in all the rooms.

    Yours sincerely,

                             Edith Chalmers.

We now looked upon Mrs. Chalmers as our best and dearest friend, and began to get under way at once. A long journey in India is a serious business, when the party comprises two ladies, two children, two ayahs, and five other servants, three fox terriers, a mongoose, and a Persian cat—all these animals going to the hills for the benefit of their health—not to speak of a ton of luggage, including crockery and lamps, a cottage piano, a goat, and a pony. Aggie and I, the children, one *ayah*, two terriers, the cat and mongoose, our bedding and pillows, the *tiffin* basket and ice basket, were all stowed into one compartment, and I must confess that the journey was truly miserable. The heat was stifling, despite the water tatties. One of the terriers had a violent dispute with the cat, and the cat had a difference with the mongoose, and Bob and Tor had a pitched battle; more than once I actually wished myself back in Lucknow.

I was most truly thankful to wake one morning, to find myself under the shadow of the Himalayas—not a mighty, snow-clad range of everlasting hills, but merely the spurs—the moderate slopes, covered with scrub, loose shale, and jungle, and deceitful little trickling watercourses. We sent the servants on ahead, whilst we rested at the *Dak* bungalow near the railway station, and then followed them at our leisure. We accomplished the ascent in dandies—open kind of boxes, half box, half chair, carried on the shoulders of four men. This was an entirely novel sensation to me, and at first an agreeable one, so long as the slopes were moderate, and the paths wide; but the higher we went, the narrower became the path, the steeper the naked precipice; and as my coolies would walk at the extreme edge, with the utmost indifference to my frantic appeals to "*Beetor! Beetor!*"—and would change poles at the most agonising corners—my feelings were very mixed, especially when droves of loose pack ponies came thundering downhill, with no respect for the rights of the road. Late at night we passed through Kantia, and arrived at Briarwood, far too weary to be critical. Fires were blazing, supper was prepared, and we despatched it in haste, and most thankfully went to bed and slept soundly, as anyone would do who had spent thirty-six hours in a crowded compartment, and ten in a cramped wooden case.

The next morning, rested and invigorated, we set out on a tour of inspection; and it is almost worthwhile to undergo a certain amount of baking in the sweltering heat of the lower regions, in order to enjoy those deep first draughts of cool hill air, instead of a stifling, dust-laden atmosphere; and to appreciate the green valleys and blue hills, by force of contrast to the far-stretching, eye-smarting, white glaring roads, that intersect the burnt-up plains—roads and plains, that even the pariah abandons, salamander though he be!

To our delight and surprise, Mrs. Chalmers had by no means overdrawn the advantages of our new abode. The bungalow was solidly built of stone, two storeyed, and ample in size. It stood on a kind of shelf, cut out of the hillside, and was surrounded by a pretty flower garden, full of roses, fuchsias, and carnations. The high road passed the gate, from which the avenue descended, direct to the entrance door, at the end of the house, and from whence ran a long passage. Off this passage three rooms opened to the right, all looking south, and all looking into a deep, delightful, flagged, verandah. The stairs were very steep. At the head of them, the passage and rooms were repeated.

There were small nooks, and dressing-rooms, and convenient outhouses, and plenty of good water; but the glory of Briarwood was undoubtedly its verandah: it was fully twelve feet wide, roofed with zinc, and overhung a precipice of a thousand feet—not a startlingly sheer *khud*, but a tolerably straight descent of grey-blue shale, rocks, and low jungle. From it there was a glorious view, across a valley, far away, to the snowy range. It opened at one end into the avenue, and was not enclosed; but at the side next the precipice, there was a stout wooden railing, with netting at the bottom, for the safety of too enterprising dogs or children A charming spot, despite its rather bold situation; and as Aggie and I sat in it, surveying the scenery and inhaling the pure hill air, and watching Bob and Tor tearing up and down, playing horses, we said to one another that "the verandah alone was worth half the rent."

"It's absurdly cheap," exclaimed my sister-in-law complacently. "I wish you saw the hovel *I* had, at Simla, for the same rent. I wonder if it is feverish, or badly drained, or what?"

"Perhaps it has a ghost," I suggested facetiously; and at such an absurd idea we both went into peals of laughter.

At this moment Mrs. Chalmers appeared, brisk, rosy, and breathlessly benevolent, having walked over from Kantia.

"So you have found it," she said as we shook hands. "I said nothing about this delicious verandah! I thought I would keep it as a surprise. I did not say a word too much for Briarwood, did I?"

"Not half enough," we returned rapturously; and presently we went in a body, armed with a list from the agent, and proceeded to go over the house and take stock of its contents.

"It's not a bit like a *hill* furnished house," boasted Mrs. Chalmers, with a glow of pride, as she looked round the drawing-room; "carpets, curtains, solid, *very* solid chairs, and Berlin wool-worked screens, a card-table, and any quantity of pictures."

"Yes, don't they look like family portraits?" I suggested, as we gazed at them. There was one of an officer in faded water colours, another of his wife, two of a previous generation in oils and amply gilded frames, two sketches of an English country house, and some framed photographs—groups of grinning cricketers, or wedding guests. All the rooms were well, almost handsomely, furnished in an old-fashioned style. There was no scarcity of wardrobes, looking-glasses, or even armchairs, in the bedrooms, and the pantry was fitted out—a most singular circumstance—with a large supply of handsome glass and china, lamps, old moderators, coffee and teapots, plated side dishes, and candlesticks, cooking utensils and spoons and forks, wine coasters and a cake-basket. These articles were all let with the house (much to our amazement), provided we were responsible for the same. The china was Spode, the plate old family heirlooms, with a crest—a winged horse—on everything, down to the very mustard spoons.

"The people who own this house must be lunatics," remarked Aggie, as she peered round the pantry; "fancy hiring out one's best family plate, and good old china! And I saw some ancient music-books in the drawing-room, and there is a side saddle in the bottle *khana*."

"My dear, the people who owned this house are dead," explained Mrs. Chalmers. "I heard all about them last evening from Mrs. Starkey."

"Oh, is *she* up there?" exclaimed Aggie, somewhat fretfully.

"Yes, her husband is cantonment magistrate. This house belonged to an old retired colonel and his wife. They and his niece lived here. These were all their belongings. They died within a short time of one another, and the old man left a queer will, to say that the house was to remain precisely as they left it for twenty years, and at the end of that time, it was to be sold and all the property dispersed. Mrs. Starkey says she is sure that he never intended it to be *let*, but the heir-at-law insists on that, and is furious at the terms of the will."

"Well, it is a very good thing for us," remarked Aggie; "we are as comfortable here, as if we were in our own house: there is a stove in the kitchen, there are nice boxes for firewood in every room, clocks, real hair mattresses—in short, it is as you said, a treasure trove."

We set to work to modernise the drawing-room with *phoolkaries*, Madras muslin curtains, photograph screens and frames, and such-like portable articles. We placed the piano across a corner, arranged flowers in some handsome Dresden china vases, and entirely altered and improved the character of the room. When Aggie had despatched a most glowing description of our new quarters to Tom, and when we had had *tiffin*, we set off to walk into Kantia to put our names down at the library, and to inquire for letters at the post-office. Aggie met a good many acquaintances—who does not, who has lived five years in India in the same district?

Among them Mrs. Starkey, an elderly lady with a prominent nose and goggle eyes, who greeted her loudly across the reading-room table, in this agreeable fashion:

"And so, you have come up after *all*, Mrs. Shandon. Someone told me that you meant to remain below, but I knew you never could be so wicked as to keep your poor little children in that heat." Then coming round and dropping into a chair beside her, she said, "And I suppose this young lady is your sister-in-law?"

Mrs. Starkey eyed me critically, evidently appraising my chances in the great marriage market. She herself had settled her own two daughters most satisfactorily, and had now nothing to do, but interest herself in other people's affairs.

"Yes," acquiesced Aggie; "Miss Shandon—Mrs. Starkey."

"And so, you have taken Briarwood?"

"Yes, we have been most lucky to get it."

"I hope you will think so, at the end of three months," observed Mrs. Starkey, with a significant pursing of her lips. "Mrs. Chalmers is a stranger up here, or she would not have been in such a hurry to jump at it."

"Why, what is the matter with it?" inquired Aggie. "It is well built, well furnished, well situated, and very cheap."

"That's just it—*suspiciously* cheap. Why, my dear Mrs. Shandon, if there was not something against it, it would let for two hundred *rupees* a month. Common sense would tell you that!"

"And what is against it?"

"It's haunted! There you have the reason in two words."

"Is that all? I was afraid it was the drains. I don't believe in ghosts and haunted houses. What are we supposed to see?"

"Nothing," retorted Mrs. Starkey, who seemed a good deal nettled at our smiling incredulity.

"Nothing!" with an exasperating laugh.

"No, but you will make up for it in hearing. Not now—you are all right for the next six weeks—but after the monsoon breaks, I give you a week at Briarwood. No one would stand it longer, and indeed you might as well bespeak your rooms at Cooper's Hotel *now*. There is always a rush up here in July, by the two months' leave people, and you will be poked into some wretched go-down."

Aggie laughed, rather a careless ironical little laugh, and said, "Thank you, Mrs. Starkey; but I think we will stay on where we are—at any rate for the present."

"Of course, it will be as *you* please. What do you think of the verandah?" she inquired, with a curious smile.

"I think, as I was saying to Susan, that it is worth half the rent of the house."

"And in *my* opinion the house is worth double rent without it;" and with this enigmatic remark, she rose, and sailed away.

"Horrid old frump!" exclaimed Aggie, as we walked home in the starlight. "She is jealous and angry that she did not get Briarwood *herself*—I know her so well. She is always hinting, and repeating stories about the nicest people—always decrying your prettiest dress, or your best servant."

We soon forgot all about Mrs. Starkey, and her dismal prophecy, being too gay, and too busy, to give her, or it, a thought. We had so many engagements—tennis-parties and tournaments, picnics, concerts, dances, and little dinners. We ourselves gave occasional afternoon teas in the verandah—using the best Spode cups and saucers, and the old silver cake-basket—and were warmly complimented on our good fortune in securing such a charming house and garden. One day the children discovered, to their great joy, that the old *chowkidar* belonging to the bungalow possessed an African grey parrot—a rare bird indeed in India; he had a battered Europe cage, doubtless a remnant of better days, and swung on his ring, looking up at us inquiringly, out of his impudent little black eyes.

The parrot had been the property of the former inmates of Briarwood, and as it was a long-lived creature, had survived its master and mistress, and was boarded out with the *chowkidar*, at one *rupee* per month.

The *chowkidar* willingly carried the cage into the verandah, where the bird seemed perfectly at home.

We got a little table for its cage, and the children were delighted with him, as he swung to and fro, with a bit of cake in his wrinkled claw.

Presently he startled us all by suddenly calling "Lucy," in a voice that was as distinct as if it had come from a human throat. "Pretty Lucy—Lu—cy."

"That must have been the niece," said Aggie. "I expect she was the original of that picture over the chimney-piece in your room; she looks like a Lucy."

It was a large, framed, half-length photograph of a very pretty girl, in a white dress, with gigantic open sleeves. The ancient parrot talked incessantly now that he had been restored to society; he whistled for the dogs, and brought them flying to his summons—to his great satisfaction, and their equally great indignation. He called "*Qui hye*" so naturally, in a lady's shrill *soprano*, or a gruff male bellow, that I have no doubt our servants would have liked to have wrung his neck. He coughed and expectorated like an old gentleman, and whined like a puppy, and mewed like a cat, and, I am sorry to add, sometimes swore like a trooper; but his most constant cry was, "Lucy, where are you, pretty Lucy—Lucy—Lu—cy?"

★★★★★★

Aggie and I went to various picnics, but to that given by the Chalmers (in honour of Mr. Chalmers' brother Charlie, a captain in a Ghoorka regiment, just come up to Kantia on leave) Aggie was unavoidably absent. Tor had a little touch of fever, and she did not like to leave him; but I went under my hostess's care, and expected to enjoy myself immensely. Alas! on that self-same afternoon, the long-expected monsoon broke, and we were nearly drowned! We rode to the selected spot, five miles from Kantia, laughing and chattering, indifferent to the big blue-black clouds that came slowly, but surely, sailing up from below; it was a way they had had for days, and nothing had come of it!

We spread the table-cloth, boiled the kettle, unpacked the hampers, in spite of sharp gusts of wind and warning rumbling thunder. Just as we had commenced to reap the reward of our exertions, there fell a few huge drops, followed by a vivid flash, and then a tremendous crash of thunder, like a whole park of artillery, that seemed to shake the mountains—and after this the deluge. In less than a minute we were soaked through; we hastily gathered up the table-cloth by its four ends, gave it to the coolies, and fled.

It was all I could do to stand against the wind; only for Captain Chalmers I believe I would have been blown away; as it was, I lost my hat, it was whirled into space. Mrs. Chalmers lost her boa, and Mrs. Starkey, not merely her bonnet, but some portion of her hair. We were truly in a wretched plight, the water streaming down our faces, and squelching in our boots; the little trickling mountain rivulets were now like racing seas of turbid water; the lightning was almost blinding; the trees rocked dangerously, and lashed one another with their quivering branches. I had never been out in such a storm before, and sincerely hope I never may again. We reached Kantia more dead than alive, and Mrs. Chalmers sent an express to Aggie, and kept me till the next day. After raining as it only can rain in the Himalayas, the weather cleared, the sun shone, and I rode home in borrowed plumes, full of my adventures, and in the highest spirits. I found Aggie sitting over the fire in the drawing-room, looking ghastly white: that was nothing uncommon; but terribly depressed, which was most unusual.

"I am afraid you have neuralgia?" I said, as I kissed her.

She nodded, and made no reply,

"How is Tor?" I inquired, as I drew a chair up to the fire.

"Better—quite well."

"Any news—any letter?"

"Not a word—not a line."

"Has anything happened to Pip"—Pip was a fox-terrier, renowned for having the shortest tail and being the most impertinent dog in Lucknow—"or the mongoose?"

"No, you silly girl! Why do you ask such ridiculous questions?"

"I was afraid something was amiss; you seem rather down on your luck."

Aggie shrugged her shoulders, and then said, "Pray, what put such an absurd idea into your head? Tell me all about the picnic," and she began to talk rapidly, and to ask me various questions; but I observed that once she had set me going—no difficult task—her attention flagged, her eyes wandered from my face to the fire. She was not listening to half I said, and my most thrilling descriptions were utterly lost on this indifferent, abstracted little creature! I noticed from this time, that she had become strangely nervous (for her).

She invited herself to the share of half my bed; she was restless, *distrait*, and even irritable; and when I was asked out to spend the day, dispensed with my company with an alacrity that was by no means flattering. Formerly, of an evening she used to herd the children home at sundown, and tear me away from the delights of the reading-room at seven o'clock; now she hung about the library, until almost the last moment, until it was time to put out the lamps, and kept the children with her, making transparent pretexts for their company.

Often, we did not arrive at home till half-past eight o'clock. I made no objections to these late hours, neither did Charlie Chalmers, who often walked back with us and remained to dinner. I was amazed to notice that Aggie seemed delighted to have his company, for she had always expressed a rooted aversion to what she called "tame young men," and here was this new acquaintance dining with us, at least twice a week!

About a month after the picnic we had a spell of dreadful weather—thunderstorms accompanied by torrents. One pouring afternoon, Aggie and I were cowering over the drawing-room fire, whilst the rain came fizzing down among the logs, and ran in rivers off the roof, and out of the spouts. There had been no going out that day, and we were feeling rather flat and dull, as we sat in a kind of ghostly twilight, with all outdoor objects swallowed up in mist, listening to the violent battering of the rain on the zinc verandah, and the storm which was growling round the hills.

"Oh, for a visitor!" I exclaimed; "but no one but a fish, or a lunatic, would be out on such an evening."

"No one, indeed," echoed Aggie, in a melancholy tone. "We may as well draw the curtains, and have in the lamp and tea to cheer us up."

She had scarcely finished speaking, when I heard the brisk trot of a horse along the road. It stopped at the gate, and came rapidly down our avenue. I heard the wet gravel crunching under his hoofs, and—yes, a man's cheery whistle. My heart jumped, and I half rose from my chair. It must be Charlie Chalmers braving the elements to see *me!*—

such, I must confess, was my incredible vanity! He did not stop at the front door as usual, but rode straight into the verandah, which afforded ample room, and shelter for half a dozen mounted men.

"Aggie," I said eagerly, "do you hear? It must be—"

I paused, my tongue silenced, by the awful pallor of her face, and the expression of her eyes, as she sat with her little hands clutching the arms of her chair, and her whole figure bent forward in an attitude of listening—an attitude of rigid terror.

"What is it, Aggie?" I said. "Are you ill?"

As I spoke, the horse's hoofs made a loud clattering noise on the stone-paved verandah outside, and a man's voice—a young man's eager voice—called, "Lucy."

Instantly a chair near the writing-table was pushed back, and someone went quickly to the window—a French one—and bungled for a moment with the fastening. I always had a difficulty with that window *myself*. Aggie and I were within the bright circle of the firelight, but the rest of the room was dim, and outside the streaming grey sky was spasmodically illuminated by occasional vivid flashes, that lit up the surrounding hills as if it were daylight. The trampling of impatient hoofs, and the rattling of a door-handle, were the only sounds that were audible for a few breathless seconds; but during those seconds Pip, bristling like a porcupine, and trembling violently in every joint, had sprung off my lap and crawled abjectly under Aggie's chair, seemingly in a transport of fear.

The door was opened audibly, and a cold, icy blast swept in, that seemed to freeze my very heart, and made me shiver from head to foot. At this moment there came, with a sinister blue glare, the most vivid flash of lightning I ever saw. It lit up the whole room, which was empty save for ourselves, and was instantly followed by a clap of thunder, that caused my knees to knock together, and that terrified me and filled me with horror. It evidently terrified the horse too; there was a violent plunge, a clattering of hoofs on the stones, a sudden loud crash of smashing timber, a woman's long, loud, piercing shriek, which stopped the very beating of my heart, and then a frenzied struggle in the cruel, crumbling, treacherous shale, the rattle of loose stones, and the hollow roar of something sliding down the precipice.

I rushed to the door and tore it open, with that awful despairing cry still ringing in my ears. The verandah was empty; there was not a soul to be seen, or a sound to be heard, save the rain on the roof.

"Aggie," I screamed, "come here! Someone has gone over the verandah, and down the *khud!* You heard him."

"Yes," she said, following me out; "but come in—come in."

"I believe it was Charlie Chalmers"—shaking her violently as I spoke. "He has been killed—killed—killed! And you stand, and do nothing. Send people! Let us go ourselves! Bearer! *Ayah! Khidmatgar!*" I cried, raising my voice.

"Hush! It was *not* Charlie Chalmers," she said, vainly endeavouring to draw me into the drawing-room. "Come in—come in."

"No, no!" pushing her away, and wringing my hands. "How cruel you are! How inhuman! There is a path. Let us go at once—at once!"

"You need not trouble yourself, Susan," she interrupted; "and you need not cry and tremble;—*they* will bring him up. What you heard was supernatural; it was not real."

"No—no—no! It was all real. Oh! that scream is in my ears still."

"I will convince you," said Aggie, taking my hand as she spoke. "Feel all along the verandah. Are the railings broken?"

I did as she bade me. No, though very wet, and clammy, the railing was intact!

"Where is the broken place?" she asked, imperatively.

Where, indeed?

"Now," she continued, " since you will not come in, look over, and you will see something more presently."

Shivering with fear, and the cold, drifting rain, I gazed down as she bade me, and there, far below, I saw lights moving rapidly to and fro, evidently in search of something. After a little delay they congregated in one place. There was a low, buzzing murmur—they had found him—and presently they commenced to ascend the hill, with the "hum-hum" of *coolies* carrying a burden. Nearer and nearer the lights and sounds came; up to the very brink of the *khud*, past the end of the verandah. Many steps and many torches—faint blue torches held by invisible hands—invisible but heavy-footed bearers carried their burden slowly upstairs, and along the passage, and deposited it with a dump in Aggie's bedroom! As we stood clasped in one another's arms, and shaking all over, the steps descended, the ghostly lights passed up the avenue, and gradually disappeared in the gathering darkness. The repetition of the tragedy was over for that day.

"Have you heard it before?" I asked with chattering teeth, as I bolted the drawing-room window.

"Yes, the evening of the picnic, and twice since. That is the reason I have always tried to stay out till late, and to keep you out. I was hoping and praying you might never hear it. It always happens just before dark: I am afraid you have thought me very queer of late. I have told no end of stories to keep you and the children from harm. I have—"

"I think you have been very kind," I interrupted. "Oh, Aggie, shall you ever get that crash, and that awful cry out of your head?"

"*Never!*" hastily lighting the candles as she spoke.

"Is there anything more?" I inquired tremulously.

"Yes; sometimes at night, the most terrible weeping and sobbing in my bedroom;" and she shuddered at the mere recollection.

"Do the servants know?" I asked anxiously.

"The *ayah* Muma has heard it, and the *khansamah* says his mother is sick, and he must go, and the bearer wants to attend his brother's wedding. They will *all* leave."

"I suppose most people know too?" I suggested dejectedly.

"Yes; don't you remember Mrs. Starkey's warnings, and her saying that without the verandah the house was worth double rent? We understand that dark speech of hers *now*, and we have not come to Cooper's Hotel yet."

"No, not *yet*. I wish we *had*. I wonder what Tom will say? He will be here in another fortnight. Oh, I wish he was here now!"

In spite of our heart-shaking experience, we managed to eat, and drink, and sleep, yea, to play tennis—somewhat solemnly, it is true—and go to the club, where we remained to the very *last* moment; needless to mention, that I now entered into Aggie's manoeuvre *con amore*. Mrs. Starkey evidently divined the reason of our loitering in Kantia, and said in her most truculent manner, as she squared up to us—

"You keep your children out very late, Mrs. Shandon."

"Yes, but we like to have them with us," rejoined Aggie, in a meek apologetic voice.

"Then why don't you go home earlier?"

"Because it is so stupid, and lonely," was the mendacious answer.

"Lonely is not the word *I* should use. I wonder if you are as wise as your neighbours now? Come now, Mrs. Shandon."

"About what?" said Aggie, with ill-feigned innocence.

"About Briarwood. Haven't you heard it yet? The ghastly precipice and horse affair?"

"Yes, I suppose we may as well confess that we *have*."

"Humph! you are a brave couple to stay on. The Tombs tried it last year for three weeks. The Paxtons took it the year before, and then sub-let it; not that *they* believed in ghosts—oh, dear no!" and she laughed ironically.

"And what is the story?" I inquired eagerly.

"Well, the story is this. An old retired officer and his wife, and their pretty niece, lived at Briarwood a good many years ago. The girl was engaged to be married to a fine young fellow in the Guides. The day before the wedding, what you know of happened, and has happened every monsoon ever since. The poor girl went out of her mind, and destroyed herself, and the old colonel and his wife did not long survive her. The house is uninhabitable in the monsoon, and there seems nothing for it but to auction off the furniture, and pull it down; it will always be the same as long as it stands. Take *my* advice, and come into Cooper's Hotel. I believe you can have that small set of rooms at the back. The sitting-room smokes—but beggars can't be choosers."

"That will only be our very last resource," said Aggie, hotly.

"It's not very grand, I grant you; but any port in a storm."

Tom arrived, was doubly welcome, and was charmed with Briarwood, chaffed us unmercifully, and derided our fears until *he* himself had a similar experience, and heard the phantom horse plunging in the verandah, and that wild, unearthly and utterly appalling shriek. No, he could not laugh *that* away; and seeing that we had now a mortal abhorrence of the place, that the children had to be kept abroad in the damp till long after dark, that Aggie was a mere hollow-eyed spectre, and that we had scarcely a servant left, that—in short, one day, we packed up precipitately and fled in a body to Cooper's Hotel. But we did not basely endeavour to sub-let, nor advertise Briarwood as "a delightfully situated *pucka* built house, containing all the requirements of a gentleman's family." No, no. Tom bore the loss of the rent, and—a more difficult feat—Aggie bore Mrs. Starkey's insufferable "I told you so."

Aggie was at Kantia again last season. She walked out early one morning to see our former abode. The *chowkidar* and parrot are still in possession, and are likely to remain the solo tenants on the premises. The parrot suns and dusts his ancient feathers in the empty verandah, which re-echoes with his cry of "Lucy, where are you—pretty Lucy?" The *chowkidar* inhabits a secluded go-down at the back, where he passes most of the day in sleeping, or smoking the soothing "*huka*."

The place has a forlorn, uncared-for appearance now; the flowers are nearly all gone; the paint has peeled off the doors and windows; the avenue is grass-grown. Briarwood appears to have resigned itself to emptiness, neglect, and decay, although outside the gate there still hangs a battered board, on which, if you look very closely, you can decipher the words "*To Let.*"

The Crooked Branch

(*A.k.a. The Ghost in the Garden Room*)
Elizabeth Gaskell

Not many years after the beginning of this century, worthy couple of the name of Huntroyd occupied a mall farm in the North Riding of Yorkshire. They had married late in life, although they were very young when they first began to "keep company" with each other. Nathan Huntroyd had been farm servant to Hester Rose's father, and had made up to her at a time when her parents thought she might do better; and so, without much consultation of her feelings, they had dismissed Nathan in somewhat cavalier fashion. He had drifted far away from his former connections, when an uncle of his died, leaving Nathan—by this time upwards of forty years of age—enough money to stock a small farm, and yet have something over to put in the bank against bad times.

One of the consequences of this bequest was, that Nathan was looking out for a wife and housekeeper, in a kind of discreet and leisurely way, when, one day, he heard that his old love, Hester, was—not married and flourishing, as he had always supposed her to be—but a poor maid-of-all-work, in the town of Ripon. For her father lad had a succession of misfortunes, which had brought him in his old age to the workhouse; her mother was dead; her only brother struggling to bring up a large family; and Hester herself, a hard-working, homely-looking (at thirty-seven) servant Nathan had a kind of growling satisfaction (which only lasted for a minute or two, however) in hearing of these turns of Fortune's wheel. He did not make many intelligible remarks to his informant, and to no one else did he say a word. But, a few days afterwards, he presented himself, dressed in his Sunday best, at Mrs. Thompson's back door in Ripon.

Hester stood there, in answer to the good sound knock his good sound oak stick made; she with the light full upon her, he in shadow.

For a moment there was silence. He was scanning the fate and figure of his old love, for twenty years unseen. The comely beauty of youth had faded away entirely; she was, as I have said, homely-looking, plain-featured, but with a clean skin, and pleasant, frank eyes. Her figure was no longer round, hut tidily draped in a blue and white bed-gown, tied round her waist by her white apron-strings, and her short red linsey petticoat showed her tidy feet and ankles. Her former lover fell into no ecstasies. He simply said to himself, "She'll do;" and forthwith began upon his business.

"Hester, thou dost not mind me, I am Nathan, as thy father turned off at a minute's notice, for thinking of thee for a wife, twenty year come Michaelmas next I have not thought much upon matrimony since. But Uncle Ben has died, leaving me a small matter in the bank; and I have taken Nab-end Farm, and put in a bit of stock, and shall want a missus to see after it. Wilt like to come? I'll not mislead thee. It's dairy, and it might have been arable. But arable takes more horses nor it suited me to buy, and I'd the offer of a tidy lot of kine. That's all. If thou'lt have me, I'll come for thee as soon as the hay is gotten in."

Hester only said, "Come in, and sit thee down."

He came in, and sat down. For a time, she took no more notice of him than of his stick, bustling about to get dinner ready for the family whom she served. He meanwhile watched her brisk, sharp movements, and repeated to himself, "She'll do!" After about twenty minutes of silence thus employed, he got up, saying:

"Well, Hester, I'm going. When shall I come back again?"

"Please thysel', and thou'll please me," said Hester, in a tone that she tried to make light and indifferent; but he saw that her colour came and went, and that she trembled while she moved about. In another moment Hester was soundly kissed; but when she looked round to scold the middle-aged farmer, he appeared so entirely composed that she hesitated. He said:

"I have pleased mysel', and thee too, I hope. Is it a month's wage, and a month's warning? Today is the eighth. July eighth is our wedding-day. I have no time to spend a-wooing before then, and wedding must na take long. Two days is enough to throw away, at our time o' life."

It was like a dream; but Hester resolved not to think more about it till her work was done. And when all was cleaned up for the evening, she went and gave her mistress warning, telling her all the history of her life in, a very few words. That day month she was married from

Mrs. Thompson's house.

The issue of the marriage was one boy, Benjamin. A few years after his birth, Hester's brother died at Leeds, leaving ten or twelve children. Hester sorrowed bitterly over this loss; and Nathan showed her much quiet sympathy, although he could not but remember that Jack Rose had added insult to the bitterness of his youth. He helped his wife to make ready to go by the waggon to Leeds, He made light of the household difficulties, which came thronging into her mind after all was fixed for her departure. He filled her purse, that she might have wherewithal to alleviate the immediate wants of her brother's family. And as she was leaving, he ran after the waggon.

"Stop, stop!" he cried. "Hetty, if thou wilt—if it wunnot be too much for thee—bring back one of Jack's wenches for company, like, We've enough and to spare; and a lass will make the house winsome, as a man may say."

The waggon moved on; while Hester had such a silent swelling of gratitude in her heart, as was both thanks to her husband, and thanksgiving to God.

And that was the way that little Bessy Rose came to be an inmate of the Nah's-end Farm,

Virtue met with its own reward in this instance, and in a clear and tangible shape, too, which need not delude people in general into thinking that such is the usual nature of virtue' s rewards. Bessy grew up a bright, affectionate, active girl; a daily comfort to her uncle and aunt She was so much a darling in the household that they even thought her worthy of their only son Benjamin, who was perfection in their eyes. It is not often the case that two plain, homely people have a child of uncommon beauty; but it is so sometimes, and Benjamin Huntroyd was one of these exceptional cases.

The hardworking, labour-and-care-marked farmer, and the mother, who could never have been more than tolerably comely in her best days, produced a boy who might have been an earl's son for grace and beauty. Even the hunting squires of the neighbourhood reined up their horses to admire him, as he opened the gates for them. He had no shyness, he was so accustomed to admiration from strangers, and adoration from his parents from his earliest years. As for Bessy Rose, he ruled imperiously over her heart from the time she first set eyes on him. And as she grew older, she grew on in loving, persuading herself that what her uncle and aunt loved so dearly it was her duty to love dearest of all.

At every unconscious symptom of the young girl's love for her cousin, his parents smiled and winked: all was going on as they wished, no need to go far afield for Benjamin's wife. The household could go on as it was now; Nathan and Hester sinking into the rest of years, and relinquishing care and authority to those dear ones, who, in process of time, might bring other dear ones to share their love.

But Benjamin took it all very coolly. He had been sent to a day-school in the neighbouring town—a grammar-school, in the high state of neglect in which the majority of such schools were thirty years ago. Neither his father nor his mother knew much of learning. All that they knew (and that directed their choice of a school) was, that they would not, by any possibility, part with their darling to a boarding-school; that some schooling he must have, and that Squire Pollard's son went to Highminster Grammar School Squire Pollard's son, and many another son destined to make his parents' hearts ache, went to this school.

If it had not been so utterly bad a place of education, the simple farmer and his wife might have found it out sooner. But not only did the pupils there learn vice, they also learnt deceit Benjamin was naturally too clever to remain a dunce, or else, if he had chosen so to be, there was nothing in Highminster Grammar School to hinder his being a dunce of the first water. But, to all appearance, he grew clever and gentlemanlike. His father and mother were even proud of his airs and graces, when he came home for the holidays; taking them for proofs of his refinement, although the practical effect of such refinement was to make him express his contempt for his parents' homely ways and simple ignorance.

By the time he was eighteen, an articled clerk in an attorney's office at Highminster,—for he had quite declined becoming a "mere clodhopper," that is to say a hard-working, honest farmer like his father—Bessy Rose was the only person who was dissatisfied with him. The little girl of fourteen instinctively felt there was something wrong about him. Alas! two years more, and the girl of sixteen worshipped his very shadow, and would not see that aught could be wrong with one so soft-spoken, so handsome, so kind as Cousin Benjamin. For Benjamin had discovered that the way to cajole his parents out of money for every indulgence he fancied, was to pretend to forward their innocent scheme, and make love to his pretty cousin Bessy Rose.

He cared just enough for her to make this work of necessity not disagreeable at the time he was performing it. But he found it tiresome to remember her little claims upon him, when she was no longer present. The letters he had promised her during his weekly absences at Highminster, the trifling commissions she had asked him to do for her, were all considered in the light of troubles; and, even when he was with her, he resented the inquiries she made as to his mode of passing his time, or what female acquaintances he had in Highminster.

When his apprenticeship was ended, nothing would serve him but that he must go up to London for a year or two. Poor Farmer Huntroyd was beginning to repent of his ambition of making his son Benjamin a gentleman. But it was too late to repine now. Both father and mother felt this, and, however sorrowful they might be, they were silent, neither demurring nor assenting to Benjamin's proposition when first he made it.

But Bessy, through her tears, noticed that both her uncle and aunt seemed unusually tired that night, and sat hand-in-hand on the fireside settle, idly gazing into the bright flame, as if they saw in it pictures of what they had once hoped their lives would have been. Bessy rattled about among the supper things, as she put them away after Benjamin's departure, making more noise than usual—as if noise and bustle was what she needed to keep her from bursting out crying—and, having at one keen glance taken in the position and looks of Nathan and Hester, she avoided looking in that direction again, for fear the sight of their wistful faces should make her own tears overflow.

"Sit thee down, lass—sit thee down. Bring the creepie-stool to the fireside, and let's have a bit of talk over the lad's plans," said Nathan, at last rousing himself to speak. Bessy came and sat down in front of the fire, and threw her apron over her face, as she rested her head on both hands, Nathan felt as if it was a chance which of the two women burst out crying first So he thought he would speak, in hopes of keeping off the infection of tears.

"Didst ever hear of this mad plan afore, Bessy ?"

"No, never!" Her voice came muffled, and changed from under her apron. Hester felt as if the tone, both of question and answer, implied blame, and this she could not bear.

"We should ha' looked to it when we bound him, for of necessity it would ha' come to this. There's examins, and catechizes, and I dunno what all for him to be put through in London. It's not his fault."

"Which on us said it were ?" asked Nathan, rather put out. "Thof, for that matter, a few weeks would carry him over the mire, and make him as good a lawyer as any judge among 'em. Oud Lawson the attorney told me that, in a talk I had wi' him a bit sin. Na, na I it's the lad's own hankering after London that makes him want for to stay there for a year, let alone two."

Nathan shook his head.

"And if it be his own hankering," said Bessy, putting down her apron, her face all aflame, and her eyes swollen up, "I dunnot see harm in it. Lads aren't like lasses, to be teed to their own fireside like th' crook yonder. It's fitting for a young man to go abroad and see the world afore he settles down."

Hester's hand sought Bessy's, and the two women sat in sympathetic defiance of any blame that should be thrown on the beloved absent. Nathan only said:

"Nay, wench, dunna wax up so; whatten's done's done; and worse, it's my doing. I mun needs make my bairn a gentleman; and we mun pay for it."

"Dear uncle! he wunna spend much, I'll answer for it; and I'll scrimp and save i' th' house to make it good."

"Wench!" said Nathan, solemnly, "it were not paying in cash I were speaking on: it were paying in heart's care, and heaviness of soul. Lunnon is a place where the devil keeps court as well as King George; and my poor chap has more nor once welly fallen into his clutches here. I dunno what he'll do when he gets close within sniff of him."

"Don't let him go, father!" said Hester, for the first time taking this view. Hitherto she bad only thought of her own grief at parting with him. "Father, if you think so, keep him here, safe under our own eye."

"Nay!" said Nathan, "he's past time o' life for that. Why, there's not one on us knows where he is at this present time, and he not gone out of our sight an hour. He's too big to be put back i' th' go-cart, mother, or kept within doors with the chair turned bottom upwards."

"I wish he were a wee bairn lying in my arms again. It were a sore day when I weaned him; and I think life's been gettin' sorer and sorer at every turn he's ta'en towards manhood."

"Coom, lass, that's noan the way to be talking. Be thankful to Marcy that thou'st getten a man for thy son as stands five foot eleven in's stockings, and ne'er a sick piece about him. We wunnot grudge him his fling, will we, Bess, my wench? He'll be coming back in a year, or maybe a bit more; and be a' for settling in a quiet town like, wi' a wife that's noan so fur fra' me at this very minute. An' we oud folk, as we get into years, must gi' up farm, and tak a bit on a house near Lawyer Benjamin."

And so the good Nathan, his own heart heavy enough, tried to soothe his womenkind. But of the three, his eyes were longest in closing; his apprehensions the deepest founded.

"I misdoubt me I hanna done well by th' lad. I misdoubt me sore," was the thought that kept him awake till day began to dawn. "Sura-mat's wrong about him, or folk would na look at me wi' such piteous-like een when they speak on him. I can see th' meaning of it, thof I'm too proud to let on. And Lawson, too, he holds his tongue more nor he should do, when I ax him how my lad's getting on, and whatten sort of a lawyer he'll mak. God be marciful to Hester an' me, if th' lad's gone away! God be marciful! But maybe it's this lying waking a' the night through, that maks me so fearfu'. Why, when I were his age, I daur be bound I should ha' spent money fast enoof, i' I could ha' come by it. But I had to am it; that maks a great differ'. Well! It were hard to thwart th' child of our old age, and we waitin' so long for to have 'un!"

Next morning, Nathan rode Moggy, the carthorse, into Highmin-ster to see Mr. Lawson. Anybody who saw him ride out of his own yard, would have been struck with the change in him which was visible, when he returned; a change, more than a day's unusual exercise should have made in a man of his years. He scarcely held the reins at all. One jerk of Moggy's head would have plucked them out of his hands. His head was bent forward, his eyes looking on some unseen thing, with long unwinking gaze. But as he drew near home on his return, he made an effort to recover himself.

"No need fretting them," he said; "lads will be lads. But I didna think he had it in him to be so thowtless, young as he is. Well, well! he'll maybe get more wisdom i' Lunnon. Anyways it's best to cu him off fra such evil lads as Will Hawker, and suchlike. It's they as have led my boy astray. He were a good chap till he knowed them—a good chap till he knowed them."

But he put all his cares in the background when he came into the houseplace, where both Bessy and his wife met him at the door, and both would fain lend a hand to take off his greatcoat.

"Theer, wenches, theer! ye might let a man alone for to get out on's clothes! Why, I might ha' struck thee, lass." And he went on talking, trying to keep them off for a time from the subject that all had at heart But there was no putting them off for ever; and, by dint of repeated questioning on his wife's part, more was got out than he had ever meant to tell—enough to grieve both his hearers sorely: and yet the brave old man still kept the worst in his own breast.

The next day Benjamin came home for a week or two, before making his great start to London. His father kept him at a distance, and was solemn and quiet in his manner to the young man. Bessy, who had shown anger enough at first, and had uttered many a sharp speech, began to relent, and then to feel hurt and displeased that her uncle should persevere so long in his cold, reserved manner, and Benjamin just going to leave them. Her aunt went, tremblingly busy, about the clothes-presses and drawers, as if afraid of letting herself think either of the past or the future; only once or twice, coming behind her son, she suddenly stooped over his sitting figure, and kissed his cheek, and stroked his hair. Bessy remembered afterwards—long years afterwards—how he had tossed his head away with nervous irritability on one of these occasions, and had muttered—her aunt did not hear it, but Bessy did—

"Can't you leave a man alone?"

Towards Bessy herself he was pretty gracious. No other words express his manner: it was not warm, nor tender, nor cousinly, but there was an assumption of underbred politeness towards her as a young, pretty woman; which politeness was neglected in his authoritative or grumbling manner towards his mother, or his sullen silence before his father. He once or twice ventured on a compliment to Bessy on her personal appearance. She stood still, and looked at him with astonishment.

"How's my eyes changed sin last thou sawst them," she asked, "that thou must be telling me about 'em i' that fashion? I'd rayther by a deal see thee helping thy mother when she's dropped her knitting-needle and canna see i' th' dusk for to pick it up."

But Bessy thought of his pretty speech about her eyes long after he had forgotten making it, and would have been puzzled to tell the colour of them. Many a day, after he was gone, did she look earnestly in the little oblong looking-glass, which hung up against the wall of her little sleeping-chamber, but which she used to take down in order to examine the eyes he had praised, murmuring to herself, "Pretty soft grey eyes! Pretty soft grey eyes!" until she would hang up the glass again with a sudden laugh and a rosy blush.

In the days, when he had gone away to the vague distance and vaguer place—the city called London—Bessy tried to forget all that had gone against her feeling of the affection and duty that a son owed to his parents; and she had many things to forget of this kind that would keep surging up into her mind. For instance, she wished that he had not objected to the home-spun, home-made shirts which his mother and she had had such pleasure in getting ready for him. He might not know, it was true—and so her love urged—how carefully and evenly the thread had been spun: how, not content with bleaching the yarn in the sunniest meadow, the linen, on its return from the weaver's, had been spread out afresh on the sweet summer grass, and watered carefully night after night when there was no dew to perform the kindly office.

He did not know—for no one but Bessy herself did—how many false or large stitches, made large and false by her aunt's failing eyes (who yet liked to do the choicest part of the stitching all by herself), Bessy had unpicked at night in her own room, and with dainty fingers had restitched; sewing eagerly in the dead of night. All this he did not know; or he could never have complained of the coarse texture; the old-fashioned make of these shirts; and urged on his mother to give him part of her little store of egg and butter money in order to buy newer-fashioned linen in Highminster.

When once that little precious store of his mothers was discovered, it was well for Bessy's peace of mind that she did not know how loosely her aunt counted up the coins, mistaking guineas for shillings, or just the other way, so that the amount was seldom the same in the old black spoutless teapot. Yet this son, this hope, this love, had still a strange power of fascination over the household. The evening before he left, he sat between his parents, a hand in theirs on either side, and Bessy on the old creepie-stool, her head lying on her aunt's knee, and looking up at him from time to time, as if to learn his face off by heart; till his glances meeting hers, made her drop her eyes, and only sigh.

He stopped up late that night with his father, long after the women had gone to bed. But not to sleep; for I will answer for it the grey-haired mother never slept a wink till the late dawn of the autumn day, and Bessy heard her uncle come up stairs with heavy, deliberate footsteps, and go to the old stocking which served him for bank; and count out golden guineas—once he stopped, but again he went on afresh, as if resolved to crown his gift with liberality. Another long pause—in which she could but indistinctly hear continued words, it might have been advice, it might be a prayer, for it was in her uncle's voice; and then father and son came up to bed. Bessy's room was but parted from her cousin's by a thin wooden partition; and the last sound she distinctly heard, before her eyes, tired out with crying, closed themselves in sleep, was the guineas clinking down upon each other at regular intervals, as if Benjamin were playing at pitch and toss with his father's present.

After he was gone, Bessy wished he had asked her to walk part of the way with him into Highminster. She was all ready, her things laid out on the bed; but she could not accompany him without invitation.

The little household tried to close over the gap as best they might. They seemed to set themselves to their daily work with unusual vigour; but somehow when evening came there had been little done. Heavy hearts never make light work, and there was no telling how much care and anxiety each had had to bear in secret in the field, at the wheel, or in the dairy. Formerly he was looked for every Saturday; looked for, though he might not come, or if he came, there were things to be spoken about, that made his visit anything but a pleasure: still he might come, and all things might go right, and then what sunshine, what gladness to those humble people!

But now he was away, and dreary winter was come on; old folks' sight fails, and the evenings were long, and sad, in spite of all Bessy could do or say. And he did not write so often as he might—so everyone thought; though everyone would have been ready to defend him from either of the others who had expressed such a thought aloud. "Surely!" said Bessy to herself, when the first primroses peeped out in a sheltered and sunny hedge-bank, and she gathered them as she passed home from afternoon church—"surely, there never will be such a dreary, miserable winter again as this has been." There had been a great change in Nathan and Bessy Huntroyd during this last year.

The spring before, when Benjamin was yet the subject of more hopes than fears, his father and mother looked what I may call an elderly middle-aged couple: people who had a good deal of hearty work in them yet. Now—it was not his absence alone that caused the change—they looked frail and old, as if each day's natural trouble was a burden more than they could bear. For Nathan had heard sad reports about his only child, and had told them solemnly to his wife, as things too bad to be believed, and yet, "God help us, if indeed he is such a lad as this!" Their eyes were become too dry and hollow for many tears; they sat together, hand in hand; and shivered, and sighed, and did not speak many words, or dare to look at each other: and then Hester had said:

"We mauna tell th' lass. Young folks' hearts break wi' a little, and she'd be apt to fancy it were true." Here the old woman's voice broke into a kind of piping cry, but she struggled, and her next words were all right. "We mauna tell her; he's bound to be fond on her, and maybe, if she thinks well on him, and loves him, it will bring him straight!"

"God grant it!" said Nathan.

"God shall grant it!" said Hester, passionately moaning out her words; and then repeating them, alas! with a vain repetition.

"It's a bad place for lying, is Highminster," said she at length, as if impatient of the silence. "I never knowed such a place for getting up stories. But Bessy knows nought on, and nother you nor me belie'es 'em; that's one blessing." But if they did not in their hearts believe them, how came they to look so sad, and worn, beyond what mere age could make them?

Then came round another year, another winter, yet more miserable than the last. This year, with the primroses, came Benjamin; a bad, hard, flippant young man, with yet enough of specious manners and handsome countenance to make his appearance striking at first to those to whom the aspect of a London fast young man of the lowest order is strange and new. Just at first, as he sauntered in with a swagger and an air of indifference, which was partly assumed, partly real, his old parents felt a simple kind of awe of him, as if he were not their son, but a real gentleman; but they had too much fine instinct in their homely natures not to know, after a very few minutes had passed, that this was not a true prince,

"Whatten ever does he mean," said Hester to her niece, as soon as they were alone, "by a' them maks and wearlocks? And he minces his words as if his tongue were clipped short, or split like a magpie's. Hech! London is as bad as a hot day i' August for spoiling good flesh; for he were a good-looking lad when he went up; and now, look at him, with his skin gone into lines and flourishes, just like the first page on a copy-book!"

"I think he looks a good deal better, aunt, for them new-fashioned whiskers!" said Bessy, blushing still at the remembrance of the kiss he had given her on first seeing her—a pledge, she thought, poor girl, that, in spite of his long silence in letter-writing, he still looked upon her as his troth-plight wife. There were things about him which none of them liked, although they never spoke of them, yet there was also something to gratify them in the way in which he remained quiet at Nab-end, instead of seeking variety, as he had formerly done, by constantly stealing off to the neighbouring town. His father had paid all the debts that he knew of, soon after Benjamin had gone up to London; so there were no duns that his parents knew of to alarm him, and keep him at home. And he went out in the morning with the old man, his father, and lounged by his side, as Nathan went round his fields, with busy yet infirm gait, having heart, as he would have expressed it, in all that was going on, because at length his son seemed to take an interest in the farming affairs, and stood patiently by his side, while he compared his own small galloways with the great short-horns looming over his neighbour's hedge.

"It's a slovenly way, thou seest, that of selling th' milk; folk don't care whether it's good or not, so that they get their pint-measure full of stuff that's watered afore it leaves th' beast, instead o' honest cheating by the help o' th' pump. But look at Bessy's butter, what skill it shows I part her own manner o' making, and part good choice o' cattle. It's a pleasure to see her basket, a' packed ready for to go to market; and it's noan o' a pleasure for to see the buckets fu' of their blue starch-water as yon beasts give. I'm thinking they crossed th' breed wi' a pump not long sin'. Hech! but our Bessy's a cleaver canny wench! I sometimes think thou'lt be for gie'ing up th' law, and taking to th' oud trade, when thou wedst wi' her!"

This was intended to be a skilful way of ascertaining whether there was any ground for the old farmer's wish and prayer that Benjamin might give up the law, and return to the primitive occupation of his father. Nathan dared to hope it now, since his son had never made much by his profession, owing, as he had said, to his want of a connexion: and the farm, and the stock, and the clean wife, too, were ready to his hand; and Nathan could safely rely on himself never in his most unguarded moments to reproach his son with the hardly-earned hundreds that had been spent on his education. So the old man listened with painful interest to the answer which his son was evidently struggling to make; coughing a little, and blowing his nose before he spoke.

"Well! you see, father, law is a precarious livelihood; a man, as I may express myself, has no chance in the profession unless he is known—known to the judges, and tiptop barristers, and that sort of thing. Now, you see, my mother and you have no acquaintance that you may call exactly in that line. But luckily I have met with a man, a friend, as I may say, who is really a first-rate fellow, knowing everybody, from the Lord Chancellor downwards; and he has offered me a share in his business—a partnership in short—" He hesitated a little.

"I'm sure that's uncommon kind of the gentleman," said Nathan. "I should like for to thank him mysen; for it's not many as would pick up a young chap out o' th' dirt as it were, and say, 'Here's hauf my good fortune for you, sir, and your very good health.' Most on 'em, when they're gettin' a bit o' luck, run off wi' it to keep it a' to themselves, and gobble it down in a corner. What may be his name, for I should like to know it?"

"You don't quite apprehend me, father. A great deal of what you've said is true to the letter. People don't like to share their good luck, as you say."

"The more credit to them as does," broke in Nathan.

"Ay, but, you see, even such a fine fellow as my friend Cavendish does not like to give away half his good practice for nothing. He expects an equivalent."

"An equivalent," said Nathan: his voice had dropped down an octave. "And what may that be? There's always some meaning in grand words, I take it, though I'm not book-larned enough to find it out."

"Why, in this case the equivalent he demands for taking me into partnership, and afterwards relinquishing the whole business to me, is three hundred pounds down."

Benjamin looked sideways from under his eyes to see how his father took the proposition. His father struck his stick deep down in the ground, and leaning one hand upon it, faced round at him.

"Then thy fine friend may go and be hanged. Three hunder pound! I'll be darned an' danged too, if I know where to get 'em, if I'd be making a fool o' thee an' mysen too."

He was out of breath by this time. His son took his father's first words in dogged silence; it was but the burst of surprise he had led himself to expect, and did not daunt him for long.

"I should think, sir—"

"'Sir'—whatten for dost thou 'sir' me? Is them your manners? I'm plain Nathan Huntroyd, who never took on to be a gentleman; but I have paid my way up to this limey which I shannot do much longer, if I'm to have a son coming an' asking me for three hunder pound, just meet same as if I were a cow, and had nothing to do but let down my milk to the first person as strokes me."

"Well, father," said Benjamin, with an affectation of frankness, "then there's nothing for me, but to do as I have often planned before; go and emigrate."

"And *what?*" said his father, looking sharply and steadily at him.

"Emigrate. Go to America, or India, or some colony where there would be an opening for a young man of spirit."

Benjamin had reserved this proposition for his trump card, expecting by means of it to carry all before him. But, to his surprise, his father plucked his stick out of the hole he had made when he so vehemently thrust it into the ground, and walked on four or five steps in advance; there he stood still again, and there was a dead silence for a few minutes.

"It 'ud, maybe, be th' best thing thou couldst do," the father began. Benjamin set his teeth hard to keep in curses. It was well for poor Nathan he did not look round then, and see the look his son gave him. "But it would come hard like upon us, upon Hester and me, for, whether thou'rt a good 'un or not, thou'rt our flesh and blood, our only bairn, and if thou'rt not all as a man could wish, it's, maybe, been the fault on our pride i' thee.—It 'ud kill the missus if he went off to Amerikay, and Bess, too, the lass as thinks so much on him!" The speech, originally addressed to his son, had wandered off into a monologue—as keenly listened to by Benjamin, however, as if it had all been spoken to him. After a pause of consideration, his father turned round: "Yon man—I wunnot call him a friend o' yourn, to think of asking you for such a mint o' money—is not th' only one, I'll be bound, as could give ye a start i' the law? Other folks 'ud, maybe, do it for less?"

"Not one of 'em; to give me equal advantages," said Benjamin, thinking he perceived signs of relenting,

"Well, then, thou mayst tell him, that it's nother he nor thee as'll see th' sight o' three bunder pound o' my money. I'll not deny as I've a bit laid up again a rainy day; it's not so much as thatten though, and a part on it is for Bessy, as has been like a daughter to us."

"But Bessy is to be your real daughter some day, when I've a home to take her to," said Benjamin; for he played very fast and loose, even in his own mind, with his engagement with Bessy. Present with her, when she was looking her brightest and best, he behaved to her as if they were engaged lovers: absent from her, he looked upon her rather as a good wedge, to be driven into his parent's favour on his behalf. Now, however, he was not exactly untrue in speaking as if he meant to make her his wife; for the thought was in his mind, though he made use of it to work upon his father.

"It will be a dree day for us, then," said the old man. "But God'll have us in his keeping, and'll may-happen be taking more care on us i' heaven by that time than Bess, good lass as she is, has had on us at Nab-end. Her heart is set on thee, too. But, lad, I hanna gotten the three hunder; I keeps my cash i' th' stocking, thou knowst, till it reaches fifty pound, and then I takes it to Ripon Bank. Now the last scratch they'n gi'en me, made it just two hunder, and I hanna but on to fifteen pound yet i' the stockin', and I meant one hunder an' the red cow's calf to be for Bess, she's ta'en such pleasure like i' rearing it."

Benjamin gave a sharp glance at his father to see if he was telling the truth; and, that a suspicion of the old man, his father, had entered into the son's head, tells enough of his own character.

"I canna do it—I canna do it, for sure—although I shall like to think as I had helped on the wedding. There's the black heifer to be sold yet, and she'll fetch a matter of ten pound; but a deal on't will be needed for seed-corn, for the arable did but bad last year, and I thought I would try—I'll tell thee what, lad! I'll make it as though Bess lent thee her hunder, only thou must give her a writ of hand for it, and thou shalt have a' the money i' Ripon Bank, and see if the lawyer wunnot let thee have a share of what he offered thee at three hunder, for two. I dunnot mean for to wrong him, but thou must get a fair share for the money. At times I think thou'rt done by folk; now, I wadna have you cheat a bairn of a brass farthing; same time I wadna have thee so soft as to be cheated."

To explain this, it should be told that some of the bills which Benjamin had received money from his father to pay, had been altered so as to cover other and less creditable expenses which the young man had incurred; and the simple old farmer, who had still much faith left in him for his boy, was acute enough to perceive that he had paid above the usual price for the articles he had purchased.

After some hesitation, Benjamin agreed to receive this two hundred, and promised to employ it to the best advantage in setting himself up in business. He had, nevertheless, a strange hankering after the additional fifteen pounds that was left to accumulate in the stocking. It was his, he thought, as heir to his father; and he soon lost some of his usual complaisance for Bessy that evening, as he dwelt on the idea that there was money being laid by for her, and grudged it to her even in imagination. He thought more of this fifteen pounds that he was not to have, than of all the hardly-earned and humbly-saved two hundred that he was to come into possession of.

Meanwhile Nathan was in unusual spirits that evening. He was so generous and affectionate at heart, that he had an unconscious satisfaction in having helped two people on the road to happiness by the sacrifice of the greater part of his property. The very fact of having trusted his son so largely, seemed to make Benjamin more worthy of trust in his father's estimation. The sole idea he tried to banish was, that, if all came to pass as he hoped, both Benjamin and Bessy would be settled far away from Nab-end; but then he had a child-like reliance that "God would take care of him and his missus, somehow or anodder. It wur o'no use looking too far ahead."

Bessy had to hear many unintelligible jokes from her uncle that night; for he made no doubt that Benjamin had told her all that had passed, whereas the truth was, his son had said never a word to his cousin on the subject.

When the old couple were in bed, Nathan told his wife of the promise he had made to his son, and the plan in life which the advance of the two hundred was to promote. Poor Hester was a little startled at the sudden change in the destination of the sum, which she had long thought of with secret pride as "money i' th' bank." But she was willing enough to part with it, if necessary, for Benjamin. Only, how such a sum could be necessary, was the puzzle. But even this perplexity was jostled out of her mind by the overwhelming idea, not only of "our Ben" settling in London, but of Bessy going there too as his wife. This great trouble swallowed up all care about money, and Hester shivered and sighed all the night through with distress. In the morning, as Bessy was kneading the bread, her aunt, who had been sitting by the fire in an unusual manner, for one of her active habits, said:

"I reckon we maun go to th' shop for our bread, an' that's a thing I never thought to come to so long as I lived."

Bessy looked up from her kneading, surprised:

"I'm sure, I'm noan going to eat their nasty stuff. What for do ye want to get baker's bread, aunt? This dough will rise as high as a kite in a south wind."

"I'm not up to kneading as I could do once; it welly breaks my back; and when thou'rt off in London, I reckon we maun buy our bread, first time in my life."

"I'm not a-going to London," said Bessy, kneading away with fresh resolution, and growing very red, either with the idea or the exertion.

"But our Ben is going partner wi' a great London lawyer, and thou know'st he'll not tarry long but what he'll fetch thee."

"Now, aunt," said Bessy, stripping her arms of the dough, but still not looking up, "if that's all, don't fret yourself. Ben will have twenty minds in his head afore he settles, eyther in business or in wedlock. I sometimes wonder," she said, with increasing vehemence, "why I go on thinking on him; for I dunnot think he thinks on me, when I m out o' sight. I've a month's mind to try and forget him this time when he leaves us—that I have!"

"For shame, wench! and he to be planning and purposing all for thy sake. It wur only yesterday as he wur talking to thy uncle, and mapping it out so clever; only thou seest, wench, it'll be dree work for us when both thee and him is gone."

The old woman began to cry the kind of tearless cry of the aged. Bessy hastened to comfort her; and the two talked, and grieved, and hoped, and planned for the days that now were to be, till they ended, the one in being consoled, the other in being secretly happy.

Nathan and his son came back from Highminster that evening, with their business transacted in the roundabout way, which was most satisfactory to the old man. If he had thought it necessary to take half as much pains in ascertaining the truth of the plausible details by which his son bore out the story of the offered partnership, as he did in trying to get his money conveyed to London in the most secure manner, it would have been well for him. But he knew nothing of all this, and acted in the way which satisfied his anxiety best. He came home tired, but content; not in such high spirits as on the night before, but as easy in his mind as he could be on the eve of his son's departure.

Bessy, pleasantly agitated by her aunt's tale of the morning of her cousin's true love for her—what ardently we wish we long believe—and the plan which was to end in their marriage—end to her, the woman, at least—Bessy looked almost pretty in her bright, blushing comeliness, and more than once, as she moved about from kitchen to dairy, Benjamin pulled her towards him, and gave her a kiss. To all such proceedings the old couple were wilfully blind; and, as night drew on, every one became sadder and quieter, thinking of the parting that was to be on the morrow.

As the hours slipped away, Bessy, too, became subdued; and, by-and-by, her simple cunning was exerted to get Benjamin to sit down next his mother, whose very heart was yearning after him, as Bessy saw. When once her child was placed by her side, and she had got possession of his hand, the old woman kept stroking it, and murmuring long unused words of endearment, such as she had spoken to him while he was yet a little child. But all this was wearisome to him. As long as he might play with, and plague, and caress Bessy, he had not been sleepy; but now he yawned loudly. Bessy could have boxed his ears for not curbing this gaping; at any rate, he need not have done it so openly—so almost ostentatiously. His mother was more pitiful.

"Thou'rt tired, my lad!" said she, putting her hand fondly on his shoulder; but it fell off, as he stood up suddenly, and said:

"Yes, deuced tired! I'm off to bed." And with a rough careless kiss all round, even to Bessy, as if he was "deuced tired" of playing the lover, he was gone; leaving the three to gather up their thoughts slowly, and follow him up stairs.

He seemed almost impatient at them for rising betimes to see him off the next morning, and made no more of a goodbye than some such speech as this: "Well, good folk, when next I see you, I hope you'll have merrier faces than you have today. Why, you might be going to a funeral; it's enough to scare a man from the place; you look quite ugly to what you did last night, Bess."

He was gone; and they turned into the house, and settled to the long day's work without many words about their loss. They had no time for unnecessary talking, indeed, for much had been left undone, during his short visit, that ought to have been done; and they had now to work double tides. Hard work was their comfort for many a long day.

For some time, Benjamin's letters, if not frequent, were full of exultant accounts of his well-doing. It is true that the details of his prosperity were somewhat vague; but the fact was broadly and unmistakably stated. Then came longer pauses; shorter letters, altered in tone. About a year after he had left them, Nathan received a letter, which bewildered and irritated him exceedingly. Something had gone wrong—what, Benjamin did not say—but the letter ended with a request that was almost a demand, for the remainder of his father's savings, whether in the stocking or the bank.

Now, the year had not been prosperous with Nathan; there had been an epidemic among cattle, and he had suffered along with his neighbours; and, moreover, the price of cows, when he had bought some to repair his wasted stock, was higher than he had ever remembered it before. The fifteen pounds in the stocking, which Benjamin left, had diminished to little more than three; and to have that required of him in so peremptory a manner! Before Nathan imparted the contents of this letter to any one (Bessy and her aunt had gone to market on a neighbour's cart that day), he got pen and ink and paper, and wrote back an ill-spelt, but very implicit and stern negative. Benjamin had had his portion; and if he could not make it do, so much the worse for him; his father had no more to give him. That was the substance of the letter.

The letter was written, directed, and sealed, and given to the country postman, returning to Highminster after his day's distribution and collection of letters, before Hester and Bessy came back from market. It had been a pleasant day of neighbourly meeting and sociable gossip: prices had been high, and they were in good spirits, only agreeably tired, and full of small pieces of news. It was some time before they found out how flatly all their talk fell on the ears of the stay-at-home listener. But, when they saw that his depression was caused by something beyond their powers of accounting for by any little every-day cause, they urged him to tell them what was the matter. His anger had not gone off. It had rather increased by dwelling upon it, and he spoke it out in good resolute terms; and, long ere he had ended, the two women were as sad, if not as angry, as himself.

Indeed, it was many days before either feeling wore away in the minds of those who entertained them. Bessy was the soonest comforted, because she found a vent for her sorrow in action; action that was half as a kind of compensation for many a sharp word that she had spoken, when her cousin had done anything to displease her on his last visit, and half because she believed that he never could have written such a letter to his father, unless his want of money had been very pressing and real; though how he could ever have wanted money so soon, after such a heap of it had been given to him, was more than she could justly say.

Bessy got out all her savings of little presents of sixpences and shillings, ever since she had been a child,—of all the money she had gained for the eggs of two hens, called her own; she put the whole together,' and it was above two pounds—two pounds five and sevenpence, to speak accurately—and, leaving out the penny as a nest-egg for her future savings, she made up the rest in a little parcel, and sent it, with a note, to Benjamin's address in London:

From a well-wisher.
Dear Benjamin,—Unkle has lost 2 cows and a vast of monney. He is a good deal angored, but more troubled. So no more at present. Hopeing this will finding you well As it leaves us. Tho' lost to site, to memory dear. Repayment not kneeded.
   Your effectonet cousin,
     Elizabeth Rose.

When this packet was once fairly sent off, Bessy began to sing again over her work. She never expected the mere form of acknowledgment; indeed, she had such faith in the carrier (who took parcels to York, whence they were forwarded to London by coach), that she felt sure he would go on purpose to London to deliver anything intrusted to him, if he had not full confidence in the person, persons, coach and horses, to whom he committed it. Therefore she was not anxious that she did not hear of its arrival. "Giving a thing to a man as one knows," said she to herself, "is a vast different to poking a thing through a hole into a box, th' inside of which one has never clapped eyes on; and yet letters get safe some ways or another." (This belief in the infallibility of the post was destined to a shock before long.)

But she had a secret yearning for Benjamin's thanks, and some of the old words of love that she had been without so long. Nay, she even thought—when, day after day, week after week, passed by without a line—that he might be winding up his affairs in that weary, wasteful London, and coming back to Nab-end to thank her in person.

One day—her aunt was up stairs, inspecting the summer's make of cheeses, her uncle out in the fields—the postman brought a letter into the kitchen to Bessy. A country postman, even now, is not much pressed for time, and in those days there were but few letters to distribute, and they were only sent out from Highminster once a week into the district in which Nab-end was situated; and on those occasions, the letter-carrier usually paid morning calls on the various people for whom he had letters. So, half standing by the dresser, half sitting on it, he began to rummage out his bag. "It's a queer-like thing I've got for Nathan this time. I am afraid it will bear ill news in it, for there's 'Dead Letter Office' stamped on the top of it."

"Lord save us!" said Bessy, and sat down on the nearest chair, as white as a sheet. In an instant, however, she was up, and, snatching the ominous letter out of the man's hands, she pushed him before her out of the house, and said, "Be off wi' thee, afore aunt comes down;" and ran past him as hard as she could, till she reached the field where she expected to find her uncle.

"Uncle," said she, breathless, "what is it? Oh, uncle, speak! Is he dead?"

Nathan's hands trembled, and his eyes dazzled. "Take it," he said, "and tell me what it is."

"It's a letter—it's from you to Benjamin, it is—and there's words written on it, 'Not known at the address given;' so they've sent it back to the writer—that's you, uncle. Oh, it gave me such a start, with them nasty words written outside!"

Nathan had taken the letter back into his own hands, and was turning it over, while he strove to understand what the quick-witted Bessy had picked up at a glance. But he arrived at a different conclusion.

"He's dead!" said he. "The lad is dead, and he never knowed how as I were sorry I wrote to 'un so sharp. My lad! my lad!" Nathan sat down on the ground where he stood, and covered his face with his old, withered hands. The letter returned to him was one which he had written, with infinite pains and at various times, to tell his child, in kinder words and at greater length than he had done before, the reasons why he could not send him the money demanded. And now Benjamin was dead; nay, the old man immediately jumped to the conclusion that his child had been starved to death, without money, in a wild, wide, strange place. All he could say at first was:

"My heart, Bess—my heart is broken!" And he put his hand to his side, still keeping his shut eyes covered with the other, as though he never wished to see the light of day again. Bessy was down by his side in an instant, holding him in her arms, chafing and kissing him.

"It's noan so bad, uncle; he's not dead; the letter does not say that, dunnot think it. He's flitted from that lodging, and the lazy tykes dunna know where to find him; and so, they just send y' back th' letter, instead of trying ira' house to house, as Mark Benson would. I've always heerd tell on south country folk for laziness. He's noan dead, uncle; he's just flitted, and he'll let us know afore long where he's getten to. Maybe it's a cheaper place, for that lawyer has cheated him, ye reck'let, and he'll be trying to live for as little as he can, that's all, uncle. Dunnot take on so, for it doesna say he's dead."

By this time, Bessy was crying with agitation, although she firmly believed in her own view of the case, and had felt the opening of the ill-favoured letter as a great relief. Presently she began to urge, both with word and action upon her uncle, that he should sit no longer on the damp grass. She pulled him up, for he was very stiff, and, as he said, "all shaken to dithers." She made him walk about, repeating over and over again her solution of the case, always in the same words, beginning again and again, "He's noan dead; it's just been a flitting," and so on. Nathan shook his head, and tried to be convinced; but it was a steady belief in his own heart for all that.

He looked so deathly ill on his return home with Bessy (for she would not let him go on with his day's work), that his wife made sure he had taken cold, and he, weary and indifferent to life, was glad to subside into bed and the rest from exertion which his real bodily illness gave him. Neither Bessy nor he spoke of the letter again, even to each other, for many days; and she found means to stop Mark Benson's tongue, and satisfy his kindly curiosity, by giving him the rosy side of her own view of the case.

Nathan got up again, an older man in looks and constitution by ten years for that week of bed. His wife gave him many a scolding on his imprudence for sitting down in the wet field, if ever so tired. But now she, too, was beginning to be uneasy at Benjamin's long-continued silence. She could not write herself, but she urged her husband many a time to send a letter to ask for news of her lad. He said nothing in reply for some time: at length, he told her he would write next Sunday afternoon. Sunday was his general day for writing, and this Sunday he meant to go to church for the first time since his illness.

On Saturday he was very persistent against his wife's wishes (backed by Bessy as hard as she could), in resolving to go into Highminster to market. The change would do him good, he said. But he came home tired, and a little mysterious in his ways. When he went to the shippon the last thing at night, he asked Bessy to go with him, and hold the lantern, while he looked at an ailing cow; and, when they were fairly out of the earshot of the house, he pulled a little shop-parcel from his pocket and said:

"Thou'lt put that on ma Sunday hat, wilt 'ou, lass? It'll be a bit on a comfort to me; for I know my lad's dead and gone, though I dunna speak on it, for fear o' grieving th' old woman and ye."

"I'll put it on, uncle, if—But he's noan dead."

(Bessy was sobbing.)

"I know—I know, lass. I dunnot wish other folk to hold my opinion; but I'd like to wear a bit o' crape, out o' respect to my boy. It 'ud have done me good for to have ordered a black coat, but she'd see if I had na' on my wedding-coat, Sundays, for a' she's losing her eyesight, poor old wench! But she'll ne'er take notice o' a bit o' crape. Thou'lt put it on all canny and tidy."

So Nathan went to church with a strip of crape, as narrow as Bessy durst venture to make it, round his hat. Such is the contradictoriness of human nature, that, though he was most anxious his wife should not hear of his conviction that their son was dead, he was half hurt that none of his neighbours noticed his sign of mourning so far as to ask him for whom he wore it.

But after a while, when they never heard a word from or about

Benjamin, the household wonder as to what had become of him grew so painful and strong, that Nathan no longer kept his idea to himself. Poor Hester, however, rejected it with her whole will, heart, and soul. She could not and would not believe—nothing should make her believe—that her only child Benjamin had died without some sign of love or farewell to her. No arguments could shake her in this. She believed that, if all natural means of communication between her and him had been cut off at the last supreme moment—if death had come upon him in an instant, sudden and unexpected—her intense love would have been supernaturally made conscious of the blank.

Nathan at times tried to feel glad that she could still hope to see the lad again; but at other moments he wanted her sympathy in his grief, his self-reproach, his weary wonder as to how and what they had done wrong in the treatment of their son, that he had been such a care and sorrow to his parents. Bessy was convinced, first by her aunt, and then by her uncle—honestly convinced—on both sides of the argument; and so, for the time, able to sympathise with each. But she lost her youth in a very few months; she looked set and middle-aged long before she ought to have done; and rarely smiled and never sang again.

All sorts of new arrangements were required, by the blow which told so miserably upon the energies of all the household at Nab-end. Nathan could no longer go about and direct his two men, taking a good turn of work himself at busy times. Hester lost her interest in her dairy; for which, indeed, her increasing loss of sight unfitted her. Bessy would either do field work, or attend to the cows and the shippon, or chum, or make cheese; she did all well, no longer merrily, but with something of stern cleverness. But she was not sorry when her uncle, one evening, told her aunt and her that a neighbouring farmer, Job Kirkby, had made him an offer to take so much of his land off his hands as would leave him only pasture enough for two cows, and no arable to attend to; while Farmer Kirkby did not wish to interfere with anything in the house, only would be glad to use some of the outbuildings for his fattening cattle.

"We can do wi' Hawky and Daisy; it'll leave us eight or ten pound o' butter to take to market i' summer time, and keep us fra' thinking too much, which is what I'm dreading on as I get into years."

"Ay," said his wife. "Thou'll not have to go so far afield, if it's only the Aster-Toft as is on thy hands. And Bess will have to gie up her pride i' cheese, and tak' to making cream-butter. I'd allays a fancy for trying at cream-butter, but th' whey had to be used; else, where I come fra', they'd never ha' looked near whey-butter."

When Hester was left alone with Bessy, she said, in allusion to this change of plan:—

"I'm thankful to the Lord that it is as it is: for I were allays feared Nathan would have to gie up the house and farm altogether, and then the lad would na' know where to find us when he came back fra' Merikay. He's gone there for to make his fortune, I'll be bound. Keep up thy heart, lass, he'll be home some day; and have sown his wild oats. Eh! but thatten's a pretty story i' the Gospels about the Prodigal, who'd to eat the pigs' vittle at one time, but ended i' clover in his father's house. And I'm sure our Nathan'll be ready to forgive him, and love him, and make much of him, maybe a deal more nor me, who never gave in to's death. It'll be liken to a resurrection to our Nathan."

Farmer Kirkby, then, took by far the greater part of the land belonging to Nab-end Farm; and the work about the rest, and about the two remaining cows, was easily done by three pairs of willing hands, with a little occasional assistance. The Kirkby family were pleasant enough to have to deal with. There was a son, a stiff, grave bachelor, who was very particular and methodical about his work, and rarely spoke to anyone. But Nathan took it into his head that John Kirkby was looking after Bessy, and was a good deal troubled in his mind in consequence; for it was the first time he had to face the effects of his belief in his son's death; and he discovered, to his own surprise, that he had not that implicit faith, which would make it easy for him to look upon Bessy as the wife of another man, than the one to whom she had been betrothed in her youth. As, however, John Kirkby seemed in no hurry to make his intentions (if indeed he had any) clear to Bessy, it was only now and then that this jealousy on behalf of his lost son seized upon Nathan.

But people, old, and in deep hopeless sorrow, grow irritable at times, however they may repent and struggle against their irritability. There were days when Bessy had to hear a good deal from her uncle; but she loved him so dearly and respected him so much, that, high as her temper was to all other people, she never returned him a rough or impatient word. And she had a reward in the conviction of his deep, true affection for her, and her aunt's entire and most sweet dependence upon her.

One day, however—it was near the end of November—Bessy had had a good deal to bear, that seemed more than usually unreasonable, on behalf of her uncle. The truth was, that one of Kirkby's cows was ill, and John Kirkby was a good deal about in the farmyard; Bessy was interested about the animal, and had helped in preparing a mash over their own fire, that had to be given warm to the sick creature.

If John had been out of the way, there would have been no one more anxious about the affair than Nathan; both because he was naturally kind-hearted and neighbourly, and also because he was rather proud of his reputation for knowledge in the diseases of cattle. But because John was about, and Bessy helping a little in what had to be done, Nathan would do nothing, and chose to assume that "nothing to think on ailed th' beast, but lads and lasses were allays fain to be feared on something." Now John was upwards of forty, and Bessy nearly eight-and-twenty, so the terms lads and lasses did not exactly apply to their case.

When Bessy brought the milk in from their own cows, towards half-past five o'clock, Nathan bade her make the doors, and not be running out i' the dark and cold about other folk's business; and, though Bessy was a little surprised and a good deal annoyed at his tone, she sat down to her supper without making a remonstrance. It had long been Nathan's custom to look out the last thing at night, to see "what mak' o' weather it wur;" and when, towards half-past eight, he got his stick and went out—two or three steps from the door, which opened into the house-place where they were sitting—Hester put her hand on her niece's shoulder and said:

"He's gotten a touch o' the rheumatics, as twinges him and makes him speak so sharp. I didna like to ask thee afore him, but how's yon poor beas?"

"Very ailing, belike. John Kirkby wur off for th' cow-doctor when I cam in. I reckon they'll have to stop up wi't a' night."

Since their sorrows, her uncle had taken to reading a chapter in the Bible aloud, the last thing at night. He could not read fluently, and often hesitated long over a word, which he miscalled at length; but the very fact of opening the book seemed to soothe those old bereaved parents; for it made them feel quiet and safe in the presence of God, and took them out of the cares and troubles of this world into that futurity which, however dim and vague, was to their faithful hearts as a sure and certain rest.

This little quiet time—Nathan sitting with his horn spectacles; the tallow candle between him and the Bible, and throwing a strong light on his reverent, earnest face; Hester sitting on the other side of the fire, her head bowed in attentive listening, now and then shaking it, and moaning a little, but when a promise came, or any good tidings of great joy, saying "Amen" with fervour; Bessy by her aunt, perhaps her mind a little wandering to some household cares, or it might be on thoughts of those who were absent—this little quiet pause, I say, was grateful and soothing to this household, as a lullaby to a tired child. But this night, Bessy—sitting opposite to the long low window, only shaded by a few geraniums that grew in the sill, and to the door along-side that window, through which her uncle had passed not a quarter of an hour before—saw the wooden latch of the door gently and almost noiselessly lifted up, as if someone were trying it from the outside.

She was startled; and watched again, intently; but it was perfectly still now. She thought it must have been that it had not fallen into its proper place, when her uncle had come in and locked the door. It was just enough to make her uncomfortable, no more; and she almost per-suaded herself it must have been fancy. Before going upstairs, however, she went to the window to look out into the darkness; but all was still. Nothing to be seen; nothing to be heard. So the three went quietly up stairs to bed.

The house was little better than a cottage. The front door opened on a house-place, over which was the old couple's bedroom. To the left, as you entered this pleasant house-place, and at close right angles with the entrance, was a door that led into the small parlour, which was Hester's and Bessy's pride, although not half as comfortable as the house-place, and never on any occasion used as a sitting-room. There were shells and bundles of honesty in the fireplace; the best chest of drawers, and a company-set of gaudy-coloured china, and a bright common carpet on the floor; but all failed to give it the aspect of the homely comfort and delicate cleanliness of the house-place.

Over this parlour was the bedroom which Benjamin had slept in when a boy—when at home. It was kept still in a kind of readiness for him. The bed was yet there, in which none had slept since he had last done, eight or nine years ago; and every now and then, the warming-pan was taken quietly and silently up by his old mother, and the bed thoroughly aired. But this she did in her husband's absence, and without saying a word to any one; nor did Bessy offer to help her, though her eyes often filled with tears, as she saw her aunt still going through the hopeless service. But the room had become a receptacle for all unused things; and there was always a corner of it appropriated to the winter's store of apples.

To the left of the house-place, as you stood facing the fire, on the side opposite to the window and outer door, were two other doors; the one on the right led into a kind of back kitchen, and had a lean-to roof, and a door opening on to the farmyard and back premises; the left-hand door gave on the stairs, underneath which was a closet, in which various household treasures were kept, and beyond that the dairy, over which Bessy slept; her little chamber window opening just above the sloping roof of the back kitchen. There were neither blinds nor shutters to any of the windows, either upstairs or down; the house was built of stone, and there was heavy framework of the same material round the little casement windows, and the long, low window of the house-place was divided by what, in grander dwellings, would be called mullions.

By nine o'clock this night of which I am speaking, all had gone upstairs to bed: it was even later than usual, for the burning of candles was regarded so much in the light of an extravagance, that the household kept early hours even for country-folk. But, somehow, this evening, Bessy could not sleep, although, in general, she was in deep slumber five minutes after her head touched the pillow. Her thoughts ran on the chances for John Kirkby's cow, and a little fear lest the disorder might be epidemic, and spread to their own cattle. Across all these homely cares came a vivid, uncomfortable recollection of the way in which the door latch went up and down, without any sufficient agency to account for it

She felt more sure now, than she had done downstairs, that it was a real movement and no effect of her imagination. She wished that it had not happened just when her uncle was reading, that she might at once have gone quick to the door, and convinced herself of the cause. As it was, her thoughts ran uneasily on the supernatural; and thence to Benjamin, her dear cousin and play-fellow, her early lover. She had long given him up as lost forever to her, if not actually dead; but this very giving him up forever involved a free, full forgiveness of all his wrongs to her. She thought tenderly of him, as of one who might have been led astray in his later years, but who existed rather in her recollection as the innocent child, the spirited lad, the handsome, dashing young man.

If John Kirkby's quiet attentions had ever betrayed his wishes to Bessy—if indeed he ever had any wishes on the subject—her first feeling would have been to compare his weather-beaten, middle-aged face and figure with the face and figure she remembered well, but never more expected to see in this life. So thinking, she became very restless, and weary of bed, and, after long tossing and turning, ending in a belief that she should never get to sleep at all that night, she went off soundly and suddenly.

As suddenly was she wide awake, sitting up in bed, listening to some noise that must have awakened her, but which was not repeated for some time. Surely it was in her uncle's room—her uncle was up; but, for a minute or two, there was no further sound. Then she heard him open his door, and go downstairs, with hurried, stumbling steps. She now thought that her aunt must be ill, and hastily sprang out of bed, and was putting on her petticoat with hurried, trembling hands, and had just opened her chamber door, when she heard the front door undone, and a scuffle, as of the feet of several people, and many rude, passionate words, spoken hoarsely below the breath.

Quick as thought she understood it all—the house was lonely—her uncle had the reputation of being well-to-do—they had pretended to be belated, and had asked their way or something. What a blessing that John Kirkby's cow was sick, for there were several men watching with him! She went back, opened her window, squeezed herself out, slid down the lean-to roof, and ran barefoot and breathless, to the shippon:

"John, John, for the love of God, come quick; there's robbers in the house, and uncle and aunt'll be murdered!" she whispered, in terrified accents, through the closed and barred shippon door. In a moment it was undone, and John and the cow-doctor stood there, ready to act, if they but understood her rightly. Again she repeated her words, with broken, half-unintelligible explanations of what she as yet did not rightly understand.

"Front door is open, say'st thou?" said John, arming himself with a pitchfork, while the cow-doctor took some other implement. "Then I reckon we'd best make for that way o' getting into th' house, and catch 'em all in a trap."

"Run! run!" was all Bessy could say, taking hold of John Kirkby's arm, and pulling him along with her. Swiftly did the three run to the house, round the comer, and in at the open front door. The men carried the horn lantern they had been using in the shippon, and, by the sudden oblong light that it threw, Bessy saw the principal object of her anxiety, her uncle, lying stunned and helpless on the kitchen floor. Her first thought was for him; for she had no idea that her aunt was in any immediate danger, although she heard the noise of feet, and fierce subdued voices upstairs.

"Make th' door behind us, lass. We'll not let 'em escape!" said brave

John Kirkby, dauntless in a good cause, though he knew not how many there might be above.

The cow-doctor fastened and locked the door, saying, "There!" in a defiant tone, as he put the key in his pocket. It was to be a struggle for life or death, or, at any rate, for effectual capture or desperate escape. Bessy kneeled down by her uncle, who did not speak nor give any sign of consciousness. Bessy raised his head by drawing a pillow off the settle and putting it under him; she longed to go for water into the back kitchen, but the sound of a violent struggle, and of heavy blows, and of low, hard curses spoken through closed teeth, and muttered passion, as though breath were too much needed for action to be wasted in speech, kept her still and quiet by her uncle's side in the kitchen, where the darkness might almost be felt, so thick and deep was it.

Once—in a pause of her own heart's beating—a sudden terror came over her; she perceived, in that strange way in which the presence of a living creature forces itself on our consciousness in the darkest room, that someone was near her, keeping as still as she. It was not the poor old man's breathing that she heard, nor the radiation of his presence that she felt; someone else was in the kitchen; another robber, perhaps, left to guard the old man, with murderous intent if his consciousness returned.

Now, Bessy was fully aware that self-preservation would keep her terrible companion quiet, as there was no motive for his betraying himself stronger than the desire of escape; any effort for which he, the unseen witness, must know would be rendered abortive by the fact of the door being locked. Yet with the knowledge that he was there, close to her, still, silent as the grave,—with fearful, it might be deadly, unspoken thoughts in his heart,—possibly even with keener and stronger sight than hers, as longer accustomed to the darkness, able to discern her figure and posture, and glaring at her like some wild beast,—Bessy could not fail to shrink from the vision that her fancy presented!

And still the straggle went on upstairs, feet slipping, blows sounding, and the wrench of intentioned aims, the strong gasps for breath, as the wrestlers paused for an instant. In one of these pauses, Bessy felt conscious of a creeping movement close to her, which ceased when the noise of the strife above died away, and was resumed when it again began. She was aware of it by some subtle vibration of the air, rather than by touch or sound. She was sure that he who had been close to her one minute as she knelt, was, the next, passing stealthily towards the inner door which led to the staircase. She thought he was going to join and strengthen his accomplices, and, with a great cry, she sprang after him; but, just as she came to the doorway, throng which some dim portion of light from the upper chambers came, she saw one man thrown downstairs with such violence that he fell almost at her very feet, while the dark, creeping figure glided suddenly away to the left, and as suddenly entered the closet beneath the stairs.

Bessy had no time to wonder as to his purpose in so doing, whether he had at first designed to aid his accomplices in their desperate fight or not. He was an enemy, a robber, that was all she knew, and she sprang to the door of the closet, and in a trice had locked it on the outside. And then she stood frightened, panting in that dark corner, sick with terror lest the man who lay before her was either John Kirkby or the cow-doctor. If it were either of those friendly two, what would become of the other—of her uncle, her aunt, herself? But, in a very few minutes, this wonder was ended; her two defenders came slowly and heavily down the stairs, dragging with them a man, fierce, sullen, despairing—disabled with terrible blows, which had made his face one bloody, swollen mass. As for that, neither John nor the cow-doctor were much more presentable. One of them bore the lantern in his teeth, for all their strength was taken up by the weight of the fellow they were bearing.

"Take care," said Bessy, from her corner; "there's a chap just beneath your feet. I dunno know if he's dead or alive, and uncle lies on the floor just beyond." They stood still on the stairs for a moment. Just then the robber they had thrown down stairs stirred and moaned.

"Bessy," said John, "run off to th' stable and fetch ropes and gearing for to bind 'em, and we'll rid the house on 'em, and thou can'st go see after th' oud folks, who need it sadly."

Bessy was back in a very few minutes. When she came in, there was more light in the house-place, for someone had stirred up the raked fire.

"That felly makes as though his leg were broken," said John, nodding towards the man still lying on the ground. Bessy felt almost sorry for him as they handled him—not over gently—and bound him, only half-conscious, as hardly and tightly as they had done his fierce, surly companion. She even felt so sorry for his evident agony, as they turned him over and over, that she ran to get him a cup of water to moisten his lips.

"I'm loth to leave yo' with him alone," said John, "though I'm thinking his leg is broken for sartain, and he can't stir, even if he comes to hissel, to do yo' any harm. But we'll just take off this chap, and mak sure of him, and then one on us'll come back to yo', and we can, maybe, find a gate or so for yo' to get shut on him out o' th' house. This felly's made safe enough, I'll be bound," said he, looking at the burglar, who stood, bloody and black, with full hatred on his sullen face. His eye caught Bessy's as hers fell on him with dread so evident that it made him smile, and the look and the smile prevented the words from being spoken which were on Bessy's lips. She dared not tell, before him, that an able-bodied accomplice still remained in the house, lest, somehow, the door which kept him a prisoner should be broken open, and the fight renewed. So she only said to John, as he was leaving the house:

"Thou'll not be long away, for I'm afeard of being left wi' this man."

"He'll noan do thee harm," said John.

"No! but I'm feared lest he should die. And there's uncle and aunt. Come back soon, John!"

"Ay, ay!" said he, half-pleased; "I'll be back, never fear me."

So Bessy shut the door after them, but did not lock it for fear of mischances in the house, and went once more to her uncle, whose breathing, by this time, was easier than when she had first returned into the house-place with John and the doctor. By the light of the fire, too, she could now see that he had received a blow on the head which was probably the occasion of his stupor. Round this wound, which was bleeding pretty freely, Bessy put cloths dipped in cold water, and then, leaving him for a time, she lighted a candle, and was about to go up stairs to her aunt, when, just as she was passing the bound and disabled robber, she heard her name softly, urgently called:

"Bessy, Bessy!" At first the voice sounded so close that she thought it must be the unconscious wretch at her feet. But once again that voice thrilled through her:

"Bessy, Bessy! for God's sake, let me out!"

She went to the stair-closet door, and tried to speak, but could not, her heart beat so terribly; Again, close to her ear:

"Bessy, Bessy! they'll be back directly; let me out, I say! For God's sake, let me out!" And he began to kick violently against the panels.

"Hush, hush!" she said, sick with a terrible dread, yet with a will strongly resisting her conviction. "Who are you?" But she knew—

knew quite well.

"Benjamin." An oath. "Let me out, I say, and I'll be off, and out of England by tomorrow night, never to come back, and you'll have all my father's money."

"D'ye think I care for that?" said Bessy, vehemently, feeling with trembling hands for the lock; "I wish there was noan such a thing as money i' the world, afore yo'd come to this. There, yo're free, and I charge yo' never to let me see your face again. I'd ne'er ha' let yo' loose but for fear o' breaking their hearts, if yo' hanna killed them already." But, before she had ended her speech, he was gone—off into the black darkness, leaving the door open wide. With a new terror in her mind, Bessy shut it afresh—shut it and bolted it this time. Then she sat down on the first chair, and relieved her soul by giving a great and exceeding bitter cry. But she knew it was no time for giving way, and, lifting herself up with as much effort as if each of her limbs was a heavy weight, she went into the back kitchen, and took a drink of cold water. To her surprise, she heard her uncle's voice, saying feebly:

"Carry me up, and lay me by her."

But Bessy could not carry him: she could only help his faint exertions to walk upstairs; and, by the time he was there, sitting panting on the first chair she could find John Kirkby and Atkinson returned. John came up now to her aid. Her aunt lay across the bed in a fainting fit, and her uncle sat in so utterly broken-down a state that Bessy feared immediate death for both. But John cheered her up, and lifted the old man into his bed again, and, while Bessy tried to compose poor Hester's limbs into a position of rest, John went down to hunt about for the little store of gin, which was always kept in a corner cupboard against emergencies.

"They've had a sore fright," said he, shaking his head, as he poured a little gin and hot water into their mouths with a teaspoon, while Bessy chafed their cold feet; "and it and the cold have been welly too much for 'em, poor old folk!"

He looked tenderly at them, and Bessy blessed him in her heart for that look.

"I maun be off. I sent Atkinson up to th' farm for to bring down Bob, and Jack came wi' him back to th' shippon for to look after t'other man. He began blackguarding us all round, so Bob and Jack were gagging him wi' bridles when I left."

"Ne'er give heed to what he says," cried poor Bessy, a new panic besetting her. "Folks o' his sort are allays for dragging other folks into their mischief. I'm right glad he were well gagged."

"Well! but what I were saying were this. Atkinson and me will take t'other chap, who seems quiet enough, to th' shippon, and it'll be one piece o' work for to mind them, and the cow; and I'll saddle old bay mare and ride for constables and doctor fra' Highminster. I'll bring Dr. Preston up to see Nathan and Hester first, and then I reckon th' broken-legged chap down below must have his turn, for all as he's met wi' his misfortunes in a wrong line o' life."

"Ay!" said Bessy. "We maun ha' the doctor sure enough, for look at them how they lie! like two stone statues on a church monument, so sad and solemn."

"There's a look o' sense come back into their faces, though, sin' they supped that gin and water. I'd keep on a-bathing his head and giving them a sup on't fra' time to time, if I was you, Bessy."

Bessy followed him downstairs, and lighted the men out of the house. She dared not light them carrying their burden even, until they passed round the corner of the house; so strong was her fearful conviction that Benjamin was lurking near, seeking again to enter. She rushed back into the kitchen, bolted and barred the door, and pushed the end of the dresser against it, shutting her eyes as she passed the uncurtained window, for fear of catching a glimpse of a white face pressed against the glass, and gazing at her.

The poor old couple lay quiet and speechless, although Hester's position had slightly altered: she had turned a little on her side towards her husband, and had laid one shrivelled arm around his neck. But he was just as Bessy had left him, with the wet clothes abound his head, his eyes not wanting in a certain intelligence, but solemn, and unconscious to all that was passing around as the eyes of death.

His wife spoke a little from time to time—said a word of thanks, perhaps, or so; but he, never. All the rest of that terrible night, Bessy tended the poor old couple with constant care, her own heart so stunned and bruised in its feelings that she went about her pious duties almost like one in a dream. The November morning was long in coming; nor did she perceive any change, either for the worse or the better, before the doctor came, about eight o'clock. John Kirkby brought him; and was full of the capture of the two burglars.

As far as Bessy could make out, the participation of that unnatural third was unknown. It was a relief, almost sickening in the revulsion it gave her from her terrible fear, which now she felt had haunted and held possession of her all night long, and had in fact paralysed her from thinking. Now she felt and thought with acute and feverish vividness, owing no doubt, in part, to the sleepless night she had passed. She felt almost sure that her uncle (possibly her aunt too) had recognised Benjamin; but there was a faint chance that they had not done so, and wild horses should never tear the secret from her, nor should any inadvertent word betray the fact that there had been a third person concerned. As to Nathan, he had never uttered a word. It was her aunt's silence that made Bessy fear lest Hester knew, somehow, that her son was concerned.

The doctor examined them both closely; looked hard at the wound on Nathan's head; asked questions which Hester answered shortly and unwillingly, and Nathan not at all: shutting his eyes, as if even the sight of a stranger was pain to him. Bessy replied in their stead to all that she could answer respecting their state; and followed the doctor downstairs with a beating heart When they came into the house-place, they found John had opened the outer door to let in some fresh air, had brushed the hearth and made up the fire, and put the chairs and table in their right places. He reddened a little as Bessy's eye fell upon his swollen and battered face, but tried to smile it off in a dry kind of way:

"Yo' see, I'm an ould bachelor, and I just thought as I'd redd up things a bit How dun yo' find 'em, doctor ?"

"Well, the poor old couple have had a terrible shock. I shall send them some soothing medicine to bring down the pulse, and a lotion for the old man's head. It is very well it bled so much; there might have been a good deal of inflammation." And so he went on, giving directions to Bessy for keeping them quietly in bed through the day. From these directions she gathered that they were not, as she had feared all night long, near to death. The doctor expected them to recover, though they would require care. She almost wished it had been otherwise, and that they, and she too, might have just lain down to their rest in the churchyard—so cruel did life seem to her; so dreadful the recollection of that subdued voice of the hidden robber, smiting her with recognition.

All this time John was getting things ready for breakfast, with something of the handiness of a woman. Bessy half resented his officiousness in pressing Dr. Preston to have a cup of tea, she did so want him to be gone and leave her alone with her thoughts. She did not know that all was done for love of her; that the hard-featured, short-spoken John was thinking all the time how ill and miserable she looked, and trying with tender artifices to make it incumbent upon her sense of hospitality to share Dr. Preston's meal.

"I've seen as the cows is milked," said he, "yourn and all; and Atkinson's brought ours round fine. Whatten a marcy it were as she were sick just this very night! Yon two chaps 'ud ha' made short work on't, if yo' hadna fetched us in; and as it were, we had a sore tussle. One on 'em 'll bear the marks on't to his dying day, wunnot he, doctor?"

"He'll barely have his leg well enough to stand his trial at York Assizes; they're coming off in a fortnight from now."

"Ay, and that reminds me, Bessy, yo'll have to go witness before Justice Royds. Constables bade me tell yo', and gie yo' this summons. Dunnot be feared; it will not be a long job, though I'm not saying as it'll be a pleasant one. Yo'll have to answer questions as to how, and all about it; and Jane" (his sister) "will come and stop wi' th' oud folks; and I'll drive yo' in the shandry."

No one knew why Bessy's colour blenched, and her eye clouded. No one knew how she apprehended lest she should have to say that Benjamin had been of the gang, if, indeed, in some way, the law had not followed on his heels quick enough to catch him.

But that trial was spared her; she was warned by John to answer questions, and say no more than was necessary, for fear of making her story less clear; and as she was known, by character, at least to Justice Royds and his clerk, they made the examination as little formidable as possible.

When all was over, and John was driving her back again, he expressed his rejoicing that there would be evidence enough to convict the men, without summoning Nathan and Hester to identify them. Bessy was so tired that she hardly understood what an escape it was; how far greater than even her companion understood.

Jane Kirkby stayed with her for a week or more, and was an unspeakable comfort. Otherwise she sometimes thought she should have gone mad, with the face of her uncle always reminding her, in its stony expression of agony, of that fearful night. Her aunt was softer in her sorrow, as became one of her faithful and pious nature; but it was easy to see how her heart bled inwardly. She recovered her strength sooner than her husband; but as she recovered, the doctor perceived the rapid approach of total blindness. Every day, nay, every hour of the day, that Bessy dared, without fear of exciting their suspicions of her knowledge, she told them, as she had anxiously told them at first, that only two men, and those perfect strangers, had been discovered as being concerned in the burglary.

Her uncle would never have asked a question about it, even if she had withheld all information respecting the affair; but she noticed the quick, watching, waiting glance of his eye, whenever she returned from any person or place where she might have been supposed to gain intelligence if Benjamin were suspected or caught: and she hastened to relieve the old man's anxiety, by always telling all that she had heard; thankful that as the days passed on the danger she sickened to think of grew less and less.

Day by day, Bessy had ground for thinking that her aunt knew more than she had apprehended at first. There was something so very humble and touching in Hester's blind way of feeling about for her husband—stern, woebegone Nathan—and mutely striving to console him in the deep agony of which Bessy learnt, from this loving, piteous manner, that her aunt was conscious. Her aunt's face looked blankly up into his, tears slowly running down from her sightless eyes, while from time to time, when she thought herself unheard by any save him, she would repeat such texts as she had heard at church in happier days, and which she thought, in her true, simple piety, might tend to console him. Yet, day by day, her aunt grew more and more sad.

Three or four days before assize-time, two summonses to attend the trial at York were sent to the old people. Neither Bessy, nor John, nor Jane, could understand this; for their own notices had come long before, and they bad been told that their evidence would be enough to convict

But alas! the fact was, that the lawyer employed to defend the prisoners had heard from them that there was a third person engaged, and had heard who that third person was; and it was this advocate's business to diminish, if possible, the guilt of his clients, by proving that they were but tools in the hands of one who had, from his superior knowledge of the premises and the daily customs of the inhabitants, been the originator and planner of the whole affair. To do this it was necessary to have the evidence of the parents, who, as the prisoners had said, must have recognized the voice of the young man, their son. For no one knew that Bessy, too, could have borne witness to his having been present; and, as it was supposed that Benjamin had escaped out of England, there was no exact betrayal of him on the part of his accomplishes.

Wondering, bewildered, and weary, the old couple reached York, in company with John and Bessy, on the eve of the day of trial. Nathan was still so self-contained, that Bessy could never guess what had been passing in his mind. He was almost passive under his old wife's trembling caresses; he seemed hardly conscious of them, so rigid was his demeanour.

She, Bessy feared at times, was becoming childish; for she had evidently so great and anxious a love for her husband, that her memory seemed going in her endeavours to melt the stoniness of his aspect and manners; she appeared occasionally to have forgotten why he was so changed, in her piteous little attempts to bring him back to his former self.

"They'll, for sure, never torture them when they see what old folks they are!" cried Bessy, on the morning of the trial, a dim fear looming over her mind. "They'll never be so cruel, for sure!"

But "for sure" it was so. The barrister looked up at the judge, almost apologetically, as he saw how hoary-headed and woeful an old man was put into the witness-box, when the defence came on, and Nathan Huntroyd was called on for his evidence.

"It is necessary, on behalf of my clients, my lord, that I should pursue a course which, for all other reasons, I deplore."

"Go on!" said the judge. "What is right and legal must be done." But, an old man himself, he covered his quivering mouth with his hand as Nathan, with grey, unmoved face, and solemn, hollow eyes, placing his two hands on each side of the witness-box, prepared to give his answers to questions, the nature of which he was beginning to foresee, but would not shrink from replying to truthfully; "the very stones" (as he said to himself, with a kind of dulled sense of the Eternal Justice) "rise up against such a sinner."

"Your name is Nathan Huntroyd, I believe?"

"It is."

"You live at Nab-end Farm?"

"I do."

"Do you remember the night of November the twelfth?"

"Yes."

"You were awakened that night by some noise, I believe. What was it?"

The old man's eyes fixed themselves upon his questioner, with the look of a creature brought to bay. That look the barrister never forgets. It will haunt him till his dying day.

"It was a throwing up of stones against our window."

"Did you hear it at first?"

"No."

331

"What awakened you then ?"

"She did."

"And then you both heard the stones. Did you hear nothing else?"

A long pause. Then a low, clear "Yes."

"What?"

"Our Benjamin asking us for to let him in. She said as it were him, leastways."

"And you thought it was him, did you not ?"

"I told her" (this time in a louder voice) "for to get to sleep, and not to be thinking that every drunken chap as passed by were our Benjamin, for that he were dead and gone."

"And she?"

"She said, as though she'd heerd our Benjamin, afore she were welly awake, axing for to be let in. But I bade her ne'er heed her dreams, but turn on her other side, and get to sleep again."

"And did she?"

A long pause,—judge, jury, bar, audience, all held their breath. At length Nathan said,

"No!"

"What did you do then? (My lord, I am compelled to ask these painful questions.)"

"I saw she wadna be quiet: she had allays thought he would come back to us, like the Prodigal i' th' Gospels." (His voice choked a little, but he tried to make it steady, succeeded, and went on.) "She said, if I wadna get up she would; and just then I heerd a voice. I'm not quite mysel, gentlemen—I've been ill and i' bed, an' it makes me trembling-like. Someone said, 'Father, mother, I'm here, starving i' the cold—wunnot yo' get up and let me in?'"

"And that voice was?—"

"It were like our Benjamin's. I see whatten yo're driving at, sir, and I'll tell yo' truth, though it kills me to speak it I dunnot say it were our Benjamin as spoke, mind yo'—I only say it were like—"

"That's all I want, my good fellow. And on the strength of that entreaty, spoken in your son's voice, you went down and opened the door to these two prisoners at the bar, and to a third man?"

Nathan nodded assent, and even that counsel was too merciful to force him to put more into words.

"Call Hester Huntroyd."

An old woman, with a face of which the eyes were evidently blind, with a sweet, gentle, careworn face, came into the witness-box, and meekly curtseyed to the presence of those whom she had been taught to respect—a presence she could not see.

There was something in her humble, blind aspect, as she stood waiting to have something done to her—what, her poor troubled mind hardly knew—that touched all who saw her, inexpressibly. Again the counsel apologized, but the judge could not reply in words; his face was quivering all over, and the jury looked uneasily at the prisoners' counsel. That gentleman saw that he might go too far, and send their sympathies off on the other side; but one or two questions he must ask. So, hastily recapitulating much that he had learned from Nathan, he said, "You believed it was your son's voice asking to be let in?"

"Ay! Our Benjamin came home, I'm sure; choose where he is gone."

She turned her head about, as if listening for the voice of her child, in the hushed silence of the court.

"Yes; he came home that night—and your husband went down to let him in?"

"Well! I believe he did. There was a great noise of folk down stair."

"And you heard your son Benjamin's voice among the others?"

"Is it to do him harm, sir?" asked she, her face growing more intelligent and intent on the business in hand.

"That is not my object in questioning you. I believe he has left England, so nothing you can say will do him any harm. You heard your son's voice, I say?"

"Yes, sir. For sure, I did."

"And some men came upstairs into your room? What did they say?"

"They axed where Nathan kept his stocking."

"And you—did you tell them?"

"No, sir, for I knew Nathan would not like me to."

"What did you do then?"

A shade of reluctance came over her face, as if she began to perceive causes and consequences.

"I just screamed on Bessy—that's my niece, sir."

"And you heard someone shout out from the bottom of the stairs?"

She looked piteously at him, but did not answer.

"Gentlemen of the jury, I wish to call your particular attention to this fact: she acknowledges she heard someone shout—some third person, you observe—shout out to the two above. What did he say? That is the last question I shall trouble you with. What did the third person, left behind downstairs, say?"

Her face worked—her mouth opened two or three times as if to speak—she stretched out her arms imploringly; but no word came, and she fell back into the arms of those nearest to her. Nathan forced himself forward into the witness-box:

"My Lord Judge, a woman bore ye, as I reckon; it's a cruel shame to serve a mother so. It wur my son, my only child, as called out for us t' open door, and who shouted out for to hold th' oud woman's throat if she did na stop her noise, when hoo'd fain ha' cried for her niece to help. And now yo've truth, and a' th' truth, and I'll leave yo' to th' Judgment o' God for th' way yo've getten at it"

Before night the mother was stricken with paralysis, and lay on her deathbed. But the broken-hearted go Home, to be comforted of God.

The Withered Arm

Thomas Hardy

1: A LORN MILKMAID

It was an eighty-cow dairy, and the troop of milkers, regular and supernumerary, were all at work; for, though the time of year was as yet but early April, the feed lay entirely in water-meadows, and the cows were 'in full pail'. The hour was about six in the evening, and three-fourths of the large, red, rectangular animals having been finished off, there was opportunity for a little conversation.

'He do bring home his bride tomorrow, I hear. They've come as far as Anglebury today.'

The voice seemed to proceed from the belly of the cow called Cherry, but the speaker was a milking-woman, whose face was buried in the flank of that motionless beast.

'Hav' anybody seen her?' said another.

There was a negative response from the first. 'Though they say she's a rosy-cheeked, tisty-tosty little body enough,' she added; and as the milkmaid spoke she turned her face so that she could glance past her cow's tall to the other side of the barton, where a thin, fading woman of thirty milked somewhat apart from the rest.

'Years younger than he, they say,' continued the second, with also a glance of reflectiveness in the same direction.

'How old do you call him, then?'

'Thirty or so.'

'More like forty,' broke in an old milkman near, in a long white pinafore or 'wropper', and with the brim of his hat tied down, so that he looked like a woman. "A was born before our Great Weir was builded, and I hadn't man's wages when I laved water there.'

The discussion waxed so warm that the purr of the milk streams became jerky, till a voice from another cow's belly cried with authority, 'Now then, what the Turk do it matter to us about Farmer Lodge's age, or Farmer Lodge's new mis'ess? I shall have to pay him nine pound a year for the rent of every one of these milchers, whatever his age or hers. Get on with your work, or 'twill be dark afore we have done. The evening is pinking in a'ready.' This speaker was the dairyman himself, by whom the milkmaids and men were employed.

Nothing more was said publicly about Farmer Lodge's wedding, but the first woman murmured under her cow to her next neighbour. ''Tis hard for *she*,' signifying the thin worn milkmaid aforesaid.

'O no,' said the second. 'He ha'n't spoke to Rhoda Brook for years.'

When the milking was done they washed their pails and hung them on a many-forked stand made as usual of the peeled limb of an oak-tree, set upright in the earth, and resembling a colossal antlered horn. The majority then dispersed in various directions homeward. The thin woman who had not spoken was joined by a boy of twelve or thereabout, and the twain went away up the field also.

Their course lay apart from that of the others, to a lonely spot high above the water-meads, and not far from the border of Egdon Heath, whose dark countenance was visible in the distance as they drew nigh to their home.

'They've just been saying down in barton that your father brings his young wife home from Anglebury tomorrow,' the woman observed. 'I shall want to send you for a few things to market, and you'll be pretty sure to meet 'em.'

'Yes, Mother,' said the boy. 'Is Father married then?'

'Yes. . . . You can give her a look, and tell me what she's like, if you do see her.'

'Yes, Mother.'

'If she's dark or fair, and if she's tall—as tall as I. And if she seems like a woman who has ever worked for a living, or one that has been always well off, and has never done anything, and shows marks of the lady on her, as I expect she do.'

'Yes.'

They crept up the hill in the twilight and entered the cottage. It was built of mud-walls, the surface of which had been washed by many rains into channels and depressions that left none of the original flat face visible, while here and there in the thatch above a rafter showed like a bone protruding through the skin.

She was kneeling down in the chimney-corner, before two pieces of turf laid together with the heather inwards, blowing at the red-hot ashes with her breath till the turves flamed. The radiance lit her pale cheek, and made her dark eyes, that had once been handsome, seem handsome anew. 'Yes,' she resumed, 'see if she is dark or fair, and if you can, notice if her hands be white; if not, see if they look as though she had ever done housework, or are milker's hands like mine.'

The boy again promised, inattentively this time, his mother not observing that he was cutting a notch with his pocket-knife in the beech-backed chair.

2: THE YOUNG WIFE

The road from Anglebury to Holmstoke is in general level, but there is one place where a sharp ascent breaks its monotony. Farmers homeward-bound from the former market-town, who trot all the rest of the way, walk their horses up this short incline.

The next evening while the sun was yet bright a handsome new gig, with a lemon-coloured body and red wheels, was spinning westward along the level highway at the heels of a powerful mare. The driver was a yeoman in the prime of life, cleanly shaven like an actor, his face being toned to that bluish-vermilion hue which so often graces a thriving farmer's features when returning home after successful dealings in the town. Beside him sat a woman, many years his junior—almost, indeed, a girl. Her face too was fresh in colour, but it was of a totally different quality—soft and evanescent, like the light under a heap of rose-petals.

Few people travelled this way, for it was not a main road; and the long white riband of gravel that stretched before them was empty, save of one small scarce-moving speck, which presently resolved itself into the figure of a boy, who was creeping on at a snail's pace, and continually looking behind him—the heavy bundle he carried being some excuse for, if not the reason of, his dilatoriness. When the bouncing gig-party slowed at the bottom of the incline above mentioned, the pedestrian was only a few yards in front. Supporting the large bundle by putting one hand on his hip, he turned and looked straight at the farmer's wife as though he would read her through and through, pacing along abreast of the horse.

The low sun was full in her face, rendering every feature, shade, and colour distinct, from the curve of her little nostril to the colour of her eyes. The farmer, though he seemed annoyed at the boy's persistent presence, did not order him to get out of the way; and thus, the lad preceded them, his hard gaze never leaving her, till they reached the top of the ascent, when the farmer trotted on with relief in his lineaments having taken no outward notice of the boy whatever.

'How that poor lad stared at me!' said the young wife.

'Yes, dear; I saw that he did.'

'He is one of the village, I suppose?'

'One of the neighbourhood. I think he lives with his mother a mile or two off.'

'He knows who we are, no doubt?'

'O yes. You must expect to be stared at just at first, my pretty Gertrude.'

'I do—though I think the poor boy may have looked at us in the hope we might relieve him of his heavy load, rather than from curiosity.'

'O no,' said her husband off-handedly. 'These country lads will carry a hundredweight once they get it on their backs; besides his pack had more size than weight in it. Now, then, another mile and I shall be able to show you our house in the distance—if it is not too dark before we get there.' The wheels spun round, and particles flew from their periphery as before, till a white house of ample dimensions revealed itself, with farm-buildings and ricks at the back.

Meanwhile the boy had quickened his pace, and turning up a by-lane some mile-and-a-half short of the white farmstead, ascended towards the leaner pastures, and so on to the cottage of his mother.

She had reached home after her day's milking at the outlying dairy, and was washing cabbage at the doorway in the declining light. 'Hold up the net a moment,' she said, without preface, as the boy came up.

He flung down his bundle, held the edge of the cabbage-net, and as she filled its meshes with the dripping leaves she went on, 'Well, did you see her?'

'Yes; quite plain.'

'Is she ladylike?'

'Yes; and more. A lady complete.'

'Is she young?'

'Well, she's growed up, and her ways be quite a woman's.'

'Of course. What colour is her hair and face?'

'Her hair is lightish, and her face as comely as a live doll's.'

'Her eyes, then, are not dark like mine?'

'No—of a bluish turn, and her mouth is very nice and red; and when she smiles, her teeth show white.'

'Is she tall?' said the woman sharply.

'I couldn't see. She was sitting down.'

'Then do you go to Holmstoke church tomorrow morning: she's sure to be there. Go early and notice her walking in, and come home and tell me if she's taller than I.'

'Very well, Mother. But why don't you go and see for yourself?'

'*I* go to see her! I wouldn't look up at her if she were to pass my window this instant. She was with Mr Lodge, of course. What did he say or do?'

'Just the same as usual.'

'Took no notice of you?'

'None.'

Next day the mother put a clean shirt on the boy, and started him off for Holmstoke church. He reached the ancient little pile when the door was just being opened, and he was the first to enter. Taking his seat by the font, he watched all the parishioners file in. The well-to-do Farmer Lodge came nearly last; and his young wife, who accompanied him, walked up the aisle with the shyness natural to a modest woman who had appeared thus for the first time. As all other eyes were fixed upon her, the youth's stare was not noticed now.

When he reached home his mother said, 'Well?' before he had entered the room.

'She is not tall. She is rather short,' he replied.

'Ah!' said his mother, with satisfaction.

'But she's very pretty—very. In fact, she's lovely.' The youthful freshness of the yeoman's wife had evidently made an impression even on the somewhat hard nature of the boy.

'That's all I want to hear,' said his mother quickly. 'Now, spread the table-cloth. The hare you wired is very tender; but mind nobody catches you.—You've never told me what sort of hands she had.'

'I have never seen 'em. She never took off her gloves'

'What did she wear this morning?'

'A white bonnet and a silver-coloured gownd. It whewed and whistled so loud when it rubbed against the pews that the lady coloured up more than ever for very shame at the noise, and pulled it in to keep it from touching; but when she pushed into her seat, it whewed more than ever. Mr Lodge, he seemed pleased, and his waistcoat stuck out, and his great golden seals hung like a lord's; but she seemed to wish her noisy gownd anywhere but on her.'

'Not she! However, that will do now.'

These descriptions of the newly married couple were continued from time to time by the boy at his mother's request, after any chance encounter he had had with them. But Rhoda Brook, though she might easily have seen young Mrs Lodge for herself by walking a couple of miles, would never attempt an excursion towards the quarter where the farmhouse lay. Neither did she, at the daily milking in the dairyman's yard on Lodge's outlying second farm, ever speak on the subject of the recent marriage. The dairyman, who rented the cows of Lodge, and knew perfectly the tall milkmaid's history, with manly kindness always kept the gossip in the cow-barton from annoying Rhoda. But the atmosphere thereabout was full of the subject the first days of Mrs Lodge's arrival; and from her boy's description and the casual words of the other milkers, Rhoda Brook could raise a mental image of the unconscious Mrs Lodge that was realistic as a photograph.

3: A Vision

One night, two or three weeks after the bridal return, when the boy had gone to bed, Rhoda sat a long time over the turf ashes that she had raked out in front of her to extinguish them. She contemplated so intently the new wife, as presented to her in her mind's eye over the embers, that she forgot the lapse of time. At last, wearied by her day's work, she too retired.

But the figure which had occupied her so much during this and the previous days was not to be banished at night. For the first time Gertrude Lodge visited the supplanted woman in her dreams. Rhoda Brook dreamed—since her assertion that she really saw, before falling asleep, was not to be believed—that the young wife, in the pale silk dress and white bonnet, but with features shockingly distorted, and wrinkled as by age, was sitting upon her chest as she lay.

The pressure of Mrs Lodge's person grew heavier; the blue eyes peered cruelly into her face: and then the figure thrust forward its left hand mockingly, so as to make the wedding-ring it wore glitter in Rhoda's eyes. Maddened mentally, and nearly suffocated by pressure, the sleeper struggled; the incubus, still regarding her, withdrew to the foot of the bed, only, however, to come forward by degrees, resume her seat, and flash her left hand as before.

Gasping for breath, Rhoda, in a last desperate effort, swung out her right hand, seized the confronting spectre by its obtrusive left arm, and whirled it backward to the floor, starting up herself as she did so with a low cry.

'O, merciful heaven!' she cried, sitting on the edge of the bed in a cold sweat; 'that was not a dream—she was here!'

She could feel her antagonist's arm within her grasp even now—the very flesh and bone of it, as it seemed. She looked on the floor whither she had whirled the spectre, but there was nothing to be seen.

Rhoda Brook slept no more that night, and when she went milking at the next dawn they noticed how pale and haggard she looked. The milk that she drew quivered into the pail; her hand had not calmed even yet. and still retained the feel of the arm. She came home to breakfast as wearily as if it had been supper-time.

'What was that noise in your chimmer, mother, last night?' said her son. 'You fell off the bed. surely?'

'Did you hear anything fall? At what time?'

'Just when the clock struck two.'

She could not explain, and when the meal was done went silently about her household works, the boy assisting her, for he hated going afield on the farms, and she indulged his reluctance. Between eleven and twelve the garden-gate clicked, and she lifted her eyes to the window. At the bottom of the garden, within the gate, stood the woman of her vision. Rhoda seemed transfixed.

'Ah, she said she would come!' exclaimed the boy, also observing her.

'Said so—when? How does she know us?'

'I have seen and spoken to her. I talked to her yesterday.'

'I told you,' said the mother, flushing indignantly, 'never to speak to anybody in that house, or go near the place.'

'I did not speak to her till she spoke to me. And I did not go near the place. I met her in the road.'

'What did you tell her?'

'Nothing. She said, "Are you the poor boy who had to bring the heavy load from market?" And she looked at my boots, and said they would not keep my feet dry if it came on wet, because they were so cracked. I told her I lived with my mother, and we had enough to do to keep ourselves, and that's how it was; and she said then: "I'll come and bring you some better boots, and see your mother." She gives away things to other folks in the meads besides us.'

Mrs Lodge was by this time close to the door—not in her silk, as Rhoda had dreamt of in the bedchamber, but in a morning hat, and gown of common light material, which became her better than silk. On her arm she carried a basket.

The impression remaining from the night's experience was still strong. Brook had almost expected to see the wrinkles, the scorn and the cruelty on her visitor's face. She would have escaped an interview, had escape been possible. There was, however, no backdoor to the cottage, and in an instant the boy had lifted the latch to Mrs Lodge's gentle knock.

'I see I have come to the right house,' said she, glancing at the lad, and smiling. 'But I was not sure till you opened the door.'

The figure and action were those of the phantom; but her voice was so indescribably sweet, her glance so winning, her smile so tender, so unlike that of Rhoda's midnight visitant, that the latter could hardly believe the evidence of her senses. She was truly glad that she had not hidden away in sheer aversion, as she had been inclined to do. In her basket Mrs Lodge brought the pair of boots that she had promised to the boy, and other useful articles.

At these proofs of a kindly feeling towards her and hers Rhoda's heart reproached her bitterly. This innocent young thing should have her blessing and not her curse. When she left them a light seemed gone from the dwelling. Two days later she came again to know if the boots fitted; and less than a fortnight after paid Rhoda another call. On this occasion the boy was absent.

'I walk a good deal,' said Mrs Lodge, 'and your house is the nearest outside our own parish. I hope you are well. You don't look quite well.'

Rhoda said she was well enough; and, indeed, though the paler of the two, there was more of the strength that endures in her well-defined features and large frame than in the soft-cheeked young woman before her. The conversation became quite confidential as regarded their powers and weaknesses; and when Mrs Lodge was leaving, Rhoda said, 'I hope you will find this air agree with you, ma'am, and not suffer from the damp of the water-meads.'

The younger one replied that there was not much doubt of her general health being usually good. 'Though, now you remind me, she added, 'I have one little ailment which puzzles me. It is nothing serious, but I cannot make it out.'

She uncovered her left hand and arm; and their outline confronted Rhoda's gaze as the exact original of the limb she had beheld and seized in her dream. Upon the pink round surface of the arm were faint marks of an unhealthy colour, as if produced by a rough grasp. Rhoda's eyes became riveted on the discolorations; she fancied that she discerned in them the shape of her own four fingers.

'How did it happen?' she said mechanically.

'I cannot tell,' replied Mrs Lodge, shaking her head. 'One night when I was sound asleep, dreaming I was away in some strange place, a pain suddenly shot into my arm there, and was so keen as to awaken me. I must have struck it in the daytime, I suppose, though I don't remember doing so.' She added, laughing, 'I tell my dear husband that it looks just as if he had flown into a rage and struck me there. O, I daresay it will soon disappear.'

'Ha, ha! Yes. . . . On what night did it come?'

Mrs Lodge considered, and said it would be a fortnight ago on the morrow. 'When I awoke I could not remember where I was,' she added, 'till the clock striking two reminded me.'

She had named the night and hour of Rhoda's spectral encounter, and Brook felt like a guilty thing. The artless disclosure startled her; she did not reason on the freaks of coincidence; and all the scenery of that ghastly night returned with double vividness to her mind.

'O, can it be,' she said to herself, when her visitor had departed, 'that I exercise a malignant power over people against my own will?' She knew that she had been slyly called a witch since hey fall; but never having understood why that particular stigma had been attached to her, it had passed disregarded. Could this be the explanation, and had such things as this ever happened before?

4: A SUGGESTION

The summer drew on, and Rhoda Brook almost dreaded to meet Mrs Lodge again, notwithstanding that her feeling for the young wife amounted well-nigh to affection. Something in her own individuality seemed to convict Rhoda of crime. Yet a fatality sometimes would direct the steps of the latter to the outskirts of Holmstoke whenever she left her house for any other purpose than her daily work; and hence it happened that their next encounter was out of doors. Rhoda could not avoid the subject which had so mystified her, and after the first few words she stammered, 'I hope your—arm is well again, ma'm?' She had perceived with consternation that Gertrude Lodge carried her left arm stiffly.

'No; it not quite well. Indeed, it is no better at all; it is rather worse. It pains me dreadfully sometimes.'

'Perhaps you had better go to a doctor, ma'am.'

She replied that she had already seen a doctor. Her husband had insisted upon her going to one. But the surgeon had not seemed to understand the afflicted limb at all; he had told her to bathe it in hot water, and she had bathed it, but the treatment had done no good.

'Will you let me see it?' said the milkwoman.

Mrs Lodge pushed up her sleeve and disclosed the place, which was a few inches above the wrist. As soon as Rhoda Brook saw it, she could hardly preserve her composure. There was nothing of the nature of a wound, but the arm at that point had a shrivelled look, and the outline of the four fingers appeared more distinct than at the former Moreover, she fancied that they were imprinted in precisely the rela-tive position of her clutch upon the arm in the trance; the first linger towards Gertrude's wrist, and the fourth towards her elbow.

What the impress resembled seemed to have struck Gertrude her-self since their last meeting. 'It looks almost like finger marks,' she said; adding with a faint laugh, 'my husband says it is as if some witch, or the devil himself, had taken hold of me there, and blasted the flesh.'

Rhoda shivered. 'That's fancy,' she said hurriedly. 'I wouldn't mind it, if I were you.'

'I shouldn't so much mind it,' said the younger, with hesitation, 'if—if I hadn't a notion that it makes my husband dislike me—no, love me less. Men think so much of personal appearance.'

'Some do—he for one.'

'Yes; and he was very proud of mine, at first.'

'Keep your arm covered from his sight.'

'Ah—he knows the disfigurement is there!' She tried to hide the tears that filled her eyes.

'Well, ma'am, I earnestly hope it will go away soon.'

And so, the milkwoman's mind was chained anew to the subject by a horrid sort of spell as she returned home. The sense of having been guilty of an act of malignity increased, affect as she might to ridicule her superstition. In her secret heart Rhoda did not altogether object to a slight diminution of her successor's beauty, by whatever means it had come about; but she did not wish to inflict upon her physical pain. For though this pretty young woman had rendered impossible any reparation which Lodge might have made Rhoda for his past conduct, everything like resentment at the unconscious usurpation had quite passed away from the elder's mind.

If the sweet and kindly Gertrude Lodge only knew of the dream-scene in the bed-chamber, what would she think? Not to inform her of it seemed treachery in the presence of her friendliness; but tell she could not of her own accord neither could she devise a remedy.

She mused upon the matter the greater part of the night; and the next day, after the morning milking, set out to obtain another glimpse of Gertrude Lodge if she could, being held to her by a gruesome fascination. By watching the house from a distance, the milkmaid was presently able to discern the farmer's wife in a ride she was taking alone—probably to join her husband in some distant field. Mrs Lodge perceived her, and cantered in her direction.

'Good morning, Rhoda!' Gertrude said, when she had come up. 'I was going to call.'

Rhoda noticed that Mrs Lodge held the reins with some difficulty. 'I hope—the bad arm,' said Rhoda.

'They tell me there is possibly one way by which I might be able to find out the cause, and so perhaps the cure of it,' replied the other anxiously. 'It is by going to some clever man over in Egdon Heath. They did not know if he was still alive—and I cannot remember his name at this moment; but they said that you knew more of his movements than anybody else hereabout, and could tell me if he were still to be consulted. Dear me what was his name? But you know.'

'Not Conjuror Trendle?' said her thin companion, turning pale.

'Trendle—yes. Is he alive?'

'I believe so,' said Rhoda, with reluctance.

'Why do you call him conjuror?'

'Well—they say—they used to say he was a—he had powers other folks have not.'

'O, how could my people be so superstitious as to recommend a man of that sort! I thought they meant some medical man. I shall think no more of him.'

Rhoda looked relieved, and Mrs Lodge rode on. The milkwoman had inwardly seen, from the moment she heard of her having been mentioned as a reference for this man,' that there must exist a sarcastic feeling among the work-folk that a sorceress would know the whereabouts of the exorcist. They suspected her, then. A short time ago this' would have given no concern to a woman of her common sense. But she had a haunting reason to be superstitious now; and she had been seized with sudden dread that this Conjuror Trendle might name her as the malignant influence' which was blasting the fair person of Gertrude, and so lead her friend to hate her for ever, and to treat her as some fiend in human shape.

But all was not over. Two days after, a shadow intruded into the window-pattern thrown on Rhoda Brook's floor by the afternoon sun. The woman opened the door at once, almost breathlessly.

'Are you alone?' said Gertrude. She seemed to be no less harassed and anxious than Brook herself.

'Yes,' said Rhoda.

'The place on my arm seems worse, and troubles me!' the young farmer's wife went on. 'It is so mysterious! I do hope it will not be an incurable wound. I have again been thinking of what they said about Conjuror Trendle. I don't really believe in such men, but I should not mind just visiting him, from curiosity—though on no account must my husband know. Is it far to where he lives?'

'Yes—five miles,' said Rhoda backwardly. 'In the heart of Egdon.'

'Well, I should have to walk. Could not you go with me to show me the way—say tomorrow afternoon?'

'O, not I; that is—,' the milkwoman murmured, with a start of dismay. Again, the dread seized her that something to do with her fierce act in the dream might be revealed, and her character in the eyes of the most useful friend she had ever had be ruined irretrievably.

Mrs Lodge urged, and Rhoda finally assented, though with much misgiving. Sad as' the journey would be to her, she could not conscientiously stand in the way of a possible remedy for her patron's strange affliction. It was agreed that, to escape suspicion of their mystic intent, they should meet at the edge of the heath at the corner of a plantation which was visible from the spot where they now stood.

5: Conjuror Trendle

By the next afternoon Rhoda would have done anything to escape this inquiry. But she had promised to go. Moreover, there was a horrid fascination at times in becoming instrumental in throwing such possible light on her own character as would reveal her to be something greater in the occult world than she had ever herself suspected.

She started just before the time of day mentioned between them, and half an hour's brisk walking brought her to the south-eastern extension of the Egdon tract of country, where the fir plantation was. A slight figure, cloaked and veiled; was already there. Rhoda recognised, almost with a shudder, that Mrs Lodge bore her left arm in a sling.

They hardly spoke to each other, and immediately set out on their climb into the interior of this solemn, country, which stood high above the rich alluvial soil they had left half an hour before. It was a long walk; thick clouds made the atmosphere dark, though it was as yet only early afternoon; and the wind howled dismally over the slopes of the heath—not improbably the same heath which had witnessed the agony of the Wessex King Ina, presented to after-ages as Lear. Gertrude Lodge talked most, Rhoda replying with monosyllabic preoccupation. She had a strange dislike to walking on the side of her companion where hung the afflicted arm, moving round to the other when inadvertently near it. Much heather had been brushed by their feet when they descended upon a cart-track, beside which stood the house of the man they sought.

He did not profess his remedial practices openly, or care anything about their continuance, his direct interests being those of a dealer in furze, turf, 'sharp sand', and other local products. Indeed, he affected not to believe largely in his own powers, and when watts that had been shown him for cure miraculously disappeared—which it must be owned they infallibly did—he would say lightly, 'O, I only drink a glass of grog upon 'em at your expense—perhaps it's all chance', and immediately turn the subject.

He was at home when they arrived, having in fact seen them descending into his valley. He was a grey-bearded man, with a reddish face, and he looked singularly at Rhoda the first moment he beheld her. Mrs Lodge told him her errand; and then with words of self-disparagement he examined her arm.

'Medicine can't cure it,' he said promptly. ''Tis the work of an enemy.'

Rhoda shrank into herself, and drew back.

'An enemy? What enemy?' asked Mrs Lodge.

He shook his head. 'That's best known to yourself,' he said. 'If you like, I can show the person to you, though I shall not myself know who it is. I can do no more; and don't wish to do that.'

She pressed him; on which he told Rhoda to wait outside where she stood, and took Mrs Lodge into the room. It opened immediately from the door; and, as the latter remained ajar, Rhoda Brook could see the proceedings without taking part in them. He brought a tumbler from the dresser, nearly filled it with water, and fetching an egg, prepared it in some private way; after which he broke it on the edge of the glass, so that the white went in and the yolk remained. As it was getting gloomy, he took the glass and its contents to the window, and told Gertrude to watch the mixture closely. They leant over the table together, and the milkwoman could see the opaline hue of the egg-fluid changing form as it sank in the water, but she was not near enough to define the shape that it assumed.

'Do you catch the likeness of any face or figure as you look?' demanded the conjuror of the young woman.

She murmured a reply, in tones so low as to be inaudible to Rhoda, and continued to gaze intently into the glass. Rhoda turned, and walked a few steps away.

When Mrs Lodge came out, and her face was met by the light, it appeared exceedingly pale—as pale as Rhoda's—against the sad dun shades of the upland's garniture. Trendle shut the door behind her, and they at once started homeward together. But Rhoda perceived that her companion had quite changed.

'Did he charge much?' she asked tentatively.

'O no—nothing, He would not take a farthing,' said Gertrude.

'And what did you see?' inquired Rhoda.

'Nothing I—care to speak of.' The constraint in her manner was remarkable; her face was so rigid as to wear an oldened aspect, faintly suggestive of the face in Rhoda's' bedchamber.

'Was it you who first proposed coming here?' Mrs Lodge suddenly inquired, after a long pause. 'How very odd, if you did!'

'No. But I am not very sorry we have come, all things considered.' she replied. For the first time a sense of triumph possessed her, and she did not altogether deplore that the young thing at her side should learn that their lives had been antagonized by other influences than their own.

The subject was no more alluded to during the long and dreary walk home. But in some way or other a story was whispered about the many-dairied lowland that winter that Mrs Lodge's gradual loss of the use of her left arm was owing to her being 'overlooked' by Rhoda Brook. The latter kept her own counsel about the incubus, but her face grew sadder and thinner; and in the spring, she and her boy disappeared from the neighbourhood of Holmstoke.

6: A Second Attempt

Half a dozen years passed away. and Mr and Mrs Lodge's married experience sank into prosiness, and worse. The farmer was usually gloomy and silent: the woman whom he had wooed for her grace and beauty was contorted and disfigured in the left limb; moreover, she had brought him no child, which rendered it likely that he would be the last of a family who had occupied that valley for some two hundred years. He thought of Rhoda Brook and her son; and feared this might be a judgement from heaven upon him.

The once blithe-hearted and enlightened Gertrude was changing into an irritable, superstitious woman, whose whole time was given to experimenting upon her ailment with every quack remedy she came across. She was honestly attached to her husband, and was ever secretly hoping against hope to win back his heart again by regaining some at least of her personal beauty. Hence it arose that her closet was lined with bottles, packets, and ointment-pots of every description—nay, bunches of mystic herbs, charms, and books of necromancy, which in her schoolgirl time she would have ridiculed as folly.

'Damned if you won't poison yourself with these apothecary messes and witch mixtures some time or other,' said her husband, when his eye chanced to fall upon the multitudinous array.

She did not reply, but turned her sad, soft glance upon him in such heart-swollen reproach that he looked sorry for his words, and added, 'I only meant it for your good, you know, Gertrude.'

'I'll clear out the whole lot, and destroy them,' said she huskily, 'and try such remedies no more!'

'You want somebody to cheer you,' he observed. 'I once thought of adopting a boy; but he is too old now. And he is gone away I don't know where.'

She guessed to whom he alluded; for, Rhoda Brook's story had in the course of years become known to her; though not a, word had ever passed between her husband and herself on the subject. Neither had she ever spoken to him of her visit to Conjuror Trendle, and of what was revealed to her, or she thought was revealed to her, by that solitary heath-man.

She was now five-and-twenty; but she seemed older. 'Six years of marriage, and only a few months of love,' she sometimes whispered to herself. And then she thought of the apparent cause, and said, with a tragic glance at her withering limb, 'If I could only be again as I was when he first saw me!'

She obediently destroyed her nostrums and charms; but there remained a hankering wish to try something else—some other sort of cure altogether. She had never revisited Trendle since she had been conducted to the house of the solitary by Rhoda against her will; but it now suddenly occurred to Gertrude that she would, in a last desperate effort at deliverance from this seeming curse, again seek out the man, if he yet lived. He was entitled to a certain credence, for the indistinct form he had raised in the glass had undoubtedly resembled the only woman in the world who—as she now knew, though not then—could have a reason for bearing her ill-will. The visit should be paid.

This time she went alone, though she nearly got lost on the heath, and roamed a considerable distance out of her way. Trendle's house was reached at last, however: he was not indoors, and instead of waiting at the cottage. she went to where his bent figure was pointed out to her at work a long way off. Trendle remembered her, and laying down the handful of furze-roots which he was gathering and throwing into a heap, he offered to accompany her in the homeward direction, as the distance was considerable and the days were short. So, they walked together, his head bowed nearly to the earth, and his form of a colour with it.

'You can send away warts and other excrescences, I know,' she said; 'why can't you send away this?' And the arm was uncovered.

'You think too much of my powers!' said Trendle; 'and I am old and weak now, too. No, no; it is too much for me to attempt in my own person. What have ye tried?'

She named to him some of the hundred medicaments and counterspells which she had adopted from time to time. He shook his head.

'Some were good enough,' he said approvingly; 'but not many of them for such as this. This is of the nature of a blight, not of the nature of a wound; and if you ever do throw it off, it will be all at once.'

'If I only could!'

'There is only one chance of doing it known to me. It has never failed in kindred afflictions—that I can declare. But it is hard to carry out, and especially for a woman.'

'Tell me!' said she.

'You must touch with the limb the neck of a man who's been hanged.'

She started a little at the image he had raised.

'Before he's cold—just after he's cut down,' continued the conjuror impassively.

'How can that do good?'

'It will turn the blood and change the constitution. But, as I say, to do it is hard. You must go to the jail when there's a hanging, and wait for him when he's brought off the gallows. Lots have done it, though perhaps not such pretty women as you. I used to send dozens for skin complaints. But that was in former times. The last I sent was in '13— near twelve years ago.'

He had no more to tell her; and, when he had put her into a

straight track homeward, turned and left her, refusing all money as at first.

7: A RIDE

The communication sank deep into Gertrude's mind. Her nature was rather a timid one; and probably of all remedies that the white wizard could have suggested there was not one which would have filled her with so much aversion as this, not to speak of the immense obstacles in the way of its adoption.

Casterbridge, the county-town, was a dozen or fifteen miles off; and though in those days, when men were executed for horse-stealing, arson, and burglary, an assize seldom passed without a hanging, it was not likely that she could get access to the body of the criminal' unaided. And the fear of her husband's anger made her reluctant to breathe a word of Trendle's suggestion to him or to anybody about him.

She did nothing for months, and patiently bore her disfigurement as before. But her woman's nature, craving for renewed love, through the medium of renewed beauty (she was but twenty-five), was ever stimulating her to try what, at any rate, could hardly do her any harm. 'What came by a spell will go by a spell surely,' she would say. Whenever her imagination pictured the act she shrank in terror from the possibility of it: then the words of the conjuror, 'It will turn your blood', were seen to be capable of a scientific no less than ghastly interpretation; the mastering desire returned, and urged her on again.

There was at this time but one county paper, and that her husband only occasionally borrowed. But old-fashioned days had old-fashioned means, and news was extensively conveyed by word of mouth from market to market, or from fair to fair, so that, whenever such an event as an execution was about to take place, few within a radius of twenty miles were ignorant of the' coming sight; and, so far as Holmstoke was concerned, some enthusiasts had been known to walk all the way to Casterbridge and back in one day, solely to witness the spectacle. The next assizes were in March; and when Gertrude Lodge heard that they had been held, she inquired stealthily at the inn as to the result, as soon as she could find opportunity.

She was, however, too late. The time at which the sentences were to be carried out had arrived, and to make the journey and obtain permission at such short notice required at least her husband's assistance. She dared not tell him, for she had found by delicate experiment that these smouldering village beliefs made him furious if mentioned, partly because he half entertained them himself. It was therefore necessary to wait for another opportunity.

Her determination received a fillip from learning that two epileptic children had attended from this very village of Holmstoke many years before with beneficial results, though the experiment had been strongly condemned by the neighbouring clergy. April, May, June, passed; and it is no overstatement to say that by the end of the last-named month Gertrude well-nigh longed for the death of a fellow-creature. Instead of her formal prayers each night, her unconscious prayer was, 'O Lord, hang some guilty or innocent person soon!'

This time she made earlier inquiries, and was altogether more systematic in her proceedings. Moreover, the season was summer, between the haymaking and the harvest, and in the leisure thus afforded him her husband had been holiday-taking away from home.

The assizes were in July, and she went to the inn as before. There was to be one execution—only one—for arson.

Her greatest problem was not how to get to Casterbridge, but what means she should adopt for obtaining admission to the jail. Though access for such purposes had formerly never been denied, the custom had fallen into desuetude; and in contemplating her possible difficulties, she was again almost driven to fall back upon her husband. But, on sounding him about the assizes, he was so uncommunicative, so more than usually cold, that she did not proceed, and decided that whatever she did she would do alone.

Fortune, obdurate hitherto, showed her unexpected favour. On the Thursday before the Saturday fixed for the execution, Lodge remarked to her that he was going away from home for another day or two on business at a fair, and that he was sorry he could not take her with him.

She exhibited on this occasion so much readiness to stay at home that he looked at her in surprise. Time had been when she would have shown deep disappointment at the loss of such a jaunt. However, he lapsed into his usual taciturnity, and on the day named left Holmstoke.

It was now her turn. She at first had thought of driving, but on reflection held that driving would not do, since it would necessitate her keeping to the turnpike-road, and so increase by tenfold the risk of her ghastly errand being found out. She decided to ride, and avoid the beaten track, notwithstanding that in her husband's stables there was no animal just at present which by any stretch of imagination could be considered a lady's mount, in spite of his promise before marriage to always keep a mare for her. He had, however, many cart-horses, fine ones of their kind; and among the rest was a serviceable creature, an equine Amazon, with a back as broad as a sofa, on which Gertrude had occasionally taken an airing when unwell. This horse she chose.

On Friday afternoon one of the men brought it round. She was dressed, and before going down looked at her shrivelled arm. 'Ah!' she said to it, 'if it had not been for you this terrible ordeal would have been saved me!'

When strapping up the bundle in which she carried a few articles of clothing, she took occasion to say to the servant, 'I take these in case I should not get back tonight from the person I am going to visit. Don't be alarmed if I am not in by ten, and close up the house as usual. I shall be home tomorrow for certain.' She meant then to tell her husband privately: the deed accomplished was not like the deed projected. He would almost certainly forgive her.

And then the pretty palpitating Gertrude Lodge went from her husband's homestead; but though her goal was Casterbridge she did not take the direct route thither through Stickleford. Her cunning course at first was in precisely the opposite direction. As soon as she was out of sight, however, she turned to the left, by a road which led into Egdon, and on entering the heath wheeled round, and set out in the true course, due westerly. A more private way down the county could not be imagined; and as to direction, she had merely to keep her horse's head to a point a little to the right of the sun. She knew that she would light upon a furze-cutter or cottager of some sort from time to time, from whom she might correct her bearing.

Though the date was comparatively recent, Egdon was much less fragmentary in character than now. The attempts—successful and otherwise—at cultivation on the lower slopes, which intrude and break up the original heath into small detached heaths, had not been carried far; Enclosure Acts had not taken effect, and the banks and fences which now exclude the cattle of those villagers who formerly enjoyed rights of commonage thereon, and the carts of those who had turbary privileges which kept them in firing all the year round, were not erected. Gertrude, therefore, rode along with no other obstacles than the prickly furze-bushes, the mats of heather, the white water-courses, and the natural steeps and declivities of the ground.

Her horse was sure, if heavy-footed and slow, and though a draught animal, was easy-paced; had it been otherwise, she was not a woman who could have ventured to ride over such a bit of country with a half-dead arm. It was therefore nearly eight o'clock when she drew rein to breathe her bearer on the last outlying high point of heathland towards Casterbridge, previous to leaving Egdon for the cultivated valleys.

She halted before a pool called Rushy-pond, flanked by the ends of two hedges; a railing ran through the centre of the pond, dividing h in half. Over the railing she saw the low green country; over the green trees the roofs of the town; over the roofs a white flat *façade*, denoting the entrance to the county jail. On the roof of this front specks were moving about; they seemed to be workmen erecting something. Her flesh crept. She descended slowly, and was soon amid corn-fields and pastures. In another half-hour, when it was almost dusk, Gertrude reached the White Hart, the first inn of the town on that side.

Little surprise was excited by her arrival; farmers' wives rode on horseback then more than they do now; though, for that matter, Mrs Lodge was not imagined to be a wife at all; the innkeeper supposed her some harum-scarum young woman who had come to attend 'hang-fair' next day. Neither her husband nor herself ever dealt in Casterbridge market, so that she was unknown. While dismounting she beheld a crowd of boys standing at the door of a harness-maker's shop just above the inn, looking inside it with deep interest.

'What is going on there?' she asked of the ostler.

'Making the rope for tomorrow.'

She throbbed responsively, and contracted her arm.

'"Tis sold by the inch afterwards,' the man continued. 'I could get you a bit, miss, for nothing, if you'd like?'

She hastily repudiated any such wish, all the more from a curious creeping feeling that the condemned wretch's destiny was becoming interwoven with her own; and having engaged a room for the night, sat down to think.

Up to this time she had formed but the vaguest notions about her means of obtaining access to the prison. The words of the cunning-man returned to her mind. He had implied that she should use her beauty, impaired though it was, as a pass-key. In her inexperience she knew little about jail functionaries; she had heard of a high-sheriff and an under-sheriff, but dimly only. She knew, however, that there must be a hangman, and to the hangman she determined to apply.

8: A WATER-SIDE HERMIT

At this date, and for several years after, there was a hangman to almost every jail. Gertrude found, on inquiry, that the Casterbridge official dwelt in. a lonely cottage by a deep slow river flowing under the cliff on which the prison buildings were situate—the stream being the self-same one, though she did not know it, which watered the Stickleford and Holmstoke meads lower down in its course.

Having changed her dress, and before she had eaten or drunk—for she could not take her ease till she had ascertained some particulars—Gertrude pursued her way by a path along the water-side to the cottage indicated. Passing thus the outskirts of the jail, she discerned on the level roof over the gateway three rectangular lines against the sky, where the specks had been moving in her distant view; she recognised what the erection was, and passed quickly on, Another hundred yards brought her to the executioner's house, which a boy pointed out. It stood close to the same stream, and was hard by a weir, the waters of which emitted a steady roar.

While she stood hesitating the door opened, and an old man came forth shading a candle with one hand. Locking the door on the outside, he turned to a flight of wooden steps fixed against the end of the cottage, and began to ascend them, this being evidently the staircase to his bedroom. Gertrude hastened forward, but by the time she reached the foot of the ladder he was at the top. She called to him loudly enough to be heard above the roar of the weir; he looked down and said, 'What d'ye want here?'

'To speak to you a minute.'

The candle-light, such as it was, fell upon her imploring, pale, upturned face, and Davies (as the hangman was called) backed down the ladder. 'I was just going to bed,' he said; '*Early to bed and early to rise*, but I don't mind stopping a minute for such a one as you. Come into house.' He reopened the door, and preceded her to the room within.

The implements of his daily work, which was that of a jobbing gardener, stood in a corner, and seeing probably that she looked rural, he said, 'If you want me to undertake country work I can't come, for I never leave Casterbridge for gentle nor simple—not I. My real calling is officer of justice,' he added formally.

'Yes, yes! That's it. Tomorrow!'

'Ah! I thought so. Well, what's the matter about that? 'Tis no use to come here about the knot—folks do come continually, but I tell 'em one knot is as merciful as another if ye keep it under the ear. Is the unfortunate man a relation; or, I should say, perhaps (looking at her dress) a person who's been in your employ?'

'No. What time is the execution?'

'The same as usual—twelve o'clock, or as soon after as the London mail-coach gets in. We always wait for that, in case of a reprieve.'

'O—a reprieve—I hope not!' she said involuntarily.

'Well,—hee, hee!—as a matter of business, so do I! But still, if ever a young fellow deserved to be let off, this one does; only just turned eighteen,' and only present by chance when the rick was fired. Howsomever, there's not much risk of that, as they are obliged to make an example of him, there having been so much destruction of property that way lately.'

'I mean,' she explained, 'that I want to touch him for a charm, a cure of an affliction, by the advice of a man who has proved the virtue of the remedy.'

'O yes, miss! Now I understand. I've had such people come in past years. But it didn't strike me that you looked of a sort to require blood-turning. What's the complaint? The wrong kind for this, I'll be bound.'

'My arm.' She reluctantly showed the withered skin.

'Ah!—'tis all a-scram!' said the hangman, examining it.

'Yes,' said she.

'Well,' he continued, with interest, 'that *is* the class o' subject, I'm bound to admit! I like the look of the place; it is as suitable for the cure as any I ever saw. 'Twas a knowing-man that sent 'ee, whoever he was.'

'You can contrive for me all that's necessary?' she said breathlessly.

'You should really have gone to the governor of the jail, and your doctor with 'ee, and given your name and address—that's how it used to be done, if I recollect. Still, perhaps, I can manage it for a trifling fee.'

'O, thank you! I would rather do it this way, as I should like it kept private.'

'Lover not to know, eh?'

'No—husband.'

'Aha! Very well. I'll get 'ee a touch of the corpse.'

'Where is it now?' she said, shuddering.

'It?—*he*, you mean; he's living yet. Just inside that little small winder up there in the glum.' He signified the jail on the cliff above.

She thought of her husband and her friends. 'Yes, of course,' she said; 'and how am I to proceed?'

He took her to the door. 'Now, do you be waiting at the little wicket in the wall, that you'll find up there in the lane, not later than one o'clock. I will open it from the inside, as I shan't come home to dinner till he's cut down. Goodnight. Be punctual; and if you don't want anybody to know 'ee, wear a veil. Ah—once I had such a daughter as you!'

She went away, and climbed the path above, to assure herself that she would be able to find the wicket next day. Its outline was soon visible to her—a narrow opening in the outer wall of the prison precincts. The steep was so great that, having reached the wicket, she stopped a moment to breathe: and, looking back upon the waterside cot, saw the hangman again ascending his outdoor staircase.' He entered the loft or chamber to which it led, and in a few minutes extinguished his light.

The town clock struck ten, and she returned to the White Hart as she had come.

9: A RENCOUNTER

It was one o'clock on Saturday. Gertrude Lodge, having been admitted to the jail as above described, was sitting in a waiting-room within the second gate, which stood under a classic archway of ashlar, then comparatively modern, and bearing the inscription, 'COVNTY JAIL: 1793.' This had been the *façade* she saw from the heath the day before. Near at hand was a passage to the roof on which the gallows stood.

The town was thronged, and the market suspended; but Gertrude had seen scarcely a soul. Having kept her room till the hour of the appointment, she had proceeded to the spot by a way which avoided the open space below the cliff where the spectators had gathered; but she could, even now, hear the multitudinous babble of their voices, out of which rose at intervals the hoarse croak of a single voice uttering the words, 'Last dying speech and confession!' There had been no reprieve, and the execution was over; but the crowd still waited to see the body taken down.

Soon the persistent woman heard a trampling overhead, then a hand beckoned to her, and, following directions, she went out and crossed the inner paved court beyond the gate-house, her knees trembling so that she could scarcely walk. One of her arms was out of its sleeve, and only covered by her shawl.

On the spot at which she had now arrived were two trestles, and before she could think of their purpose she heard, heavy feet descending stairs somewhere at her back. Turn her head she would not, or could not, and, rigid in this position, she was conscious of a rough coffin' passing her borne by four men. It was open, and in it lay the body of a young man, wearing the smockfrock of a rustic, and fustian breeches. The corpse had been thrown into the coffin so hastily that the skirt of the smockfrock was hanging over. The burden was temporarily deposited on the trestles.

By this time the young woman's state was such that a grey mist seemed to float before her eyes, on account of which, and the veil she wore, she could scarcely discern anything: it was as though she had nearly died, but was held up by a sort of galvanism.

'Now!' said a voice close at hand, and she was just conscious that the word had been addressed to her.

By a last strenuous effort, she advanced, at the same time hearing persons approaching behind her. She bared her poor curst arm; and Davies, uncovering the face of the corpse, took Gertrude's hand, and held it so that her arm lay across the dead man's neck, upon a line the colour of an unripe blackberry, which surrounded it.

Gertrude shrieked: 'the turn o' the blood', predicted by the conjuror, had taken place. But at that moment a second shriek rent the air of the enclosure: it was not Gertrude's, and its effect upon her was to make her start round.

Immediately behind her stood Rhoda Brook, her face drawn, and her eyes red with weeping. Behind Rhoda stood Gertrude's own husband; his countenance lined, his eyes dim, but without a tear.

'D—n you! what are you doing here?' he said hoarsely.

'Hussy—to come between us and our child now!' cried Rhoda. 'This is the meaning of what Satan showed me in the vision! You are like her at last!' And clutching the bare arm of the younger woman, she pulled her unresistingly back against the wall. Immediately Brook had loosened her hold the fragile young Gertrude slid down against the feet of her husband. When he lifted her up she was unconscious.

The mere sight of the twain had been enough to suggest to her that the dead young man was Rhoda's son. At that time the relatives of an executed convict had the privilege of claiming the body for burial, if they chose to do so; and it was for this purpose that Lodge was awaiting the inquest with Rhoda. He had been summoned by her as soon as the young man was taken in the crime, and at different times since; and he had attended in court during the trial. This was the 'holiday' he had been indulging in of late. The two wretched parents had wished to avoid exposure; and hence had come themselves for the body, a wagon and sheet for its conveyance and covering being in waiting outside.

Gertrude's case was so serious that it was deemed advisable to call to her the surgeon who was at hand. She was taken out of the jail into the town; but she never reached home alive. Her delicate vitality, sapped perhaps by the paralysed arm, collapsed under the double shock that followed the severe strain, physical and mental, to which she had subjected herself during the previous twenty-four hours. Her blood had been 'turned' indeed—too far. Her death took place in the town three days after.

Her husband was never seen in Casterbridge again; once only in the old market-place at Anglebury, which he had so much frequented, and very seldom in public anywhere Burdened at first with moodiness and remorse, he eventually changed for the better, and appeared as a chastened and thoughtful man. Soon after attending the funeral of his poor wife he took steps towards giving up the farms in Holmstoke and the adjoining parish, and, having sold every head of his stock, he went away to Port-Bredy, at the other end of the county, living there in solitary lodgings till his death two years later of a painless decline. It was then found that he had bequeathed the whole of his not inconsiderable property to a reformatory for boys, subject to the payment of a small annuity to Rhoda Brook, if she could be found to claim it.

For some time, she could not be found; but eventually she re-appeared in her old parish—absolutely refusing, however, to have anything to do with the provision made for her. Her monotonous milking at the dairy was resumed, and followed for many long years, till her form became bent, and her once abundant dark hair white and worn away at the forehead—perhaps by long pressure against the cows. Here, sometimes, those who knew her experiences would stand and observe her, and wonder what sombre thoughts were beating inside that impassive, wrinkled brow, to the rhythm of the alternating milk-streams.

Thurnley Abbey

Perceval Landon

Three years ago, I was on my way out to the East, and as an extra day in London was of some importance, I took the Friday evening mail-train to Brindisi instead of the usual Thursday morning Marseilles express. Many people shrink from the long forty-eight-hour train journey through Europe, and the subsequent rush across the Mediterranean on the nineteen-knot *Isis* or *Osiris*; but there is really very little discomfort on either the train or the mail-boat, and unless there is actually nothing for me to do, I always like to save the extra day and a half in London before I say goodbye to her for one of my longer tramps.

This time—it was early, I remember, in the shipping season, probably about the beginning of September—there were few passengers, and I had a compartment in the P. & O. Indian express to myself all the way from Calais. All Sunday I watched the blue waves dimpling the Adriatic, and the pale rosemary along the cuttings; the plain white towns, with their flat roofs and their bold *duomos*, and the grey-green gnarled olive orchards of Apulia. The journey was just like any other. We ate in the dining-car as often and as long as we decently could. We slept after luncheon; we dawdled the afternoon away with yellow-backed novels; sometimes we exchanged platitudes in the smoking-room, and it was there that I met Alastair Colvin.

Colvin was a man of middle height, with a resolute, well-cut jaw; his hair was turning grey; his moustache was sun-whitened, otherwise he was clean-shaven—obviously a gentleman, and obviously also a pre-occupied man. He had no great wit. When spoken to, he made the usual remarks in the right way, and I dare say he refrained from banalities only because he spoke less than the rest of us; most of the time he buried himself in the Wagon-lit Company's time-table, but seemed unable to concentrate his attention on any one page of it. He found that I had been over the Siberian railway, and for a quarter of an hour he discussed it with me. Then he lost interest in it, and rose to go to his compartment. But he came back again very soon, and seemed glad to pick up the conversation again.

Of course, this did not seem to me to be of any importance. Most travellers by train become a trifle infirm of purpose after thirty-six hours' rattling. But Colvin's restless way I noticed in somewhat marked contrast with the man's personal importance and dignity; especially ill-suited was it to his finely made large hand with strong, broad, regular nails and its few lines. As I looked at his hand I noticed a long, deep, and recent scar of ragged shape. However, it is absurd to pretend that I thought anything was unusual. I went off at five o'clock on Sunday afternoon to sleep away the hour or two that had still to be got through before we arrived at Brindisi.

Once there, we few passengers transhipped our hand baggage, verified our berths—there were only a score of us in all—and then, after an aimless ramble of half an hour in Brindisi, we returned to dinner at the Hôtel International, not wholly surprised that the town had been the death of Virgil. If I remember rightly, there is a gaily painted hall at the International—I do not wish to advertise anything, but there is no other place in Brindisi at which to await the coming of the mails—and after dinner I was looking with awe at a trellis overgrown with blue vines, when Colvin moved across the room to my table. He picked up *Il Secolo*, but almost immediately gave up the pretence of reading it. He turned squarely to me and said:

"Would you do me a favour?"

One doesn't do favours to stray acquaintances on Continental expresses without knowing something more of them than I knew of Colvin. But I smiled in a noncommittal way, and asked him what he wanted. I wasn't wrong in part of my estimate of him; he said bluntly:

"Will you let me sleep in your cabin on the *Osiris*?" And he coloured a little as he said it.

Now, there is nothing more tiresome than having to put up with a stable-companion at sea, and I asked him rather pointedly:

"Surely there is room for all of us?" I thought that perhaps he had been partnered off with some mangy Levantine, and wanted to escape from him at all hazards.

Colvin, still somewhat confused, said: "Yes; I am in a cabin by myself. But you would do me the greatest favour if you would allow me to share yours."

This was all very well, but, besides the fact that I always sleep better when alone, there had been some recent thefts on board English liners, and I hesitated, frank and honest and self-conscious as Colvin was. Just then the mail-train came in with a clatter and a rush of escaping steam, and I asked him to see me again about it on the boat when we started. He answered me curtly—I suppose he saw the mistrust in my manner—"I am a member of White's. I smiled to myself as he said it, but I remembered in a moment that the man—if he were really what he claimed to be, and I make no doubt that he was—must have been sorely put to it before he urged the fact as a guarantee of his respectability to a total stranger at a Brindisi hotel.

That evening, as we cleared the red and green harbour-lights of Brindisi, Colvin explained. This is his story in his own words:—

"When I was travelling in India some years ago, I made the acquaintance of a youngish man in the woods and forests. We camped out together for a week, and I found him a pleasant companion. John Broughton was a light-hearted soul when off duty, but a steady and capable man in any of the small emergencies that continually arise in that department. He was liked and trusted by the natives, and though a trifle over-pleased with himself when he escaped to civilisation at Simla or Calcutta, Broughton's future was well assured in Government service, when a fair-sized estate was unexpectedly left to him, and he joyfully shook the dust of the Indian plains from his feet and returned to England. For five years he drifted about London. I saw him now and then.

"We dined together about every eighteen months, and I could trace pretty exactly the gradual sickening of Broughton with a merely idle life. He then set out on a couple of long voyages, returned as restless as before, and at last told me that he had decided to marry and settle down at his place, Thurnley Abbey, which had long been empty. He spoke about looking after the property and standing for his constituency in the usual way. Vivien Wilde, his fiancée, had, I suppose, begun to take him in hand. She was a pretty girl with a deal of fair hair and rather an exclusive manner; deeply religious in a narrow school, she was still kindly and high-spirited, and I thought that Broughton was in luck. He was quite happy and full of information about his future.

"Among other things, I asked him about Thurnley Abbey. He confessed that he hardly knew the place. The last tenant, a man called Clarke, had lived in one wing for fifteen years and seen no one. He had been a miser and a hermit. It was the rarest thing for a light to be seen at the abbey after dark. Only the barest necessities of life were ordered, and the tenant himself received them at the side-door. His one half-caste manservant, after a month's stay in the house, had abruptly left without warning, and had returned to the Southern States.

One thing Broughton complained bitterly about: Clarke had wilfully spread the rumour among the villagers that the abbey was haunted, and had even condescended to play childish tricks with spirit-lamps and salt in order to scare trespassers away at night. He had been detected in the act of this tomfoolery, but the story spread, and no one, said Broughton, would venture near the house except in broad daylight. The hauntedness of Thurnley Abbey was now, he said with a grin, part of the gospel of the countryside, but he and his young wife were going to change all that. Would I propose myself any time I liked? I, of course, said I would, and equally, of course, intended to do nothing of the sort without a definite invitation.

"The house was put in thorough repair, though not a stick of the old furniture and tapestry were removed. Floors and ceilings were relaid: the roof was made watertight again, and the dust of half a century was scoured out. He showed me some photographs of the place. It was called an abbey, though as a matter of fact it had been only the infirmary of the long-vanished Abbey of Clouster some five miles away. The larger part of the building remained as it had been in pre-Reformation days, but a wing had been added in Jacobean times, and that part of the house had been kept in something like repair by Mr. Clarke. He had in both the ground and first floors set a heavy timber door, strongly barred with iron, in the passage between the earlier and the Jacobean parts of the house, and had entirely neglected the former. So, there had been a good deal of work to be done.

"Broughton, whom I saw in London two or three times about this period, made a deal of fun over the positive refusal of the workmen to remain after sundown. Even after the electric light had been put into every room, nothing would induce them to remain, though, as Broughton observed, electric light was death on ghosts. The legend of the abbey's ghosts had gone far and wide, and the men would take no risks. They went home in batches of five and six, and even during the daylight hours there was an inordinate amount of talking between one and another, if either happened to be out of sight of his companion.

On the whole, though nothing of any sort or kind had been conjured up even by their heated imaginations during their five months' work upon the abbey, the belief in the ghosts was rather strengthened than otherwise in Thurnley because of the men's confessed nervousness, and local tradition declared itself in favour of the ghost of an immured nun.

"Good old nun!' said Broughton.

"I asked him whether in general he believed in the possibility of ghosts, and, rather to my surprise, he said that he couldn't say he entirely disbelieved in them. A man in India had told him one morning in camp that he believed that his mother was dead in England, as her vision had come to his tent the night before. He had not been alarmed, but had said nothing, and the figure vanished again. As a matter of fact, the next possible *dak-walla* brought on a telegram announcing the mother's death. 'There the thing was,' said Broughton. But at Thurnley he was practical enough. He roundly cursed the idiotic selfishness of Clarke, whose silly antics had caused all the inconvenience. At the same time, he couldn't refuse to sympathise to some extent with the ignorant workmen. 'My own idea,' said he, 'is that if a ghost ever does come in one's way, one ought to speak to it.'

"I agreed. Little as I knew of the ghost world and its conventions, I had always remembered that a spook was in honour bound to wait to be spoken to. It didn't seem much to do, and I felt that the sound of one's own voice would at any rate reassure oneself as to one's wakefulness. But there are few ghosts outside Europe—few, that is, that a white man can see—and I had never been troubled with any. However, as I have said, I told Broughton that I agreed.

"So the wedding took place, and I went to it in a tall hat which I bought for the occasion, and the new Mrs. Broughton smiled very nicely at me afterwards. As it had to happen, I took the Orient Express that evening and was not in England again for nearly six months. Just before I came back I got a letter from Broughton. He asked if I could see him in London or come to Thurnley, as he thought I should be better able to help him than anyone else he knew. His wife sent a nice message to me at the end, so I was reassured about at least one thing. I wrote from Budapest that I would come and see him at Thurnley two days after my arrival in London, and as I sauntered out of the Pannonia into the Kerepesi Utcza to post my letters, I wondered of what earthly service I could be to Broughton. I had been out with him after tiger on foot, and I could imagine few men better able at a pinch to manage their own business. However, I had nothing to do, so after dealing with some small accumulations of business during my absence, I packed a kit-bag and departed to Euston.

"I was met by Broughton's great limousine at Thurnley Road station, and after a drive of nearly seven miles we echoed through the sleepy streets of Thurnley village, into which the main gates of the park thrust themselves, splendid with pillars and spread-eagles and tom-cats rampant atop of them. I never was a herald, but I know that the Broughtons have the right to supporters—Heaven knows why! From the gates a quadruple avenue of beech-trees led inwards for a quarter of a mile. Beneath them a neat strip of fine turf edged the road and ran back until the poison of the dead beech-leaves killed it under the trees. There were many wheel-tracks on the road, and a comfortable little pony trap jogged past me laden with a country parson and his wife and daughter. Evidently there was some garden party going on at the abbey. The road dropped away to the right at the end of the avenue, and I could see the abbey across a wide pasturage and a broad lawn thickly dotted with guests.

"The end of the building was plain. It must have been almost mercilessly austere when it was first built, but time had crumbled the edges and toned the stone down to an orange-lichened grey wherever it showed behind its curtain of magnolia, jasmine, and ivy. Farther on was the three-storied Jacobean house, tall and handsome. There had not been the slightest attempt to adapt the one to the other, but the kindly ivy had glossed over the touching-point. There was a tall *flèche* in the middle of the building, surmounting a small bell tower. Behind the house there rose the mountainous verdure of Spanish chestnuts all the way up the hill.

"Broughton had seen me coming from afar, and walked across from his other guests to welcome me before turning me over to the butler's care. This man was sandy-haired and rather inclined to be talkative. He could, however, answer hardly any questions about the house; he had, he said, only been there three weeks. Mindful of what Broughton had told me, I made no inquiries about ghosts, though the room into which I was shown might have justified anything. It was a very large low room with oak beams projecting from the white ceiling. Every inch of the walls, including the doors, was covered with tapestry, and a remarkably fine Italian four-post bedstead, heavily draped, added to the darkness and dignity of the place. All the furniture was old, well made, and dark. Underfoot there was a plain green pile carpet, the only new thing about the room except the electric light fittings and the jugs and basins. Even the looking-glass on the dressing-table was an old pyramidal Venetian glass set in heavy *repoussé* frame of tarnished silver.

"After a few minutes' cleaning up, I went downstairs and out upon the lawn, where I greeted my hostess. The people gathered there were of the usual country type, all anxious to be pleased and roundly curious as to the new master of the abbey. Rather to my surprise, and quite to my pleasure, I rediscovered Glenham, whom I had known well in old days in Barotseland: he lived quite close, as, he remarked with a grin, I ought to have known. 'But,' he added, 'I don't live in a place like this.' He swept his hand to the long, low lines of the Abbey in obvious admiration, and then, to my intense interest, muttered beneath his breath, 'Thank God!' He saw that I had overheard him, and turning to me said decidedly, 'Yes, "thank God"' I said, and I meant it. I wouldn't live at the abbey for all Broughton's money.'

"'But surely,' I demurred, 'you know that old Clarke was discovered in the very act of setting light on his bug-a-boos?'

"Glenham shrugged his shoulders. 'Yes, I know about that. But there is something wrong with the place still. All I can say is that Broughton is a different man since he has lived there. I don't believe that he will remain much longer. But—you're staying here?—well, you'll hear all about it tonight. There's a big dinner, I understand.' The conversation turned off to old reminiscences, and Glenham soon after had to go.

"Before I went to dress that evening I had twenty minutes' talk with Broughton in his library. There was no doubt that the man was altered, gravely altered. He was nervous and fidgety, and I found him looking at me only when my eye was off him. I naturally asked him what he wanted of me. I told him I would do anything I could, but that I couldn't conceive what he lacked that I could provide. He said with a lustreless smile that there was, however, something, and that he would tell me the following morning. It struck me that he was somehow ashamed of himself, and perhaps ashamed of the part he was asking me to play. However, I dismissed the subject from my mind and went up to dress in my palatial room.

"As I shut the door a draught blew out the Queen of Sheba from the wall, and I noticed that the tapestries were not fastened to the wall at the bottom. I have always held very practical views about spooks, and it has often seemed to me that the slow waving in firelight of loose tapestry upon a wall would account for ninety-nine per cent. of the stories one hears. Certainly, the dignified undulation of this lady with her attendants and huntsmen—one of whom was untidily cutting the throat of a fallow deer upon the very steps on which King Solomon, a grey-faced Flemish nobleman with the order of the Golden Fleece, awaited his fair visitor—gave colour to my hypothesis.

"Nothing much happened at dinner. The people were very much like those of the garden party. A young woman next me seemed anxious to know what was being read in London. As she was far more familiar than I with the most recent magazines and literary supplements, I found salvation in being myself instructed in the tendencies of modern fiction. All true art, she said, was shot through and through with melancholy. How vulgar were the attempts at wit that marked so many modern books! From the beginning of literature, it had always been tragedy that embodied the highest attainment of every age. To call such works morbid merely begged the question. No thoughtful man—she looked sternly at me through the steel rim of her glasses—could fail to agree with me.

"Of course, as one would, I immediately and properly said that I slept with Pett Ridge and Jacobs under my pillow at night, and that if Jorrocks weren't quite so large and cornery, I would add him to the company. She hadn't read any of them, so I was saved—for a time. But I remember grimly that she said that the dearest wish of her life was to be in some awful and soul-freezing situation of horror, and I remember that she dealt hardly with the hero of Nat Paynter's vampire story, between nibbles at her brown-bread ice. She was a cheerless soul, and I couldn't help thinking that if there were many such in the neighbourhood, it was not surprising that old Glenham had been stuffed with some nonsense or other about the Abbey. Yet nothing could well have been less creepy than the glitter of silver and glass, and the subdued lights and cackle of conversation all round the dinner-table.

"After the ladies had gone I found myself talking to the rural dean. He was a thin, earnest man, who at once turned the conversation to old Clarke's buffooneries. But, he said, Mr. Broughton had introduced such a new and cheerful spirit, not only into the abbey, but, he might say, into the whole neighbourhood, that he had great hopes that the ignorant superstitions of the past were from henceforth destined to oblivion. Thereupon his other neighbour, a portly gentleman of independent means and position, audibly remarked 'Amen,' which damped the rural dean, and we talked to partridges past, partridges present, and pheasants to come. At the other end of the table Broughton sat with a couple of his friends, red-faced hunting men. Once I noticed that they were discussing me, but I paid no attention to it at the time. I remembered it a few hours later.

"By eleven all the guests were gone, and Broughton, his wife, and I were alone together under the fine plaster ceiling of the Jacobean drawing-room. Mrs. Broughton talked about one or two of the neighbours, and then, with a smile, said that she knew I would excuse her, shook hands with me, and went off to bed. I am not very good at analysing things, but I felt that she talked a little uncomfortably and with a suspicion of effort, smiled rather conventionally, and was obviously glad to go. These things seem trifling enough to repeat, but I had throughout the faint feeling that everything was not quite square. Under the circumstances, this was enough to set me wondering what on earth the service could be that I was to render—wondering also whether the whole business were not some ill-advised jest in order to make me come down from London for a mere shooting-party.

"Broughton said little after she had gone. But he was evidently labouring to bring the conversation round to the so-called haunting of the abbey. As soon as I saw this, of course I asked him directly about it. He then seemed at once to lose interest in the matter. There was no doubt about it: Broughton was somehow a changed man, and to my mind he had changed in no way for the better. Mrs. Broughton seemed no sufficient cause. He was clearly very fond of her, and she of him. I reminded him that he was going to tell me what I could do for him in the morning, pleaded my journey, lighted a candle, and went upstairs with him. At the end of the passage leading into the old house he grinned weakly and said, 'Mind, if you see a ghost, do talk to it; you said you would.' He stood irresolutely a moment and then turned away. At the door of his dressing-room he paused once more: 'I'm here,' he called out, 'if you should want anything. Goodnight,' and he shut the door.

"I went along the passage to my room, undressed, switched on a lamp beside my bed, read a few pages of *The Jungle Book*, and then, more than ready for sleep, turned the light off and went fast asleep.

******

"Three hours later I woke up. There was not a breath of wind outside. There was not even a flicker of light from the fireplace. As I lay there, an ash tinkled slightly as it cooled, but there was hardly a gleam of the dullest red in the grate. An owl cried among the silent

Spanish chestnuts on the slope outside. I idly reviewed the events of the day, hoping that I should fall off to sleep again before I reached dinner. But at the end I seemed as wakeful as ever. There was no help for it. I must read my *Jungle Book* again till I felt ready to go off, so I fumbled for the pear at the end of the cord that hung down inside the bed, and I switched on the bedside lamp. The sudden glory dazzled me for a moment. I felt under my pillow for my book with half-shut eyes. Then, growing used to the light, I happened to look down to the foot of my bed.

"I can never tell you really when happened then. Nothing I could ever confess in the most abject words could even faintly picture to you what I felt. I know that my heart stopped dead, and my throat shut automatically. In one instinctive movement I crouched back up against the head-boards of the bed, staring at the horror. The movement set my heart going again, and the sweat dripped from every pore. I am not a particularly religious man, but I had always believed that God would never allow any supernatural appearance to present itself to man in such a guise and in such circumstances that harm, either bodily or mental, could result to him. I can only tell you that at the moment both my life and my reason rocked unsteadily on their seats."

★★★★★★

The other *Osiris* passengers had gone to bed. Only he and I remained leaning over the starboard railing, which rattled uneasily now and then under the fierce vibration of the over-engined mail-boat. Far over, there were the lights of a few fishing-smacks riding out the night, and a great rush of white combing and seething water fell out and away from us overside.

At last Colvin went on:—

"Leaning over the foot of my bed, looking at me, was a figure swathed in a rotten and tattered veiling. This shroud passed over the head, but left both eyes and the right side of the face bare. It then followed the line of the arm down to where the hand grasped the bed-end. The face was not entirely that of a skull, though the eyes and the flesh of the face were totally gone. There was a thin, dry skin drawn tightly over the features, and there was some skin left on the hand. One wisp of hair crossed the forehead. It was perfectly still. I looked at it, and it looked at me, and my brains turned dry and hot in my head. I had still got the pear of the electric lamp in my hand, and I played idly with it; only I dared not turn the light out again. I shut my eyes, only to open them in a hideous terror the same second. The thing had not moved. My heart was thumping, and the sweat cooled me as it evaporated. Another cinder tinkled in the grate, and a panel creaked in the wall.

"My reason failed me. For twenty minutes, or twenty seconds, I was able to think of nothing else but this awful figure, till there came, hurtling through the empty channels of my senses, the remembrances that Broughton and his friends had discussed me furtively at dinner. The dim possibility of its being a hoax stole gratefully into my unhappy mind, and once there, one's pluck came creeping back along a thousand tiny veins. My first sensation was one of blind unreasoning thankfulness that my brain was going to stand the trial. I am not a timid man, but the best of us needs some human handle to steady him in time of extremity, and in this faint but growing hope that after all it might be only a brutal hoax, I found the fulcrum that I needed. At last I moved.

"How I managed to do it I cannot tell you, but with one spring towards the foot of the bed I got within arm's-length and struck out one fearful blow with my fist at the thing. It crumbled under it, and my hand was cut to the bone. With a sickening revulsion after my terror, I dropped half-fainting across the end of the bed. So, it was merely a foul trick after all. No doubt the trick had been played many a time before: no doubt Broughton and his friends had had some large bet among themselves as to what I should do when I discovered the gruesome thing. From my state of abject terror, I found myself transported into an insensate anger. I shouted curses upon Broughton. I dived rather than climbed over the bed-end of the sofa. I tore at the robed skeleton—how well the whole thing had been carried out, I thought—I broke the skull against the floor, and stamped upon its dry bones.

"I flung the head away under the bed, and rent the brittle bones of the trunk in pieces. I snapped the thin thigh-bones across my knee, and flung them in different directions. The shin-bones I set up against a stool and broke with my heel. I raged like a Berserker against the loathly thing, and stripped the ribs from the backbone and slung the breastbone against the cupboard. My fury increased as the work of destruction went on. I tore the frail rotten veil into twenty pieces, and the dust went up over everything, over the clean blotting-paper and the silver inkstand. At last my work was done. There was but a raffle of broken bones and strips of parchment and crumbling wool. Then, picking up a piece of the skull—it was the cheek and temple bone of the right side, I remember—I opened the door and went down the passage to Broughton's dressing-room. I remember still how my sweat-dripping pyjamas clung to me as I walked. At the door I kicked and entered.

"Broughton was in bed. He had already turned the light on and seemed shrunken and horrified. For a moment he could hardly pull himself together. Then I spoke. I don't know what I said. Only I know that from a heart full and over-full with hatred and contempt, spurred on by shame of my own recent cowardice, I let my tongue run on. He answered nothing. I was amazed at my own fluency. My hair still clung lankily to my wet temples, my hand was bleeding profusely, and I must have looked a strange sight. Broughton huddled himself up at the head of the bed just as I had. Still he made no answer, no defence. He seemed preoccupied with something besides my reproaches, and once or twice moistened his lips with his tongue. But he could say nothing though he moved his hands now and then, just as a baby who cannot speak moves its hands.

"At last the door into Mrs. Broughton's rooms opened and she came in, white and terrified. 'What is it? What is it? Oh, in God's name! what is it?' she cried again and again, and then she went up to her husband and sat on the bed in her nightdress, and the two faced me. I told her what the matter was. I spared her husband not a word for her presence there. Yet he seemed hardly to understand. I told the pair that I had spoiled their cowardly joke for them. Broughton looked up.

"'I have smashed the foul thing into a hundred pieces,' I said. Broughton licked his lips again and his mouth worked. 'By God!' I shouted, 'it would serve you right if I thrashed you within an inch of your life. I will take care that not a decent man or woman of my acquaintance ever speaks to you again. And there,' I added, throwing the broken piece of the skull upon the floor beside his bed, 'there is a souvenir for you, of your damned work tonight!'

"Broughton saw the bone, and in a moment it was his turn to frighten me. He squealed like a hare caught in a trap. He screamed and screamed till Mrs. Broughton, almost as bewildered as myself, held on to him and coaxed him like a child to be quiet. But Broughton—and as he moved I thought that ten minutes ago I perhaps looked as terribly ill as he did—thrust her from him, and scrambled out of bed on to the floor, and still screaming put out his hand to the bone. It had blood on it from my hand. He paid no attention to me whatever. In truth I said nothing. This was a new turn indeed to the horrors of the evening. He rose from the floor with the bone in his hand and stood silent. He seemed to be listening. 'Time, time, perhaps,' he muttered, and almost at the same moment fell at full length on the carpet, cutting his head against the fender. The bone flew from his hand and came to rest near the door. I picked Broughton up, haggard and broken, with blood over his face. He whispered hoarsely and quickly, 'Listen, listen!' We listened.

"After ten seconds' utter quiet, I seemed to hear something. I could not be sure, but at last there was no doubt. There was a quiet sound as one moving along the passage. Little regular steps came towards us over the hard oak flooring. Broughton moved to where his wife sat, white and speechless, on the bed, and pressed her face into his shoulder.

"Then, the last thing that I could see as he turned the light out, he fell forward with his own head pressed into the pillow of the bed. Something in their company, something in their cowardice, helped me, and I faced the open doorway of the room, which was outlined fairly clearly against the dimly lighted passage. I put out one hand and touched Mrs. Broughton's shoulder in the darkness. But at the last moment I too failed. I sank on my knees and put my face in the bed. Only we all heard. The footsteps came to the door and there they stopped. The piece of bone was lying a yard inside the door. There was a rustle of moving stuff, and the thing was in the room. Mrs. Broughton was silent: I could hear Broughton's voice praying, muffled in the pillow: I was cursing my own cowardice. Then the steps moved out again on the oak boards of the passage, and I heard the sounds dying away. In a flash of remorse, I went to the door and looked out. At the end of the corridor I thought I saw something that moved away. A moment later the passage was empty. I stood with my forehead against the jamb of the door almost physically sick.

"'You can turn the light on,' I said, and there was an answering flare. There was no bone at my feet. Mrs. Broughton had fainted. Broughton was almost useless, and it took me ten minutes to bring her to. Broughton only said one thing worth remembering. For the most part he went on muttering prayers. But I was glad afterwards to recollect that he had said that thing. He said in a colourless voice, half as a question, half as a reproach, 'You didn't speak to her.'

"We spent the remainder of the night together. Mrs. Broughton actually fell off into a kind of sleep before dawn, but she suffered so horribly in her dreams that I shook her into consciousness again. Never was dawn so long in coming. Three or four times Broughton spoke to himself. Mrs. Broughton would then just tighten her hold on his arm, but she could say nothing. As for me, I can honestly say that I grew worse as the hours passed and the light strengthened. The two violent reactions had battered down my steadiness of view, and I felt that the foundations of my life had been built upon the sand. I said nothing, and after binding up my hand with a towel, I did not move. It was better so. They helped me and I helped them, and we all three knew that our reason had gone very near to ruin that night.

"At last, when the light came in pretty strongly, and the birds outside were chattering and singing, we felt that we must do something. Yet we never moved. You might have thought that we should particularly dislike being found as we were by the servants: yet nothing of that kind mattered a straw, and an overpowering listlessness bound us as we sat, until Chapman, Broughton's man, actually knocked and opened the door. None of us moved. Broughton, speaking hardly and stiffly, said, 'Chapman you can come back in five minutes.' Chapman, was a discreet man, but it would have made no difference to us if he had carried his news to the 'room' at once.

"We looked at each other and I said I must go back. I meant to wait outside till Chapman returned. I simply dared not re-enter my bedroom alone. Broughton roused himself and said that he would come with me. Mrs. Broughton agreed to remain in her own room for five minutes if the blinds were drawn up and all the doors left open.

"So, Broughton and I, leaning stiffly one against the other, went down to my room. By the morning light that filtered past the blinds we could see our way, and I released the blinds. There was nothing wrong with the room from end to end, except smears of my own blood on the end of the bed, on the sofa, and on the carpet where I had torn the thing to pieces."

★★★★★★

Colvin had finished his story. There was nothing to say. Seven bells stuttered out from the fo'c'sle, and the answering cry wailed through the darkness. I took him downstairs.

"Of course, I am much better now, but it is a kindness of you to let me sleep in your cabin."